Project Daily Grind

a novel
by Alexey Osadchuk

To my Dear Reader, with gratitude,
Alexey Osadchuk.

Mirror World
Book#1

Magic Dome Books

Project Daily Grind
Mirror World, Book # 1
Second Edition
Published by Magic Dome Books, 2017
Copyright © A. Osadchuk 2016
Cover Art © V. Manyukhin 2016
English Translation Copyright ©
Irene Woodhead, Neil P. Mayhew 2016
All Rights Reserved
ISBN: 978-80-88231-13-4

Table of Contents:

For my beloved wife

Chapter One

"You need to understand, Mr. Ivanenko, that our bank can't see you as a potential borrower," the teller looked into my eyes, faking sympathy. A drop of sweat rolled down his fat clean-shaven cheek. The man stretched his plump pink lips in a buttery smile. His little white hand which never could have held anything heavier than a knife and fork kept tweaking the knot of his tie. Even when he clenched it occasionally, I couldn't see the knuckles of his plump fist.

"Why, have I ever missed a payment?"

My wife and I make sure we always have an emergency fund on our account at all times. We call it our "last resort": we must have the money, come hell or high water. On the first of each month, the bank always gets its pound of flesh, whatever the circumstances.

"No, not at all!" the clerk threw his chubby hands in the air. "I wish we had more clients as punctual as you are."

"So what's the problem, then?" I touched the bridge of my nose, trying to rearrange the non-existent glasses.

Talk about the power of habit. The glasses had bitten the dust two weeks ago, when I'd fainted for the first time in my life. I wasn't taken ill, no. According to the doctor, this was exhaustion (as he'd put it). My nerves were in tatters. And what with all the insomnia, no wonder I'd fainted. Plus I'd broken my glasses, which had been a shame indeed. Now I had to squint whenever I wanted to see anything. But I just couldn't afford a new pair. Every bit of money available had to go on my daughter's treatment.

"You need to understand," the clerk continued. "Even if you had three lives, you'd never be able to pay back the kind of sum that you're asking for plus what you already owe us. You've got nothing to remortgage anymore. You have no relatives who could act as guarantor. Your wages are below average. Your wife doesn't work, if you excuse my indiscretion-" this cute and cuddly individual promptly shut up, apparently reading something unkind in my glare. I heaved a sigh, trying to calm down, and looked aside.

Losing it now would be the worst thing to do. This loan was vital for us. For my daughter, rather.

It had all started with some heart murmurs she'd had. According to the doctor, it was perfectly normal in a three-year old. She'd grow out of it, he'd said. She hadn't. Christina was now six, and her heart—her *second* heart—wasn't doing too well. Her own had burned out within the first year.

To raise money for the surgery, we'd promptly sold our apartment and our country cottage. We'd had a quiet celebration away from prying eyes when we'd learned that there was a donor heart available. Others might judge us: having a donor heart meant that someone's child had just died. Those who never spent nights by their dying daughter's bedside will never understand me. I didn't care what they might think. All I cared was that my baby lived.

The surgery had been performed in Germany by a team of expert surgeons working for a top clinic. The doctor had assured us that if the transplanted heart took, our girl would live happily ever after. Tearful with joy, we'd believed him. During the first year our faith in his words had taken root in our own hearts. Christina's health had largely improved. She wasn't short of breath anymore. Her nails were now pink, not blue. My girl was strong. The doctors kept telling us that a young body like hers was bound to overcome the disease.

Then the troubles had returned.

Chronic rejection, we'd been told. Apparently, her blood was the problem.

They'd implanted my girl with a prosthetic heart complete with a twenty-five pound battery to be recharged every twelve hours. We'd been told this was the latest breakthrough in medicine. A temporary measure while they looked for a new donor heart. If ever they found one.

We'd been waiting for a week when Dr. Klaus came to see us. He told us we'd been put on their "risk book". In other words, they'd blacklisted us.

Christina's body had rejected the very first donor heart, thus bringing her back to the bottom of the queue.

I remember the pain and tears in my wife's eyes silently asking, *'So this is the end, is it?'* Mechanically her pale lips kept counting the number of extrasistoles of the prosthetic heart ticking loudly in my daughter's chest. They'd warned us that patients who'd undergone this kind of surgery were prone to psychopathological disorders. But in our case, Christina had taken the ticking and slight vibration in her chest all in her stride. She even joked that she had a "ticking heart bomb". But Sveta—my wife—wasn't so strong. She'd check the battery and all the connectors every half-hour and almost stopped sleeping at night listening to the beat of the mechanical heart. Only when the first orderlies arrived early in the morning, would she doze off despite the sounds of the television, her hand still resting on her daughter's chest.

Dr. Klaus had finished his sales pitch, but he wasn't in a hurry to leave. We tensed up like two hyenas about to charge their prey. Was there hope after all? According to him, there was.

With his every word, my wife's brow cleared. Apparently, about a year ago a Japanese laboratory had succeeded in growing a functioning human heart. And more importantly, it had been successfully implanted in a patient here, in this very clinic, by Dr. Klaus himself. The Japanese used the patient's own DNA which in our case was a perfect solution.

This was a miracle—the one we so desperately

needed. Dr. Klaus kept talking, describing the whole procedure. We listened to him, already visualizing our baby alive and healthy.

His mention of the expenses brought us swiftly back to earth. Dr. Klaus had already contacted the Japanese. The whole process, from the initial "conception" stage until the realization of the grownup organ, took about two months, give or take a week. If you counted the cost of the procedure itself including the transportation and surgery plus the hospital bills and the unavoidable taxes, we were looking at two hundred fifty thousand dollars. That's with all the discounts offered, both by the Japanese and the clinic itself. When later I checked their price list, I discovered that they basically shared the profits. To grow a heart cost just a tad more than implanting it.

Had we been shocked by the price? Honestly, we hadn't. We were happy. When Dr. Klaus had tactfully left, giving us some time to consider his offer, we hugged and cried. At that moment, we hadn't even thought where the money was going to come from. All we were thinking about was that our girl was going to live. Gone would be this piece of steel ticking like a time bomb in her chest. Gone would be the bed. Christina would have a proper human heart! She would live!

We'd signed the full board contract with the German clinic. They'd sent a DNA sample to the Japanese but they wanted an advance payment of fifty thousand dollars to proceed. They'd asked for seventy thousand first, but the Germans had helped us to bring it down. And once we transferred the money into the Japanese account, my girl's heart would start to grow.

I'd signed all the papers, kissed my family and took the first flight home. Hope gave me wings.

My wife Sveta had stayed on in the clinic. We had just enough money for three more weeks in the hospital. I had to hurry.

"Mr. Ivanenko!" the cuddly clerk gingerly touched my hand. "Are you all right?"

I startled. "What is it? Sorry..."

The clerk snatched his hand back in a very feminine gesture. "I thought you were unwell."

"Well," I said, peering at his name tag, "Mr. Antonov, you have no idea how unwell I am. Never mind."

I slapped my knees and rose. "I suppose I'll be off, then."

"Have a nice day," he mumbled at my back.

As I walked out of his cubicle, my gaze alighted on a colorful poster: smiling faces, medieval attire. I didn't read what it was about. I had other things to do.

I lingered on the bank's doorstep, holding the door open for a portly lady, when I heard,

"Mr. Ivanenko! Please wait!"

Mr. Shantarsky, the bank's manager, stood in the doorway of his office, smiling at me. An imposing face, a touch of gray at his temples, an expensive suit and good shoes. Everything about him told you that this forty-five-year-old man was perfectly happy.

Oh, well. I really should go and speak to him. You never know. He might help.

Shantarsky swung his office door open wide, letting me in. "Do come in and take a seat."

A gold watch clinked on his groomed hand as he gestured to a soft chair. "Would you like a coffee?"

"I'd rather have some water, thank you," I said while my mind raced, coming up with suitable arguments for the forthcoming conversation.

He closed the door. "A coffee for me, please," he addressed his secretary, "and some water for Mr. Ivanenko."

I caught a whiff of his expensive aftershave as he walked around my chair and lowered his agile body into his seat. His vivid blue eyes stared at me with compassion.

I didn't for one second doubt he was sincere in his sympathy.

"I bet you're angry with me," he smiled. "You probably already have a conspiracy theory about it. You must be thinking that I decided to get rid of you and sent a clerk to deal with you."

I waved his suggestion away. "The thought didn't even cross my mind. You're too busy. Nobody expects a bank manager to wait hand and foot on his every client."

"I can if the client needs me," he grinned. "In the West, apparently every client has access to the bank manager's office. No one would even dare object. We here in Russia still live in the Middle Ages."

I smiled back. I couldn't agree more. I remembered a bank back in Dresden: I'd gone there to change some money and I was watching this old lady who'd barged into the reception like an icebreaker and headed directly for the manager's office without as much as a knock on the door. The manager had jumped up and begun fussing around her, offering her a chair. At the time, I'd thought she was their millionaire client but no, they'd explained to me later, she was a regular retired old lady like any other.

The door opened, letting in the secretary with a cup of coffee and a glass of water on a tray.

"Thank you," Shantarsky said.

"Thanks," I repeated, reaching for my glass.

"Actually," Shantarsky went on, "back in Europe I've never seen a bank manager have his own secretary, let alone one who'd make him coffee."

"Neither have I," I agreed.

We paused, sampling our drinks, then continued our conversation.

"Back to what I just said," Shantarsky continued, "I think I owe you an explanation. I've only just flown back from Munich an hour ago. I've only had time to take a shower and down a quick breakfast. I haven't even seen my family yet but went straight to the office. And there you were, just leaving. Had I not known about your problem, I wouldn't have stopped you."

"Thank you. I really appreciate your concern."

"We do care for our customers and their problems."

There it was, the rush for all things Western rearing its ugly head. He was sitting here repeating stale catchphrases and referring to Western work ethics while I wasn't really sure how he'd have behaved in the above retired-lady scenario. I could see that he was trying to force his own agendas on me. Most likely, she'd have never made it past his secretary. He was too used to the luxury of a personal assistant's services which he'd have never been entitled to had he really worked in the West. There, only top directors had personal assistants. I knew this from experience. I'd done my fair share of traveling and been to all sorts of offices, bank outlets included. Everybody needs an expert interpreter like myself. And here I was sitting opposite this small fry that felt entitled to his own secretary and unlimited supplies of coffee and brandy... enough.

What was wrong with me today? I really should watch my tongue. None of this was any of my business. I had other objectives to take care of.

"Thank you," I repeated. "I really appreciate it."

Shantarsky regally accepted my gratitude. "So you need a loan," he said with a smug expression.

I nodded but said nothing. Straight from Munich, yeah right. Pull the other one. He'd been sitting in his office all along, following my conversation with the clerk. I just couldn't work out what he wanted from me. I was as poor as a church mouse. My houses had been sold, my money spent.

'I do indeed," I finally said.

"My colleague has explained our situation to you, hasn't he?"

I nodded again. At some point, the tables had turned. Only a moment ago I was quite prepared to plead and beg. Now something had changed. He needed something from me.

The thought was relaxing. I had nothing he

could take from me. It made me curious.

"I'm terribly sorry but we don't decide these things. We follow orders," he pointed a meaningful finger at the ceiling.

"So nothing can be done?" I played along.

He shrugged. His cold blue eyes locked into mine. "If you had a guarantor..."

So that's what it was about! Come on, spit it out. "I'm afraid I've got no one who could stand guarantee," I said. "Apart from my wife, of course."

"And your brother?"

At this point, I could see through his little scheme. "We don't have much to do with each other."

Dmitry was my brother in name alone. I'd been nine when Dad had left us. I'd only met his other son decades later. The meeting had been neither particularly warm nor cold—it had been bland. He was the one who'd found me. We'd met, seen each other and parted. Just before we left, he told me that Dad had died fifteen years ago. Before he died, he'd asked him to find and meet me. That was it, basically. I was curious though how they knew about him. Then again, why should that have surprised me?

"What a shame," Shantarsky chanted. "According to our information, your brother is doing very well. He has an apartment in the center of Moscow and a large country house. With him as guarantor, your loan is as good as settled."

Something clicked in my head. My first impulse was to grab the phone and call him. Thank God I still had his number! He'd given it to me just in case. The solution was so simple!

Then I felt as if someone had thrown a bucket of cold water over me. This just wasn't right. I smelled a rat there somewhere. Did they really take me for an idiot? Or did they think I was that desperate?

"I'm afraid it's not that simple," I said. "I'm sorry. I do appreciate your concern."

He gave me a look of disappointment. Oh well. Sorry to have rained on your parade, mister. But I still had to call my brother. He needed to know about this conversation.

Shantarsky sprang from his chair making it clear our meeting was over. We shook hands and I headed for the exit—again.

I needed money. I needed it now. We had very little left, barely enough to keep Christina in the clinic for two more weeks. That was all we had left in our bank account. Then we still had to find the fifty thousand dollars for the advance payment to the Japanese. And even more money to pay for the clinic.

I staggered. Was I shaking? It didn't look as if anyone in the bank had noticed. Good. Sympathy was the last thing I needed now.

Call my brother. The thought filled my mind, drilling through it. That could be a way out. Surely he'd understand our situation. Of course he would. I wasn't asking him to gift it to us. I'd work to pay it back. All of it, interest included. I'd work my butt off for him.

As I stepped out, my eye fell on the same poster with its medieval costumes and happy smiles. I slowed down. I might as well check it out.

I reached into my pocket for my broken

glasses. Only one glass had survived my fall even though it had cracked in the process. Had someone told me ten years ago that I wouldn't be able to afford a new pair of glasses! Having said that, of course I could. But I didn't want to. I could do without them. Every cent we spent was shrinking Christina's time in the clinic.

So, what did we have here?

The virtual lands of Mirror World await you!

Live out your most secret dreams in the realm of Sword and Sorcery!

Become a Great Wizard or a Famous Warrior!

Build your own castle! Tame a dragon! Conquer a kingdom!

All those desperate, lonely and insecure— Mirror World offers you a chance!

There you can start to-

I didn't read any further. What a lot of bull. Strange that the bank was hung with these ridiculous offers. Strange? Wait a second...

Normally, all such glamorous offers have strings attached. The said strings are usually denoted in a very fine inconspicuous print, like Times New Roman. Let's see...

Ah, there it was:

Industrial Mega Bank offers consumer loans to finance your work and account upgrade in the Mirror World virtual game.

What did they mean by "loans to finance work?" Logically, the game probably needed programmers and web designers. Would they be interested in interpreters, I wonder? Actually... what was the point? So they might offer me work for a wage, then what? I needed an enormous amount of money and I needed it now. The money left from the sale of our apartment and country house was dwindling rapidly.

Never mind. First things first. I had to talk to my brother, and then we'd see. I could use a well-paid job anyway. Asking for a loan was one thing, but then I'd have to pay it back somehow.

If the truth were known, I'd be happy to sell myself into slavery for my daughter's sake. Then again, who would need a nerd slave like myself? I'd pop my clogs the very next day in hard labor.

I walked out onto the street and took in a lungful of fresh air. Then I took out my cell and scrolled through my contacts for *Brother*.

The phone was ringing. That was a good sign: the number was still in use.

"Hi Oleg," Dmitry's voice was as strong and confident as I remembered it.

"Hi. How d'you know it's me?"

"Easy," he chuckled. "I've got your number listed as *Brother*."

"I suppose I should be happy to hear it," I said with a bitter smile.

"That's up to you."

"I've got you listed as *Brother* too."

"I know."

"Do you really?"

"I watched you enter my number into your phone that day."

"I see."

I paused and took a deep breath before speaking.

He beat me to it. "You have problems?"

"You can say that."

"Are you in town?"

"Yeah."

"Got something to jot my address down on?"

I got there in no time. In fact, I'd splurged on a taxi. My inner money counter was spinning, deducting minutes from my daughter's hospital stay.

Finding my brother's workplace proved almost too easy, for me at least, despite my failing eyesight. You had to be blind not to notice the familiar medieval fonts.

The sign on the front door read,

Mirror World. Terminal #17

The door was flanked by announcements identical to those in the bank, only these were the size of a movie poster.

I stopped at the reception to explain my business to a security guard. He made a phone call, received a confirmation over an intercom and let me through with detailed directions.

I took the elevator to the fifth floor and looked for #105. The total absence of any signs puzzled me.

Only numbers. Then again, what did I care?

Dmitry rose from his desk. We shook hands. His palm was dry and warm. And strong, just like Dad's. When I was little, neighbors still used to tell each other how he could bend nails with his bare hands just for the kicks of it. I was pretty sure Dmitry could do so too. Me, I took after Mom: both in physical and in mental build.

"You don't look well," he stared at me, his steely gray eyes unblinking. His face was big and rough. Broad shoulders. Not an ounce of fat anywhere.

"Thanks," I mechanically touched the bridge of my nose, readjusting the non-existent glasses. "You really took after Dad."

"I know," he said, pointing at a soft chair. "Go ahead, spit it out."

He was never one to mince words.

I began tactically. I told him about my conversation in the bank, mentioning the bank manager's knowledge of his financial situation and his suggestion to involve him as a guarantor. In doing so, I was steering him toward the only question he was bound to ask. Which he promptly did.

"I'll look into it. What did you need the money for?"

I'd rehearsed my spiel several times on my way there and until now, everything had gone as I'd planned. I gave him a brief run-down of Christina's situation: her heart, Germany, the Japanese, her life...

When I stopped speaking, Dmitry sat

thoughtful, staring out of the window. Finally, he seemed to have come to a decision. He turned to me. "I don't think I can be your guarantor."

It took all of my self-control not to crumble. Never mind. I'd have to find another way.

"But," he interrupted my train of thought, "I can get you a job."

I sighed. "Thanks. God knows I need one. But to be brutally honest, this advance payment is much more important-"

"You don't understand," he interrupted me. "I'll help you get a job here in Mirror World and I'll pay for your account."

"No, wait..."

"*You* wait. Just listen. The moment Shantarsky finds out you work here in the Glasshouse—that's our insider slang for Mirror World—he'll give you the loan. Maybe not all of it but I'm sure he'll give you thirty thousand at least."

"Yes, but-"

"You did say you still had something in the bank, didn't you?"

I nodded. "Seven thousand two hundred twenty-three dollars and thirty-four cents."

"Love it! Add to it the thirty thousand the bank will give you. I'll top it up. Plus I'll pay for your account which is another twenty grand."

I whistled in amazement.

"That's including my discount as a company worker," he explained. "The standard Daily Grind package costs twenty-five grand."

"That's why all the banks are promoting it like

crazy!" I said. "Question is, is it really worth it?"

"What do you think? Why would your bank collect all that intel on me?"

"So you're in it too?"

He nodded.

"How does it work?"

He rubbed his chin. "Imagine a virtual world inhabited by a multitude of races, where every character is controlled by a living person. The immersion is so realistic you risk forgetting your real life. Imagine if you used to be a hen-pecked bookkeeper, and here in the Glasshouse you become the best swordsman in the whole kingdom. You choose your own build and appearance. Once a nerd and a loser, you're now handsome and rich, one of the best warriors, enjoying both property and the attentions of the opposite sex. The only problem is the cost of the account itself—but as you probably understand, some spoiled daddy's boy has no problem with that. And as for a regular Tom, Dick or Harry whose thirty-day trial period is about to expire, where would he go? He'd go cap in hand to the bank. He's already an addict, see, dreading to lose what he's gained."

"That's crazy."

"Not really. A money-making scheme, yes. We're talking billions here."

"I see. But what about a job?"

"That's not a problem. The game developers have thought of everything. In the game, everything is just as complex as it is in real life. Imagine for a second that you're a spoilt rich kid buying yourself an account. For you it's peanuts. So you've created a super warrior char for yourself. You buy a castle for him and some land. Rich people keep investing in the game all the time, by the way. The developers even had to introduce a monthly payment limit in order to prevent inflation. So your character keeps growing but you can't level him up properly without, say, improving your reputations. Lots of them there, as you can imagine. In order to improve a reputation, you need to complete certain quests which in a hundred percent of cases suggest collecting some resources or crafting something. Besides, this is still a world, however virtual, so its streets need sweeping, its plants need watering, and so on and so forth. Because if your castle or town is dirty and unkempt, it'll begin losing its reputation and with it, a certain number of bonuses. Lots of bonuses there, by the way. It's enough to make your head go round. So do you really think that this spoilt rich kid would buy himself an account just to become a street sweeper or a stable hand? No, what he does he hires other players to do his dirty work for him and pays them in the in-game currency which can be exchanged for real-world money. At the moment, the exchange rate is 1:1. That is to say, one gold piece is worth one dollar. Every bank in the world will accept it."

I paused, digesting it all. "What other accounts are there?"

"There're also Bronze, Silver and Gold ones."

"What's the difference, then?"

"The price, the plan, the initial configuration, lots of things."

"Can you explain?"

"All right, there's the Bronze plan. It costs fifty grand. The initial configuration includes a basic set of gear. Access to the game from public modules. In other words, you start as a pauper. Silver costs a hundred and fifty grand. They'll install your personal virtual class B module in your home. You'll have the right to choose your own seigneur. Then there's Gold. Half a million bucks for the rich and famous. It offers all sorts of bonuses and freebies, including your own plot of land. Its size can be upgraded for an extra charge."

"This is crazy," I repeated, dumbfounded. "Very well, so what about this Daily Grind account?"

"Daily Grind is a zero-level account. The player can't kill anyone but he can't die, either. He's technically immortal. This type of account is created for work alone. The plan includes the profession itself, some tools and a free access to public modules. Or rather, it's the char's employer who pays for all that, allowing his employee to work on his territory without a care in the world. If it's a mine or a corn field, then they should already be mopped up, free from any potential mobs. Oh, and another important thing. The char's level of skill keeps growing regardless of his level."

"How does that differ from Bronze?"

"Like all other regular players, they have to wait till they make level 10 to choose a profession. They'll have to pay for their choice and for the toolkit, too. And their level of skill is directly linked to their own level."

"What does that mean?"

"Well, the game has a multitude of resources of every level, from zero to relic."

"I see. A level-10 player can't farm a relic resource."

"Exactly. I'll tell you more: even a level-200 player can't do so."

"And what's the top?"

"At the moment, there's nobody in the game above level 300. The top player is level 285, I think. His name is Romulus from the Steel Shirts clan. They're known as SS to common players."

"Jesus."

"But you don't really need to know that. You just do your work and that's it."

"Deal."

He glanced at his watch. "Let's do it this way. I'll take you to my assistant now. She'll show you exactly how it works. It's her job, anyway. I mean, she can do it much better than I can. I'm afraid I'm a bit pressed for time. Agreed?"

I nodded. "Thanks. I really appreciate it."

For the first time, he gave me a warm smile. "It's all right. We're brothers, aren't we?"

Chapter Two

"Oleg, have you ever played computer games?"

Dmitry's colleague Zoriana sat by her computer entering my data into the company's database. First name, family name, date of birth, social security number, that sort of thing.

She had cropped hair and funny earrings shaped as iridescent butterflies. Intelligent eyes glistened behind glasses. Twenty years old max.

"Do Tetris and tank simulators count?" I asked.

She smiled without taking her eyes off the monitor. "Any bad habits?"

"Not that I'm aware of."

She typed away. "Good. Basically, that's it. All I need is your signature."

"Be my guest."

"Not so fast," she smiled. "I know you're serious about it. Dmitry told me. It's not that. First you need to familiarize yourself with the game's content. You need to choose a race and profession."

"Does it really matter?" I asked.

"You see, Oleg," Zoriana adjusted her glasses and smiled condescendingly, "computer games of today are a far cry from those like Tetris. They are millions of years apart, so to say."

Unwilling to argue, I raised my hands in the air. "I give up! Let's choose a race."

"Excellent. I like your attitude. I'm going to take you to a class A test module so you can see for yourself."

The test module looked like a cross between a dentist's chair and—I couldn't help laughing at the thought—one of those hairdresser's chairs from the 1970s with a huge bucket-shaped bowl over your head.

Ignoring my merriment, she walked over to the machine and began keying in some information on the monitor built into the "bucket". She must have probably heard her fair share of clumsy jokes about the machine's weird shape.

"Make yourself comfortable, Oleg. The process will take much longer than you might think. I suggest you use the bathroom first."

I shook my head and climbed onto the hard seat.

She finished adjusting the settings. "Relax," she said, "and don't turn your head. It's not dangerous. Now close your eyes."

With a quiet beep, the "bucket" came down, covering my head all the way to the chin. I felt Zoriana take my hand and press my fingers against a hard surface.

"You can open your eyes now. The sensor panel is next to your right hand. The panoramic screen is right in front of you. Do you have a cell phone?"

"Yes."

"It's the same principle. I'm uploading the content. That's it. I'm leaving you to study it. If you need me, there's an icon with a ring bell in the top right corner of the screen."

"I see. Thanks."

"See you later."

The program upload bar began to grow, changing its light from yellow to green as the percentage increased. It felt like sitting in a 3D theater. I even lifted my hand, hoping to touch the image.

99%...
100%...

The speakers exploded with a fanfare riff. I hurried to put the sound down. Basically, the thing was quite easy to use—no more difficult than my phone. The interface pleased the eye. The font was clear, the graphics high quality. Apparently, people enjoyed playing games in these machines. If they spent so much money on it—actually *investing* in it—then they must have. Whatever. So far, I wasn't that impressed.

Never mind. Let's do it.

The world's history came first. But I had no interest in all those myths and chronicles. They must have been packed solid with useless information dear to the hearts of some die-hard fantasy fans. Me, I preferred facts. What's there?—Aha, *Newbie Guide*. *Professions*. Let's click it.

Farming, crafting, services... So! Each category had hundreds of pages! Blacksmith, Street Sweeper, Stable Hand, Fisherman, Herbalist, Water Carrier, Sewage Collector, Farmer, Gardener...

The mind boggles. Zoriana was right: I wasn't going to leave this place any time soon.

I clicked on the filter: *Most Popular*.

A hair stylist, a landscape designer, a manager... Okay...

Filter: *Best Paid*.

Number one on the Best Paying list was Mine Digger. I didn't look any further. Mine Digger it was.

Now race. Which ones were the most popular for this particular profession?

The huge bulk of racial choice #1 filled the screen. Muscles bulged under his gray hairless hide. His sinewy arms wound with veins hung to his knees. A walking shovel, like. What's your name, handsome? A Cave Horrud. Basic characteristics: Strength, Speed, Survivability, Defense, Agility. As for his additional abilities, I really needed to look into them.

Additional Ability: Force of the Mountains
Effect: +0.5% to Strength with every new skill level

Additional Ability: Willpower

Effect: +0.8% to Speed with every new skill level.

This was more or less clear. The guy was strong but too slow. Next. A Rock Rhoggh. More of the same, only a tad smaller. Slightly less Strength, a bit more Speed.

The next down the list was Dark Gnome. What about you, buddy?

Additional Ability: Free Miner.

Effect: +0.5% to chance to mine twice as many resources in one swing of the pick.

Additional Ability: Dark Vision.

Effect: +0.1% to chance to mine a higher-level resource in one swing of the pick.

He was followed by a Dwarf with similar characteristics. Basically, the bulk of players seemed to prefer strong and slow guys. They apparently thought that speed had no use in underground mines. Others went for dwarves and gnomes whose additional abilities offered resource bonuses.

I checked their contracts. They offered three types of payment: by the hour, by piecework and "extracted value". Now what was that? Aha, I see. Same as the two above but it also took into consideration the resources' price. I might take piecework plus extracted value.

So where was I? Oh yes. A dwarf or a gnome? I definitely wasn't going for the first two beefcakes. As far as I was concerned, too much muscle never solved a problem.

I repeated my search, adding Strength and Speed to the search characteristics. Same story. Oh well. I'd have to go for Dwarf, then. Why not? His characteristics were not bad. Also, as far as I remembered, these were underground dwellers, a race of mine diggers—at least if the game developers stuck to the traditional mythology.

I clicked Reset Settings. Wait a bit. What's that now?

I repeated my search. Indeed, the moment I filtered search results by popularity, I got 124 search results. But the moment I removed it, the search came back with 125 results. Same thing happened when I tried to filter the search results by Strength. Why? The search filter seemed to have overlooked a race. Was it a glitch? It shouldn't be. This was a big corporation.

So how was I supposed to find the missing race? Did they expect me to scroll through all the pages? No. There had to be a better way.

Then I figured it. I filtered the search results by page views. Got it. I entered 0 into the page view results and waited. There! But... was this a joke?

The picture of a puny little man appeared on the screen. He had a shaggy beard and unkempt hair. I gave him a closer look. His shoulders were narrow but his forearms were rather strong. All he needed was a sailor's uniform complete with hat and pipe to look like the epitome of a weathered seafarer.

His complexion was tinged gray; his eyes glared

at me from under his bushy eyebrows. His hands were large. Actually... it all fit. What would that ten-foot monster of a Horrud do in a narrow low-ceilinged mine? Together with the other one, the Rock Rhoggh, he was destined to farm cheap ore. And both dwarves and gnomes looked like sawn-off wardrobes with knee-long beards—way too broad around the beam to toil in narrow tunnels. Even if creatures like these had indeed existed, they must have looked different.

Never mind. No sense in me getting so wound up. So what's your name, buddy?

An Ennan.

Okay. And how about your abilities?

Additional Ability: *Shrewd Operator*
Effect: +1% to your chance of raising skill level with every 20 resources farmed
Additional Ability: True Heroes Take Devious Routes
Effect: +2% to your chance to raise the Shrewd Operator ability 1 level with every 100 resources farmed

Did that mean that the second ability affected the first one? In other words, I'd only have one because they were interconnected. And in terms of skill... what a shame I couldn't try it out.

I spent at least another hour reading up on the Ennan. As if it could change anything.

I peered into his sullen face. "What do you say,

---

buddy? Should we try it?"

He didn't say anything, just kept staring into space.

I gave it some more thought and calculation. Finally, I pressed Select.

You've chosen the profession of Mine Digger. Confirm: Yes/No.

Yes.

You've chosen the race of Ennan. Confirm: Yes/No.

Yes.

Enter the name by which you would like to be known in the game.

Oleg.

We're sorry. The name is already in use. Would you like to enter another name?

Good question. A small window popped up: Ennan Name Generator. Let's try it. I entered *Oleg* and cringed at the results. No good... definitely no... but this one might actually work. And this one? *Olgerd...*

Welcome, Olgerd! Well done!

Right. I clicked on the bell. Time to get out of this contraption.

Zoriana reappeared after a few minutes. "Are you all right? I was worried. I was about to check on you myself."

"Why?"

"You've been sitting here for nearly four hours!"

"No way! I thought it was thirty minutes at most."

"Yeah right! And you haven't even started playing yet. This was only a test module. Now I would ask you to follow me."

"What do you mean, I wasn't playing?"

She gave me a funny look, then turned round and headed for the exit. I shrugged and tagged along.

We came back to my brother's office. He sat there staring thoughtfully at the monitor. The silence was only disturbed by the quiet hum of the computer cooler and the clicking of a mouse.

I sat in front of him waiting. They were taking themselves too seriously here. No idea what all this hype around this Mirror World was about. If you asked me, this was just a flea circus. And a very expensive one at that.

My brother kept staring at my results. What was wrong? What could he see there?

He rubbed his forehead. "I see, said the blind man."

"That's what Dad used to say. His favorite expression."

"It was," he agreed without taking his eyes from the monitor. "He couldn't just say *'I see'*, he absolutely had to add *'said the blind man'*. I got the habit from him."

"Me too," I said.

He smiled bitterly. "We have a lot in common, don't you think?"

I paused. "How's your Mom?"

"Sick. And yours?"

"She died seven years ago."

"I'm sorry."

We fell silent. The mouse kept clicking. The cooler switched off.

"All done," Dmitry finally looked up at me. "I've saved your escapades in our database. Where did you find him? I didn't even know this race existed."

I shrugged. "Pure chance."

"Never mind. Now it's only the checkup left to do and we can sign you up. That's tomorrow. Now you need to go and get some rest."

"What checkup?"

"Just a few tests. It's obligatory. Government's requirement."

"Is it so serious?"

"It is. There were certain problems just after the game's release," he waved my silent question away. "It's nothing, really. That's it for today. I'll be expecting you tomorrow at nine a.m. Go and get some rest now."

I struggled to my feet. "Thanks, man," I offered him my hand.

"Don't mention it. I just hope it works out for you."

I smiled and nodded, then headed for the door.

Things got rolling.

I couldn't wait to share the news with my wife. All the way back to my rented apartment I imagined her eyes and her smile when she hears the news. I couldn't stop thinking about how it all was finally over. We'd be together. Sveta was bound to be happy for me and my brother getting to know each other. I was already forty; he thirty-five. We were grown-up people now. We had to understand that our parents must have had their own agendas that had nothing to do with their children.

I couldn't wait till tomorrow. Time was an issue.

Chapter Three

The checkup was a joke. I received the once-over from a doctor and had to fill in a few questionnaires. Then I was taken to a gym where I was fitted up with sensors and instructed to lift weights, run and do sit-ups. I even managed to do six pull-ups. Zoriana watched my exploits closely, marking something down on a clipboard.

Finally they released me. It took them another hour to calculate the results.

Dmitry entered the office, beaming from ear to ear. What was he celebrating? Then again, he was probably just happy for his brother.

"You got twenty-five points! Not bad at all. I've seen fitter people never make twenty. That's what I call letting your head do the work!"

"Why, does it matter?"

"Well, for one, had you failed to make fifteen points, you'd have been disqualified."

"Wow. Why didn't you tell me so?"

"I couldn't. We have very strict rules about that. The fine print. Spontaneous testing. But it doesn't matter. Everything's fine. I was sure you'd make it."

"Me too, sort of. And secondly?"

"Secondly, the developers have a rule. The test points are a bonus added to the players' main characteristics. Now when you log in, apart from the standard initiation package, you'll also have these twenty-fine points. It's up to you how you're going to distribute them."

I shrugged. What did he expect me to say? I didn't have the slightest idea what I was getting into. Sveta had told me she'd seen their ads on TV. The thing looked legit. Then again, gone were the days when you could actually believe what they said on TV. Or should I say, you could never believe it.

"Once you get to the Glasshouse, you'll wish you'd earned more points. Everyone does. They even joke about it. One thing I can tell you, you can never have too many bonus points."

Again I shrugged.

"Very well," he said, "let's get on with it. Your account is halfway complete. All you need to do now is confirm your settings, and off you go. Next thing. The actual hiring, the signing of the contract and the distribution of tools take place in Mirror World. Here we can't influence your decision. One word of advice.

Keep an eye on the in-game news. Try to deal only with established players. Find a way to join a strong clan or guild. The first day is crucial. Today you'll be logging in from here. Next time you'll already be using your employer's module. Your objective is to land a work contract in Mirror World. The longer its term, the bigger loan they'll offer you. And one last thing. Don't overexert yourself. The human mind is an unpredictable and poorly studied piece of gear. Everything you do in the game affects your body. That's just the way it works. Remember the other thing Dad used to say?"

"A sound mind in a sound body?"

"Exactly. Only here it's the other way round, sort of. As long as your mind is sound, so is your body. You'll see what I mean. Good luck."

The GT class module resembled a horizontal sunbed. I faltered. I had this funny feeling... it looked too much like a coffin.

"Are you okay?"

I startled. A young guy of about twenty-five looked at me sympathetically. I lowered my eyes at his name tag, squinting.

Andrew
Module unit controller

"I'm fine, thanks," I said. "Just a bit dizzy."

He smiled. "It's all right. It happens. People do get last-moment jitters. And then you just can't pull them out by their ears. Please remove your clothes and take your place."

I did as he asked of me. The warm gelatinous bed enfolded over my body. It felt like lying in plum jelly.

"Please don't move."

I froze. Andrei crowned my head with a complex-looking device. "Close your eyes."

I did as I was told.

"I'm going to count to ten. One. Two. Three. Four. Five..."

His voice began to distance.

"Six..."

Now I had to strain my ears to hear him.

"Seven. Eig-"

Silence fell, boundless and perfect. Had I just died? I was enveloped in pitch darkness. No, I couldn't have been. My thinking was perfectly clear. I tried to speak but I couldn't. I tried to turn my head after a fashion. It felt as if my body was gone.

My glance chanced on a tiny white spot. I focused. It kept growing. Now it was the size of a tennis ball... a saucer... looming ever closer until it had grown to the size of a window.

Closer.

Light consumed me.

The sound of falling water assaulted my eardrums. A fresh breeze touched my face, mixed with a veil of moisture. My body convulsed. I sensed a few pebbles under my open hand. All of a sudden I could feel them throughout my entire body.

I pushed away from the ground and sat up.

Jesus Christ almighty!

Somehow they had magically transported me

from their labs to this beautiful waterfall. The rocks felt warm to touch. I brushed my hand over some shrubs growing in a crevice in the cliff. This was a hundred percent real. Impossible!

I took in a deep breath. The air was sweet. Trees rustled in the wind. I could hear birds chirruping. The waterfall rumbled away.

I must be going mad!

Confounding me even more, a 3D sign appeared before my eyes. I startled. The letters faded, then filled again with color.

Welcome to Mirror World, Olgerd!
In order to enjoy the world in its entirety, please complete your account registration.
Would you like to complete your account registration now?
Yes/No

I focused on *Yes*.

Congratulations! Registration complete!
You have 15 points available!
You have 25 bonus points available!

This would have to wait. I wasn't in a hurry. I tried to get up and failed.

You cannot move.
Strength: 0
Speed: 0

Ah, so that's how it worked, then. I invested one point into each. My body began to obey me albeit reluctantly, as if in slow motion.

I added another point to speed. Much better, but still too slow.

Two more. Excellent. It wasn't as if I needed to run around here. I tried to walk about for a bit. It felt okay.

Now Strength. I picked up a rock small enough to close my hand around it. Good.

How about this one the size of my head? As if! But my trade as mine digger called for some serious weight lifting.

I added one point to Strength. I still couldn't lift the bigger rock. Another one. Yes! Perfect.

From what I'd read the day before, I had to go easy on points. If I wanted to bring a characteristic back to zero, I was going to lose half the points I'd invested in it. So I had to give it a good think. Just imagine how many points I'd have had to invest in Cave Horrud, with his bulk? And here I'd gotten away with only a few.

So, what did we have here?

Strength: 3 pt.
Speed: 4 pt.

I had 33 points left. Not bad.

I walked over to the water and peered at my reflection. An Ennan stared back at me. He had my face and body build by default—I made sure not to change the settings. So there we were! As large as life and twice as ugly!

I touched the water. It was cool to touch, the kind you'd expect water to be in the mountains. How did they do it? Was it my mind with its knowledge of what water should be like, affecting my perception? Or was it some different mechanism entirely?

I had a good eyeful of the new me. Then I checked the map. It offered a helpful view of all the nearby settlements. The largest of them, Leuton City, was about two miles away. So that's where I decided to go.

I marched away: first along a trail winding around cliffs, and then through a forest, turning my head this way and that like a five-year-old boy on his first trip out of town. The area was admittedly impressive. Giant ancient trees loomed overhead, threatening to squash me with their bulk. The numerous meadows were crowded with flowers of every color of the rainbow. This riot of color was astounding. And even more amazing was the world's authenticity.

After some ten minutes, I began to feel fatigued. My breathing became labored. My legs grew heavy. I had a splitting headache. It felt as if I'd just single-handedly unloaded a truckful of bricks. Something was going wrong.

Aha! I saw it:

Energy: 5/40

Basically, a ten-minute walk had just consumed almost all of my energy. Not good.

I perched on a large fallen tree covered in thick moss. Time to look into this. Where was it now... aha!

Stamina
Effect: each point gives +20 to Energy

Let's do some math. Ten minutes of brisk walking equaled 35 Energy. So! Apparently, walking was a luxury in this world.

I splurged three points on Stamina. Which gave me:

Stamina, 3
Energy, 12/100

Wow! Twelve already? I'd had five only a moment ago!

I could breathe easier now, even though my legs were still heavy. Which meant that sitting still restored your Energy. Finally some good news!

Never mind, I'd apparently have to travel in stops and starts. Yes, it would take me some time. But I couldn't help it.

And that's how I continued on my way: the moment I started feeling tired, I immediately found myself a nice comfortable spot to rehabilitate.

When I was crossing a large field, a colorful cavalcade of riders in shiny armor caught up with me. I'd just sat down to recuperate. No idea what prompted them to stop. Could be either my unkempt looks or the silent amazement in my stare. Whatever.

The enormous head of a black horse hovered

---

over me, glaring at me with its evil eye and quite prepared to trample me. The smiling face of a perfectly beautiful young girl beamed at me from behind the horse's back. Emerald eyes, golden locks, a full bosom, a rod-straight back and a perfectly shaped body.

"Greetings, O wanderer!" she had a musical voice, strong and cheerful.

"You shaggy dog! You should bow when you see a lady!"

Another horse soared over me. Its rider looked utterly awesome in his head-to-toe armor.

"Please don't, Lord Melwas," the girl's voice chimed again. "Can't you see he's a newbie? Aren't you, my good man?"

She seemed to be addressing me. "I am. You're absolutely right."

"I am, *my lady!*" the man snapped at me. "Then bow as low as you can, peasant!"

The bully's horse seemed about to crush me like a walnut. "Young man," I addressed the rider, "how dare you talk to me like that!"

His black eyes turned into slits. "Oh, I dare!" his steel-clad hand reached for his sword.

"Melwas! Please don't!" the musical voice assaulted my eardrums.

"Only for you, Lady Isa," the bully lost all interest in me and nudged his horse forward, covering me with a thick cloud of dust. I burst out coughing.

"Thank you, my lady," I said, trying out new forms of speech. "It's my first day today."

"We've all had our first day here," she flashed

me a winning smile. "I can see you're all empty. Hey, Aragorn!"

Another rider approached. His armor was different from a knight's traditional suit. Navy blue, it was covered in some fancy script. Beautiful.

"Yes, my lady," Aragorn lowered his head.

"Please help this poor soul," Lady Isa made a cute face.

The dark knight smiled. Silently he reached his hand out to me.

The entire cavalcade raced off, leaving me to choke in the filthy dust.

I began cleaning myself up. It took me some time to notice a system message that had apparently been there for some time,

You've received a blessing: Dark Hand.
Effect: +10 to Energy every 30 seconds.
Duration: 2 hrs.

I stood there blinking like an idiot, watching my Energy bar approach the 100% mark.

"So, noob, are you sufficiently impressed?" someone growled behind my back.

I swung round. A Cave Horrud in the flesh stood not five paces away from me. He was at least ten foot tall. Powerful muscles rippled under his thick grey hide. I'd seen a rhino in a Madrid zoo once: that's the kind of hide he had.

Most of all he resembled a large chunk of rockfall.

The Horrud grinned, exposing his crooked

---

fangs, "Enjoying the view?"

I gulped. Looking at computer pictures while wearing that stupid bucket on my head was one thing. Encountering this monster in the flesh was quite another.

"Cat got your tongue?"

"Eh, sor-sorry," I mumbled.

"Look at this noob," he growled, baring his teeth. "Never seen a Horrud before?"

"Only in pictures in the test module," I admitted.

"Is this your first day in the Glasshouse, then?"

"My first hour, more like."

"Aha, that's what it is! I see. A Daily Grinder. A fellow mine digger! Er... an Ennan? What the hell is that?"

"How d'you know all this?" I asked him.

"Jesus," the Horrud rolled his eyes. "You *are* a noob, aren't you? Focus on the space just over my head."

Name: Grryrsch
Race: Cave Horrud
Account type: Daily Grind
Level: 0
Profession: Mine Digger
Skill level: 9

"How interesting," I said pensively.

"Nice to meet you, Olgerd," he roared.

"Nice to meet you too, Gr... Grrych..."

"It's Greg actually," he waved his bucket-sized

hand in the air.

"I'm Olgerd," I proffered mine.

"Not a good idea," Greg grinned. "You risk losing your mitt. The Horrud race is quite strong."

I snatched my hand away.

"That's right. So where are you heading, Olgerd?"

"I'm off to Leuton. Looking for work."

"So! Same here! We can go together if you want. We could chat about the game."

I nodded eagerly, grinning. How great was that? How was I supposed to know that Mirror World was *this* authentic?

"I can see you've no idea what a cool goodie you've just got," Greg boomed, thumping along.

"I've no idea of lots of things."

"You're dead right there. The Dark Hand is an expensive buff. About fifty gold normally. It's rare. Perfect for working underground. Can keep you going for two hours without grub. And that's an extra slot in your bag any way you look at it. Talking about grub..."

He reached into his bag and threw something into his mouth. I focused on the item.

A Rosy-Cheeked Apple
Effect: restores 100 pt. Energy

"Wow," I enthused.

"My point entirely," Greg grinned. "You're a noob if ever I've seen one."

"Mind telling me what *noob* means?"

He stared at me. "Have you ever played before?"

Having heard my explanation about "tank games", he shook his head. "Hopeless case, you. Go to the info portal and look it up. There's lots of stuff there. It's the icon with the mirror."

"Does the game have Internet access?"

"Not into the real world, no. But it has its own network."

It didn't take me long to locate the icon with the mirror. "This is crazy," was all I could say when a browser window opened up right before my eyes.

Local news, translators, weather, maps and apps – tons of useful tools, perfectly downloadable and usable. Provided you had money, that is.

"So?" my new friend grinned. "Have you looked up *noob*?"

Okay. I opened the dictionary. Oh, well. I couldn't agree more.

"Greg, you've no idea how right you are," I said.

"How old are you in real life?"

"Almost forty-one."

"I see. Now everything becomes clear. Then again, they say that Romulus is fifty-plus but he's one of the top players."

"The one with the Steel Shirts?"

"Ha! You're full of surprises. Not all's lost, then."

"And how old are you?"

"Almost twenty. The best age, as they say, LOL."

I didn't ask him any further questions. He

didn't look too eager to open up either. I got the impression that people here weren't too willing to exchange personal data. I, for one, didn't want everyone and their grandma to know who I was.

"Have you already decided on an employer?" Greg asked.

"Not yet. Why? Did I have this option?"

"You're too much, you. Are you sure you know how to use the Internet?"

Yes, I'd admittedly been slow on the uptake, as today's youngsters say. The thought of looking it all up and checking a few forums hadn't even occurred to me. It must have had something to do with my being so preoccupied with my daughter's condition. Also, to be brutally honest, I hadn't taken any of this seriously. I hadn't expected it to be so... so incredibly awesome. Never mind. I was sure I'd sort it all out somehow. I had to.

"Any advice for me?" I asked.

"Leuton isn't much of a city even though it's the capital of the cluster. Not much choice there. You either try the dwarves' guild or go cap in hand to the father of that idiot who very nearly gave you a taste of his Lash of Fury."

"I was told that Daily Grinders can't kill anyone and can't be killed."

"They can't, no, but he could have whacked you with it and very hard, too," seeing the incomprehension in my stare, Greg began to explain. "He could give you an injury debuff – in other words, cripple you for a limited period of time. He's level 130 so his lash is quite a bitch. One blow would have been

---

enough to finish you off. These kinds of weapons increase Fury – and we here try not to annoy any characters who might happen to level it. He can give you a Class 9 injury and that's the end of you. They normally last over twenty-four hours. You'll spend all your money on quacks and healing spells. Actually, the highest-level healer I know in Leuton is the Mayor himself. He heals all the injuries up to Class 7."

"These injuries, what do they do?"

"Normally, it's minus to Life, Energy, Speed and such. Works the same as your blessing."

"My what?"

"The blessing, I mean the buff you've received."

"I see. Sorry. It's all a bit confusing."

"Never mind. You'll work it all out in the end. It's your first day, after all. You're a big guy. You'll make it."

"That's settled, then. Off to the dwarves we go. Somehow I'm not so keen on having to constantly watch my back."

"Can't say I blame you. He's sixteen in real life, by the way. His dad is a bank manager. But strangely enough, his mines are a better workplace. I work for him and I'm still alive and in one piece. Money just keeps falling into my account."

"What's so good about it?"

"First, we all work for a set wage. The money's very good. You just keep picking at the rock without a worry in the world. They have all sorts of bonuses too. Clothing and tools on the house. And the food."

"Sounds good. How about the dwarves?"

"At the dwarves, it's exactly the opposite. You

get paid for what you produce. Gear, tools, you pay for everything yourself."

"Now I see why your Strength is so high."

"Ah, so you noticed," he grinned with pleasure. "What would I need Speed for? At the dwarves you do need to move it, but here... I get paid for hacking at the rock and keeping an eye on the clock. After a week, I installed this little piece of software my bosses suggested, the Merry Digger. Once you activate it, your char can work on his own. The program keeps an eye on him, restoring his Energy, sitting him down to rest or taking him out for a pee. And I can browse the Net to my heart's content while I wait for my wage to drop into my account."

He leaned close to me and whispered conspiratorially, "I'm saving up to buy myself a Bronze account. The moment I pay off my Daily Grind plan, I'll start putting the money aside for it. That's a totally different ball game! That's why I do my research and visit all those sites and forums. I need to come up with a strategy. From what I've heard, even Romulus himself started off as a Daily Grinder—he played a Horrud too. Maybe they're just rumors but I read about these things in some quite reliable sources.

Aha. So that's why this race was so popular. Romulus, of course! How childish. The rich characters benefited from cheap labor. Mindless cheap labor even, considering they'd built all these stupid programs. I wouldn't have been surprised if they'd advised Greg to invest most of his points into Strength. One more argument for my joining the

---

dwarves. Finally, the pieces of the jigsaw puzzle began falling into place.

"Hey," I said, "Mind if I add you as a friend?"

"Not a problem."

I entered his name. Access denied. And again. Denied again. How weird. "Why do you keep rejecting my friend request?"

He smiled. "Which name did you enter?"

I slapped my forehead. "I am a noob, really!"

"You said it."

Right. I entered *Grryrsch*.

Friend request accepted.

Greg didn't send me his. Apparently, he wasn't interested in the likes of useless first-timers like myself. That was only fair.

An hour later we walked out into a large river valley. Leuton City stood on a river bank, looking utterly beautiful. The game designers had done a fine job. Neat towers topped city walls built of perfectly smooth slabs of stone. The houses' colored domes peeked out from behind the wall, most of them flying bright flags. This was a nice and neat version of the Middle Ages.

"That's it, Olgerd," Greg said. "Good luck! From here you're on your own. I still have quite a hike to get to Lord Shantar's estate."

"Thanks, Greg. I really appreciate your help," I gingerly touched his broad forearm.

I meant it. I'd met him in the right place at the right time.

"Ah, one more thing," he growled from afar. "Go directly to the Mine Diggers' Guild. They'll give you your first profession quest. From then on, you'll be fine."

"Thanks!" I waved my hand to him. "Good luck!"

Chapter Four

As you'd expect, guards stood like statues by the city gates. Three of them were clad in steel suits of armor and one in a navy blue one, like I'd seen on the guy who'd accompanied Lady Isa. I focused on the guards. All four were level 200: three warriors and a wizard. No one paid any attention to me. The wizard gave me the once-over and turned back to the others, talking heatedly.

The moment I entered the city, a system message popped up,

We welcome you, O traveler, to the glorious City of Leuton! Would you like to make our city your permanent or temporary resurrection point?

I clicked *No*. That was one thing I didn't need.

Free apps available: Leuton and Its Environments *and* A History of Leuton.

This I couldn't refuse.

Would you like to install our free apps: Leuton and Its Environments *and* A History of Leuton*?*

Yes, please. A map was exactly what I needed.

New app available: Streets and Dark Alleys of Leuton. Price: 5 gold.

No, thank you.

I had no money. Dmitry had tried to talk me into putting a couple of hundred dollars onto my in-game account. I'd refused. My daughter needed that money.

I just hoped that I could borrow some basic gear from the dwarves until I could pay it back.

More messages kept popping up, offering me all sorts of undoubtedly useful apps – for money, of course. I kept waiting for them to come up with another freebie, but no such luck. Apparently, that was all there was.

I pressed *No* one last time. The system bade its farewell and left me well alone.

I opened the map. The guild... there it was. *Mine Diggers of Leuton.* Off we go.

The artist in me thoroughly enjoyed my stroll

through town. Those programmers, developers or whoever they were had done a fine job. Everything was well-written and thought out. I felt like a tourist in one of those medieval cities. Shame I didn't have a camera. My girls would have loved to see it. Having said that... there must be a camera there somewhere. Eh... found it!

New app available: Screenshot. Price: 3 gold.

What were you supposed to do with them? Oh, well. Once I got a bit of money behind me I would surely buy it. Three dollars weren't going to break the bank. Then I could take all the screenshots I wanted.

The Satnav app cost five gold. I looked at its properties. This was a very useful little piece of software that recognized all the maps I had. Never mind. Later, all later.

In full accordance with the city plan, I crossed the Refraction Square and took Air Street. A few blocks later I saw a squat two-story building with a fancy sign that read,

Mine Diggers Guild

I walked in. The place looked quite busy. Their main hall reminded me of the Railway Post Office back in my home town. Several dozen vaulted ticket windows lined the walls, complete with tellers behind little desks. Lines of players snaked toward each and every window. All those races! Indeed, human imagination knew no bounds. Stocky dwarves and black-bearded gnomes, green-skinned Rhogghs, a dozen Rock Dwandes and a few of Greg's fellow Horruds.

"Jesus," I whispered for the umpteenth time.

I joined one of the lines and decided to check the Net. I was so engrossed in my browsing that I didn't even hear the teller calling me,

"You deaf?"

"Eh? 'xcuse me?"

"You noobs are all the same," a pair of very black and very angry eyes glared at me. A bulbous nose, a black beard and a dark gray complexion. The gnome rubbed his forehead in anger.

"Excuse me," I said. "I got side-tracked."

"You sure did," he mumbled under his nose, sorting through the scrolls on the desk in front of him. "Olgerd, an Ennan, that's strange... never heard of that race... Now... Characteristics... I see... that's all right... Here. This is your first quest."

Find your way to the nearest Mine Diggers' Guild and confirm your chosen profession.
Accept: Yes/No

Yes.

Congratulations, Olgerd! From now on you're a Mine Digger!

"Now the next quest," he continued matter-of-factly, rummaging through his papers.

Enroll in the Mine Diggers Guild (required).

Yes.

Congratulations, Olgerd! From now on you're a member of the Mine Diggers Guild!

"And another one," the dwarf grumbled.

Please confirm your willingness to pay weekly subscription dues into the Guild's treasury (required). Every due paid gives +50 to your Mine Digger reputation.

"All done," I said.

"Will you pay now or after you receive your first wage?" he asked.

"After."

"I knew it," he grumbled. "Now a bit of free advice. If you decide to seek employment at Lord Shantar's, you should invest in Strength. But as for my fellow Stonemasons, they have the obligatory 10 pt. Speed. They don't need no slouches. That's all for you. Next!"

I mumbled my thanks and hurried toward the exit. Only when I walked out onto the street, did I realize the significance of the dwarves' 10-point Speed requirement. By raising your Speed to 10, you automatically had to increase Stamina. In other words, in order to be faster, you needed more energy. Then you'd have to raise Strength too: the higher the Strength, the faster your energy restoration times are.

I could already see I'd have to part with my points – there just was no way around it.

It didn't take me long to find the Dwarves' office. A large sign hung next to the front door – provided this masterpiece could be called a sign. It was a large slab of stone seven feet by three and a half, as thick as the upper arm of my new friend Greg. Masterfully carved, the sign read:

Stonefoot Clan

The street around their front door was swarming with players. Remarkably, I didn't see a single Horrud, Dwand or Human – only dwarves and gnomes. I liked their cheerful faces, their slapping of shoulders, their constant joking and guffawing. These guys were nice. As I walked past them, a ginger-haired dwarf slapped my shoulder; a gnome gave me a wink as in, *cheer up, don't be shy.* They were probably celebrating something. I just hoped the office wasn't closed yet.

To my question of where I could find their HR, a stocky dwarf pointed at the staircase. I hurried up the steps.

The next floor was surprisingly quiet. Everybody must have already gone down. It was almost lunch time. My heart raced. I just hoped I'd make it.

I hurried along the wide corridor, desperately peering at the signs on large carved doors – also made of stone, by the looks of them.

One of the doors a few paces ahead of me

swung open, letting out a gnome and a dwarf. They spoke in low voices, demonstratively ignoring me.

"Excuse me," my voice broke, betraying my true feelings.

Two pairs of eyes focused on me.

"Could you be so kind as to tell me whom I should address regarding employment..."

"Too late," the gnome said calmly. "All vacancies have been filled."

"We posted a notice on our site three days ago," the other one added.

I heaved a disappointed sigh. Three days ago I'd known nothing about their existence.

'Try Lord Shantar's," the dwarf said with a crooked grin. "They always have vacancies."

Oh well. Exactly what I didn't want to do.

As I watched the celebrating dwarves back in the street, I couldn't help thinking: only a few minutes ago I'd felt myself part of their crowd. Now there I was again, alone. It looked as if they were celebrating the discovery of a new mother lode. Their warriors had already mopped it up. The mine diggers were going to make a pretty penny. What a shame. I'd as good as been part of it.

I heaved a sigh and opened the map. Let's see... Shantar's estate... it was a thirty-minute hike from here. My buff was to last another twenty minutes. I had to move it.

Chapter Five

As I walked, I decided to message Greg. *Hi there. Didn't work out with the dwarves. I'm coming over.*

He took his time to answer. He'd probably already forgotten me. Or he might have been ignoring me. I was no family of his, after all.

Finally, he wrote back.

Hi noob! So you've changed your mind then? You'd better hurry up, it's lunch time in an hour and our HR is only open in the mornings. If you fail to get hired today, you'll have to shell out tomorrow for the capsule.

Thanks Greg. I won't be a mo.

My pleasure. When you enter the settlement, just ignore the system's greeting. You'll sort it out later. Just keep going straight ahead until you see the town hall. It's easy to find. The place is called The Ruby. That's it. I'll let you know if I'm in the area. Good luck... noob."

It took me longer than expected. The blessing had expired after twenty minutes – and one becomes very quickly used to such things. I tried to keep up the pace but only brought myself down to near zero. I had to stop, then continue on my way in a more relaxed tempo. I'd never forget those last fifteen minutes. I was fighting off the desire to invest another two points into each characteristic. Still, I restrained myself.

As I walked through the gate, I followed Greg's advice and disregarded the system's greeting. It only took me a few minutes to reach the town hall, wasting a few more precious Energy points on it. It wasn't the right time to skimp. Getting a job was critical. I'd hate to have exited the game with nothing to show for it.

The settlement was a cross between a very small town and a rather large village. Closer to its center the streets grew wider, the small houses giving way to taller, more imposing edifices. The place was clean – cozy.

The multi-racial folk I met on my way were more on the smiley side. Then again, why would they frown? This was only a game. They didn't have a care in the world. Judging by their clothes and the abundance of zero levels, the bulk of the settlement was comprised of Grinders—mainly gatherers. About 70% of them must have been Mine Diggers—prospectors. There were also lots of herbal doctors. One was busy sweeping the street. I could hear the clanging of hammers and the ringing of an anvil. No one seemed to be lazing about or shirking their work. They really gave it their all and didn't slow down for a minute. If only everyone worked like this in real life!

It didn't take me long to find The Ruby. It would have been hard not to have noticed Greg's massive bulk hovering next to it. A slightly smaller species of his race was standing next to him, listening to whatever Greg was passionately telling him.

Hi Greg I'm here! – no, I didn't shout it across the square. I simply PM'd him.

He swung round, his gaze searching me out in the crowd, then waved hard with his shovel of a hand.

"I told you he wouldn't take long," Greg bellowed to his partner when I finally stopped next to them, gasping for breath.

His partner wasn't exactly a partner—or rather not in the sense you'd think. He turned out to be female—a female Horrud... what would you call them—a she-Horrud? A Horrudess? The reason I was curious was because I was probably risking my own skin as a wrongly uttered word might earn me a hearty punch from this ten-foot lady built like a hippo.

"Hi, I'm Olgerd," I hurried to introduce myself.

"As if I didn't know," she bellowed, then bared a row of small fangs in a smile. "It's written all over your face."

"Oh. I still can't get used to it."

"You will, don't worry. Never mind. Come along, then, I'll sign you up. You're lucky you got me on my good day."

"Thanks," I said.

"You'd better thank your friend," she grumbled, unlocking the door. "He's been on my case for the last hour: *oh please let's take him, he's a total newb, he's such a sorry sight...* As if I have nothing better to do with my time! My friends have almost given up waiting for me while I'm busy here with you two..."

"Come on, Sandra babe," Greg butted in. "You know I can be grateful," he glared at me meaningfully, nodding at the lady's monstrous bulk striding next to him.

"Of course," I awoke from my stupor. "I owe you. The first payday, I'll be around with a box of chocolates and a bottle of champagne," I faltered and added, "or whatever you guys give to each other here."

"Yeah, something like that," she swung her fifty-pound hand in the air, waving my suggestion away. "Real-life stereotypes die hard."

Her office was as massive as its owner, with a heavy desk, a powerful chair and several crudely made cabinets.

Sandra—which was apparently her name—laid her hand on a dark panel built into the wall. After a brief pause, a translucent screen materialized over the desk.

"We need to wait for it to boot up," she explained, studying herself in a wide mirror. Our eyes met. "You're probably wondering what a woman would want with an avatar like this?"

I gave an embarrassed nod.

"Don't," she said. "Your reaction is perfectly normal. I'm actually twenty-five and blonde with legs that go on forever. Can you imagine how fed up I am with all the idiots, with all those *Hi beautiful* and all that stuff? Now imagine me as a freakin' Elfa or a Dryad. I need to work, you know. My mom's sick; every minute is precious. That's why I chose this little gal. This way I can kick any butt that shows disrespect."

"I know what you mean. Excellent decision," I said and I really meant it.

"I like you the way you are," Greg offered jokingly.

"Yeah right, pull the other one. Wait... aha, it's up and running. Now, name: Olgerd. Race: Ennan," she peered at the roller captions on the screen. "Why did you go see the midgets first? What was wrong with us?"

"You see, Sandy, he'd managed to run into our rich daddy's boy within his first hour in the game. That idiot had very nearly given him a dose of his Lash of Fury."

"The guy is a first-rate freak," Sandra commented without taking her eyes off the monitor. "I think everyone here's fed up with him like you wouldn't imagine. Had it not been for his daddy, we'd have long shoved his head up his butt... know what I mean?"

I didn't but I got the idea.

"The dwarves keep themselves to themselves.

Greg, you really should have told him!"

"I didn't know, did I?" Greg mumbled. "I thought he was one of those..."

"Thinking isn't your forte, buddy. Now, what next? How many points have you got left?"

"Thirty," I said.

"Really?" she turned away from the screen. "How many did you start with?"

"Forty."

"Which means you had twenty-five test points. Not bad. But I'm surprised you've made it here at all. Did you take frequent breaks?

Greg laughed. "No, he didn't. He used the Dark Hand. Aragorn bestowed it on him."

"What, that cheapskate? He's tighter than a duck's backside!"

"It was Lady Isa who asked him to do so," I said.

"Ah yeah. Our lord's daughter. That explains it. She's a nice girl. So how are you going to distribute your points?"

"Depends on the contract," I said.

I'd already come up with a strategy. Now all I had to do was double-check it.

"What kind of contract do you want, then?"

"I'd like piecework plus extracted value."

"You've come prepared, eh?"

"Purely by chance," I shrugged. "I checked the contract types when I was choosing my char. But I still don't understand what extracted value means."

"It means you get a bonus from the resource's market price. Which in our case is one percent."

"How interesting," I said.

"Useless, more like," she snapped. Seeing my puzzled face, she began explaining. "You see, your lord's mines are poor in precious stones. And whatever's available is only worth something in large quantities."

"In other words," Greg added, "had I signed this type of contract, I'd have had to toil in the mines day and night—and I'm not even sure I'd be able to earn what I'm earning now."

"But it's your decision," Sandra summed up.

"Is it possible to sign a contract, then cancel it and sign a new one?"

"You mean you'd like to try it?"

"Yeah."

"You can, of course, but you'd have to pay the cancellation fee."

"I see."

"But you can in fact try without canceling the contract. Thing is, you are required to sign a two-week contract first. This is sort of trial period. Then if both worker and employer are happy, they can make a longer contract—say, for six months. After that they can make an even longer one... you get the picture. I think two weeks will be well enough for you to make up your mind."

"I agree."

"Excellent. So what do you choose?"

"Piecework plus extracted value."

Greg gasped.

Sandra hummed sarcastically. "I had a funny feeling you would. Just something my delicate stone heart tells me. Trust my word, dude: they'll carry you out of the mine feet first."

"Let's see if I make it," I whispered.

My hands shook with excitement. This was probably what a gambler feels when he bets everything he has on zero. I risked everything, but it was worth it. I wasn't going to raise enough money promptly just by working. And *promptly* was the key word. I needed the money fast. I needed my girl to live.

"Right, I'm sending you the contract. Yes... good. Press *Accept* here and here. Yes... all done!"

"Sandra?" I said. "I wonder if you could forward a copy to my bank, please?"

"Absolutely. Here you are. And one more thing. We have several in-game banks here. You'll need to open an account with one of them and send me the number. That's where we'll send your wages. Pay packets are paid every week. I'll expect you at our office tomorrow to confirm your data. Here's the address. Your module number is 345C. As for your working schedule, it's entirely up to you. This idiot needs to show up at eight every morning," she nodded at Greg, "but you have a different set of problems entirely. You're entitled to a start-up kit: gear, clothes, tools and food. It won't last forever, as you understand, so any new or replacement items are your responsibility. Now. You can get it all at Digger's Store—that's our local minimarket. Apart from that, there're loads of various little bits of software: bots, maps, resource guides, satnavs, music players..."

"I'm all right, thanks."

"That's it, then!" Sandra squeezed her bulk out of the chair. "Congratulations on your first job in Mirror World! I'm not shaking hands with you, otherwise you'll be walking round with an injury debuff for the rest of the day. Now a word of advice. You can pick up your gear tomorrow if you wish. It's better you quit the game for today. You've been here long enough for Day One as it is. Plus all your experiments with energy. You'll know what I mean when you're back. See you tomorrow. Good luck!"

We thanked her again and walked out onto the street.

My new friend smiled. "So, Mister Mine Digger, see you tomorrow? Once you log out, get yourself a nice big meal and go to bed. Tomorrow will be a big day for you. Oh, and one more thing. Before you log out, I suggest you bind your login to this place. That way you won't find yourself God knows where next time you enter."

I nodded. "Will do. I really appreciate it, man. No idea what I'd have done without you."

"That's nothing," he waved my words away. "Now press the logout button."

Just before I did, I received a system message,

Grryrsch would like to be your friend!
Accept: Yes / No.

I smiled and pressed *Yes*, then logged out.

Chapter Six

My awakening, or whatever you might call it, was instant. One moment I was standing in the middle of the mining village, then I pressed *Confirm Log Out* and here I was, stirring in the plum jelly like a beetle in a jam jar.

The lid of my "coffin" was already open. My vision was blurred, as if underwater. But of course! This was my bad eyesight coming back. I'd been so busy in the game I hadn't even noticed that I could see perfectly well.

My body shuddered as the real world flooded over me.

A dull throbbing in my temples came first. My blood pressure was off the scale—and I'd left the pills in the rented apartment that morning. Never mind, there's nothing a hot shower can't fix. It had always worked for me before.

Gradually, the pain began to subside but it was still there. I clambered out of the capsule. My poor legs! What had those people been doing to my body while I was playing? Had they sent it to unload cement trucks? I'd been told it might feel bad but I hadn't expected it to be so freakin' awful!

How long might I last like this? No, no, thinking like that wasn't going to help anything! I *had to* last—as long as was necessary!

I felt at least five years older. My joints ached, my muscles felt leaden. My head was splitting, my eyesight was failing and my hands shook. I could clearly hear my heart beating.

Someone supported me by the elbows.

"Ah, you've come round?" I saw my brother's blurred smiling face. "Welcome back!"

* * *

A soft chair hugged my body. A cup of hot strong tea; a warm blanket wrapped around my legs. My brother's office was cozy and quiet. Night had fallen behind the window. I hadn't even noticed the day go by.

"Feeling better?" Dmitry was sitting opposite, nursing an identical tea cup.

"Sort of," I croaked. "But I feel like I've been through the mangle."

"Nice simile. You did well calling it short."

"It was a tip from some good peop- er, good Horruds."

"Who did you join?"

"Some dude called Lord Shantar."

"Good," he nodded. "You'll have a fixed wage and will be able to pay off your loan just nicely."

"I've chosen piecework plus extracted value."

He choked on his tea. "Are you mad? You won't survive this week! Everybody knows how poor his mines are. It's basically just refuse rock they sell on an industrial scale. I'm sure the bank will bring your loan amount down now..."

"You didn't tell me that," I whispered. "You didn't tell me lots of things."

Was it my imagination or had he really shrunk under my gaze?

"Listen," I began. "My wife and I really appreciate what you've done for us. You're literally bringing our daughter back from the grave. This is your game and your money. I'll never be able to repay you. We may be half-brothers but we are basically strangers. You don't owe me anything but still you're helping me. The only excuse I have is the fact that I met you so late. Then there was Christina's illness... even though it was my responsibility as your elder brother to call you and stay in touch. I'm very sorry about it. But Dmitry, you shouldn't have done it the way you did. You just threw me in at the deep end, as if you wanted to see whether I'd sink or swim. Like a blind kitten, you know. I understand all this about the company's policy but Dmitry, this isn't the right way to do these things, is it? I've been in many European countries where I'm pretty sure your company has its fair share of terminals too, but somehow I don't think they treat their clients the same way. All I've heard was some vague hints, like *don't worry, you'll soon find out*, and a few very economical pieces of advice. Is this your company policy or our traditional Russian recklessness? Don't forget I'm a total noob as someone's already called me!"

"That's exactly what you are," Dmitry answered calmly.

I choked on my soliloquy and stared at him.

"Why do you think I took you to Zoriana? What were you doing in that test module all that time, tell me? Did you read the game's story? Did you peruse the in-game news? No good blaming me for not taking it seriously. A newb is all well and good but how was I supposed to know you were completely virgin? Apparently, you don't even watch TV or check online news! Our ads take up more TV time than women's tampons! As you've just said, this isn't the right way to do these things."

A long silence hung in the air. Finally I took in a deep breath, wishing to speak first. However, he beat me to it.

"Never mind," Dmitry said. "We're both to blame, probably. We can't undo it. Drink your tea. Try to get some rest. You can sleep here. This chair is convertible. You can't go anywhere in that state. I've already ordered you a dinner from the Ukrainian restaurant. Nothing like a bowlful of Ukrainian borsch to cheer one up! You'll chase it down with some smoked lard on rye bread followed up by a dish of potato dumplings with crackling, then wash it all back down again with some kvass. That'll put you right. Then have some more tea before you go to bed— and tomorrow you won't know yourself!"

He was already reaching for the door when I finally said, "Thanks... brother. I'm sorry."

"I'm sorry too. Actually, how did you like Mirror World?"

"Honestly? Not special. The real world is better, simply because both my girls are here."

"You know something? You've no idea how much we have in common."

He gave me a wink and left.

I attacked my food as if I'd been starving for several days. I could barely remember ever having this kind of appetite. Finally I sat back, feeling drowsy. No, wait. First I had to give Sveta a ring. She was awake, anyway, listening to little Christina's heart.

"How are you, sweetheart?" her anxious voice demanded.

I grinned into the receiver. "I'll live."

"I've checked a few sites and forums. There're lots of pictures there. Is it as real as they say it is?"

"You can't even imagine. You're much smarter than I am, by the way. I haven't even thought of looking it up. I might do some browsing now before going to bed."

"Please take good care of yourself," her voice quivered. "People say lots of things."

"I've already worked that out. Something is

rotten in the state of Denmark."

"They say you need to eat a lot when you log out."

"I've just wolfed down three times my usual portion—and I think I'm hungry again."

"Please don't! I'm telling you that as a doctor! You'll be sick!"

"It's all right, don't worry. I'll grin and bear it. How's our Little Rabbit?"

"She's still the same," she said softly.

"It's going to be all right, sweet, I assure you. Tomorrow first thing I'm going to the bank to sign for the loan. Dmitry is topping it up so they can start growing our baby's little heart. She'll make it, I know it."

She gave a sob. "It feels as if I'm losing both of you."

"What are you saying, babe? You know I'm strong. I only look like a wuss."

"I know... that's why I'm worried. You might overdo it. I know you. When it's for us, you'll do anything."

We talked for a long time—crying, laughing and dreaming. Finally, Sveta cut it short and demanded I hang up, making me promise I wouldn't stay up too late with the computer.

The Internet, indeed, was packed with the information about the game. Everything you needed, it was there. Players' blogs bursting with pictures, clan sites, employment sites and forums... I found the official Stonefoot Clan's site. Indeed, they had no vacancies; a small announcement promised potential openings next year. A whole year! This was a huge amount of time in gaming terms. Would the game even be here in a year's time?

Never mind. As I looked up my employer's site, I was chewing on the last slice of rye bread. Waste not, want not. But when I opened the biography of Lord Shantar, I very nearly choked on my fare. This Lord Shantar was none other than my very own bank manager friend Mr. Shantarsky! That's what had been giving me this constant déjà vu feeling all day.

All right. So that's what it was, then. I didn't even know what I was supposed to feel about it. The next morning I'd have to raise the subject in the bank. I was dying to call my wife but stopped myself.

Dmitry must have known all along. But he'd said nothing to me, the fox. Never mind.

I went on reading. Lord Shantar, level 210. When did the guy find the time to play? A member of the Gold Guild clan which in turn made part of the Alliance of Light—was in its top 10, in fact. They looked like serious people. Apparently, the game was divided into the two sides of Light and Darkness respectively, constantly feuding with each other. Not that it had anything to do with me: I was a humble level-0 Grinder.

So I gave that bit of info a miss. I couldn't care less about their petty clan wars.

The game's official site informed everyone of the beta testing of their water world. According to the news, it had been successfully tested on several local servers with a preliminary release date in roughly three months' time. Nice job. Those game developers didn't rest on their laurels.

From there, I switched to studying the various stats: professions, gear and point distribution.

Apparently, I'd done rather well on my first day in the game. Some had it much worse. I read in a blog about an Italian, a total newb like myself, who'd managed to splurge all his points on Strength—naturally, completely immobilizing himself. After having sat still for two hours, he'd been forced to reset his characteristics, losing 20% in the process.

A chill ran down my spine. I wouldn't have liked to have been in his shoes, that's for sure.

I also found out that the few lucky ones who'd managed to reach level 3 in farming—which seemed virtually impossible doing standard mining—received access to a second profession: a crafting one. Its choice depended on one's racial characteristics. In other words, I wouldn't be able to choose freely anymore: I had to accept what I was offered. According to the bloggers, this second profession was akin to a ticket to heaven. It took a lot of elbow grease, but in another year or two such a hard-working bastard could afford a Silver plan, no less.

I whistled with surprise. My hands shook as I entered my race in the search box. Right...

Excuse me? *No results found?* None at all? I checked the connection. It was working. What was wrong, then?

I entered the word into the advanced search. Aha! One of the forums seemed to have the search term mentioned in a dialogue—the whole two lines of it. A certain MedVed was writing,

Hi all,

Checked the admins site today. They've introduced this new race, the Ennan. I mean, WTF? What's wrong with all the dwarves and other underground midgets? Nothing about their abilities anywhere. Just another stupid beta they'll have to delete after a while.

A certain Ginger Dwarfa answered,

Who are you calling midgets, jerk?

That was about it. I stared at their brief teenage squabble trying to work out what was going on.

I did another check, just in case, of some of the biggest and most influential sites and forums. Nothing.

That was a let-down! Did that mean I'd chosen a non-existent race? How on earth had I managed to do that? I'd already spent half a day playing it!

Finally I located the info that comforted me somewhat. Apparently, the game included lots of races that hadn't become part of it. That didn't mean anything. Quite a few players were happy about it. Choosing one of the so-called "dead races" was even trendy in a way. But being a single player of some esoteric dead race was admittedly weird.

As I fell asleep, I kept thinking about my wife and daughter. Strangely enough, I was looking forward to the next morning. The Ennan's gloomy glare puzzled me. What kind of beast are you? How am I supposed to level you? You don't even have a simple manual, let alone a guidebook.

I'd managed to stake everything on a dark horse. Just my luck.

Chapter Seven

Next morning, I couldn't get to the bank fast enough. I was standing at its doors twenty minutes before opening time.

As it turned out, my loan was already halfway through. Sandra hadn't let me down and sent the contract in. Even though Shantarsky wasn't in the office, one of the girls there told me that he'd okayed my loan yesterday and authorized her to offer me nineteen thousand dollars.

Deep inside, I was jumping for joy. No, it wasn't the amount I'd initially counted on. But after my escapades in the game I hadn't counted on more than fifteen thousand. That's what Dmitry had thought, too. But I was lucky: I'd got another four thousand on top.

The paperwork didn't take long. I was already their client, anyway: I'd been with them for over four years.

So now I had thirty-six thousand two hundred dollars on my account. The agreement with Dmitry was for eleven thousand but he'd transferred twelve saying the extra thousand was just emergency money to make sure I had a bit of extra cash to spend.

I gave Sveta a quick ring. She cried with joy. Managing the money was her job. Ecstatic about my first victory, I hurried to the address Sandra had given me.

As I rode the bus, my cell rang. Sveta's number appeared on the screen. I could hear her triumphant voice, "The money's on its way! Her heart is already growing!"

I felt tears well up in my eyes.

"You've done it! We love you!"

"I love you too," I managed.

"I need to go, sweetheart," she said. "The doctors will be doing their rounds in a moment. You take care of yourself. If something happens to you, I'll never forgive myself. Do you hear me?"

"Yes, baby."

We said our goodbyes. By then, the bus was almost empty. I stared at the houses behind the window, the passersby and the traffic lights flashing past. An autumn drizzle was in the air. I tried not to think that I only had twelve hundred dollars left on the account. Or that I had to pay the loan back somehow. Too much thinking might burn me out— and then I'd be sorry. I needed to stay healthy more than anything now. I was facing a problem that didn't seem to have a solution—but I was going to brave it no matter what.

The communal module center was in the industrial zone almost out of town. My module was located on the second floor of a refurbished building of what used to be a clothes factory. Now it looked modern and spanking-new. I dreaded to even think how much money they'd poured into it. The place was swarming with staff and security. Little wonder: all that equipment must have cost millions.

Each module was located in its own small space, a bit like a hotel room with a shower and a toilet. A small fridge sat in one corner next to a microwave and an electric plate. A bed; a table; two chairs and a narrow wardrobe. Once again I tried to imagine the scope of the company's investment in all this—and failed.

At the reception, they'd given me a user's manual. It looked pretty straightforward.

All the modules were connected to the host computer. A special program monitored each client's bodily functions: their pulse, blood pressure, body temperature and such. The building had its own medical center with doctors on call day and night just in case someone overdid it. The whole thing ran like clockwork... or like an assembly line. And I was quickly becoming a cog in their works.

Already at the bank they'd told me that I could move into the center permanently. All out-of-town clients did so. Both the room and the module were paid by the employer—who, I suppose, would later deduct it from my wages. A health check was also included.

It was pointless dragging it out. I packed up my things, gave my heartfelt thanks to the landlady and hurried on to the center. As I stepped into my room, I tried to get used to the thought that it was to become my home for a very long time.

It was already half past midday and I hadn't shown up at work yet. I set my suitcase down in the corner: I could unpack later. I undressed, kissed the picture of my two girls, then plunged into the gelatinous bed.

I pressed *Start.*

All systems go! Time was an issue.

The familiar darkness enveloped me, followed by the approaching light. This time I logged in much quicker. Dmitry had told me that every time I entered the game, the contrast between the two realities would continue to erode: very soon it would feel like walking from my lounge into the bedroom.

I was standing in the square, on the exact same spot where I'd logged out yesterday. I had Greg to thank for that—among other things.

Actually, he was offline despite the fact that the workday was in full swing. Could he have taken a day off? Never mind. That could wait.

I opened the courtesy map of the settlement. The Digger's Store was two blocks away from the town hall. Off we go, then.

In the morning, my wife had insisted I put a hundred dollars on my in-game account. I'd protested but she would hear nothing of it. She wanted me to deposit more money but then it was my turn to refuse point blank. That's how it happened that I had a hundred gold glittering in my purse. I just hoped I wouldn't have to spend much.

Remembering my earlier mistakes, I walked in a controlled even pace. I had to go easy on my energy resources. Today I felt a bit more confident: the world around me had lost some of its absurd mystery. The Internet was a great thing any way you looked at it: I'd gleaned a lot of useful intel last night. So now as I headed for the shop, I already had a strategy.

The Diggers' Store reminded me of its counterparts in cowboy movies. Wooden shelves lined the walls. Hooks were hung with clusters of boots. Tools everywhere: from fishing rods to hoes and spades. The mannequins in the shop window were kitted out in all sorts of gear complete with bags and belts.

As I walked in, I had to slip past two very unpleasant fanged individuals. Their animal glares drilled holes in me. I pretended I hadn't noticed, just brushed past them through the closing doors. A conflict was the last thing I needed right now.

"Morning, sir," a Rock Dwand said from behind the counter. The shop owner was rather small, with gray skin and small pointy ears. He beamed, exposing a row of small but very sharp teeth within his wide frog-like mouth. "How can I help you? Ah, don't bother. An Ennan, a Mine Digger, current profession level: zero."

I smiled back. "You've nailed it," I said, then hurried to add, "A very good morning to you too."

"So! At the moment, you have three sets of clothes available, a tool and a shoulder bag. What exactly do you have in mind? A Hulk? Speedo? A Duracell Bunny? Or is the price an issue?"

"The price?"

"Exactly. I can offer a Goner's Universal kit. Its elements fit any kit without affecting its bonuses. Its pros: low price and zero durability. Which means it's fatigue-free, if you'll excuse the pun. You just can't wear it out. Its cons: a drop in characteristics and no bonus. What would you prefer?"

Eh," I faltered. "Honestly, I've looked it up and I was thinking about the speedy one. Doesn't it have an energy bonus?"

"Absolutely," the Dwand said. "I can tell you more: all the chars of your build seem to go for it,"

"You mind if I give it some thought?"

"Of course," he smiled. "To tell you the truth, it's the first time I see someone contemplating the purchase of a zero-level kit. You'll kill it in a week and be back here with me."

"Pardon me?"

"You heard. It only has 20 pt. Durability. The first rockfall, a ricocheting pick or even a friendly slap on the shoulder from a Horrud will all shave some off. An herbalist can afford to roam around the fields in the same gear week in, week out. A Mine Digger can't. It's a dangerous trade—accident-prone, if you know what I mean."

"I see," I said. "So this generous promise of 'gear kit on the employer' has strings attached."

"Heh! You haven't read the fine print. The *start-*

up gear kit is on the employer."

"Very well. So how much is this Speedo kit?"

"Let me see. The start-up kit contains five pieces: some clothing plus a pick which too has a tendency to break often. It is... thirteen gold and seventy silver."

"Which makes it about sixty gold a month. Plus energy restoration. So!"

"Well, at an average wage of four hundred and fifty gold a week, it won't break the bank, will it?"

"I'm getting paid piecework plus extracted value," I mumbled, desperately trying to find a solution.

"You don't mean it!" the Dwand shook his head. "Talk about bad luck!"

"I know, I know," I waved his sympathy away. "Everybody and their grandmother have already told me about the local mines."

"Here, if you're paid piecework, the most you can make is two hundred gold a week after taxes. Give or take a few. I might be wrong, of course. Eight hundred gold a month," he paused and added, "That's if you live that long."

"Is it so bad?"

He shrugged. "You won't understand until you try."

I sighed. "Four hundred and fifty a week just won't cut it, I'm afraid."

He chuckled. "You have some appetite!"

I looked up at him. He promptly shut up.

Apparently, there was something in my stare these days. That's the second time it had happened to me here. I couldn't remember any such reactions to my gaze in the past. But then again, imagine a sullen Ennan with a pitch-dark glare... it couldn't be that nice.

I felt awkward. "My daughter's dying," I explained.

He nodded. What did I care about his feelings? And if so, why should he care about my problems?

He stepped back behind the counter, giving me some space to think. I concentrated on the gear's stats. The five items of Speedo, counting the pick, offered 25 to Speed, 11 to Strength and a bonus of +5 to Stamina. I opened the stat simulator and did a rough calculation. This was what I had:

Speed: 29
Strength: 15
Stamina: 8

I had 30 points left to spare, but I'd better save those for any additional skills. I had big plans regarding them. I opened the Goner's kit. This was how it looked:

Speed: 19
Strength: 9
Stamina: 3

Stamina was so low because the Goner had no bonus. So I'd have to splurge on it from my reserve. Apart from that, the Goner looked rather decent. Why not? Indestructible duds, what's there not to like? I could use some in real life, that's for sure. No idea about down the mine though. What if I died within the first hour just through wearing the kit? I needed to do something about my energy levels.

"So? Have you decided?" the vendor's voice made me jump.

"I think so."

This was one choice I was going to regret. "I think I'll take the Goner."

The Dwand—I focused to read his name tag—aha, Rrhorgus—stared at me. This was the kind of gaze one reserves for idiots or suicide cases.

A system message helpfully popped up.

Congratulations! You've just acquired a Goner's Universal gear kit.
A Ragged Shirt: receipt confirmed.
A pair of Worn-Out Pants: receipt confirmed
A Creased Jacket: receipt confirmed
A Misshapen Hard Hat: receipt confirmed
An Old Pick: receipt confirmed

I just hoped I wasn't going to regret my decision.

I hurried to change. My new togs fit nicely. I chose not to check them out in the mirror, though. I must have looked a sight. But I wasn't here for a fashion show.

Your characteristics have grown!
Speed: +15
Strength: +6

My old zero-level clothes that I'd received at the start of the game had now disappeared. I did a few jumps and squats and touched my toes a few times, noticing with delight that Strength had positively affected my energy restoration times.

And?" Rrhorgus asked doubtfully. "Fit okay?"

"Fine," I ignored the sarcasm in his voice.

"Shoulder bags are standard-issue for all zero-level players," he continued. "Durability: 30. Holds forty items. Not bad at all, if you ask me. Quite resistant. Normally, it's the last item to break. Take it, you won't regret it. Now this..."

He reached under the counter and produced a small box divided into eight compartments. Round brown stoppers just showed above them. I focused.

Name: Stamina Elixir
Effect: Restores 200 pt. Energy

"A word of warning," the vendor said. "Don't overdo them. You might regret it later in real life."

"Thanks for the tip," I said as I remembered my last-night's logging out experience. No, thanks.

"Your contract specifies that your employer only pays for the start-up gear kit. After that, it's your responsibility. We have a rather wide range of elixirs and other restoring products. These are ten silver a piece. Using one or two a day, you don't run the risk of damaging your physical body. Any more than that, and the consequences can be hard to predict. Can I help you with something else?"

"Only if you tell me if the catalog download is free."

"Absolutely. Here."

I confirmed its installation and was about to leave when my eye chanced on a neat row of wooden boxes on one of the shelves. "What's that you've got there?"

The vendor turned to look. He chuckled in confirmation of his own thoughts, headed for the shelves and began rummaging through them. Soon he was back with a beautifully carved brown box.

He opened it, showing me ten green tablets the size of a five-year-old child's palm, each about a finger thick. The material looked like stone. A few pictograms were carved at their centers—whether runes or hieroglyphics, I couldn't tell.

"The Malachite Runes," Rrhorgus said. "They boost items' characteristics. Not the most popular thing among Mine Diggers. By themselves they're indestructible, but once applied to an item, in case of its destruction they disappear as well. A costly toy, let me tell you. These ones over here are from fifty gold up."

I focused on one of the tablets.

Name: Malachite Rune of Strength
Effect: +10 to Strength
Level restriction: Seasoned Mine Digger

That was worth having. "How many of them can you use?" I asked.

He grinned, seeing my interest. "One per item...

the problem is, you'll never make it to Seasoned in these here mines. Wait a sec."

He disappeared in his storeroom and stayed there for a good ten minutes. He reemerged all sweaty, his right sleeve covered in dust, a piece of cobweb clinging to his left shoulder. Had it not been for his gray skin tone, I'd have thought he had turned crimson from the effort.

"Here," he said victoriously, setting a dusty wooden box onto the counter. "I thought I wouldn't find it. This is a relic, heh!"

He wiped the box clean with his sleeve. "Yet another beta testing sample. You can't imagine how much of this junk has gone through my hands. Look," he opened the lid. Four gray—or rather, earth-colored—runes lay at the bottom of the box.

"Zero-level Clay Runes," he grinned. "I don't think anyone still has any of these anymore. They're ancient. The admins got rid of them at an early stage as no one used them. But I stashed them away... just in case."

"Why did no one use them?"

"Why would they? The zero-level gear has a week's durability. Once the item's broken, the rune's gone with it. And they're fifteen gold each. Seasoned Diggers don't need clay: they can afford the malachite ones. No idea why the admins decided to get rid of them. Wouldn't it have been easier to simply drop the price? Never mind."

"I beg your pardon, sir," my voice began to shake, "Do you think these runes might fit my gear?"

"That's exactly what I'm driving at," he said.

"I've never in my life seen anyone install runes on zero-level items. It's actually the first time I see a Goner's kit in the flesh, if you know what I mean. All thanks to you—a player who thinks out of the box."

I forced a skittish grin, unable to take my eyes off the clay tablets. Three runes of +3 to Strength each and one of +7 to Stamina. This was a treasure trove! Installing these runes would have considerably boosted my gear stats—without leaving me out of pocket, either. If my items were indestructible, the runes too would last me an eternity! If only they fit!

"So what do you think? Would you like to try them?"

I gave a nervous nod.

"Do you have the money?" the Dwand double-checked. "Once a rune is installed, it can't be removed."

"I do have the money," I reassured him. "If it works, I'll buy all four of them."

"Let's do it, then," he said. "Take a rune. The system will ask you to choose an item you'd like to use it on. After that, you know what to do. God bless!"

I reached out and picked up a clay tablet. Was it indeed warm or was it my imagination?

The rune began to glow.

Name: Clay Rune of Strength.
Effect: +3 to Strength
Restrictions: None
Choose the item you would like to install the rune on.

I chose the shirt.

Congratulations! You've received +3 to Strength!

The rune crumbled in my hands and disappeared without a trace. A complex earth-color sign appeared on my shirt above my heart.

"I got it!" I raised my hands, celebrating.

Strangely enough, Rrhorgus seemed to be celebrating with me.

I hurried to shell out sixty gold and installed the remaining runes. This was how my stats looked now:

Speed: 19
Strength: 18
Stamina: 10

My Energy bar had grown to 240. Excellent. All wasn't as bad as I'd thought. I compared my finished kit to the Speedo and was pleasantly surprised. I had 10 pt. less Speed but 3 pt. more Strength and 2 pt. more Stamina. So even without a bonus my kit was nothing to sniff at.

On Rrhorgus' advice I also purchased a 10-slot leather belt to stash away elixirs. It also had 30 pt. Durability. We spent the next quarter of an hour chatting. I bade him a warm farewell and walked out of the shop. Hope gave me wings.

Chapter Eight

I perched myself on a bench in the shade of a large tree and tried to calm down. I was done with the shopping. Now all I had to do was distribute the additional skills.

Thirty points was desperately not enough, but I hoped this was only the beginning. Let's do it, then.

I invested 20 pt. into the True Heroes Take Devious Routes skill. The catchy phrase belonged to a Soviet-era song lyricist Vadim Korostylev who'd apparently been poking fun at the so-called *Homo Sovieticus* behavioral patterns. I had no idea who'd created my character but he definitely had a good sense of humor.

Done it!

Congratulations! You've received +20 to your additional skill! Name of skill: True Heroes Take Devious Routes

Congratulations! You've received +10 to your additional skill! Name of skill: Shrewd Operator

I took stock of my mental exercise. My chances of raising my skill level by collecting twenty rocks had increased to 10%. Also, collecting 100 resources improved my chances of adding one point to Shrewd Operator 40%. I just hoped that this estimate would be worth the effort. That was it. I had no reserve points left.

Now, mining. The previous night I'd read in one of the forums that there were five zero-level minerals: aquamarine, turquoise, agate, granite and marble. Lord Shantar's mines mainly specialized in the two latter ones. Loaded individuals were quick to find their place in the gaming world. Demand and supply walked hand in hand, as Shantarsky surely knew. All he'd done, he'd created a low-scale mining business as his personal retirement fund.

Still, neither granite nor marble suited me. They were too heavy. Only the Horrud-like races could do this kind of work. The lightest mineral was turquoise, followed by aquamarine and agate as a close third. Those were the minerals used by zero-level crafters: jewelers, sculptors, blacksmiths, alchemists and such. Nothing was wasted. The game developers had taken good care of that.

The market dictated its own terms. A thousand points of marble cost more or less the same as a thousand turquoise—a tad more even. But as for demand... If both granite and marble were bought by the thousand, things like turquoise, agate and aquamarine were sold by the hundred, if not less. Which was why everyone considered me either a noob or an idiot—a suicide case even—whenever I mentioned my contract.

Still, this noob had a plan. The noob was about to take the devious route. They knew nothing of my additional characteristics. I'd kept them to myself. I just didn't appreciate people's stares focusing on me.

My plan was both simple and potentially damaging—to my health first and foremost. I decided to gamble on quick skill leveling which directly depended on the quantity of minerals farmed. Being the lightest of the lot, turquoise fitted my plan perfectly. Yes, I was in for quite a bit of running and weight lifting and I was quite prepared to gulp my share of energy-boosting elixirs if it helped me improve the skill. Once I made the first level, I could count on higher earnings.

This was my plan. Very soon I was going to find out if it had any weak points.

As I rummaged through the maps of Shantar, I decided to download the Satnav app, after all. I paid the three gold and clicked *Install*. The app dutifully analyzed the precious few maps I had and came up with the following message,

Would you like to install the Voyager bot?
I leafed through the user's guide. All you had to do was enter your itinerary, then the bot would take

---

over your char and take him there saving the maximum of energy by using "low calorie" elixirs. Some sort of auto pilot, basically.

I downloaded that too. The app kept showering me with more offers but I paid no heed to those. I only had thirty gold left in my pocket.

I opened the maps. Now. The Marble Mines... The Granite Mines... More marble... and again... and some granite... Aha, finally some agate! But where were the turquoise and aquamarine?

Oh. *No results found?* And the aquamarine? Same? How strange. I tried the agate and the search results came back with the name of a mine. What, only one? It must have been a glitch.

Never mind. Whatever. Once I got to the mine, I'd see for myself. Off we go, then.

The route has been calculated.
Would you like to activate the Voyager bot?

Yes, please.

Choose the mode.

I chose Economy mode that didn't call for any boosts or stopovers.

Time en route: 30 min.
Accept: Yes/No
I was all set.

My body made a smooth turn around and began walking rather energetically. The feeling was strange: it was still me walking, as if someone invisible was pulling—or rather, pushing—me forward. I decided to test it and tried to stop myself. It worked. Excellent. I leaned forward and touched my toes. Not a problem. I stood up, listening to my body. Thirty seconds later, it resumed its progress. So! Not bad at all!

It hadn't taken me long to get to the mine. As I traveled, I used the time to study the app's menu and found lots of useful features. Good. I was finding my way around. And the best part was still to come!

I came across many miners walking in the opposite direction returning from work. All zero levels, they plodded along, exchanging unenthusiastic comments. I noticed one guy being carried along, so badly had he overdone it. Mainly beefcake races, but I also saw a few punier types, all sporting every possible kind of tool and gear.

My kit brought smiles to their faces. Someone pointed their finger at me; I could hear a few jokes and jibes coming from the crowd. I must have looked a sight. It was a good job I'd changed the stats settings to "private", otherwise I'd have spent the rest of the day answering their questions.

I reached a place where the route forked. Much to my relief, the bot turned right, leaving me alone on the road. It felt too empty—even the trail had overgrown as if no one had used it for a long time. Behind it, I glimpsed a few cliff tops.

After ten more minutes, I finally stood by the entrance to a mine. The place looked as if it had been really busy once—a long long time ago. Apparently, there used to be quite a demand for agate for a while. The entrance was littered with rock debris and rotting old trolleys. A row of derelict workers' barracks could be seen behind them, black with age.

Oh. The place gave you that spooky feeling. The cave's dark mouth breathed damp and cold.

Never mind. One can get used to anything. Still, knowing how it worked would be useful.

I opened the info portal. So... Mines, yes... Farming... Got it!

According to the user's guide, a worker was supposed to sign on in a terminal that was located near the mine somewhere. Right... All I could see was an apparatus that looked a bit like a parking meter. What if I tried to approach it?

I stopped within an arm's reach of the terminal. After a short pause, it sprang to life.

Greetings, Olgerd!
This is Mine Terminal #12.
Levels: 0 to 35
Resource: Agate
Press Confirm to begin farming.

I'd failed to locate turquoise. Ditto for aquamarine. I had no time to go search for them now, either. I'd been in the game for several hours already and I hadn't even started working yet.

I heaved a sigh. *Confirm.*

Chapter Nine

My first step into the dark depths of the cave was wary. It might have been a game but it felt just as spooky as in real life.

Once I blinked the darkness from my eyes, I realized that I could see perfectly well in the gloom. It must have been one of my racial properties. The mine that looked so scary and damp on the outside turned out to be warm and inviting. I remembered reading that the Ennans were natural cave dwellers. The game developers had apparently paid great attention to detail. Wonders will never cease! I'd never been known to enjoy closed spaces but here I was, loving the dark confines of the cave.

The abandoned location was in complete disarray. Oh well. Apparently agate wasn't the flavor of the day. Just my luck.

Yes! I saw my first stone! I took a powerful swing with the pick and grunted victoriously as I buried its blade in the ground. I tried to pull it out— no way. Admittedly, this was the first time I had ever had to handle one. I'd even watched a couple of online tutorials the previous night explaining how to use a pick.

As I repeatedly pulled at the handle, I began to panic. What had I thought I'd been doing, choosing this as my trade of choice? A Gardener or a Street Sweeper sounded much more like myself. But no, I'd had to join the Mine Diggers, then sign the most lethal of contracts.

Cursing myself to hell and back, I spent the next five minutes trying to prize the wretched pick free. The freakin' stone would not give. With an angry gasp, I dropped to the ground, about to howl like a wolf. No amount of four-letter words could express the degree of my agony. Wretched Mine Digger!

Mine Digger? That rang a bell. I frowned, trying to remember... got it!

I opened the info portal and selected the Apps tab. Where was it now?

There!

The Merry Digger bot
Price: 3 gold
Download: Yes/No

Yes. I downloaded and opened it. I thought I'd go mad in the time it took the program to install.

Finally, it was ready. I pressed *Run*.

> *Greetings, Olgerd!*
> *This is Merry Digger!*
> *Please select mode:*
>
> *Economy Mode*
> *Rational Mode*
> *Speed Mode*
> *No Mercy Mode. Warning: Not Recommended!*

I'd have to do it by trial and error. I forced a nervous grin. Then again, why not? That's exactly how jurors are elected, isn't it? Actually, it was irrelevant. I had to test this bot now.

I selected Economy Mode.

> *Please wait. Data analysis in progress.*

The bot took over my body. It turned me around in the air, then froze me in place.

> *Data analysis completed.*
> *Resources found in this location: agate.*
> *Quantity: 2456 pcs.*

So! And I'd only noticed one stone!

> *Would you like to calculate the time necessary to farm this resource?*

That was useful. I pressed *Confirm*.

Please wait. Data analysis in progress.
Data analysis completed.
Economy Mode: 29 hrs 48 min (time calculated without the use of elixirs, with occasional breaks for energy restoration)
Rational Mode: 15 hrs 12 min (with a minimum of 1 elixir; no breaks allowed)
Speed mode: 7 hrs 15 min (with a minimum of 2 elixirs; no breaks allowed)
No Mercy Mode: analysis failed. 85% probability of total energy depletion before farming process is completed.

Would you like to choose Economy Mode?

So that's how it was, then. This bot only gave me a 15% chance of not popping my clogs in the process of farming this wretched agate. Shame I couldn't check the approximate output and timeframe just for future reference. Apparently, the game developers were playing it safe. If not, why would they have created this No Mercy mode at all? By the same token, even cigarette packs came with warnings and all sorts of blood-curdling little graphics.

Let's give it a think. My contract specified that I'd be paid six and a half gold per thousand of resource value. Plus an extra percent for the resource's rarity. Last night I'd checked the auction prices for zero-level stones. Prices per thousand were eighty to a hundred gold. Ironically, Agate was one of the cheapest. Which only served to prove my [insert air quotes] remarkable good luck and observation skills. Or their complete lack thereof. What had I been doing, plunging into the mine head first without first checking which locations had turquoise and aquamarine?

Today I'd have to work here, but the following morning I was definitely going to search for turquoise.

According to Rrhorgus, the best I could make in a week was two hundred gold after taxes. If you deducted the expenses, then in order to make thirty gold a day I'd have to farm about forty-five hundred stones. Which meant brandishing my pick in Speed Mode for fifteen hours or so.

Oh. They might just as well bury me right here. Having said that... I remembered how I'd spent several months in Spain as a student, working in a field. We used to harvest onions. I still have dreams of those never-ending fields. You placed a six-gallon plastic basket between your feet, bent your body until your torso was parallel to the ground and started moving forward in a half-squatting position, wearing out a pair of thick leather gloves a day. The scorching Spanish sun blazed away overhead, a behemoth tractor followed you unhurriedly while you scooped the onions filling your basket, then poured them into the tractor's bottomless bucket. In order to earn five thousand pesetas—which had been the equivalent of twenty-five US dollars at the time—we all had to meet a quota of seven tons each.

I still shuddered remembering my first days at work. My muscles hadn't hurt anymore. My bones had. We slept on average four or five hours a night. Still, I'd made it. My body had been young and I'd been reckless enough to eagerly test its limits.

Ironically, now I'd ended up in a game where I'd have to live up to my old feat. My face dissolved into a smile. They say that the virtual world makes everything possible. Still, my virtual body's stats didn't offer much against the old me—the real-life Grinder of flesh and blood, young, reckless and tough.

I heaved a sigh and selected Speed Mode. After a thirty-second pause, my body began to move toward the pick still stuck in the rock.

It came out with surprising ease. I hadn't even made any considerable effort. It felt almost like cheating.

The thought surprised me. Was I going slightly mad? Sveta was going to laugh her socks off when I told her. Was I cheating on myself?

While I was thus busy soul-searching, my bot had already produced five little stones. No—six!

You've received a resource: Agate.
You've received +1 to your skill.

Yesterday morning I might have been dancing around the room, overjoyed, but today all that forum-reading had left its mark. Even a noob like myself gains a bit of confidence having spent some quality online time perusing the wealth of blogs, guides and user's manuals.

All of them claimed that although profession leveling in Mirror World was admittedly boring and mind-numbing, at the end of the day it paid for itself. Provided you did level up, of course. Zero-level resources only provided the base of your future prosperity. Farming them was in equal doses important, dangerous, cheap and tedious.

Location owners were the only people who profited from start-up resources. Forum members engaged in lukewarm discussions saying that it wasn't fair when one had everything and all the rest had to bust their guts for him for peanuts. They were predictably told that no one prevented players from buying Gold plans and paying extra for their choice of minerals, then they'd be all set to make a quick buck.

When the game had only just started, they apparently used to have some sort of a free zone. Still, it didn't last. The stronger players formed several powerful clans and indulged in turf wars, plunging the area into the Middle Ages. The game developers' mail boxes were snowed under by tens of thousands of complaints and letters of protest against this breach of justice. As I'd read these forum comments, I'd been dying to add my two cents and ask them if they thought there was any difference between Mirror World and real life. Did they really think there were any unclaimed territories left on Earth? Didn't the whole world abide by the same principle, *one man rakes it in while millions have to toil*? And where could I find an admin to complain to about this disparity?

Not everyone had been interested in joining clans, and not all clans could boast any clout. Still, everyone needed to level up professions: this was one thing you couldn't get around. Either the admins felt the pressure from all the complaints or for whatever reasons of their own, but they'd created a large gaming territory and packed it chock full of mobs, resources and all sorts of instances. Now anyone could take the risk of visiting the new neutral zone nicknamed No-Man's Lands in order to farm a rare piece of armor, an expensive resource or just earn a few week-long injuries.

Congratulations! You've received a resource: Agate
You've received +1 to your Skill

Excellent. This was a good start. Forum gurus had warned newbs against celebrating too soon when their skill began to grow after the first few farmed resources. Apparently, the first ten points came relatively quickly, but after that, a player would hit a plateau when he would have to pay with his own blood (sometimes literally) for every point earned. The overall advice was to *be patient, make sure you ate well and above all, keep your head on.*

Only when I'd read this did I begin to realize the significance of my additional skills. In light of this, I was even more surprised why no one had chosen an Ennan as their char.

Your bag is full!

The moment the message popped up, the Merry Digger bot turned my body around to face the exit. I decided not to resist it. I was quite curious about what I was supposed to do next. I hadn't even had time to mull over anything—and I'd already farmed forty stones! I dreaded to think how long it would have taken me without this undoubtedly useful app.

Two Skill points into the kitty.

I left the cave and headed for the terminal. A message appeared on the screen,

Greetings, Olgerd!
Would you like to declare your resource? Name: Agate. Quantity: 40 pcs.

I pressed *Confirm*.

As I waited, I watched my Energy bar grow. The bot knew what it was doing.

Thank you for your work! You now have 40 pcs. of Agate.

Rinse and repeat. My body turned round and headed for a new helping of pale blue stones the size of a small cantaloupe melon. Had I farmed turquoise, I wouldn't have had to spend so much energy— according to forum posts, it was even smaller. I definitely had to find a turquoise mine first thing tomorrow.

* * *

...Six hours of work had flown by. I had eighteen hundred-plus stones in the kitty. Skill level

6. Plus 1 point to Shrewd Operator. As for True Heroes Take Devious Routes, I was in for a surprise. Five out of eighteen attempts had been successful, raising my Shrewd Operator skill to 15. And this was only my first day at work! I could literally feel my virtual heart jumping in my chest with joy.

How had they created this illusion? Or was it my mind playing up? My own heart was far away now, deep inside my physical body floating in that gelatinous goo.

Your energy level has dropped to 40.
Would you like to drink a Stamina elixir: Yes/No
Tick the box if you don't want to see this message again.

I confirmed elixir drinking but I wasn't going to tick any boxes. I wasn't going to give this bot any more independence than was absolutely necessary. I preferred keeping an eye on everything myself.

The contents of the fat vial proved tasteless. Once I'd drunk it, the vial disappeared, leaving me for some glass blower who too had to level up his or her chosen profession.

* * *

... I'd been at it for thirteen hours now. The location's resources kept restoring promptly. It had been two hours since I'd drunk the second vial. My energy kept dropping, and even my frequent stops by the terminal didn't help anymore. It was probably my physical body reminding me of itself. I was pretty sure that if I drank another elixir, its effect wouldn't last for longer than an hour. Now I understood the connection between our physical and virtual bodies like never before. Or was it again my mind playing up?

Now I could understand why the No Mercy mode was "Not Recommended". What was the point? All it meant was that you'd have to OD on elixirs until every new stone began to cost you dearly. That's exactly how others must have burned out—and for what? It only meant more money spent on elixirs to ruin your health faster. All to farm some agate? Please.

Very well. It was time I stopped. Enough for my first day.

I switched off the bot and staggered out. Night had fallen over Mirror World. An enormous moon bathed this weird land in its pale light. The sound of my footsteps alone disturbed the silence that had enveloped everything around.

The terminal habitually greeted me with the phrase I couldn't hear any more,

Greetings, Olgerd!
Would you like to declare your resource? Name: Agate. Quantity: 40 pcs.

Yes, damn you!

Thank you for your work! You now have 3968 pcs. of Agate.

Not good. Just falling short of my quota. All I'd earned was twenty-five gold. Not much at all. Two more hours would have done it. But no. It wasn't worth risking it. I could barely stand on my feet.

Before leaving, I checked my skill and ability levels.

Current skill: 12 pt.

Maximal skill pt. for your current profession level: 35

Another twenty-three points, and I'd become a Seasoned Digger. And that was totally different money. I'd have to spend some quality time studying resources and weigh up all the pros and cons. With any luck, I might start looking for a new mine the day after tomorrow.

My girls only had to brave it for a little bit longer. I was almost there. I shook the thought away. Were they all right? They were probably already fast asleep—but not Sveta, no. In any case, I wasn't going to disturb her. I'd give her a call in the morning.

I checked on my Shrewd Operator. Twenty-two points. That's a result! Talk about devious routes. Time to quit.

I cast one last glance at the moon. Wasn't it beautiful! Never mind it wasn't real.

Chapter Ten

Darkness enveloped me. I was already getting used to it. What a weird sensation. Scary. You didn't feel your body at all. I couldn't see anything. I didn't breathe.

Logging out was taking a while. I couldn't see the light. What was going on—were they all asleep or something? Hey! Where's my light?

It felt a bit like waiting for an elevator: you knew it was there somewhere, shuffling its cables in the dark, but you couldn't tell its exact location because some idiot had melted the elevator button with his lighter and then an alcoholic neighbor had cannibalized the floor display. His wife would stand next to you also waiting for the elevator, cursing the anonymous vandals just to check if you knew who the true culprit was. The funny thing was, she would know you knew it and you'd know she knew it too, and still your good manners wouldn't allow you to confront her story and you'd just stand there nodding as she heaped accusations onto the unknown bastards who deserved "having their arms ripped off".

Finally, my "elevator"! The light approached gradually—too slowly, really. It hadn't been like this before. Hadn't Dmitry said things were only going to happen quicker?

Then the light came crashing down on me, consuming me. Blurred images appeared before my eyes. My vision seemed to be failing alarmingly fast. I couldn't do without glasses anymore. If I still had time today, I'd go and see an optician.

My body shuddered. I regained control over it.

Jesus, what was that pain? I'd once read an interesting article about Medieval torture tools. Some people had a truly sick imagination. They used to have this rack on which they used to stretch a victim's limbs while stabbing or roasting him or her. For some reason, I immediately remembered that rack when the pain flooded over me.

All my joints were screaming. My head was going round. My arms felt like two unmanageable oak beams. My eyesight had dropped considerably. What was wrong with me?

"So, you're back now, Mister Hard Worker?" my brother's voice came from somewhere to my right. "I tell you now, Oleg, you're a freakin' idiot!"

"Why... what happened?" I managed.

"He's asking me what happened! What

happened is that somebody decided to become the first virtual champion mine digger and has very nearly busted his backside in the process. Not nearly even— you *have* busted it. Did you decide to remember the old days and die in style?"

"No, wait... please... what happened?"

"What happened?" he snapped. "I'll tell you now. What happened is that one inappropriately forward individual, despite everything that had been said to him, spent thirteen hours of the in-game time brandishing his pick in an agate mine! That's considering his own weight is a whopping hundred fifty pounds! He didn't give a damn about the two-week adaptation period, did he? He just sank his dentures into the rock and away he went! Your new buddy Greg, too much muscle and not enough brains, even he took three weeks to adapt until he gradually eased himself into using boosting elixirs. And what did you do? You've downed two Stamina elixirs and used it to turn out almost four thousand resource units! Which incidentally is unheard-of for a normal production procedure. Those guys do their four or five hundred stones a day and don't give a damn! And what have you earned today? A measly twenty-seven bucks? You're not a noob, brother. You... do you know who you are? Have you thought of your wife? Of your daughter? They're beyond themselves with worry these last two days!"

I startled. "*Two days*? No!"

"Oh, yes!" Dmitry's eyes glistened with glee. "Can't you see where you are? Yeah, right, as if! It's your wretched eyesight..."

He sniffed and shut up. I heard the rustling of a paper bag, followed by quick footsteps in my direction. "Here, try them on."

I sensed the familiar feeling of glasses hugging my temples. "I found your old pair and took it to the optician's on my way. They patched up the frame a little and put a new pair of lenses in. You look just like a mole!" he waved away my attempts at gratitude. "Ah, we'll sort the cost out later."

The glasses changed everything. I took a look around me. I was hung with all sorts of tubes and wires. A hospital bed complete with a control desk allowed me to change my position any way I wanted. An IV drip needle was stuck in my arm. Some machine kept beeping rhythmically next to me.

I looked out of the window. The sun blinked back at me. I smiled. This was the real sun. Warm and beckoning.

"Whatcha grinning at?" Dmitry asked in a calmer voice. "Then again, why not, now that the local doctors have brought you back from the dead."

I carefully removed the glasses, wiped them on autopilot, then put them back on. My eyesight had indeed deteriorated. I'd have to get a new prescription. Later. All later...

"How are they?" I asked.

Dmitry knew what I meant. "There's no change in Christina. She's a very clever child."

I nodded and smiled. It was a pleasant compliment. It's always nice to hear your children being praised when you know the speaker means it.

"Your Sveta is already threatening to sue

---

everyone in sight if anything happens to you. She promises to raze the whole place to the ground."

I grinned. "You'd better believe her."

"I do. Your wife is a fighter. All those years of battling for your daughter's life have left their mark."

"They have indeed," it felt good knowing my girls were trying to protect me.

"The doctor said, two more weeks of this masochism and you'll waste yourself into an early grave," he pulled his chair closer to the bed. "Listen, brother-" he began.

"Listen, brother-" I said simultaneously.

We both shut up. Then we burst out laughing. The pressure seemed to have eased off a little.

"You first," I offered.

"No, you speak," he said. "I've been doing all the talking for an hour now. I'm not a freakin' stand-up comedian. But just before you say anything, tell me: WTF? Are you raving mad? Busting your guts for twenty bucks? Why won't you work for a regular wage? They love your kind of speedy idiots."

"I got my skill up to 12," I said.

Dmitry choked on his words. For a while he just stared at me, bug-eyed and open-mouthed. Then he stood up, strode toward the door, opened it and looked outside. He closed it shut, walked back to me and pulled himself and his chair as close to me as he could.

"Go ahead," he whispered.

Surprised at this turn of events, I too switched to whispering. "Nothing to tell. It's the additional skills. I told you."

He shrugged. "Do you think I remember? If I looked into every little trick that came with every race, I'd scorch my brain. You saw how many they were. What about those abilities?"

"Firstly," I said. Shrewd Operator improves your chances to raise your skill with every twentieth resource you farm. And secondly, Devious Routes works in tandem with Operator, improving your chances of raising it 1 pt. with every hundredth resource."

"Twelve points," Dmitry whispered musingly. "So Pierrot was right then. That son of a bitch!"

I stared at him. Seeing my confusion, Dmitry hurried to explain,

"Remember the morning you came to see me? An hour earlier we'd held a board meeting. The CEO had a field day ripping the programmers apart, namely Pierrot. That's Andrew Petrov, but everybody calls him Pierrot. Most heads of terminals took part in the discussion. We have this virtual conference room, you know—it's very convenient. It was Pierrot who dealt with race development. He's a bit of a nutcase. All programmers are."

He shuddered. "Basically, once the meeting was over, Pierrot laid his resignation on the CEO's desk and walked out, just like that. Didn't say a word to anyone. Packed his stuff and left."

"Let me guess. The Ennan was his work, wasn't it?"

Dmitry nodded. "Exactly. You might call it his swan song. He introduced it just as you connected to the test module. You weren't the only one who chose

---

it. A hundred and twenty-five players also did so, but then they all reconsidered. You were the first one. You found the Ennan through a number of backdoors thus making it visible in the Search. The developers reacted just in time and removed the Ennan from the game."

"Why did the others reconsider?"

"The developers applied a bit of pressure telling them this was a glitchy defective race. They said they couldn't be held responsible for any malfunctions. They sugar-coated it of course by throwing a few bonuses into the swap—nothing ground-breaking but enough to make one's life considerably easier at level zero. The players got the message—especially because you were the only one who'd already managed to try this race out. Actually, I have the authority to offer you the same. If you refuse, the responsibility is entirely yours. No one knows what this nutty programmer had in mind when he was writing it. Or what kind of grass he smoked. On one hand, such an impressive raise in skill is awesome. But what's gonna happen to you next? What if you level your char up only to discover he comes with a nice little glitch no one knows about? He offered you this char on a silver platter but what if the platter has strings attached? Plus you'll be constantly monitored by the admins. I don't think your activity can damage the game's economy—you're only a grain of sand in this ocean. But hundreds and thousands of you—that's a totally different ball game. So what do you say?"

"Oh," I said. "I've already invested so much into him. It would be a shame."

"As you wish. The admins can't force you."

"Does that mean it's up to me whether I want to abandon the char or not?"

Dmitry nodded. "It does. Once we've removed the race, the danger of any potential glitch will be neutralized. You're the only one left. They don't give a damn what you decide. They have much bigger fish to fry. They think in hundreds of million dollars. They're not interested in one particular character with a slightly elevated chance of skill raising. You, pottering away in your measly mine somewhere in the outskirts of the game? Please. All they'll do they'll assign a bot to tail you to make sure you they keep tabs on you. Especially because they're more than sure that Pierrot has some sick surprise in store for you that would make you crawl back to them on your knees. It's not the first time this has happened, you know. The game keeps improving. True, there're some dedicated beta-testing servers but you can't provide for every eventuality. There's always something nasty coming to light, all the time. Talk about trial and error! The situation in your favorite Europe is no better. So basically, it's up to you."

That got me thinking. No, I didn't for one second want to abandon my char. That little was clear. I'd invested too much heart and effort into him already. No. I had other things to consider.

Dmitry seemed to have second-guessed my plans. "You aren't going to change char, are you?"

I shook my head.

"Then I have some advice for you. Keep your head down. Pretend you're not even there. It'll only take a while. It's a good thing you keep your stats private. Most newbs do. This way you can stay off their radars. Otherwise... they'll be after you. Your gear is decent. Excellent idea with the runes, by the way."

"The power of joint thinking," I shakily raised an authoritative finger. "We thought it up together: Rrhorgus the vendor and myself."

"I see," Dmitry nodded. "Now, the short-term goal: you'll have to stay in bed for a few days, I'm afraid. You need some treatment. If you play at all, it must be in Economy Mode. Don't worry about the money. I've just sent you anther three grand. Lie still, you! I know you appreciate it. Down, I say! We'll settle our accounts later. Your Shantarsky's just called. He's asking you not to exert yourself on the work front anymore. I told him you overdid it a little. It happens all the time. So he's quite happy now. He's expecting you back to work tomorrow morning."

"How nice of him," I forced a sarcastic grin. "I haven't seen him in the game yet, by the way."

"What do you want him to do in Leuton? It's the ultimate backwater. Our Lord Shantar lives in Mellenville, the great capital of Mirror World. He has about half a dozen such properties all around the game. The Gold Guild is a very influential clan."

"Why did I arrive at Leuton on my first day, then?"

"Because that's the cluster associated with our terminal."

"I see."

The phone rang. My heart clenched: it was

Sveta calling.

"Right, I'll leave you to it," Dmitry handed me the phone. "We'll talk later. I don't want to see you anywhere near the capsule, understood?"

"Which capsule? Can't you see I can't move?" I managed a smile as I took the phone and pressed the button. "Hi babe, you okay?"

Quietly Dmitry left the room and closed the door tactfully behind himself.

My girls and I talked for a good three hours. Sveta was crying, desperate to join me, but I knew that as she spoke, her hand lay on our little Christina's chest.

Chapter Eleven

I'd been lazing around in the virtual center's hospital for three days now. My body was gradually recovering from the mining marathon. According to some forum discussions, that's how people called these things. Which meant I wasn't the only wussy Grinder around.

I spent some time reading the comments. Apparently, my exploits would need a two-week recovery period. But if someone wanted to go back to work, no one could stop him. All I had to do was sign a disclaimer and I could head back to the mine.

A special clause in the contract specified that the hospital treatment was free. No wonder I received daily phone calls from the bank asking after my health! I couldn't help smiling. I'd earned all of twenty-five dollars but I'd already cost my employers hundreds. Some employee! Who would want me?

I had a funny feeling that once my two-week contract with Lord Shantar expired, he'd show me the door. I was nothing but a headache for them. So the next morning I was going back—and that was non-negotiable.

"Hey, dude," a hoarse two-packs-a-day male voice disrupted my musings.

I was lucky with my hospital roommate, wasn't I? Skinny, about five foot eight, with a crew cut, he was stooping, his narrow shoulders shaking in constant bouts of coughing. He must have had TB or something. Probably caught it in some seedy jailhouse. He called everyone "dude". The hospital staff didn't give a damn. They reminded me of in-game Grinders: same emotionless smiles, all their movements well-calculated, their every action well-rehearsed. They probably earned a nice buck here—excellent working conditions, security at the gate, hefty advance payments and regular wages. Which probably allowed them to suffer idiots like this Vova quite gladly, just by ignoring him.

"Vova, what is it?" I asked.

"Got a smoke?"

"I told you I didn't."

"Ah, sorry dude."

They'd brought him in last night, bandaged all over like some Egyptian mummy. According to him, he'd been victim of a rockslide while mining. His injured char was out of action for a week and the man himself was sent to the hospital ASAP. His whole body was black and blue—and his head too had apparently taken a beating.

The same evening, a doctor had come to see him. He'd explained to Vova that he might suffer memory lapses for a while. In return, the doctor was called *dude*, after which he bid a hasty goodbye.

Once back in the game, I'd have to be doubly careful. My roommate was living proof of that.

I didn't waste time. I attacked the new information like a hungry cat attacks a bowlful of minced steak. I tried to find out something about the Ennans, anything at all. Nothing. Even the dialogue I'd seen a couple of days ago had disappeared from the search engine. The admins were cleaning up after themselves.

I checked the Dead Clan site. This was a meeting place for all the races already removed from the game—and all the players who'd been too happy with their stats to promptly delete their unwanted chars.

Talk about a motley crew. They had all sorts: red-skinned four-armed Narchs, hairy Tarks, small Grolls and mysterious Ralds. They shared useful links as well as their own experiences, and posted ads in search of compatible weapons, gear and rare elixirs.

Vova tried to bum a smoke off me at least five more times, then began snoring peacefully. Poor wretch. He probably had a family. His wife and children must have been worried out of their minds. I'd have to ask him about them when he woke up.

In the meantime, I found some info on level-one stones. They were: amethyst, obsidian, sapphire and malachite. I checked their prices: excellent. The former three cost almost three times more apiece than marble or granite. Malachite was cheaper but the demand for it was higher because almost thirty percent of all crafters needed it. Virtually all of it was used in crafting—for instance, for the making of the runes like I'd seen earlier. In the context of Mirror World, malachite was apparently a much-sought after resource.

Still, it wasn't good enough for me. I had my sights set on sapphire. The lightest and the most expensive of them all. Mining sapphire could easily give me six hundred bucks a week after taxes. And that was a totally different ball game.

For someone it might have been good enough. No pressure: with a bit of work you could pay off your credit and take regular days off to be with your family. But this didn't apply to me. I had both the Germans and the Japanese on my case, about to procure new payments.

I located a few maps of Shantar's estate. I wasn't going to repeat my first-day error. I had no right to make mistakes anymore. My third day in the Glasshouse was going to pay.

Once I'd studied the map, my enthusiasm all but disappeared. There was neither turquoise nor aquamarine in Shantar. It had seven marble mines, four granite ones and the sole agate mine I'd already discovered. My search for either sapphire, amethyst or obsidian returned zero results. That left me with malachite. Shantar had just two mines of this: the heaviest and the cheapest of all four. Just my flippin' luck.

A quick estimate showed that this way I could earn five hundred gold a week at best: the same as Greg was making on an hour wage. This was a Catch 22 situation: my plan was admittedly good but it only worked with the lightest and most expensive of resources.

Had Sveta heard it, she'd have nodded her understanding. I did have this flaw: I always considered the best-case scenarios. Should I really switch to an hourly wage to level up a little, then go back to piecework? The problem was, no one in Shantar mined malachite on an industrial scale. In fact, no one mined it, period. Everyone had their hands full with marble and granite. No one was interested in busting their respective backsides. Was I the only one who wanted too much too quickly?

Right, let's see what else Shantar's estate had to offer. Wait a minute... wow! Wasn't I the lucky one! Emerald fields! The most expensive level-two mineral in Mirror World! Very light and always in high demand. I could easily make fifteen hundred dollars a week mining it. There was one little thing left to do: I had to make Seasoned Digger first and not pop my clogs in the process. And yes, I had to keep a low profile as Dmitry had told me.

That was it, then. Tomorrow I was going back. Enough lazing about.

Vova mumbled something in his sleep, as if in agreement.

* * *

"Are you sure?" Dmitry asked politely.

"I am. I don't have much time left."

"Promise me you aren't gonna kill yourself."

I pressed a clenched fist to my chest and eased my body into the gelatinous goo.

"Good luck."

Log in.

* * *

The doors of the Digger's Store opened without a sound. Hearing my footsteps, Rrhorgus emerged from the storeroom. He beamed on seeing me.

"Howdy, Olgerd! Where've you been?" he asked, wiping his hands on a rag.

"Well, you know," I faltered. "I suppose I bit off more than I could chew. Spent the last week in hospital."

He looked upset. "Was it so bad?"

"I set the bot to Speed Mode."

He shook his head. "Why didn't you set it to Jump Off a Cliff mode? Same effect, only quicker."

I waved his sarcasm away. "Never mind. I'll be more careful this time. I've only popped in to say hello and buy a few more elixirs. You okay?"

He sighed. "Boring. No custom worth mentioning. I kill time by polishing this junk. How many elixirs do you want?"

"Four. To fill up my belt."

He nodded. "I can see they're not damaged yet: neither the belt nor the bag. Don't forget they're going to take all the damage now. Seeing as they're level zero and all."

"Not a scratch on them yet, touch wood. Listen, I meant to ask you..."

He smiled. "Go ahead. I think I know what it's about."

I grinned back. "What is it about, then?"

"You're gonna ask me if I have anything else like those Clay Runes."

"Exactly. You know that's the only way for us to raise characteristics, by using gear and runes. So I just thought you might have something for me."

He shrugged guiltily. "You won't believe me but after you left, I checked the whole place. I've got all sorts of junk, I told you."

"You did. I just don't understand how you managed to keep all the items. Didn't the admins remove them one by one?"

"Sure. But they removed them from the listings. And those that vendors already had in stock stayed in the game. You understand? Later they sent us a half-assed order to destroy them. But I didn't have the heart. That's how you got the runes."

I chuckled. "I've been lucky to meet you, then."

He grinned back.

'How much of that junk do you have, actually?" I asked. "I think I have an idea."

"About five hundred items," he grunted, pleased with himself. "What kind of idea? Tell me!"

"Five hundred? Wow!" I couldn't conceal my surprise. "Not bad at all."

"What do you think? Come on, spit it out!"

"I will. I think it might be interesting—for you mainly. You never know, it might prove quite lucrative."

He laughed. "I can see you're already going to hassle me for a bargain! Come on, say it. I won't leave you out, I promise. You can trust me."

I chuckled. I couldn't haggle to save my life. It just wasn't my thing. I was too timid. "What do you know about dead races?"

"You mean guys like you?"

I nodded.

"Well," he began, "I know that they exist. We actually call them "discarded races". That's all I know. I've never really been interested in them. I know it might sound weird. In all my time in the game, we've only had three chars like that in our cluster, you included. No idea what happened to the other two. I know they're not here anymore. Haven't been for a long while—in the in-game time, I mean. Terminal #17 mainly sends us warriors as well as dwarves and gnomes. That's the way the cookie crumbles. You really think someone needs any of this junk? Please."

"Okay then," I decided to try a different approach. "Question: do you happen to have any Rocky Tail elixirs?"

That got the attention of this rarity connoisseur. "I do. Three of them. It was a set of three. Sort of."

"How much are they?"

His eyes glinted. "Seventy gold each."

I ventured a dramatic pause, just to prolong his agony. "I've been at the Dead Clan forum," I finally said, "They offered three hundred gold for one Rocky Tail."

He gasped.

Someone might say it wasn't very clever of me leaking important information just like that. They might be right, too. I should have probably made a list of the costliest artifacts, then visit Rrhorgus and buy them all wholesale, then sell them on to the Dead Clan for a nice bit of profit. The vendor wouldn't have very easily refused me: the shop wasn't his property, after all. He was just a Grinder like myself.

Sorry, but that was something I couldn't do. It just didn't feel right. Besides, it looked as if I might be stuck here for a while. And you never know when I might need a friend or at least an ally.

The vendor seemed zoned out. He must have been busy leafing through the inventory of his "treasures".

"Right, I'm off then," I said. "Here's the link to the forum. I suggest you check it out once you come round."

He nodded absent-mindedly. I smiled at his salt-pillar countenance, said my goodbyes and walked out of the shop. Time to get back to work.

As I followed the route I'd mapped out earlier, I couldn't help wondering what had stopped Rrhorgus from looking into it himself. Vendors were an entrepreneurial bunch, normally. How strange.

The mine welcomed me by its already-familiar

desolation. I said hello to the terminal and hurried inside. As I walked, I tweaked the bot's settings on Dmitry's suggestion, changing the mode to Economy which only needed one elixir. That would bring me around eighteen hundred stones a day, give or take a few. Still exhausting, but I could do it. I could always increase pressure afterwards, depending on my condition.

Two hours later, my bag had lost two points Durability: first time when I'd dropped a hefty rock onto my foot and the second when my arm brushed a sharp ledge. Had I worn a standard gear kit, the damage would have been distributed equally among my clothes, including the jacket and the hard hat. But just as Rrhorgus had warned me, in my case it was the bag and the belt that took all the strain.

Yesterday I'd been farming stones in the center of the location but today I'd decided to work near the walls and had suffered accordingly.

I switched off the bot and moved into the center. Loads of stones here. Off we go!

An hour later I'd gravitated back to the wall and grazed a knuckle of my right hand against a sharp rock. Another minus 1 to the Bag. If it went on like this, there wouldn't be much left of it soon.

I tried to switch off the app and work on my own. Oh well. As far as mine diggers went, I was rubbish. I turned the bot back on. I'd have to be more careful, that's it. Let's give it our all!

Chapter Twelve

I wish I could say that the four days in the agate mine had flashed by. True, man has a general tendency to want a lot but somehow his abilities tend to fall short of his expectations.

Today was my fifth day in the mine. I'd developed a strong allergy to the sight of agate. The terminal's system messages were already coming out of my ears. The only thing that still made me happy was the constant rise in my skill and abilities. They were the ones I looked forward to with an almost maniacal anxiety. And it was this anxiety that made me dig my pick into the rock time and time again. And again. And again!

Instead of adapting, my physical body kept deteriorating. Dmitry was only shaking his head: like,

I was working myself into an early grave. Each day I raised about fifteen hundred stones—peanuts but I was making some progress.

Yesterday my secret fears had come true as the ghost of Pierrot had raised its ugly head. Once the system informed me that Shrewd Operator had grown to 59 pt, a new message appeared below,

That's it, noob! End of the free ride!

The message blinked and disappeared. With it, True Heroes Take Devious Routes also disappeared from the characteristic menu. A very real chill ran down my virtual spine. It felt as if I'd had a truss rod removed from my back.

Dmitry spent all evening trying to talk me into discarding my char and starting afresh. The developers' offer was still there, he said.

"Why don't you choose a Gnome?" he kept saying. "Its characteristics are quite decent. You have some experience in distributing them now so you can do it wisely. Didn't I tell you that Pierrot was a nutcase? You have any idea what might happen next? Eh? Cat got your tongue? What's that smile on your face for?"

The secret was, as I'd listened to Dmitry I'd mechanically checked my bank account. Just out of habit.

"What are you smiling at?" he repeated.

Without saying a word, I turned the laptop to him, still smiling.

Dmitry whistled. "So! Ten grand! Have you sold

a kidney or something?"

I shook my head. Dmitry leaned toward the monitor. "Look, there's a message here. *With compliments from Rrhorgus the Dwand.* So it looks like he did appreciate the tip. Still I don't think it's enough. Not for that kind of idea."

I shook my head. "I kept asking myself why he'd never thought about it himself. But apparently, both the Dead Clan and their site only existed for a short while. I'm pretty sure he monitored other sites and forums and sold them an occasional item. But it was a drop in the ocean. There aren't that many chars that need them. And I introduced him to an entire site that was doing just that. He would have found it sooner or later, with or without my help. I just happened to be the first. He had a field day there for the first couple of days. Then other vendors started coming which dropped prices considerably. Honestly, I don't know all the details nor do I want to. It's the outcome that matters. And I have to admit I'm very happy with it. Another good mensch I've met on my travels."

"And ten grand on your bank account," Dmitry laughed. "Still I don't think he paid you enough. I can only imagine how much he's made this week... and how much more he's yet gonna make."

I shrugged. "You know, I don't think I'm going to change my char. I'm used to this one. Pierrot was right, by the way. That's exactly what this second ability was: a free ride."

"You should have invested all thirty points into it straight away. That way you might have leveled your first ability better."

"Possible," I said. "Very possible."

"How many points have you got now?"

"Thirty-three."

"Which means that tomorrow Mirror World will be one Seasoned Digger richer!"

* * *

I did the last two points by the skin of my teeth. It had been nine hours since I'd entered the mine. I was about to give up and drink a second elixir when I finally saw a new system message,

You've received a resource: Agate.

You've received +1 to your Skill.

Congratulations! Your professional level has grown! You're a Seasoned Digger now!

I'd done it...

I sank to the ground. The first stage was over. To tell you the truth, I'd been all nerves, expecting that nutcase Pierrot to offer me a new surprise. Luckily, there'd been none. According to Dmitry, there was no way the disgraced programmer could have changed the main profession's characteristics. They were the same for everyone. Now the individual racial settings, that was different.

Once I'd got over the initial shock caused by the ability's disappearance, I had to admit that so far nothing had been done to harm me. On one hand, I'd lost it but on the other, it had allowed me to level the rest up quite nicely.

In any case, if my brother were to be believed, nothing could be done to strip me of my skill level. So even if Shrewd Operator had followed suit and left me, it would be annoying but not too serious. I was already a Seasoned Digger anyway; if push came to shove, I could always command an hourly wage in some malachite mine and just keep raising skill. I'd have a word with Shantarsky—he wouldn't say no. But even if he did, I could always go to the dwarves. I'd done the first level already. Admittedly it meant losing time, changing the module center and moving in there.

I had a funny feeling that Mr. Shantarsky wasn't one to ignore any potential gains. From what I'd sussed out by listening in to forum conversations, Lord Shantar regularly rented his emerald fields out to the Stonefoot. He simply didn't have his own workers of the same level. Once I became a Seasoned Digger, I could be allowed into the fields with a team of porters. Why not? Okay, a wage was a wage, as long as they agreed on the loan I needed.

In any case, what was I doing sitting here? I had to visit Rrhorgus and thank him—and probably check out any new gear. Compare his prices with the auction, too. You never know, he might have something interesting there... something not listed in his catalog.

Having declared the last forty stones, I waved goodbye to the terminal and hurried over to the miners' settlement.

It didn't take me long to get to the shop. You could say I skipped all the way there, impatient to choose some new gear and log out. I couldn't wait to give Sveta a call and hear her news—and share my own. Yes, I wanted to boast a bit, why not?

Rrhorgus met me standing behind the counter as usual. "Why are you beaming like a new penny?"

"What do you mean, why? Can't you see?"

He grinned. "No, I don't. Guess why?"

"Oh," I slapped my forehead, then switched off the private stats setting.

Rrhorgus applauded, smiling. "Congratulations! You *are* persistent, aren't you?"

"Thank you, Rrhorgus the Dwand," I said with a smile.

He chuckled. "Ah, so you've received it, then. Don't say anything. It's me who should thank you. You couldn't have appeared on my doorstep at a better time. Didn't I tell you I knew how to be grateful? Oh, one more thing. Wait a sec."

He dove into the storeroom. After a short while, he reappeared with the familiar carved box in one hand and a smallish pick in the other. I focused on it.

Name: Infallible Pick

Effect: +5% to your chances of finding an additional resource.

Restriction: Seasoned Digger

A runic script snaked along its blade,

Name: Pit Rune
Effect: +100 pt. to Durability
Restriction: Seasoned Digger

He chuckled, watching me. "I can see you're interested. I don't think you've ever seen anything like it at an auction, have you?"

I shook my head.

"I'm not finished yet," he laid the box on the counter.

I prized the lid open. A set of malachite runes nestled inside.

"Once you decide on your kit, you can choose seven of them, one for every item of your gear. Plus the pick. It's a gift. Have you decided what you want to choose?"

"Yeah," I said, studying the carved green tablets. "I need a Hardy Digger kit. It has a bonus to Speed plus an excellent rise in both Stamina and Strength."

"Good decision. I'll tell you more: this is the most popular kit of all. If you distribute the runes wisely, that will allow you to stay in game up to forty-eight hours. You can check out all sorts of instances."

As I'd studied the game's sites, I'd discovered that my rise in profession offered me quite a few interesting opportunities. Apart from working in the mine, I could now visit the so-called "instances"—locations inhabited by mobs. Swarming with them, in fact. Being a Grinder, I couldn't fight them—this pleasure was saved for the players with paid account plans. But apart from smoking monsters, these locations were excellent farming sources.

Mirror World had developed its own practice of completing instances. The paid players entered them first and mopped the location up from all sorts of nasty critters. Once the location's boss was killed, the location—a cave or some abandoned castle—stayed deserted for a few days. Two or three days normally. That's when Grinders stepped in and farmed whatever resources were available.

There were certain rules, of course. You couldn't enter an instance alone, only as part of a group of five players. Secondly, to make the experience as realistic as possible, the admins had decreed that once inside an instance, a player could neither log out nor quit the group. If you got fed up and decided to go home, you either had to exit the location or ask the group leader to delete you from the group. And normally, picky players like those didn't get a repeat invitation to join. Naturally, things happened—a leader could even disband the group by mutual agreement when all group members would be moved to the exit. There were lots of little rules like those.

The beauty of group farming was in the fact that instead of using the bag, the farmed resources were placed into special trolleys that could hold up to a thousand pieces. Which was why normally, a group consisted of diggers and haulers who pushed the trolleys to the exit. The profits were either shared equally between the group members by default, or distributed by the group leader according to prior arrangements. As a rule, the player who quit both the instance and the group could lose all of his or her earnings.

As for the resources themselves, for me this was especially important. The level-one stones farmed in instances cost about the same as sapphires. That looked very promising.

Now that I'd leveled up a bit, I had the right to use another very important in-game feature: the auction. Naturally, it had some level restrictions. Also, according to my contract, I couldn't sell resources I'd farmed in my employer's mine. Which meant that had I wanted to sell, say, some malachite myself, I couldn't do so—neither at auction nor via Rrhorgus or whoever else. The system was ruthless about that. Special filters had been installed to combat any pilfering. On Lord Shantar's estate, all resources belonged to its owner alone.

I turned my stare away from the runes. "I really appreciate it, Rrhorgus."

"Call me Ruslan."

"I'm Oleg."

We shook hands. It felt as if we'd only just met.

"Every cent is vital for me at the moment," I said.

"I know."

I sighed and looked at the pick. He pushed it toward me. "Oh by the way, what are you going to do with your Goner's kit?"

"Actually, I was thinking of selling it to you. Would you be interested?"

"Six days ago I would. Would have made a nice profit at your expense."

"What about today?"

He grinned. "Today I can't. My conscience won't let me. Take my advice. Auction the whole lot off and sell it separately. Set a starting bid at twenty-five gold on your runic items—you have four of them, don't you? You might be in for a pleasant surprise."

"But how about the "no-pilfering" rule?

"No problem. The kit is your property. It may have been a free gift but it's yours anyway. Now: the Hardy Digger. A seven-item kit will cost you forty-five gold. You already have the runes and the pick. We'll kit you out like a dream."

He beamed, exposing his sharp teeth. "Another thing. The Strength runes give you ten points each while the Stamina ones give you nine. I'd suggest taking four Strength ones and the rest as Stamina."

"Why? Wouldn't it be better to invest into energy?"

He shook his head. "No, it wouldn't. It'll create a misbalance. How are you going to sustain these levels of energy without Strength? You'd have to drink elixirs non-stop. I should even take five to Strength although four to three is a good enough ratio too. I also suggest you check the auction for any second-hand Hardy Digger items. Players sell them all the time. And you'd better dump both your bag and the belt. You can buy new Seasoned Digger ones—either from me or also at auction, even though they're likely to have lower Durability there. They might also have runic bags and belts too, but you can't get them at the moment. You still need to level up your guild Reputation first."

"Yes, I think I read about that somewhere."

"It's a good job you're such a diligent reader," he grinned. "When are you planning to celebrate?"

"How about tomorrow after work?" I said.

"Will do. Leuton has a few decent places with nice food and drink."

"Excellent. Actually, do you mind if I invite another couple of peop- er, Horruds?"

"What, Greg and Sandra?" he smiled. "Absolutely not. They're nice kids."

"Good," I said with relief. "They helped me a lot in my first few days."

"That's settled, then."

We shook hands again.

"Talking about gear," I returned to the subject. "I actually might do as you suggested. I'll check out the auction first and if I don't find anything good there, I'll get back to you."

"Good decision," he agreed. "You're not working today anymore, are you? So you can auction your Goner straight away."

"I'm not sure I want to use the malachite runes with second-hand gear."

"You never know, you might not have to. They do have runic items in the auction as well. If you like the prices, you might go for it even if it means the items have lower durability."

I smiled. "I really should visit you more often. You've given me all sorts of tips already. On my own, I'm sure I'd have messed it all up."

"Come and visit me then, don't just say it!" he jokingly threw his hands in the air. "If you find any decent runic items in good condition, I suggest you auction off the malachite runes too. Waste not, want not."

"It actually looks pretty promising," I murmured.

"You bet! You've left the hardest stage behind you now. And you did it in record time, I must say. Talk about workaholics."

"That's what my brother calls me," I said. "That's when he doesn't call me an idiot or suicide case."

Rrhorgus guffawed. "He might be right. But you're still alive, aren't you?"

"I'm obliged to be," I said firmly.

"Excellent," he rubbed his hands. "Come on, accept my gifts."

Rrhorgus has offered you a Wholehearted Gift.
Accept: Yes/No

I smiled. No need to ask me.

You've received a Wholehearted Gift!
Name: Infallible Pick
Name: A Malachite Rune of Strength, 4 pc.
Name: A Malachite Rune of Stamina, 3 pc.

We bade our goodbyes, then I walked out onto the street. A light pick snuggling in my hand, a boxful of malachite runes rattling in my bag—I was definitely making some progress! The main thing was not to get into any more trouble. And if their Pierrot kindly forgot all about me, that would be even better.

I stopped by a miniature fountain and took a lungful of virtual air. It tasted almost like the real stuff, the bastard! I opened the chat window. Greg was online—excellent.

Hi there Greg!

He replied straight away.

Howdy noob! Are you still alive?
Looks like it, I added a smilie.
That's good news.
Whatcha doing tomorrow after work?
Nothing, why? Wassup?
Just a bit of a party for my Seasoned Digger.
No! No way! You're not a noob, you're... you're...Way to go! Count me in!

I grinned at the flow of emoticons. *I wonder if you could invite Sandra for me. She's not on my friend list and I won't be able to see her today. I still need to go to Leuton.*
No prob. She keeps asking me about you.
See you tomorrow, then!
See ya, Mr. Seasoned Noob!

Still smiling, I quit the chat. Tomorrow we'd talk about everything. Shame Sveta couldn't be with us. I missed her already. How was Christina doing?

The thoughts of my family made me double my pace. It took me fifteen minutes to get to Leuton.

What a difference! I remembered my first journey. Today's trip felt more like a walk in the park rather than the perverted form of punishment I'd had on my first day. And once I got my Hardy Digger kit, it would be even better!

Guards stood watch by the town gate, talking, just like on the first day. This time no one paid any attention to me. Admittedly my Goner's kit made me look less of a noob, even though I must have still been a sight.

First things first: I had to pop into the guild and pay my weekly dues of twenty-five gold. It gave +50 pt. to one's Reputation with the Mine Diggers Guild. Ten such payments would earn me an Order of Recognition. Five hundred Reputation gave a player access to the guild store. For the time being, all I could get there was some Capacity Runes, but it opened up some interesting perspectives for the future. So today I was going to get my first 50 pt. Reputation. Shame you couldn't pay all of it at once: you'd shell out 250 gold and they'd present you with your brand new Order of Recognition. But Mirror World had its own rules geared up to keep players in the game for as long as possible. Which meant that if I paid my twenty-five gold every week and not a second earlier, it would take me two and a half months to earn my first Order. From there it got even more complicated. If the second step—the Order of Friendship—took you two months to achieve, the following ones—the Orders of Respect, Merit and Veneration—cost a thousand points each. Which in total meant four thousand points. A year and a half of playing! That was crazy. I had a funny feeling that this was the developers' way of sugar-coating the in-game charges.

Naturally, the guild store had all sorts of cool stuff like jewelry, cloaks, runes and tools. Then again, all of them had profession level restrictions. So it was really a Catch-22 situation. Still, as the saying goes, a journey of a thousand miles begins with a single step. Admittedly Mirror World was known for its abundance of various reputations, and every year they introduced something new. The game kept evolving. As the players' levels and demands grew, so did the game.

The Guild's reception was predictably packed with queues of zero-level workers snaking from the entrance. I joined one of them and prepared for a long wait. Still, as the novelty of the motley crowd had worn off a little, I noticed a few empty teller's windows. I took a closer look and noticed signs that said, *Seasoned Digger*, *Experienced Digger*, *Master Digger* and *Expert Digger*. Oh! That was where I was supposed to go!

I left the mass of waiting players and headed tentatively for the window that said, *Seasoned Diggers*. The players who'd a moment earlier given me looks of contempt worthy of my noobish Goner attire followed my progress with sarcastic anticipation. They probably expected the noob to venture to the window "just to ask a question" and looked forward to my receiving a good dressing-down. I'd made my stats private, hadn't I? So no good staring at me or my Shrewd Operator like that. In all honesty, their smirks didn't add to my confidence.

A skinny ginger-haired she-dwarf was peering at me from behind the locket. She flashed me an open smile. "Greetings, Sir Olgerd! Congratulations on your new profession level!"

"So!" I was taken by surprise. "So that's how it is, then."

"Of course," the lady dwarf nodded her ginger head of hair. 'What did you think? We're a serious organization. By joining the Guild, you automatically put your name on our lists. This way a special program can monitor our workers' progress."

"All right..." I managed.

"Don't worry, we have no access to your characteristics—only your profession level."

"Well, I suppose it's good news."

"It is," she flashed me another smile as she nodded at the line of players. "I don't think you had time to kit yourself out?" she asked knowingly.

I shook my head. "It can wait. I decided to come here first thing. Seeing as I have a couple of matters to settle with you."

"Which are?"

"Firstly, I need to pay my weekly dues. And secondly, I'd like to make an application for a level-appropriate instance."

She nodded her understanding. A system message popped up,

Would you like to pay the Guild dues of 25 gold?

Yes, I would. I had forty gold on my gaming account. This was the little cache I'd made from the money I'd earned in the agate mine, to pay for elixirs and other emergencies. It was already good news that I could make do on what I earned. The rest was forwarded to the in-game bank then further into the real world.

Congratulations! You've received +50 to your Reputation with the Mine Diggers Guild!

The lady dwarf smiled at me again. "Congratulations."

"Thanks," I flashed back.

"Now, your instance application. Any resource preference?"

"Not really. As far as I know, prices are all more or less the same."

She nodded, staring into the monitor on the desk in front of her. "You're going to dig, aren't you?"

"Exactly."

She spent a minute entering the data, then turned away from her monitor. "That's it. Your application has been filed. The contract you'll make directly with the group leader. Once we receive a suitable request, we'll send you an email. Anything else I can do for you?"

"That's it. Thank you. Have a nice day."

"It's been a pleasure. Enjoy the game!"

As I walked toward the exit, I caught a few envious glances from the zero-level players. Sorry, guys. No circus show for you today!

Now I only had to pop into Leuton City Chamber of Commerce, then I could finally log out.

Actually, the auction dealings didn't require a building as all transactions were made online. I didn't yet know how exactly it was all supposed to happen but I fully intended to try it. But in order to participate in the bidding, I first had to register with the Chamber of Commerce. No idea why they called it such because in my opinion, the place was none other than a tax office. Somebody at the forum had suggested that this name would have evoked unpleasant sentiments in players. A taxman sounds a bit—how can I put it—a bit too real-world, if you know what I mean. But a "Chamber of Commerce representative" was supposed to elicit different kinds of emotions... having said that, it was still a bit too real for comfort. Never mind. What was the point in pondering over it? I had too many other problems to worry about.

The building looked least of all what I'd expected it to be. It was a miniature Disney logo castle replete with little towers and weathercocks. It was begging you to walk in and investigate. I couldn't help smiling as I remembered the forum member's comment: this was the proverbial witch and her gingerbread house.

In we go, then! I just hoped they weren't going to fatten me up for the witch's pot.

Forty minutes later, I'd finalized all my financial affairs in this "gingerbread castle". I'd only had to sign a tax agreement on 1% of each transaction. They'd also given me a list of resources banned from the auction and another one of various helpful—or so they thought—services they provided.

As an example, the Chamber of Commerce could act as a guarantor and contract witness in case of particularly large transactions—and that's considering that Mirror World was packed with all sorts of lawyers and notary offices.

I reached the park and looked for a large enough tree. Hiding behind its broad trunk, I began to undress. This was a good place. No one was going to interfere. As I removed the last piece of my Goner's kit and stuffed it into the bag, I discovered I was once again dressed in my decorative start-up zero-level kit.

It felt as if something invisible was pressing down on me. I had trouble breathing. The absence of the kit's characteristics showed. These things got you hooked really quickly. Never mind. This was only a temporary measure.

I had to sit down. As my back leaned against the giant tree's powerful trunk, I heaved a sigh.

I opened the auction menu. The runeless clothes would be the first to go. I was going to price them slightly lower than they were in the shop. I didn't want to risk it: I'd have to pay the tax even if I failed to sell the item. The admins always wanted their pound of flesh.

Now, the four runic items. I set the starting bid at twenty-five gold apiece. Done. I ticked the "pay tax after completing the transaction" box. All ready.

Then I began checking the auction for a Hardy Digger kit. Most of the items were quite worn-out. Not a single one had more than 50% Durability. But quite a few had runes on them. Actually... how about these gloves? They had a rune on them, too. Only minus 10

Durability but the price was way too high. No idea who would buy them. If you worked it out, you could easily see the item would still be cheaper than if you had to separately buy the rune and the item new from the shop. But me, I already had the runes, that was the problem.

After delving into it a bit more, I finally worked it out. I had to go for Durability. The next morning I'd have to buy some new gear from Rrhorgus, apply the runes to it and stop pondering over it. Still, I was curious what else they might have.

I set up the search results filter to "zero level, seasoned digger". Picks, clothes, elixirs. The picture was pretty clear. I left the level filter on but removed the elixirs. Strangely enough, here they were ten times cheaper than in the shop. Apparently, everybody was interested in crafting professions. The scrolls were prohibitively expensive... Stamina and Life stones... everything way too dear. But if I wanted to do the instance, I'd have to buy them. At least that was the forum members' collective wisdom. My level was too low to hope for any jewelry. Having said that... I ran a quick search...

I couldn't believe my eyes. I blinked to make sure I was actually seeing it. The park was quite warm but I felt a cold chill run down my spine.

A single offer hovered on the screen,

Type of item: Ring
Name: Truth Will Out
Effect: unknown
Restriction: Only Ennan Race

Mechanically I shifted my gaze to the vendor's name.

Sold by: Torreip

Chapter Thirteen

I quit the game like a scalded cat. My brother's cell phone was out of range. I paced my temporary dwelling until I'd calmed down a little. Never mind. A shower first. Then I'd have to try Dmitry's number again.

As I stood under the shower's cooling jets, I kept humming an old song from a Russian fantasy movie. *Magic ring, magic ring, take this man, bind him tight...tie his legs, chain his feet...* Oh. I was definitely getting old. The way I was shaking you'd think I'd found Tolkien's Ring of Power.

Gradually I felt better. The day in the mine had taken its toll. This kind of job could finish you off, no problem. The game developers preferred to hide behind complex terminology, hiring high-brow professors to brainwash gullible TV viewers into buying the "Mirror World phenomenon" story. Just the other day I'd seen two such learned members on YouTube having an altercation as one of them insisted that Mirror World's creators had somehow managed to penetrate the players' brains to create a copy of the so-called virtual world. The other foamed at the mouth trying to assure the audience that this was due to the discovery of a time portal into another dimension. What a circus.

I always wanted to know why the powers that be considered all common people a bunch of brain-dead idiots. If one kept his mouth shut while watching a show like that, it didn't mean he or she believed it. It was just something in our nation's genes—the aftershock of several generations of Russians fighting and dying in several murderous continental wars. Our fathers and grandfathers had only one argument to counter the Soviet authorities' tyranny with: *Please, not another war.* We'd been raised with this phrase, passing it down to our own children and grandchildren. *Please not another war, the rest we can manage; we'll grin and bear whatever it is—we're a nation of survivors, after all.*

So now, watching Mirror World developers' attempt to sugar-coat the truth, I realized that no one would ever discover the real story. The program made me understand one thing, though: apparently, whatever happened in the virtual world directly affected the state of our physical bodies. All this uncertainty, this ambiguity and lack of information worried me. Still, I had my own story. I needed the money.

As I rubbed myself red with the towel, I kept thinking about everything that had just happened. Having said that, what *had* happened? Nothing really. I hadn't bought the dodgy ring. Too risky. I hadn't had the heart. This ring was bad news. *Magic ring, magic ring, take this man, bind him tight...* Oh well. Any other gamer would have snatched it even without thinking. A goodie like that?—sure! Wasn't it what gamers called things like this: a goodie?

But I wasn't a gamer, was I? Not by any stretch of the imagination. The shock of the Devious Routes skill disappearing had been too much for me. Constantly feeling that someone was playing with you like a cat with a mouse was beginning to take its toll. It made you nervous. And it's common knowledge that a nervous person starts making mistakes.

Enough. I had to calm down. Sveta was already waiting for my call. My voice had to be calm and cheerful. Otherwise she was bound to smell a rat. She had a knack of sensing these things.

* * *

I awoke in the morning feeling broken. I'd had all sorts of sick dreams the whole night.

I dialed my brother's number. Same story. True, he'd said that he'd be out of town for a couple of days but he hadn't told me he was going to switch off the phone.

Never mind. I had a big breakfast, called my wife, tried Dmitry again, then headed off to work.

Mirror World greeted me with a pleasant surprise. The in-box icon blinked with new messages. Was it reporting my future profits? It was indeed. Everything I'd put up for auction had sold. On top of that, the runic items had gone for almost twice the price. All in all, I was two hundred ten gold and some small silver change richer.

I grinned. No need to buy second-hand gear now: I could comfortably afford new items.

Rrhorgus wasn't in that morning. A young Dwand served customers instead. He bore a fleeting resemblance to my friend.

Finally, I faced the vendor. He grinned politely,

"Hi, Olgerd, how are you today? How can I help you?"

I still couldn't get used to the fact that my name was literally written over my head. "Where's Rrhorgus?"

"Dad's taken a day off. I'm filling in for him. He told me you'd be coming."

"I see... er... Max. I meant to..."

"You've come to buy the Hardy Digger kit, haven't you?"

"Yeah. Plus a level-appropriate bag and belt."

"Let's start with them then, shall we? This is a Capacious Backpack for 70 slots. Durability 50 pt. Next... a Stitched Leather Belt—fifteen pockets, durability 50. Plus a complete Hardy Digger kit. Would you like something else?"

"That's it," I said.

"That'll be fifty-four gold."

"Here."

"I suggest you auction off your old belt and bag," he said. "They're always sought after, even if low on Durability."

"Got it. Thanks."

"Here you are."

My virtual wallet became fifty-four gold poorer. A system message popped up, reporting the purchase. Without leaving the shop, I distributed the runes between the items and hurried off to change into my new best.

The lack of energy weighed down on me. Only when I put the shirt on did I sense a relief. The pressure was gone. With every new item donned, my body shed some of the weight. The energy bar hit the green.

Max gave me a cheerful smile. "Feeling high? I bet."

"Yeah, sort of," I smiled back.

So what did we have here? This seven-item kit added +25 to Strength, +10 to Stamina and a bonus +18 to Speed. The three Stamina runes of nine points each and four Strength runes of ten each added their weight to the gear. All in all, my new stats began to look like this:

Strength, 68
Stamina, 40
Speed, 22

The kit's Durability was 70 which once again convinced me that I'd made the right decision buying new stuff. My Energy bar was especially pleasing to the eye with its 840-point calibration. Now I'd be able to spend more time working. I wouldn't have to quit the game so often. The only problem was, now I'd have to move into another room with a different type of capsule. The one I had now wasn't suitable for extended immersion.

And now down the malachite mine we go! Time to try out my acquisitions. I asked Max to remind his dad of our RV that evening and hurried out.

You could say I had a spring in my step all the way to the mines. They were situated at the same location. Already as I approached, I realized that something was wrong. If the agate mine had looked like a horror movie setting, the malachite fields were swarming with activity. Why all these people? Hadn't I read only the day before yesterday that no one was interested in mining malachite? And now it looked as if this place was experiencing some kind of industrial revolution!

As I moved closer, I was already getting some idea of what was going on. The place was packed with dwarves and gnomes. How many of them were there? Dozens? Hundreds?

I counted fifteen terminals in total, each with a small line of people in front of it. The queues moved and grew equally as fast, new diggers taking the place of those who'd declared their spoils.

The trolleys were brought out to special dedicated terminals that looked just like the one I'd been using. Wherever I turned, I saw none other than dwarves, gnomes and yet more dwarves. I remembered reading somewhere that the Stonefoot clan made up part of the Alliance of Light even though it didn't participate in any of its armed conflicts. The clan counted a handful of warriors but its bulk was made up by Grinders. They were actually more like a guild than a clan. And a very rich guild it was, too.

At first, no one paid any attention to me. Only when I finally stood in line at one of the terminals did I catch dozens of stares focusing on me—annoyed, indignant and openly sarcastic.

My turn came. I could physically sense the line behind me grow tense: I'd slowed their routine up.

Greetings, Olgerd!
This is Mine Terminal #22
Levels: 35 to 85
Resource: Malachite
Press Confirm to begin farming.

"Come on, move it!" voices shouted behind me. "Wretched noob! Quit stalling!"

I pressed *Confirm*. Still, the terminal wasn't in a hurry to let me go,

As of the latest lease agreement between the Stonefoot Clan and the Lord of Shantar, the clan's workers are denied access to the mines' three upper levels. You're welcome to farm resources at levels 4 and 5. Thank you for your consideration.

I stepped away from the terminal. The crowd heaved a sigh of relief. Yesterday I'd had no idea of

---

any contract. The news had said nothing about it. Having said that, who'd be interested in a level-zero mine? Compared to breaking news of a conflict between the forces of Light and Dark in No-Man's Lands or a report about the discovery of an ancient artifact in a sleeping god's tomb, a petty lease agreement would look admittedly out of place.

As for me... I knew of course I was just a nobody but had it really been so difficult to either send me a quick email or post a message on my page, informing me of these changes? I refused to believe I was the only Seasoned Digger working for Shantarsky. But still, as I climbed down the mine, I didn't see any of his employees. Only when I reached Level 4 did I understand why.

The descent had taken me about ten minutes—which meant that the round trip to the terminal and back would cost me twenty minutes of my time. I could already see that Level 4 wasn't equipped for using trolleys. And I dreaded to even think about Level 5.

The most I could take out on me would be 70 stones. Farming them would take me about ten minutes. So in theory, that meant 140 stones an hour. Minus queuing time, the stones' regeneration time and other emergencies. Didn't leave much. But at least I had a trump card up my sleeve: the Shrewd Operator. Plus my new gear kit which allowed me not to skimp on energy.

That's it! Enough procrastinating! Time to do some mining!

When I climbed out with my first dose of

Malachite and lined up for the nearest terminal, I couldn't but notice their smirks. A comment reached my ears: *He'll burn out by his third delivery and go for a beer.*

Yeah yeah. They could laugh all they wanted. They hadn't seen me back in the agate mine, that's what it was. My new skill, all three points of it, pleased me even more. And this was just the beginning!

By my fifth trip, the dwarves glanced at me with undisguised curiosity. I must have looked like an idiot. So what? I'd already farmed 350 stones and raised my skill to 11 pt. I didn't even feel any energy loss. After the agate mine, this was a pleasure cruise.

I kept at it for almost nine hours. Finally, I exited the mine for the sixteenth time. My last trip. My skill was at 53. Shrewd Operator began glitching with a worrying regularity. It was probably some admins' regulation. According to my own count, I should have made much more already. I'd have to discuss this with Dmitry, even though he was unlikely to tell me. Possibly, he didn't even know. I was still pleased with the results. I'd already earned seventy gold. Had it not been for my friends and our outing, I'd have stayed in the mine for a little longer.

Dwarves cast respectful glances my way. And they hadn't even seen my stats! I waved to the terminal—it had already become a habit—and set off for Leuton.

My PM box pinged with a message from Rrhorgus.

We're in the Old Bell tavern. Waiting for you.

I'm on my way!

I entered the tavern's name into my satnav. It was within fifteen minutes' brisk walk. Excellent. I strode faster.

As I walked, I checked my email. Both the bag and the belt had sold. Good. I had a hundred seventy gold in my purse. Tonight we'd party, and tomorrow I'd transfer the extra to the bank. I didn't need so much money in the game.

I tensed as I checked on Pierrot's ring. Nothing. The ring was gone. Probably, the bidding time was up. That was good news. One trouble less. I was doing perfectly fine without any suspect artifacts. If it all went like this, very soon I'd move on to emeralds. That would allow me to resume my loan negotiations with Shantarsky.

The Old Bell tavern was a very picturesque place—like everything in Mirror World, really. It sported wide lattice windows made of hundreds of tiny colored glass panes. Red rounded tiles covered the roof. Little bells laced with fancy patterns hung from the roof ridges.

Virtually every part of the building was marked with a small picture of a bell. Its massive front doors, carved shutters and wrought railings all bore the same logo.

A system message greeted me at the doors,
Welcome to the Old Bell Tavern!
Would you like to download and install our free

Menu app?

I accepted.

The tavern met me with a cloud of tantalizing aromas and the hubbub of voices. Players were chilling out after another hard day. No one was making trouble. Little wonder: two wardrobe-sized Horruds levels 40-plus kept the room peaceful. This was the first time I saw Greg's fellow counterparts in full combat gear: weapons, armor and all. They looked impressive. Apparently, the tavern owner was on the rise. It must have cost him a pretty penny to hire two such hulks as bouncers. Or was I missing the point?

I looked around me. The customers were mainly Grinders. Two level-forty men would be well enough to bring any number of trouble-makers to heel. Their service was excellent too: a bunch of petite Alven girls fluttered around the room in their uniforms resembling that of the German national costume: calico aprons embroidered with little bells and navy pinafores with full skirts worn over white wide-sleeved blouses with demure cleavages. Men cast surreptitious glances at the pretty girls but didn't allow themselves anything immoderate. Rrhorgus had chosen a very decent place. I really liked it here. If only I could bring my two girls here one day! We'd have had a lovely evening, the three of us.

Greg rose from a far table and waved his shovel of an arm at me. I threaded my way between the tables trying not to inconvenience anyone.

"What took you so long?" Greg thundered.

I smiled. "Sorry I'm late."

Sandra, Greg and Rrhorgus stared at me cheerfully.

"You don't mess about, Mister Goner, do you?" Sandra said. "We thought we'd have to chip in for a nice little coffin for you—and you're a Seasoned Sonovabitch already! Congrats!"

"Thanks! As the classic said, reports of my death have been greatly exaggerated."

"You like it here?" Rrhorgus asked.

"Very much. Sort of like Munich away from Munich."

"You got it," Rrhorgus nodded. "The owner is German. He started off as a Grinder too."

Greg rolled his eyes. "One day I'm gonna save enough money for a Bronze plan. Then I'll spend some quality time mopping up dungeons until I make enough gold to open something like this. What do you think, Sandy? Would you marry a well-fed *sour craft* lover? We could make a few baby Horruds, brew beer and live happily ever after."

"It's *sauerkraut*, stupid, not sour craft," she corrected him. "Making babies and drinking beer, that's all you can think of. You seem to be too content to stick to your hourly wage. Look at our Grinder friend here and try to level your skill up a bit too. You need to start growing otherwise you risk lugging granite around for the rest of your life."

"It's all right," Greg waved her words away. "Every dog has its day."

"If you say so," she murmured. "So do groundhogs."

Three girls fluttered out of the kitchen carrying

large trays groaning with food. Expertly navigating the room, they headed for our table.

Noticing their advance, Greg tensed in anticipation.

"I wish you were as enthusiastic when you saw a slab of rock," Sandra commented.

While they exchanged quips, I leafed through the menu. Oh well. It looked very respectable, neat and quite cheap too.

Rrhorgus smiled at the other two's banter. "We've already ordered while we waited for you."

The table began to fill with various dishes. A deep clay bowl was filled to the brim with sour... er, sauerkraut. An oblong plate heaving with fried sausage of every kind and shape stood next to it. Pig shanks and spare ribs were followed by a few misted pitchers of light beer. The whole caboodle looked and smelled delicious.

I surveyed the table in bewilderment, then looked at my friends. All three stared at me in anticipation. "What?"

"Just waiting for you to try," Rrhorgus said. "As far as I understand, this is your first meal in Mirror World."

"Ah yeah," I forked the nearest sausage. "That's good. Why? What's wrong?"

"*Good?* Is that all you can say?" Sandra couldn't conceal her disappointment.

"Our Olgerd must be so used to his virtual body now he can't even understand what we expect from him," Rrhorgus explained.

"Honestly, I can't," I admitted. "What's all this

about?"

"It's about you sitting here eating virtual food. And the fact that you can smell and taste it," Sandra couldn't help herself.

"Ah. I see."

Rrhorgus smiled and sent a piece of bread tumbling into his mouth. "It's just that your reaction is unusual," he said. "One might think you've been a gamer for at least a couple of years."

"I remember the shock I had the first time," Greg confirmed, necking down some pork and potatoes.

I shrugged. "I never looked at it that way."

"It's all right," Sandra summarized. "What difference does it make? The main thing is, he's enjoying it."

Rrhorgus swigged some beer from his mug. "What have you done over there at the malachite mine?"

I didn't understand the question. "What *have* I done?"

"While I was waiting, I got a message from Flint, one of the Seasoned players, a nice guy. He told me about a certain Olgerd who apparently got one over on the dwarves. The guy walked in, checked in as if it was the most natural thing in the world, went down to Level 4 without as much as breaking into a sweat, delivered a very decent turnover, finished his work and left without saying a word."

I could have done more had it not been for this particular appointment, I wanted to say but kept it to myself. I didn't want to hurt their feelings.

"Flint?" Sandra said. "I know him. Nice guy, a Dwand. His group are all nice."

Greg nodded. "I know him too."

I shrugged and said what I'd been thinking, "After the agate mine doing malachite is a walk in the park. Not even to mention my gear."

"You see?" Sandra turned to Greg. "That's the attitude!"

"Flint would like to see you tomorrow," Rrhorgus said.

"Why?"

"He's the permanent leader of the Dungeon Busters group."

"But there have always been four of them," Sandra sounded surprised.

"Apparently, he was sufficiently impressed by the escapades of our Seasoned friend."

Mechanically Greg raised his enormous paw to slap my shoulder. I squeezed my eyes shut. My jacket's Durability was about to take some damage. Still, he stopped himself just in time.

"Sorry," he said, embarrassed. "I won't do it again."

"Please don't," Sandra giggled. "Our dear Olgerd still has a few years' life in him."

Rrhorgus paused and went on. "Flint knows about your instance application. The guild included it in the newsletter it sends out to all group leaders. It's basically just a lucky coincidence. For my part I can say that both Flint and his guys are very correct."

Sandra and Greg nodded their agreement.

"I'm all for it," I said. "I was quite prepared to

join any group at all."

"Excellent," Rrhorgus said. "I want you to come over to see me tomorrow. I'll introduce you."

"That calls for a toast," Greg announced. "To the future dungeon buster!"

Our clay mugs thudded their fat sides in unison.

"That's not all," Rrhorgus continued once we'd drunk the toast. "We have a gift for you. You're a Seasoned Digger now, after all."

"What kind of gift?" I asked.

Greg grinned. "It's a surprise!"

"Come on, give it to him already!" Sandra opened her eyes wide in anticipation.

What were they up to? Judging by their hyped attitude, it must have been something interesting.

"Here, take it," Rrhorgus said.

Rrhorgus would like to give you a Surprise Gift.
Accept: Yes/No

I smiled. This was an easy choice.

You've received a Surprise Gift!
Would you like to open it?

"Come on, open it already!"
"Go ahead, dude!"

"You're like children, really," still smiling, I opened the gift.

You've opened a Surprise Gift!
You've received the Truth Will Out Ring!

Chapter Fourteen

"That bastard!" Dmitry fumed, pacing his office. "You wait till I get my hands on him! I'll rip his head off!"

He looked the spitting image of our father now: the same brisk walk, the same large hands clenched into sledge-hammer fists. This one could rip the head off anyone. I had no doubts about it.

"But what's he up to, d'you think?" I reached for my glasses and wiped them mechanically.

"Do I know? Does anyone know? The guy is a nutcase!" he finally slumped into his chair opposite the small couch by the window where I was sitting.

"Not necessarily," I said. "He might have his reasons."

Dmitry waved my argument away. "Please. He

was always slightly off his trolley. I could never understand him."

"Your not understanding him doesn't make him, as you call it, slightly off his trolley."

"Personally, I know very little about him. He's from a foster family. I've never seen him with a girl. Not that I'm surprised, but then again, who knows. I'm pretty sure that those at HQ could tell you much more about this loon and his private life."

"Is that it? How about a few character traits? Apart from him being a "loon" and "off his trolley"—I heard you perfectly well the first time."

He smiled sarcastically and shook his head.

"What, nothing at all?" I insisted.

He shrugged. "His workmates used to say he was very greedy. He would count every penny, whether it was his or somebody else's."

"Well, I have to count every penny too."

"You have a good reason," Dmitry dismissed my argument.

"How do you know? He too might have a reason."

He shook his head. "Not him. The guy is seriously deranged. He is a true penny pincher, literally. Either he's a control freak or deluded, one of the two. Then again, he used to spend all his paycheck on himself and his favorite gadgets."

"Why, was he supposed to share his earnings with anyone who asked?" I quipped.

"I didn't say that. Still, he could walk over to you and remind you you'd borrowed five rubles from him a couple of weeks ago."

"Right," I shrugged. "Anything else?"

"He couldn't take criticism. None at all. You couldn't tell him anything."

"Do you mean he expected everyone to praise him?"

"Not necessarily. I don't think he cared about it that much. I saw him once when the boss praised him. Zero reaction. Judging by his expression, he considered it his due."

"Anything else?"

"Haven't you had enough?"

"Personally, I don't think I have. I'm trying to work out his motives."

"His motives are to damage the company, that's what I think. Imagine an army of Ennans rapidly leveling up their respective skills. That might crash the market!"

"Then how do you explain the disappearance of my second skill? I'm pretty sure this was a premeditated trick, not just something he willed to happen! And now this ring... Didn't you say the admins were on it?"

"I just don't know what to think any more. All I know is that Pierrot is an expert. Just look how he keeps showering you with surprises."

I winced. "How does he do that?"

Dmitry shrugged. "I'm not a programmer. I'm good at other things. The game is still developing. They keep fine-tuning it all the time. You should expect some problems and errors."

"Talking about problems. Have they identified the auction vendor?"

He flinched. "Yes and no. Torreip is Pierrot's old char he used at the testing stage. He created it when the game was only just starting out. He hadn't used it for ages. Until recently, that is. I'll tell you more: God only knows how many toons he's got. The guys kindly checked the logs for me. They say that Torreip discovered the stash containing this ring a few months ago. He then lay low for a while until a week ago when he began showing up in the game on a daily basis. Guess what he was doing?"

I shrugged, then offered something that had occurred to me on my very first day in the game, "Monitoring the auction."

"Exactly. As soon as you began putting up your stuff, he put up the ring. And there was only one ring of this kind at the auction. Which meant he initially targeted the first Ennan who'd made Seasoned Digger. Had there been more of them, one of them would have bought it anyway."

"So if I understand correctly, if even one Ennan laid his or her hands on this ring, it would affect the whole race?" I asked.

"Something like that," Dmitry muttered. "What a shame we failed to ID him. He must have his own jailbroken capsule, I think. But my guys are still working on it. I'm pretty sure they'll dig something up."

"Oh."

"What did I say? You should have changed race when you still could."

"Yeah, but you also said that my skill points were safe."

"That's true. Even Pierrot can't get to them."

"In that case, I don't have to worry about it."

We fell silent. The day before, it had taken all of my self-control not to reveal my emotions at receiving the gift. Luckily, my friends hadn't noticed anything. They must have thought that my shaken expression was caused by their gift's sheer value. Which was good. They didn't need to know anything about my problems.

And as for their gift—the disgraced programmer left me with no choice, really. As soon as I'd confirmed acceptance, the ring clung to my index finger like a hungry tick, much to my and the others' astonishment.

"Have you tried to remove it?" Dmitry asked.

"You can't. According to Rrhorgus, the ring's setup works similarly to that of a rune. The only difference being, you apply your runes to your items and this bastard snatched my finger instead."

"Any effect?"

I shrugged. "None whatsoever. All my skills and other stats are still the same. I haven't grown a pair of donkey ears, either."

He guffawed. "It's early days still."

I cracked a sad smile.

'It's okay," he grinned. "The administration express their appreciation of your cooperation and suggest, for the umpteenth time, that you change your race."

"They appreciate it, yeah right. Appreciating the cooperation of their guinea pig. I don't think so. I'm meeting up with Flint tomorrow. I might sign up for an instance."

He shrugged. "Whatever. So," he sat up straight, rubbing his hands, "how about another one to celebrate your new level?"

We spent the next hour appreciating his excellent brandy. I wasn't sure about Dmitry, but personally I'd forgiven Dad a long time ago. When I'd been a little boy I think I'd even hated him. As I'd grown up, my hatred had dulled into indifference. And once Christina got sick, all earlier problems had seemed like... like they hadn't been problems at all. I'd suffered a complete reality shift.

It didn't take me long to get to the module center. I had a late-night conversation with my girls and sent them a few screenshots of the streets of Leuton and of the Old Bell Tavern complete with my smiling friends. My girls laughed looking at them; predictably, they wanted to come and see me in "fairy land", as Christina put it. Also predictably, I promised that things were going to work out just fine, adding that we might be together soon.

* * *

I met Flint in the Golden Sturgeon—a small cozy tavern in the miners' settlement. Our previous agreement was to meet up at Rrhorgus' store. But Rrhorgus, having introduced us to each other via his PM box and having sent us our respective mug shots for easier identification, had closed his shop for inventory. The looming introduction of the water world meant that all the vendors would have their hands full. To put it nicely, Rrhorgus had more important things to do with his time than shepherd us around.

The tavern was empty: at eleven in the morning, everybody was busy working. Apart from me and Flint drinking our coffees, the only other customers were a couple of dwarves talking in the far corner.

"Why don't you work for the dwarves?" Flint asked me once our introductions were over.

I shrugged. "They didn't hire me. I came to them on my very first day in the game. They said something about all vacancies already being filled."

"I see. You came to see them wearing your zero-level clothes, didn't you? No wonder. They have a competition for newbs: if you win, their guild will accept you on probation—depending on race, of course. I would have stood zero chance. They only want dwarves and gnomes, but your race has more in common with them."

I dismissed his suggestion. "Whatever. It's done now."

"True. I'm quite happy without them. We keep doing instances—there're loads here—and earn some decent money, similar to what they make farming sapphires. No one standing over you. Lord Shantar's boys keep mopping up the dungeons and bringing newbs in for a bit of leveling, so we get our share, at least two trips a week. Our group keeps in Shantar's good books so we have everything covered without having to go cap in hand to those Stonefoot pigs."

"Flint, mind me asking? Why me?"

He chuckled, then ran his hand under his chin, checking the non-existent stubble. "That's straightforward enough."

I shrugged. "Why wouldn't it be?"

He took a sip from a miniature cup and spoke. "Ever since our fifth member has left, we've been passively looking for a new group member. We have a tight team. No free riders trying to capitalize on fellow players' hard work. We can afford working the four of us. There is no rush. But as you understand, four isn't the same as five."

"From what I understand, a group of your reputation should have no problem hiring honest hard-working people."

"It's not that easy, Olgerd. It may sound like fantasy, but there *are* a lot of honest people around. But... there's always a "but". We need someone who can keep up with us. None of us want to take on a slow Moe, even if he's as honest as the day is long."

"I see."

"And as for you... Rrhorgus recommends you. Plus there's your malachite stint. Basically, me and my guys would like to offer you a trial period. If everything works out, we might make a team of five, why not?"

"Indeed, why not. What are your terms?"

"Between the four of us, we work three to one."

"Three with picks and one lugging?"

"Exactly," Flint nodded. "Actually, we have two haulers. But Sprat is also speedy. He has no problem keeping up with the three of us. Sir Tristan is strong but not as fast. And Knuckles and I, we just keep chipping away at the rock. If you join, it'll be three to two—perfect. Each does his job according to his characteristics, and we'll split the earnings."

"Does that mean that the three of us will have to meet five people's quota?"

He shook his head. "It doesn't quite work like that. It isn't like in a regular mine. Our objective is to do the instance. The resources are non-restorable, don't forget. We begin afresh at the level before last— usually, it's level five or six."

"Why the one before last?"

"Because if we mine ordinary resources, once we reach the last level, we might get a bonus of some quest stones. On one condition, though: the instance has to be already completed."

"I see."

"Exactly. And from our experience, five diggers just can't do it. Too much running to and fro. These aren't your malachite mines: quest locations are much deeper normally."

"All right. Are there many bonus resources, then?"

He pushed the cup away from him. "That's His Majesty Chance. Can be twenty, can be fifty. Even a hundred sometimes if you're lucky."

We fell silent. Seeing my pensive face, he added, "Take your time. We're gonna go on a raid tomorrow. We'll be incommunicado for thirty-six hours. That gives you two days to ponder over it. And if you make up your mind, we'll do our next instance together, you and us."

"I'm too short of thinking time," I said firmly. When I'd submitted my application, I was quite prepared to join anyone. But these guys were too good. I simply had to accept. "Count me in."

He nodded, then gave me a long look. "Before we sign the agreement, there's something I want to ask you. Is there anything I should know before we enter the instance?"

I expected something like that. Sooner or later the truth would come out, anyway. You can't keep a meteoric rise in skill a secret for too long. People start asking questions. And it was never a good idea to start a new friendship with ambiguity and secrets. I wasn't going to tell him everything, but I had to let him in on some of it at least.

"As a matter of fact, there is," I said. "But... I know it would be stupid asking you to keep your mouth shut. Share a secret with a friend, you share your secret with the whole world. No good grinning, man. I'm sorry if I offended you but that's what my experience has taught me."

He shrugged. "I'm not going to argue. You don't know us, that's all. Go on."

"Basically, my char belongs to one of those dead races."

He nodded. "And?"

"The programmer who created it has recently quit over some disagreement with the top brass. The admins then removed Ennans from the game just to avoid any potential problems. They offered me a swap but I refused."

He grinned. "Too greedy to lose your skill points?"

"Exactly," I nodded. "The first day I nearly snuffed it but I almost did four thousand agate. Then they suggested I change race!"

Flint whistled with amazement. "So basically, you're sitting on a ticking bomb. Is that it?"

I forced a smile. "Sort of."

"Any nasty surprises?"

"Not yet," I lied.

That was it, sorry, bro. I knew it wasn't honest but I wasn't going to tell him anything else. What I'd said was well enough in case something happened to me during the raid.

"I'm ready to join," I said instead. "It's up to you. I can only add that according to the admins, my main characteristics are immune."

In all honesty, I expected him to say no. Who would need a group member whose future was so insecure? Still, Flint surprised me.

"Take it easy," he said. "I have a few friends who play for dead races too. It's what admins always do: the moment there's a bug somewhere, they're offering you to turn coat. In your case it's only a few skill points, but imagine someone with a level-100 char who's suddenly told, *would you mind changing your race for a safer one because there might be a glitch there somewhere?* Heh. That's not a problem, man. Here, I'm sending you the contract, have a look. I'm gonna order us some more coffee."

The contract seemed legit. Besides, it was a one-off. I only had to do one instance. I signed it.

"Excellent," Flint smiled. "Welcome to the group! Tomorrow morning I'll send you an invitation from the entrance to the grotto."

"Where're we going?"

"Our boss' little boy is going to take some newb girls to the Spider Grotto for a bit of leveling. Hey, what's up? What's the sad face for?"

True, the name of Shantarsky Jr. had dampened my excitement which must have reflected in my facial expression. "There's something else I forgot to tell you."

His stare grew serious. "Which is?"

"I'm not his flavor of the month."

Flint guffawed. Then he surprised me again. "Ha! That only proves you're exactly who we're looking for!"

I ventured a smile as he went on,

"This little brat is only friends with his toads and brownnosers. We all have a bone to pick with him, so welcome to the club!"

We killed some more time over our coffees discussing various important details, then parted friends.

Flint definitely left a positive impression. What I liked about the group was that all its members seemed to be the same age as myself. Each of them had a family and a goal. Each of them took this seriously. Once again, I had Rrhorgus to thank for that.

I didn't go to the mine. I had too many real-world questions to sort out. The main one being, I had to change the capsule. The one I'd been using wasn't suitable for my new tasks. I had to move one floor up.

It didn't take me long to hang my hat in my new quarters—which incidentally were identical to my old lodgings. I decided against unpacking. You never know, I might need to move again. So I set my suitcase down in the corner to wait for further developments.

First of all I opened the Internet and started researching the Spider Grotto. It turned out to be the most common instance in the whole of Mirror World. Every cluster had one or more of them. I gave the mobs a cursory check: levels 20 to 35. The boss: Steel Widow. I didn't check the compensations—I wasn't entitled to them, anyway—but I did study the resources info.

Gray Crystals. A tad cheaper than sapphires, they were used mainly by alchemists and jewelers. A popular commodity on Mirror World's market. Notably, their dust was used in the making of stones of Strength, Life, Stamina and Speed.

Just as Flint had said, the Spider Grotto also offered bonus stones—the so-called Twilight Crystals. Their value lay in the fact that they were mentioned in several major quests. In other words, they weren't used in crafting—but several major NPCs wanted players to bring them these stones as offerings or gifts. I'd already noticed that quest resources were highly valued in Mirror World. This was a rare and much sought-after commodity. Oh well. This played right into my hands. The only thing left to do was actually get them.

Chapter Fifteen

We kept a safe distance from Lord Melwas and Co. as we watched their pompous departure from the Spider Grotto. The men's handsome faces flashed cheerful smiles as they bowed gallantly to the ladies in riding habits. My eyes watered with the sheer quantity of stabbing and slashing weapons.

"Freakin' boy scouts," a Rock Rhoggh growled, stretching his broad shoulders.

"You shouldn't say that, dear Sprat," said his bigger counterpart. "Nothing of boy scouts left in that lot. With boy scouts, you can still influence their baby minds. These are fully grown bastards. I'm afraid they are fully formed now."

"Fully formed idiots," a slight skinny Dwand finished his sentence.

"I have to admit I completely agree with you on this one, dear Knuckles."

"So!" Flint said in mock surprise. " Sir Tristan has agreed on something! That's a first!"

Grim bodyguards exited the dungeon next, following their master.

"These are Specters," the skinny Knuckles screwed up his face in disdain.

"Meaning?" I asked, peering at their dark figures hung with cold steel.

"The thing is, dear Olgerd," Sir Tristan began, "that the Mirror World phenomenon has led to the creation of all sorts of parties and movements in every shade of religious and political hue. Such formations are especially popular amongst the younger generation."

"Do you mean that these Specters are some kind of sect?"

"It wouldn't be exactly accurate to call them that," Sir Tristan objected. "Firstly, because they don't represent the result of some religious schism and secondly, because they aren't religious at all. They don't possess any particular teaching—neither founder nor any clear-cut tradition."

"That'll come," Flint said. "All they need is some time. They have their ideology basically shaped. Whoever compiles it into a concise formula will become their founder. And he won't be short of followers, trust me. As long as the idea is loud and attractive enough."

"What kind of idea?" I asked.

It was Flint who answered my question. "To put

it short, a reality swap. These people view the Glasshouse as a new real world."

"How about their bodies?"

"They stay IRL in some sort of induced coma," Sir Tristan replied. "There's no precise data yet."

"From what I heard, those who were forced out of this state have developed mental problems," Knuckles added. "Something like substance dependency."

"It's only rumors, mind you," Flint added. "They try not to draw the public's attention to it. The powers that be don't want any negative publicity. Right, enough shirking. The grotto is ours now. Off we go! It's do or die, LOL!"

As we marched toward the mine, I tried to stay behind, shielded by the Rhogghs' broad backs. Just in case. I couldn't be too sure if Shantarsky Jr. wouldn't want to take it out on me. New problems were the last thing I needed at the moment, and neither did my new group mates. Talking of whom—I'd turned out to be the youngest in the group. Knuckles who used to bear this title before me was two years my senior. Despite his guttersnipe nickname, he impressed me as serious—ruthless even.

For some reason, I'd expected to see Horruds as the group's haulers. But Flint explained to me that Rock Rhogghs could beat even the strongest race with their hands tied behind their backs. To run up and down the levels pushing heavy trolleys, this race was absolutely the best. Flint couldn't tell me anything about Sir Tristan—he didn't know much himself. The man kept his true occupation under wraps. Still, judging by his manner, our strongest team member was unlikely to indulge in heavy labor in real life.

As for Sprat, he was his complete opposite, a simple and straightforward menial worker, a true Grinder. For some reason I got a feeling that he was just as burly in real life, with two callous spade-like hands and a cocked flat cap.

In other words, I was very happy I'd landed in an experienced group—and their age suited me to perfection.

As I stepped over the invisible line separating the instance from the rest of the location, I had a stupid urge to look back at the departing company of Lord Shantar Jr. He stood there watching me intently as he was saying something to one of his minions.

A hand touched my shoulder. I flinched, betraying myself.

"I don't think he recognized you," Flint said reassuringly. "I wouldn't be surprised if he's already forgotten all about your first-day encounter on the road."

I chuckled. "Had anyone told me I'd be scared of some little bastard, I'd have laughed long and hard. But it is what it is, I'm afraid. I can't afford to lose time."

Flint nodded. "That's right. Come on, then. The clock is ticking. We have thirty-six hours tops."

"Who was it with him?" I asked as I hurried to catch up with the rest.

"That was Slayer, a level 80 wizard. One of his brownnosers."

"Is he also a *specter?*"

"Yeah, sort of," Flint answered. "An aspiring one, so to say. You'd better stay out of his way."

We caught up with the rest of the group as they descended the stairs between levels one and two. A set of narrow gauge rails ran parallel to the steps. Very soon they would groan under the weight of our loaded trolleys. Here, the terminals were located inside the grotto itself which made this mine different from the others.

Thirty six hours: the countdown began. Mechanically I checked the belt stuffed with elixirs. This was my first extended immersion experience. My bag contained energy food: apples, bread, meat and water. At Flint's suggestion, I'd also bought a few stones of Stamina, fifteen gold each, just in case. If I was lucky, by the end of the raid I might get a buff of +3 to Energy every 40 seconds for half an hour.

The Spider Grotto wasn't at all what I'd expected it to be. I'd imagined it as a nasty place blocked with cobwebs to the point of being impassable. A kingdom of arachnid monsters, so to say. In a way I'd been right, of course. The cave was hung with cobwebs complete with skeletons still clinging to them. The size of some of the bones was impressive. The designers had done an excellent job. No; it was something else that I found interesting. The spiders weren't the original inhabitants of this place. Judging by the ruins, the crumbling monuments and the dilapidated roads and sidewalks, once this place had been occupied by sentient beings.

"I wonder," I decided to share my deductions with the group, "why is this place called a Spider

Grotto?"

"Ah, you noticed it too, didn't you?" Sir Tristan replied readily.

"Oh, no," Knuckles said jokingly. "Here it starts again."

"There you go, Olgerd," Flint laughed. "Get ready for a lecture."

"Brace yourself, man," Sprat shouted to me from the front. "He'll turn you into a smartass like himself!"

Sir Tristan didn't bat an eyelid. "I simply have the habit of refreshing each location's story before I go there."

"I do too," I admitted, then corrected myself. "Since recently, anyway. But this time I gave it a miss. I know I should have looked into it. But Spider Grotto sounded self-explanatory."

"Look at those two!" Sprat cheered. "Kindred souls meet!"

"I just don't bother to read that nonsense," Knuckles said. "Usually what it says is just to pull the wool over your eyes."

"I am sorry to disappoint you, dear Knuckles, but sometimes this wool, as you eloquently put it, can tell a lot about a location. And even offer a few tips."

"Oh, no," Flint mumbled. "Here comes the Pearl Citadel stash story."

As if in confirmation of his words, Sir Tristan said, "And the Pearl Citadel stash can serve as a dramatic example of the latter."

"What do you mean?" I asked.

"Jesus," Knuckles groaned.

Regally ignoring his friends' jibes, Sir Tristan began to explicate,

"A few months ago, a certain low-level player discovered a one-off stash in one of the rooms of the Pearl Citadel. At the risk of preempting myself, let me tell you that the sum raised from the auction sales of the stash's contents had resulted in some sort of gold rush as everyone in Mirror World set off in search of new stashes. And what was especially instrumental in creating this kind of reaction, was an interview the lucky player had given to some local blogger. In it, he admitted that he'd come across a helpful tip in an article about the location's history."

I grinned. "I can imagine what happened next."

Knuckles nodded. "Everybody went mad!"

"All the forums and blogs, everything was packed with all sorts of interpretations," Flint added.

"Each even more stupid then the next," Sir Tristan said.

"So how did it all end?"

"It didn't," Knuckles said. "No one has found anything ever since."

"I don't think the player told us everything he knew," Sir Tristan objected.

"I think he was pulling the journalist's leg," Sprat said.

"That would be too much," I said.

"It would," Flint agreed. "I've known people's bones being broken for less."

"Back to the subject," Sir Tristan continued. "Talking about the Spider Grotto. From what I read, initially these dungeons used to domiciliate a certain clan Under the Mountain. The Black Axes, to be precise."

"Dwarves again," Knuckles spat.

"They're everywhere," Sprat agreed. "Bunch of bearded tight-ass bastards."

I'd already noticed that my new workmates seemed to have a thing about dwarves. I didn't dare ask, hoping to glean some information from their conversations. Instead, I said, "What's so special about these Black Axes?"

"And how can it help us discover treasure stashes?" Knuckles added with a grin.

"I don't think it can," Sir Tristan answered pensively. "The chronicles say that these Black Axes were rebels."

"What did they do?" Flint asked.

"You see, it was about that time when the Alven Race and the Highlanders made an alliance against a strong kingdom of humans."

"Let me guess," Knuckles grinned. "Our midgets sided with the humans?"

"Exactly," Sir Tristan nodded. "But they didn't even get the chance to warn the human king about the looming war. The clan was brutally massacred. I can tell you more: the clan had already been doomed."

"Why?" Sprat asked.

"Apparently, the clan's artifact makers had learned to build some kind of battle machines but they weren't in a hurry to share their secrets with other clans."

"If I can't have you, no one will!" Flint said theatrically.

"Not really," Sir Tristan corrected him. "The great master and his best apprentice had been taken hostage."

"Good!" Sprat exclaimed. "That's the spirit!"

"End of the line!" Flint suddenly announced. "Level six, everyone's invited to disembark!"

"Oh," Knuckles said. "I didn't even notice! Time flies when you're enjoying yourself."

I glanced at the clock. Our descent had taken thirty-five minutes in total. Holy cow. Good job I wasn't alone here.

"To work, comrades!" Flint exclaimed mockingly.

The level six cave was enormous. By my estimation, its ceiling reached to the height of a nine-story building. Its walls were streaked with stalactites as if some mythical giant had tried to melt them with a blow torch.

I suppressed a sarcastic grin. What was I thinking of! This was only a game, a set of clever stage props. But still it looked so real it sent shivers down your spine.

The cave was the size of two football pitches, its floor littered with rock debris and the remains of crumbled columns and statues.

"Impressive, eh?" Sir Tristan asked, smiling.

I nodded. "It is. I have to remind myself that all this was created by computer designers and not by some mythical ancient beings."

"Heh! That's right!" he agreed. "The location looks very believable."

"Never mind," I said. "Let's do it!"

Chapter Sixteen

At three in the afternoon we decided to stop for a lunch break. We deserved it. We'd done the whole of level 6. Predictably, our haulers had suffered the most. Still, they didn't complain—they even tried to be cheerful about it. As far as I could understand, we were making good progress. If we kept it up, we could mine more Twilight Crystals.

We also celebrated Knuckles' new skill point. Twenty more, and he'd make a new level. Everyone seemed sincerely happy for him. I sat there keeping a low profile. I'd already done nine skill points. And the best was still to come.

Only now did I realize the true value of my Shrewd Operator. Knuckles had the highest skill numbers in the group but he'd remained a Seasoned

Digger for two months already—and that's considering he was only doing the mining!

I didn't disclose my stats. Not that anyone had asked me about them. They seemed to be seriously thinking I'd only just got a new level. The few precious crumbs they received to their skill were a pittance. For the first time in the cave I wished that my Operator slowed down a bit. The cave was crammed full of crystals and I kept hacking at them non-stop. Both Sir Tristan and Sprat kept a watchful eye on the scene to make sure everyone had a trolley at hand. I winced and rubbed my chin.

Apparently, Knuckles misread my body language. "Cheer up, Olgerd," he gave me a friendly slap on the shoulder. "We'll level you up so you won't know yourself! You, and Sprat, and Sir Tristan too!"

"Oh yeah," Flint agreed. "I can already see our group of Experienced Diggers doing level-two instances. That's better than climbing down some spider's hole!"

"You can make good money with emeralds too," Sprat suggested. "Lord Shantar has this mine..."

"Please," Flint winced. "Rubbing shoulders with those midgets, thanks but no thanks! Great deeds await us!"

I listened in to their conversations, faking a self-conscious smile. I tried so hard to play the part of a newbie embarrassed by the attention of his more experienced colleagues. Even as I did so, I realized this was our last outing. More than that: I realized that if I happened to make Experienced Digger here in this cave, I'd have to disappear from Leuton. Here, it took people months of daily grind to earn their skills, point by miserable point. And here I was, rising through levels faster than some magic goose could lay golden eggs. Was I really a fraud—or as they called them here, a cheater? I didn't know. I'd chosen a race. I'd registered my account. I'd done some cruel things to my char trying to save every point in order to invest it in my future characteristics. Had I used any dirty tricks?—I didn't think so. I'd been offered a choice. So I'd done what everybody did when joining the game: I'd made my choice. Theoretically, everything was kosher. But it's true that most of the time theory disagrees with practice. I was 200% sure that had the true nature of my skills become known, it would have created quite an uproar. And that was the last thing I needed. Really.

"Cool," I tried to change the subject. "What comes after Experienced Digger, then? Isn't it Master Digger?"

Sprat guffawed. "Won't you be happy with Experienced?"

"Oh, I will," I smiled. "Just curious. There isn't much about it on the Internet."

Flint grinned. "That's all you'll find. Firstly, because clans treasure their Masters. They keep their names under wraps. They provide them with bodyguards, individual capsules and whatnot."

I whistled in surprise. "Why?"

Sir Tristan answered for everyone, "The answer to this question is pretty obvious. See for yourself: here we are in one of the most basic quest instances. But its resources cost like the most expensive class-one stones. There are certain locations in Mirror World that are the dream of every advanced player but venturing there is pointless without having a top-level digger to do the mining. The resources in such locations can be incredibly valuable. Without certain quest stones, for instance, you can't level up your mount or improve your castle's defenses. The examples are legion. People pay a king's ransom for the opportunity to lay their hands on resources like these. And in their turn, they protect and value the workers capable of obtaining them."

"I see," I said. "And secondly?"

"Pardon me?"

"Flint said, 'firstly'. What's secondly, then?"

"Ah," Sir Tristan's voice rang with understanding. He turned to Flint. " May I, sir?"

Flint nodded again. "Completely forgot. Masters have access to a second profession."

"Exactly," Sir Tristan said. "Normally, whoever gets access to a second profession concentrates on it and only agrees to clans' occasional requests to mine a particularly rare resource. The rest of the time Masters spend in the comfort of their workshops-"

"... crafting stuff like our runes and elixirs," Knuckles finished his phrase.

"Interestingly," Sir Tristan went on, "other professions have more than their fair share of Masters. But amongst Mine Diggers they are few and far between."

"That's because our profession is the most dangerous and accident-prone!" Sprat announced.

"Absolutely," Sir Tristan agreed. "Most people

prefer an easier job even if it doesn't pay as well."

"As for Master Diggers," Flint said, "you don't need to be a brain surgeon to realize these people are quite wealthy. They aren't interested in busting their humps in the mines anymore. Nor in running around instances like we do."

"They definitely aren't," Knuckles rolled his eyes in anticipation. "Once I become a Master Digger, I'll grow myself a big fat belly and get myself a personal assistant. I'll buy myself a waistcoat like they wear in the movies, with little pockets and a gold watch on a chain. Then I'll do nothing all day but saunter about like I don't have a care in the world. That's life!"

"Just make sure you don't get promoted while working the instance," Sprat said sardonically.

I pricked up my ears. "Why's that?"

"What do you mean?" Sprat sounded surprised. "The moment you reach a new level, the system throws you out of the group."

"Why?"

"Because an Experienced Digger can't be subordinate to a Seasoned one. Likewise, a Master can't be subordinate to an Experienced one," Flint explained.

"I see," I said. "I'd missed that somehow. What's the problem, then?"

"The problem is, a rise in levels incurs the player's deletion from the group and automatically teleports him back to his or her starting point," Flint said.

"The biggest bastard is the fact that I would

lose all the resources I'd already farmed during the raid," Knuckles added.

"Everything you've done in the last thirty-six hours? Really?" I asked, dumbfounded.

"Not everything, no. The stuff already declared is immune," Flint reassured me.

Sprat nodded at Knuckles' trolley filled to the brim with gray crystals. "But this isn't."

Bummer! More food for thought.

Gradually the conversation faded. Each of us was busy doing his own thing. Then Flint turned to me,

"Actually, Olgerd, there's something we'd love to know..."

I tensed. Here come the questions. I nodded for him to go on.

"How do you like Mirror World?" Flint asked.

It took me all of my composure to suppress a sigh of relief. Unpleasant questions were being put off. "What do you mean?"

"What he wants to say," Sir Tristan butted in as was his habit, "is that this game has a very high addiction rate. You have the developers to thank for that. They created a week's free trial—perfectly functional with all the trimmings, mind you—in a special dedicated server."

"Normally, a week's enough for a player to get seriously hooked," Flint said. "From what we've heard, ninety-nine people out of a hundred can't imagine their lives outside Mirror World anymore. So we're curious how it happened in your case."

I chuckled. "I see. Well, I'm afraid my answer

might disappoint you. I don't like it here."

They exchanged meaningful smiles.

"Please don't get me wrong," I said. "I fully appreciate the entire experience. I still can't believe it's possible. Everything's so real. Too real. It's like..." I paused, searching for the right words.

"Like visiting another planet?" Knuckles offered. "Or a parallel world?"

"Exactly," I nodded. "Not even. My job requires a lot of traveling. I've seen lots of different places—lots of strange people and unusual cultures. I've been to some amazing places. But strangely enough, coming back to my family was always the best part."

"A family?" Sprat asked.

"Yeah. A wife and a little girl."

"So you miss them but not the real world as such? Not your home?" Knuckles asked. "Me, I'm homesick like you won't believe."

"I'm not," I said. "You're right: I miss them, not our home."

"Are they away, then?"

I nodded, suppressing a sigh. The others fell silent, each thinking his own thoughts.

"And still," Sprat broke the silence, "I don't understand those specters. How can you swap the real world for this cage? The admins can interfere when you least expect it. What kind of life is that?"

"You think in real life you're free?" I said. "D'you want to say we aren't puppeteered around in the real world? That we don't have to obey their sick rules and regulations?"

"I couldn't agree with you more," Sir Tristan

turned to me. "Absolute freedom is the politicians' notion helping them to massage the voters' egos. Nobody votes as eagerly as a free idiot."

"In a way, I can understand those who've chosen this project to replace their real-world lives," I said. "I'll bet all you want that they're desperate. Mirror World allows them to experience something they're deprived of in real life. I keep thinking about my next door neighbor. The smartest guy you've ever met, handsome as hell and a mountain ski freak. One day he left on a ski holiday. A few days later they brought him back to his mother almost a vegetable. Completely paralyzed. He spent years on medications. His mother fought for his every breath. She placed him in all sorts of clinics and occupational therapies. Finally he could walk—after a fashion, moving around on crutches, all crooked like a bonsai. He can't speak anymore, he hums. But at least he can move around!"

"Let me guess," Knuckles said. "His friends gradually stopped coming. His girlfriend disappeared. He was all alone, if you don't count his mom and his computer. Right?"

"Yeah, sort of," I said. "At first he kept fighting. He walked a lot and he did all the exercises. Then one day his doctor said this was his limit."

"And he believed him and gave up?" Sprat said.

"It's not a question of believing," I said. "He'd already done everything he was supposed to have done. Oh, no. He just joined an online game. Made quite a few friends there," I smiled. "One day he even said to me that he'd got married... in the game. It may sound sick but I understood him. And as for Mirror

World... I wouldn't be surprised to find out that my next-door neighbor is here somewhere, walking around as some paladin in shiny armor."

"You might be right," Flint said pensively.

"Whether I'm right or not is of no consequence. I just think these people deserve some understanding. Having said that... I don't think my neighbor cares that much about what other people think. It's not going to change his life, that's for sure."

Chapter Seventeen

We'd reached level 7. We had another hour and a half until the first mobs reappeared. We had 118 Twilight Crystals in the kitty. Everyone was tuckered out but it felt good. The guys were happy. According to my calculations, we'd earned about four hundred gold each and had done a bit of skill leveling. As for me... each swing of my pick sent cold shivers down my spine. Eighty-three points! Two more points, and I'd get a new level.

I took a heavy, purposefully slow swing. My pick lingered in mid-air.

You've received a resource: Gray Crystal.
That was close.
By mutual agreement, we did level 7 all by

---

ourselves. As the other guys explained to me, you didn't get as many bonus resources when you let the bots to do the job.

Another swing.

You've received a resource: Gray Crystal.

Big sigh of relief.

Level 7 was one huge throne hall. Admittedly it looked more like a mass grave. Its floor was littered with skulls and bones, pieces of rusty armor and broken shields, swords, axes, halberds, arrows and spear tips. This disgusting mix was generously garnished with stiff gray cobwebs.

I'd mined thirty-four Twilight Crystals. I'd lost count of the Gray ones. If I made Experienced Digger now, I'd ruin the whole raid, both for myself and for the others. I'd already decided to tell them the truth once I made level 84. I just hoped they'd understand. That wasn't what worried me. But where four people shared a secret, it was only a question of time before it became common knowledge.

Should I keep it under wraps, maybe? Should I hit 85 points, get my new level, then promptly quit both the group and the game and start over in some other cluster as far from here as possible? Never mind the crystals—never mind what the guys were going to think about me. But this way my secret definitely wasn't safe. It wouldn't take Flint and the others long to put two and two together. And then they wouldn't keep their mouths shut, if only just to punish the jerk who'd done the dirty on them.

No. This wasn't an option. I hated the very idea of it.

Another swing.

You've received a resource: Gray Crystal

"Keep going, guys!" Flint cheered. "I got another Twilight one!"

"Olgerd, hold on!" Knuckles shouted to me from the opposite side of the hall. "We're nearly there!"

"Leave him alone," Sprat interfered. "Can't you see he can barely lift his pick? First time is never easy!"

"Don't shortchange him, man," Flint joined the quip exchange. "He's gonna surprise us all, trust me!"

Sullenly I kept picking at the rock. He didn't even know how right he was.

You've received a resource: Gray Crystal.
Your tool slipped as you picked at the slab of dark rock.
You've received a resource: Twilight Crystal.

"I got another one!" I wheezed.

"So!" Flint echoed. "What did I tell you?"

He had indeed. And the worst was still to come. I could imagine his face once I started telling them my story.

A swing.

"Comrades," Sir Tristan called out, "our time is up! One last swing and we're out of here!"

A swing.

You've received a resource: Gray Crystal.

Saved by the bell.

I stopped. I was heaving. For the first time in the last two hours I cracked a happy smile, meeting my friends' cheerful eyes. Yes: my *friends*. Nothing brings people closer than hard work. Especially when you know that each of them, you included, had given it their all.

I noticed an enormous carving in the rock wall a few paces away from me. It depicted a battle of dwarves with hordes of Rhogghs and Horruds. That was unusual. As I'd worked, I hadn't even had time to cast a look around. But now I could finally enjoy a bit of local artwork, why not? I still had a couple of minutes to catch my breath.

"Olgerd!" Flint called out. "Whassup?"

"Just a sec! I need a breather!"

"I see! All right then! We're going up! You'll have to catch up with us! Don't forget that the spiders will be here in forty minutes!"

"They're the biggest ones in there!" Sprat added, grinning.

I waved their warnings away: like, *don't worry, I have plenty of time.* Then I stepped toward the carving. I couldn't yet understand what it was but my eye had caught on something very... very *familiar*.

I had three more paces to take when I sensed a light prickling in my right hand. My ring finger.

Surprised, I pulled off the glove. The ring. The

fine runic script encircling it glowed an intense blue.

I took another step. The ring prickled my hand again. Another one of Pierrot's tricks.

I immediately remembered the conversation we'd had earlier about stashes and things. What if I managed to find a treasure as well? But what if it was a trap?

I took another step. The ring gave me one last prickle and became inanimate again. Not that I needed its warnings now. I'd already worked out what it was in the carving that had seemed so strange to me.

The warriors fighting the hordes of fanged Rhogghs and thick-skinned Horruds were no dwarves.

They were Ennans.

I peered closer at the scene. No, I wasn't mistaken. A squat figure of a warrior at my eye level was clad in a set of armor, his helmet in his right hand, his left one reaching for his face. Just like my own Ennan: a sullen stare, an aquiline nose. This one didn't have a shock of hair, though: his was neatly braided into lots of plaits, both his head and his beard. A tattoo on his cheek looked very much like a rune.

What an interesting individual. He wasn't in the thick of battle but it somehow seemed to flow around him. I got the impression that the Rhogghs and the Horruds seemed to be trying to get to him, hindered by the thick ranks of squat broad-shouldered Ennan soldiers bristling with long spears and blocking the way with their tall shields.

I couldn't see any archers. Ah, there they were.

Not archers: crossbowmen.

A group of bearded midgets hovered around the Ennan leader. Cassocks, long beards, twisted staffs in their hands. They carried neither armor nor weapons. These must have been wizards.

I stepped ever closer to the picture. I wanted to see everything in every detail.

But... what was this? It couldn't be! Then again... who did I think I was fooling? Apparently, whoever had created Ennans had his own far-fetched plans for their race. The Ennans' leader sported the exact same ring on his hand as I did.

Could I have been wrong? I raised my hand and took a look. The ring was identical.

I'd been expecting what happened next with a complex mix of fear and impatience. Both our rings glowed with the familiar blue hue. Fine blue threads emanated from the Ennan's ring. Mine followed suit, the threads reaching out for each other. It was fascinating.

I nearly missed the moment when they met. I snatched my hand away. The light went out. Gasping, I looked around me but saw no one.

What could this mean? Was it yet another surprise from the disfavored programmer? Or was it a complex activation of something very dangerous—or alternatively, very useful?

Later, I kept asking myself the question hundreds of times. What had triggered my next action? Could it be the guys' talks of hidden treasures? Or my constant musings to the point that Pierrot or what's his name, Andrew Petrov, hadn't done anything that could have hurt me yet?

I really couldn't tell. I only remember thinking clearly that if the ring would allow me to earn a bit more money, I shouldn't let this chance slip.

I raised my hand. The threads of blue light reappeared, reaching toward each other even faster than the first time. It was as if they were scared to fail again.

Finally, they met. For a while nothing happened. I admittedly thought this was the end of it. As if! A system message popped up,

Greetings, O Olgerd, from the guardian spirit of the Der Swyor Clan!

Would you like to download the clan's app suite?

Accept: Yes/No

An app suite. What harm could an app suite do to me? An expert would probably warn me against it. But once I started, I had to complete this route. The first thing that sprang to mind was a treasure map of the notorious cursed clan.

I pressed *Yes*.

A download bar came on. Oh. The download was big. I'd have to wait. And I really had very little time.

As if in confirmation, Flint PM'd me,

Olgerd, where the hell are you? What do you think you're doing?

I'm coming!

Drop everything and get here quick! The spiders will be there in a minute! Then you're dead!

54% downloaded. If I broke the fine thread now, the download would stop. Just one more minute...
75%...
89%...
96%...
Finally—100%!
Yes!
The fine thread disappeared. My little ring followed suit and crumbled into dust. So that's how it was, then? A single-use ring? Never mind. I'd think about it later.

Would you like to install the Der Swyor app suite?

Not now. It would have to wait until a more convenient opportunity. Time was an issue.
I was about to reply to Flint's message when I heard a rustling noise behind my back. Had the mobs already arrived? I still had about forty minutes, hadn't I?
Chill poured down my spine. My heart fluttered.
I swung round.
"Whatcha stalling for, you idiot?"
Yes, he had remembered me alright. And he'd

noticed me outside earlier that morning. Vindictive bastard. I didn't envy his father.

His wizard minion Slayer stood slightly aside. A nasty smirk curved his lips. He had the typically slanted eyes of an Alven and a navy suit of armor that all the magic classes wore in Mirror World. He stood there with his arms crossed, glaring at me from under his eyebrows. I really didn't like what I read in his glare.

"What's that for a tone?" I tried to browbeat him as I stepped toward the exit.

Slayer only grinned, then waved his hand as if brushing aside an annoying fly.

A system message popped up,

You've been cursed! Name of curse: Midday Shroud.

Effect: From now on, you can't talk to other players.

Duration: 2 hrs.

Then another,

You've been cursed! Name of curse: Wasted Prisoner

Effect: From now on, you cannot leave the location.

Duration: 2 hrs.

"That's better," Slayer smirked, then added, "Don't even try to escape. It won't work. And I can see in your face that you realize it already. Your chat isn't available, is it? Cool, eh? Your stupid friends must be spamming you with messages. And you can't write back like the dumb idiot that you are. Can you or can't you? The Shroud is an excellent thing. Especially when one needs to talk. To teach some cheeky noobs to show some respect to their superiors."

I could feel my face turn crimson. I wasn't afraid, no. I was enraged. I took a better grip of my pick.

Seeing this, Slayer shook his head. "Once a noob, always a noob. Don't stare at my lash. I'm not going to soil my hands on you. All I want is to teach you a lesson. Next time you'll be more respectful," he started for the stairs, speaking as he climbed, "All right, time for me to go. I'm not wishing you good luck but trust me you'll need it. See you later! Repeat after me: respect!"

All my attempts to break through the invisible wall failed. All I achieved was a nasty fall and a few points' drop in my pants and jacket's Durability.

Flint kept flooding my PM box with messages while all I could do was open my mouth soundlessly like a fish out of water.

Damn that carving on the wall! Damn Shantarsky and his sorry excuse for a son! Damn this sadist Slayer!

Gasping, I sat on the floor by the wall. I tried not to think what was going to happen once the instance came back to life. One thing I knew was that this was the top level and top mobs. Plus Steel Widow, the instance boss. I wasn't going to like it, that's for sure. It was going to hurt. A lot. I didn't even want to think how it was going to feel. Shame about my clothes. Their Durability was about to suffer somewhat.

What could I do? Had I had a standard account, I could have promptly "died", then resurrected at the main square. But now... How was I going to survive the two hours until the curse wore off? And once it did, how was I supposed to battle my way out of a dungeon swarming with spiders? Now my hopes lay with Flint. If he disbanded the group quickly, I might get off easy. But they had to declare the stones first. They were still on their way to the exit—and would be for the next half-hour. Then they would have to use the terminal. They weren't going to lose their haul—what was the point? I wouldn't want to, either. So I'd have to suffer in silence. I had no other way.

So what did we have? It would take the group another thirty minutes to get to the terminal. Give it five more minutes to declare their spoils. Then they'd walk out. The spiders would arrive. And then-

A message from Flint interrupted my calculations.

Olgerd, we've just seen Slayer going out past us. I think we know why you don't answer.

The bastard must have cast a Gag on you! Knuckles butted in.

I beg of you to hold on, Sir Tristan added. *Please listen to us—or rather, read the messages. I*

---

know you can see them even though you can't answer. Most likely, he cast one of those virtual curses on you. According to the instance map, you must still be at level 7. Which means you aren't just gagged but also immobilized. In the worst-case scenario, the scoundrel cast a Ball and Chain on you which means you're standing there unable to take a single step. The best-case scenario, however, could be one of the minor curses that block the instance's exits. I'm going to pre-empt your question as I know you can't ask it yourself. Judging by your references to online games, you're apparently not familiar with combat tactics. Here in Mirror World, they're basically the same as in all other game worlds. You must know then that all monsters possess a quality commonly known as aggression...

He means aggro, Flint butted in.

Exactly. This is a particular mob's radius of vision. In your case, it's spiders'. If he cast a Ball and Chain on you and if you're located at the center of the hall, this is very bad news. Very. The moment the monsters arrive, they'll attack you. As long as a group member is engaged in combat, Flint as the group's leader can't disband it. But if you're only denied exit from the location—as we all hope you are—you need to find the most inconspicuous cranny in the whole location and keep quiet. In that case there's some chance they might not notice you at all.

Hold on man, we're gonna get you out! Sprat assured me.

Even if we dump the haul! Knuckles promised.

Oh no. Anything but that. All that work! My mind was screaming as I desperately tried to find a safe spot in the cave.

As if listening in to my thoughts, Sir Tristan added,

Please don't worry. I'm sure it won't come to that. We've doubled up speed so we might gain about ten minutes. I'm pretty sure you'll come out unscathed.

I could sense he was struggling to add, *provided you're not under Ball and Chain.* I couldn't suppress a nervous grin. Wasn't I the lucky one?

As far as this shameful incident is concerned, Sir Tristan went on, *we're going to file a collective complaint. Both with the admins and with our employer.*

I'm fed up with his little skunk and his pranks! Sprat vented his indignation. *About time I look for a new job.*

Me too, Knuckles added.

So we'll just quit, all of us, Flint summed up. *A group of Seasoned Diggers is always welcome. Shantarsky can do what he wants.*

I'm more than sure that our collective complaint will give us enough ground to cancel our employment agreement, Sir Tristan informed us. *I suppose, quite a few other players in this cluster will follow suit. Many of them have a bone to pick with Shantarsky Jr.*

Their support made me feel so good. These were guys you could follow through hell and high water.

Their idea made sense. Why not? I'd been thinking about quitting too, hadn't I? In any case, I couldn't stay in this cluster for much longer. And now I had a perfect official excuse. I wouldn't be quitting on my own even but as part of a top group. Stupid as it might sound in my situation, whatever happened would be for the best. My cheat ability wasn't exactly welcome here.

Wait! A cheat ability? Of course! My Shrewd Operator! Why hadn't I thought about it earlier!

I grabbed my pick and ran toward the trolley, pulling a Stamina stone out of my pocket as I ran. Now was the time to use it!

You've used a magic stone of Stamina.
Effect: +3 to Energy every 40 sec.
Duration: 30 min

Excellent. I screeched to a halt next to the trolley and hurried to change the bot's settings to Speed Mode. Off we go!

You've received a resource: Gray Crystal

My idea was simple. The same thing that I'd been trying so desperately to avoid could now save me. If I leveled up now, I'd be thrown out of the instance. By then the guys would have their haul safely in the terminal. Counting on the mobs not noticing me wasn't a particularly smart idea.

Okay, so I'll blow my secret, big deal. I was going to quit anyway.

You've received a resource: Gray Crystal

Fifteen minutes had elapsed. I gulped an elixir. The bot was taking one hell of a lot of energy. Never mind. A couple of days in bed, that's all.

We've reached level 2! Flint reported.

Hold on, man, Knuckles added.

I chuckled nervously. All that time I'd been trying not to get a new level—and now my counter seemed to have frozen.

You've received a resource: Gray Crystal.
Your tool slipped as you picked at the slab of dark rock.
You've received a resource: Twilight Crystal.
This was our twentieth. What a shame. It felt weird: I was about to face murderous monsters capable of ripping me to shreds, and I was mourning the loss of some stupid stones.

I wondered whether they were indeed going to

rip me to shreds or whether they would choose some different kind of torture.

You've received a resource: Gray Crystal.
Your tool slipped as you picked at the slab of dark rock.
You've received a resource: Twilight Crystal.
You've received +1 to your skill.

Yes! Got it. Just one more level, then I'd be free!

I gulped yet another elixir. The trolley was heaped with stones. I ran toward the next one.

Never mind! We'll make it!

The bones of my long dead fellow Ennans crunched underfoot. I understood of course that this was the work of my imagination, nothing else. Everything around me was naught but designer stage settings. They just looked so impossibly real.

My mind must have kept immersing deeper and deeper into the virtual world. Another year, and I might end up like one of those Specters. And it was pretty clear to me now that I was stuck here for quite a while. Getting the loan was one thing. Now I had to pay it back. Which might take years—decades.

You've received a resource: Gray Crystal.

I didn't hear the other guys anymore. What were they up to? I was beginning to miss Sir Tristan's preaching.

Five minutes until the spiders respawned.

Where the hell were they? I cast a scared glance around me. By my calculations, they must have already declared their spoils about five minutes ago. I swallowed another elixir. The bot kept crashing through the rock, quickly and efficiently.

You've received a resource: Gray Crystal.
Your tool slipped as you picked at the slab of dark rock.
You've received a resource: Twilight Crystal.

I didn't care! I'd stopped counting crystals a long time ago. A sense of doom washed over me. The guys must have had a problem. What a shame I couldn't even open the map. That way I might at least see where they were. It was high time they rescued me.

Grinning sarcastically, I looked over the loaded trolleys. What a waste. Only a few seconds left. I had to go look for cover. You never know, they might indeed not notice me.

Closer to the carved picture in the rock I noticed a small niche. Good place. A nice little deposit of crystals. I might keep hacking at them. You never know...

Sorry, guys. If you don't answer, it can only mean you have problems because of me.

I darted for the niche. There! I made it. Slowly I reached into my bag.

You've used a magic stone of Stamina.
Effect: +3 to Energy every 40 sec.

Duration: 30 min

I froze.

Spiders began appearing. I clasped my pick handle. Holy mama mia, how many were they? Ten... eleven... exactly fifteen.

I took a closer look. All of them were the same race: Red Widow. All level 35.

Compared to their bellies, their heads were tiny. All had eight legs, sharp as spears. Their color was fiery red. I remembered reading somewhere that some spiders had excellent vision while others could detect sounds with the little hairs on their legs. Those game developers were full of sick ideas.

I could see fifteen of them, all staring at me. Where was their boss? She was probably lying in hiding, studying me.

I cast a look around. She was nowhere to be seen. The monsters were busy peacefully spinning cobwebs. Even from where I stood I could see that each thread was an arm's width.

Now where was this lady lurking now? It didn't really matter, did it? As long as she stayed there for as long as she could.

Ten minutes elapsed. I kept nice and quiet, trying not to breathe. This must have something to do with the fact that I was still in one piece. The spiders weren't paying any attention to me. If it went like that, I could stay in my hidey hole until the cows came home.

Guys, where are you? Now was a perfect moment to disband the group and head home. But I had a funny feeling I wouldn't forget this quiet evening in a hurry.

Having finished their work, the spiders hung motionlessly in their freshly-spun webs. I made a quick estimate. If I managed to get out of this particular cave, the remaining levels were bound to be easier. I had to wait till the curses wore off and then try to advance toward the exit. By then, the guys were bound to remember me. I still didn't think they'd forgotten, though. Something must have happened— something quite serious, too.

Fifteen minutes elapsed. Everything remained the same. The eight-legged behemoths froze statue-like.

I was stiff all over. Strangely, my body felt real. Or was it my imagination playing up? The moment I'd thought that staying motionless for a couple of hours was a hard call, my brain must have reacted accordingly, sending my body an impulse to move.

Whatever the reason, it did feel real. My shoulders ached like hell.

No idea what could have triggered what happened next. It must have either been my attempts to move my stiff neck or my bad choice of a hiding place. In any case, I didn't get the chance to contemplate: I beheld Steel Widow in all her awesome glory.

Chapter Eighteen

Something snapped within my chest.

The steel Leviathan moved unhurriedly towards me. If the other mobs looked like regular spiders the size of a family car, their Queen resembled a robot rather than an insect.

Her head and belly appeared to be armored. Her eight legs carried her enormous body across the ceiling with remarkable ease. Now I knew why all that time I hadn't seen her. The wretched thing had been hanging right above me.

Now I was in trouble.

I had only one way out. I shifted the pick in my hand for a better grip.

I swung and hit the rock.

You've received a resource: Gray Crystal

The Widow doubled her step.
I swung and hit the rock.

You've received a resource: Gray Crystal

I kept watching her out of the corner of my eye as she was creeping sideways toward me. Only a dozen paces left between us.
I took a swing.

You've received a resource: Gray Crystal.
Your tool slipped as you picked at the slab of dark rock.
You've received a resource: Twilight Crystal.

As if anyone needed them now!
I took a swing.

You've received a resource: Gray Crystal.

The Widow stopped, tensing like a taut spring. I squeezed my eyes shut. My heart was pounding, about to explode. My hands shook. She was bound to lunge at me.
I took a swing.

You've received a resource: Gray Crystal.

And again.

You've received a resource: Gray Crystal.

Come on, you bitch! Don't drag it out!
I swung and hit the rock.

You've received a resource: Gray Crystal.

The Widow hadn't lunged at me. She'd done it differently.

You've been attacked!
Your feet are bound with Venomous Cobwebs
Effect: -5 pt. Life every 25 sec
Duration: 30 min

Immediately my boots lost 5 pt. Durability. Dammit!
I swung and hit the rock.

You've received a resource: Gray Crystal.

The monster withdrew—apparently waiting for me to pop my clogs. Oops, not really. She tensed again.
I swung and hit the rock.

You've received a resource: Gray Crystal.
You've been attacked!
Your shoulders are bound with Venomous Cobwebs
Effect: -5 pt. Life every 25 sec
Duration: 30 min

Minus 7 Durability to my jacket. You bitch! That way I'd walk out of here naked!

You've been attacked!
Your hands are bound with Venomous Cobwebs
Effect: -5 pt. Life every 25 sec
Duration: 30 min

Bye, gloves. The sticky whitish threads now entwined most of my body. A few more attacks like these, and I'd look like a friggin' Egyptian mummy.
I took a swing.
My bag was almost full.
The Widow looked puzzled. She crept closer but she didn't attack me again quite yet. She was watching me. How I understood her! All that effort on her part had done zilch damage to me, only to my gear. Or had it?
I took a swing.

You've received a resource: Gray Crystal.

Come on now! Was my Shrewd Operator asleep or something?
I took a swing.

You've received a resource: Gray Crystal.
Your tool slipped as you picked at the slab of dark rock.
You've received a resource: Twilight Crystal.

What was I supposed to do with their stupid crystals?

The Widow shifted her position. Still, she seemed reluctant to approach me. Or was this her normal behavior? The other spiders positioned themselves next to the exit. Apparently, they were supposed to attack an entering group *en masse* while the Widow sat coyly in one corner throwing Venomous Cobwebs over any newcomers. That was the most realistic scenario.

I swung but failed to hit the rock.

You've been attacked!
Your feet have been burned with Toxic Saliva
Effect: -2 pt. Energy every 50 sec
Duration: 30 min
You've received Burns to both feet.
Effect: -15 pt. Life every 40 sec

So that's her new tactic, then. My feet felt on fire. I'd once experienced something similar when I'd scalded my hand. Oh, bummer. I shouldn't have thought about it.

You've been attacked!
Your hands have been burned with Toxic Saliva
Effect: -2 pt. Energy every 50 sec
Duration: 30 min
You've received Burns to both hands.
Effect: -15 pt. Life every 40 sec

Both my boots and my gloves lost a few more Durability points and were automatically moved into my bag. According to the rules, any injury prevented the use of clothes or armor. Luckily, the rule didn't apply to weapons and tools.

The game developers had it all covered. An injured player offered work to several professions. A healer would have to heal him or her, an alchemist would have to make a necessary potion while an herbalist would have to find an herb suitable for healing. There had to be even more links to this moneymaking chain. But at least in this particular case, they could forget sponging off me. The moment I left the instance, all the negative effects I'd received were bound to wear off. I remembered it well from the guide book.

My stats kept dwindling. I was overcome by fatigue—and pain, an unbearable and supposedly never-ending agony burning through me.

Dammit! I had very few crystals left in this particular spot. If I tried to move to the next deposit, I could trigger the other spiders.

I took a swing.

A few minutes ago, I'd poured the contents of my bag onto the floor, emptying it completely. A few of the Venomous Cobwebs had already landed on the bag. It wouldn't survive another attack. In that case, I'd have to bolt for the trolley standing by the opposite wall.

You've been attacked!
Your chest has been burned with Toxic Saliva
Effect: -2 pt. Energy every 50 sec
Duration: 30 min

You've received a Burn to your chest.
Effect: -15 pt. Life every 40 sec

That was it. My bag was gone. I watched miserably as it crumbled to dust. The gloves and the boots dropped to the ground. My injuries didn't allow me to put them on.

I used another Stamina stone and downed another elixir. I had only one left now. I heaved a sigh. Now I had to make a dash for the trolley.

I looked up. My torturess wasn't in a hurry. She seemed to be watching me with curiosity.

All right. I took in a deep breath, let the air out, then darted.

Darted probably wasn't the right word. *Hobbled* was more like it. Stooped like an old man, I limped toward the trolley—my last chance and my saving grace as I thought—struggling to overcome the agonizing pain and losing precious Energy points.

Come on now! I was almost there! I ran around a particularly large heap of bones, steel and cobwebs: the ancient arena of a major battle. What was I saying? This was only stage scenery! This was a game, dammit! But why oh why did it hurt so much?

I glanced up at the rock ceiling. The Widow followed me closely. You bitch!

I stepped it up. Faster! Faster! Move it!

My haste played a bad trick on me. I stumbled over a skeleton and collapsed to the floor right in the middle of the room. The deafening clangor of deformed suits of armor echoed off the walls. Someone's radio helmet rattled across the floor like an old tin bucket. Like a child, I squeezed my eyes shut and shrank my head into my shoulders.

The wretched piece of metal seemed to rattle forever. But I was still in one piece. The helmet rolled in between some rocks and came to a halt. Silence hung in the cave.

I glanced up. The Widow was right there, tensed and ready to spit at me again. I had to be quick.

Gingerly I raised my head. The spiders hung motionlessly in their cobwebs. That was good. That was very good! That was exactly what we needed.

I scrambled to my feet, trying not to stumble against any of the steel junk lying around. The trolley was about twenty paces away. Never mind. I'd make it. Come what may!

My chest was heavy. I was dangerously low on oxygen. No wonder. My Energy levels were dropping fast. The Stamina stone couldn't handle all the numerous poisons the wretched Widow had cast on me. I gulped down my last elixir. That was a bit better.

I went for it. I'd never forget those last twenty paces.

Gasping, I took a swing with my pick.

You've received a resource: Gray Crystal.

Come on, Operator, man! Do it!
I swung and hit the rock.
You've received a resource: Gray Crystal.

Come on, bro!

You've received a resource: Gray Crystal.

Come on, you bastard!

You've been attacked!
Your back has been bound with Venomous Cobwebs
Effect: -5 pt. Life every 25 sec
Duration: 30 min

Yeah, yeah. Sorry, spider lady, but you're wrong. Your cobwebs can't stop me anymore. Shame about the jacket. But I was long past caring about such details.

The trolley began filling with crystals. The Widow hurled a few more cobwebs at me. Then she quieted down—probably waiting for me to pop my clogs. You preprogrammed bitch!

I swung and hit the rock.

You've received a resource: Gray Crystal.

I couldn't do it for much longer. This nightmare seemed to never end. My movements slowed down. I'd never felt so bad in my life. I didn't even want to think about the consequences. All I wanted was to get out of this cave. The pain was mind-boggling. Bright circles span before my eyes. My hands were shaking. My legs felt leaden. I was on the brink of fainting. I stubbornly shook my head and took another swing.

You've received a resource: Gray Crystal.

A few more swings, and I was going to die right there. That was it. I closed my eyes and drew in a strained breath. I swung.

You've received a resource: Gray Crystal.

I glanced at my torturess. I didn't care anymore.

Wait a sec. What was that? Something was wrong. Something was going on. Until that moment, the Widow had been sitting still after her last cobweb attack. But I'd never seen anything like what was happening to her now. Her gigantic steel body was vibrating silently—no, not silently. I could hear the sound it made: disgusting and barely audible, as if someone was rubbing two pieces of foam plastic together.

My body hair stood on end.

What happened next was something I must have subconsciously feared all along. I heard a similar sound coming from the entrance, only louder—more aggressive. And it was louder for a reason. This unbearable rustle consisted of many separate sounds.

I turned round, already knowing what I was going to see. I was right. The Widow must have got tired of watching me, so she'd called her little helpers. All fifteen spiders were slowly climbing down their webs.

I watched helplessly as the giant spiders

approached, moving faster and faster. That was it. End of game for me. With a strange clarity I thought that it might have been better for me to receive a few lashes of Slayer's whip. It wouldn't have been as bad.

Oh, no. I wasn't going to give up that easily. I got a better grip on my pick and struggled to take a swing. And another. And again. My Energy was at zero. Three spiders had already lunged at me, about to stab me with their sharp spearlike legs. I might have time for just one more stone.

I invested the last of my strength into the swing. Then I tensed my back, expecting to turn into a shapeless lump of flesh. The sharp edge of my pick dug into the rock.

You've received a resource: Gray Crystal.
Your tool slipped as you picked at the slab of dark rock.
You've received a resource: Twilight Crystal.
You've received +1 to your skill.

Congratulations! Your professional level has grown! You're an Experienced Digger now!

We're sorry to inform you that the game rules don't allow you to remain a group member.

Reason: the profession level of the group's leader has to be equal to or above yours.

You've received a fine! You are removed from the group and will now be transported to your chosen resurrection point.

With any questions or complaints, please contact Support. Thank you.

Chapter Nineteen

Scientists say that a dream is a sequence of images drawn from our memory. Apparently, we don't realize we're asleep and believe the dream to be part of real life.

I'm not sure if being chased by gigantic spiders clad in rusty armor can qualify as part of real life. It was the bit with a girl in a wheelchair that had bothered me most in my dream: she was someone I'd been trying hard to remember—and couldn't.

Then at a certain point everything had disappeared: both the girl and the spiders, replaced by tranquility. I dreamed of our old country cottage and the times when Sveta and I had just got married. Her, sitting on the river bank with a bamboo fishing rod. Me, lying on the soft grass watching her inconspicuously. Her small nose, her intense stare; her wavy hair pulled into a nice little ponytail. Me, smiling; calling her *my little angler*. She seemed to love it. Finally, sensing my stare on the back of her head, she turned around and made a face at me, bringing a warning finger to her lips. As in, *be quiet, I'm about to catch a huge one!*

I was happy. I knew it was only a dream and still I was happy. I lowered my eyelids with pleasure, then heard Sveta's voice,

"Wake up, sleepy head! The fish are biting! Wake up now!"

A hand on my shoulder. A strange voice. "Wake up! Please wake up!"

"No," I croaked with my eyes shut. "Why couldn't you have woken me up when I was dreaming all sorts of junk..."

"I can see you've decided to move to the clinic permanently," somebody else said.

I knew this voice. "Not my fault," I wheezed. "The credit is all yours, Mr. Shantarsky, sir."

"Please don't say that," Shantarsky's voice kept urging. "What have I got to do with that? On the contrary—my workers keep me informed that you seem to be bent on working yourself into an early grave."

I opened my eyes. I lay on a bed in a spacious single hospital room. Medical equipment beeped next to my headrest. Shantarsky sat on a chair in the far corner with his arms crossed, looking respectable and dignified as usual. He reeked of an expensive aftershave. His gold watch and cufflinks glistened in the sunlight.

A man in a lab coat was busy with the equipment. A doctor, probably—who else? Then again, nothing would surprise me after the trick Slayer had played on me.

I suppressed a sarcastic grin. Yeah, right. Talk about paranoid.

Apparently, Shantarsky misinterpreted my smirk. "Did I say something funny?"

"Oh no, not at all. Must be nerves."

"I understand."

"Do you really?"

Shantarsky must have picked up on the sarcasm in my voice. He winced. "Dear Oleg, you're the last person I'd expect to lose his cool."

"That's because you didn't have to prance around the cave in the company of jumbo spiders," I blurted out.

The doctor—or whoever he was—finished whatever he was doing and left without a word. Once the door closed behind him, Shantarsky spoke apologetically,

"You have to believe me: I'm really, really sorry about what happened."

I felt the blood pulsing in my face. My jaws clenched. I had to watch out not to tell him everything I thought about him. And about his son. And that bastard Slayer. Wait a sec... What was he going on about?

"I have to admit," Shantarsky said, deliberately ignoring my mental state, "that you've found a very elegant solution to the problem. Bravo! Can you imagine the amazement of my men when they discovered there was virtually nothing left of you?"

"What do you mean, nothing?" I asked coldly.

"*Virtually* nothing. The moment I heard about my son's escapades, I sent a rescue group to get you out. They promptly mopped up the instance—but by the time they'd reached level 7 they only discovered a few pieces of your gear. I had to pay them extra by way of apology for wasting their time—for my failing to let them know your group leader had already discarded you."

He rubbed his clean-shaven chin, pensive. "The only problem is," he said softly, "I had to lie to my employees. And that, as you can well imagine, is not the most pleasant thing in the world."

Our eyes met. He knew everything, I could see that. But I could also see one other thing: the duel between keeping my secret and claiming compensation for damages was about to end in the former's victory.

I heaved a sigh and leaned back against the pillows. "Before we go on," I began, all businesslike, "I need to make sure that none of the other group members have been hurt. I need to know where I am and contact my family and my brother. I suppose, your little son will come out of it smelling of roses. So it would be pointless to demand that justice be done. The other group members must have already been sufficiently warned off, I suppose. I just hope they're all right. That's all I have to say. So what is it you want?"

He flashed a smile. "You're remarkably quick

on the uptake. I didn't even say anything."

I just shrugged. For a while, he waited for me to continue.

"Very well," he finally said. "If that's how you want it. Your friends are fine. They've even been transferred to another job in a different cluster. Once they received compensation and found out that you had no claims against them, they shut up."

"Did they?" I asked with a crooked smile.

"Oh, yes," he hadn't noticed my sarcasm. "Why not?"

I kept grinning. "Indeed, why not?"

"And as for where you are... You're in my personal capsule center. As you can imagine, it's considerably more comfortable that the ones you had to use before."

"I was comfortable enough there."

"Don't speak too soon. You'll see tomorrow."

"You and I, do we *have* a tomorrow?"

"Absolutely," he smiled. "Most definitely. Now, your family. As soon as we finish talking, you'll be able to speak to them."

"Can't we do it now?"

"I don't think so."

"Am I your prisoner?"

"You're joking, aren't you? It's only because if you speak to them now, we might not be able to have a constructive discussion later. Which is only in your own interests, mind you."

"Only mine?"

"And ours too."

"*Ours*?"

"Yes. I speak not only of myself now."

"It's getting interesting. So what is it you want?"

Shantarsky rearranged the right cufflink. "We need an Expert Digger."

It took me some effort to suppress a gasp.

"I thought you'd be surprised," he continued. "Or did you really think your secret would be safe for much longer? Mirror World is just one big village. Every high level player, be he a warrior or an honest laborer, immediately comes to the attention of the stronger clans."

"So what's that got to do with me?"

He shook his head. "Please. I thought we had an understanding."

I heaved a sigh and waved to him to get on with it.

"Very well," he continued. "I've weighed up all the options and come to the conclusion that your character is in possession of some unique abilities. You've only been in the game for a month and you're already an Experienced Digger!"

'So what? I didn't break the rules, did I?"

He smiled again. "Oleg, please don't get so het up."

He had a really creepy smile.

"It's only that I," Shantarsky continued, "have the necessary power to offer you an opportunity to make full use of these abilities of yours."

In other words, to work me into an early grave. "Providing that this full use of me doesn't include me popping my clogs in your service," I said.

"Oh no, we can't make that happen. You're too valuable to us."

"Us? Who do you mean?"

"The administration of the alliance that unites the strongest clans of Light."

I whistled with surprise. "So!"

"What did you think I was talking about?"

"Well, I suppose I thought you'd come to apologize for your son and his actions," I said.

He sat back and grinned again. "Now that you've mentioned him, my stance in his respect is quite clear. My son's too young and too quick off the mark. Power is the only language he understands. For him, you're nothing. There's no way to convince him otherwise. You might say you're a human being—which should be enough. Well, you might be right in your own way. But this philosophy doesn't sit well with him. So I'm not going to discipline him, no. Why should I? I've been raising him a leader, proud and strong. I've taught him to never bow his head to any Tom, Dick or Harry. Are you angry? That's good. But I don't care what you think. I'll tell you something else: you'll have to swallow your pride. You'll have to do what you're told. And you know the funny thing about it? I'm going to tell you now so we can laugh together: strangely enough, you'll be only too eager to obey my orders."

I was furious.

"No need to blow a fuse," he continued in a calm voice. "Keep your hair on. You're only slowing up your own recovery. As for Slayer—you might be happy to know that he's been fired. Not because of you, actually. In your case he was only following my son's orders. And he's done an excellent job, I have to admit. No; it was his drug habit that was his undoing. We found out too late. Our clan has no place for drug abuse. But you know something? He seems to think it's because of you. He blames it on you, heh! Talking of which, I know it may sound stupid but you have to thank this little incident in the Spider Grotto for your being able to stay in Mirror World at all. Surprised? I'll explain it to you in a minute. Such a meteoric rise through levels couldn't have remained unnoticed for much longer. Sooner or later, other players would have started asking questions. Or even filing complaints against you. I'm pretty sure that in less than a month, the admins would have been forced to delete your account. You'd have never been able to keep your abilities under wraps. Impossible. Those in the know would have found out. Just like I did."

"What do you want?" I asked icily, shaking with fury.

Shantarsky raised a surprised eyebrow. "You can't have already forgotten, surely! Didn't I just tell you? We're looking for an Expert Digger. Granted you're only Experienced, but I can offer you every opportunity to level up."

"And what if I refuse?"

"You sure you need it? We're not forcing you to work with us. But you're going to do your best anyway."

"Why should I?"

He gave me a friendly smile. "We've signed a contract, haven't we? Or did you think we'd use you

---

as slave labor?"

"Sorry, I don't understand."

"Nothing to understand, really. Your contract with me is still valid. All we'll do, we'll extend it and tweak it in a few places. You have your daughter's medical bills to pay, don't you? That's why you applied for a loan, right? The paperwork is on the table over there. Once we sign it, my bank will wire the money to Germany. All your problems will be solved with one stroke of a pen."

I tensed; I even craned my neck, looking for the ominous contract. So this was my ticket into slavery? It couldn't be. I could smell a rat there somewhere. I was only an ordinary Grinder. There were hundreds of thousands of them in Mirror World. True, Pierrot had endowed me with a few so-called cheat skills, but my experience had already taught me that his gifts were treacherously short-lived.

Plus Shantarsky had been threatening me with publicity. He'd said they might delete my account. But was it really possible? Publicity yes, why not—even though neither of us profited from it. But deleting my account? I'd signed a user's agreement. I'd broken no rules. I'd chosen a character based on the characteristics offered to me by the system. There was no problem there.

Yes, I needed the loan. Or rather, I needed to raise the money for Christina's hospital treatment. If it involved a stretch of slavery, so be it. Humiliation was nothing. I was quite prepared to eat dirt if it helped. My pride had died with my daughter's first heart.

Still, there was something else I had to consider. I had a funny feeling that this contract was going to differ from the generic ones quite a bit. I was pretty sure it was stuffed with all sorts of restrictive conditions. *I wasn't a slave*, yeah right! Had this snake spoken to me in the presence of my brother and and in somewhere neutral—maybe. Oh no siree, instead you'd kidnapped me and hadn't allowed me to contact my family. Judging by the way my head was spinning, you might have even plied me with some nasty substances while I'd lain here unconscious. No, this was no way to conduct business.

There was also another argument against it, something that had kept bugging me since my flight to Germany. At first I'd tried not to even think of it, but little by little I'd forced myself to face it. The thing was... what if Christina's body rejected the Japanese heart? What then? No one had promised us a 100% success rate. The odds were indeed very high, but still not a 100%. Been there. So what if this heart died too? And I'd be stuck here in Shantar's mines working off the loan with my hands tied? Someone might say, never mind, I could always apply for another loan even if it meant selling myself down the river and becoming Shantar's property. But what if my child's body rejected this second heart too... and the third one... and the fourth one... What then? Sooner or later, I'd just choke on it all. Not because I'd give up— no, I just wouldn't be in a position to help her anymore.

I firmly believed her new heart was going to take. Christina would get better. Then we'd be looking at a long-winded recovery process. We'd need money to buy groceries and pay the bills; we'd have to find a place for us all to stay; we'd also need to pay for her education. Life would have to go on. We'd need to give our girl a good start in life. We could finally live. Just *live*, dammit!

Somehow I doubted that I could achieve all this working for Shantarsky. And there was also another thing to consider. Something that I hadn't noticed until now—because I'd been either too thick or too set in my ways. For hundreds of thousands of people, this wasn't a game anymore. Take Shantarsky himself, for instance. What was he doing playing a game, with his money? What kept drawing him here? How much money had he already invested into this project? And how much did he intend to invest still? Was it because he enjoyed it? Or was it because he liked spending time here? The list could go on, but still I had the strange feeling he was in it for the money. Because the potential money turnover here was huge.

My not taking Mirror World too seriously had prevented me from asking myself the very important question: what if I too could achieve something bigger in this world? Yes, the *world*. It had become one for me, anyway. The downside was that I'd only realized the fact now, imprisoned by that bastard Shantarsky and under his control, facing slavery.

Never mind. I'd have to bide my time. The most important thing to do now was to get in contact with Dmitry. Together we could sort it all out.

"You'll keep on working and leveling up as

usual," Shantarsky continued his sales pitch. "You'll have a special module center at your disposal. Everything will remain the same. The only things that will change are zero risks and a minimum of interactions with other players. You'll be working in the most remote cluster of our alliance."

Oh. He hadn't even mentioned the pay yet. I had a bad feeling about this contract already. I needed to prize some more intel out of him. "But this, as far as I understand, is only the beginning?"

"Exactly," he beamed. "Do you know anything about the neutral zone?"

I shook my head. Let him tell me himself.

"Even the very greenest of newbs knows about it," he said. "The neutral lands are virtually uncharted. Our groups venture there to gradually explore the most inaccessible areas."

"What's that got to do with me?"

"You'll see in a moment. We've discovered quite a few instances that offer some really rare resources in addition to the usual loot. We're especially interested in gem stones."

"I see. Mining in combat conditions, eh?"

"You could say that," he admitted. "But it's worth it."

I smiled. *Worth it*—for whom? And at what price? And more importantly, what would it cost me?

"As far as I understand, Expert Diggers are quite well-off," I repeated what I'd heard from the other guys. "And they don't seem to be particularly interested in risky schemes like mining to the accompaniment of volleying cannons and bullets whizzing past."

What would he say to that?

"Overall, what you've just said makes sense," Shantarsky said calmly. "But from experience I can tell you that your logic is slightly flawed. There are certain stones that keep resurfacing at our closed auctions—the kind of stones only Expert Diggers can mine. Take a guess: do you think you can name a game where an especially rare stone can fetch a million bucks?"

So that's what he wanted me for. To tie my loan to a new work contract—thus leaving me no room for maneuver.

I frowned, faking disbelief, "You're joking, aren't you?"

"Do I look like I am?"

"Sorry. It's just that that kind of money-"

"I need to tell you something," he leaned closer. "There're many people for whom Mirror World is much more than a game. And some of them are prepared to pay tenfold more than the sum I've just mentioned," he smiled carnivorously. "There're some top level players in our alliance. We guard those people closely. No one knows they exist. You might call us conspiracy freaks and you'd be right in your own way. You might say we've taken the joke too far. But I believe that given another month, you might catch up with them."

Yeah right, Mister Snake. He wanted me to be his personal Expert Digger! Bound hand and foot by the promise of a loan? I beg to differ. His pitch was well-rehearsed but not subtle enough.

I decided to check. "I don't need so much."

"So much what?" he asked, uncomprehending.

"If you give me everything I need, I won't need a month to make Expert level."

I could see dollar signs flash in his eyes. "I'm all ears," Shantarsky said.

Time to fly the coop, as the saying goes. "I'd like to call my wife," I said aloud. "She must be worried out of her mind. How long have I been here, actually?"

"Less than twenty-four hours," Shantarsky said. "No need to indulge in conspiracy theories. The only reason we've had you moved here from the communal center was to provide better conditions for your recovery."

Sure. Those eyes couldn't lie. Freakin' snake. Kidnapper. He had no idea he was playing with fire. Either he was so cock sure of himself and his connections or he didn't expect me to decline his offer. Him blackmailing me! Threatening me with "publicity"! Actually, this could be his cover story: he could always say he'd had me moved to his place out of fear for my well-being. I'd love to know how the center's security had allowed him to do so... then again, I was working for him, wasn't I? He must have sent some goons in lab coats to collect his employee, as simple as that. As in, he was worried about me! He must have had his people among the center's security, too.

Just you wait till Dmitry finds out. Heads will roll, that's for sure.

They'd try to sweep the whole thing under the carpet, of course. There must have been some very

---

influential people standing behind all of this. They didn't need unwanted publicity. Kidnapping an innocent player out of a communal module center in broad daylight? Please. Who would trust them after that? So yes, they would definitely try to sweep the whole thing under the carpet. Even if it meant hurting me.

So I'd have to swallow my pride. It wasn't the right moment to blow the whistle. But still, I'd have to send Dmitry a word somehow.

"I'm going to send somebody to your module now to collect your things," Shantarsky said. "In the meantime, you can take a look at the contract."

He rose and walked out of the room.

Once I was alone, I sprang from my bed. No, *sprang* was probably the wrong word choice. *Scrambled* was more like it. Wheezing and ouching, I crawled from under the blanket. Why was I so weak? They must have slipped me a Mickey Finn somehow. Then again, this was probably how I was supposed to feel after my Spider Grotto escapades.

I walked over to the window. I was on the third floor. A lawn; some trees; a river or a lake glistening at a distance. I was out of town, that little was clear. The window wasn't barred. I suppose I had to be grateful for small mercies.

I turned around. What was that over there? Aha, a bathroom. No window.

I went back into the room. The window frames were blocked. If I wanted to get out, I'd have to break the glass. And then what? Jump? I'd only break my legs. No, I couldn't escape that way.

How about the door?

A burly individual sat in the corridor just outside the door. He glared at me like a python at a rabbit.

"Whassup?" his voice rang with threat. "Go back in."

"I need to use the bathroom," I pleaded shyly.

"Use the one in your room. Good enough. Now get in and stay in before I tear you a new one. Understood?"

I pulled the door shut. I was trapped. Might Dmitry be looking for me already? He was supposed to have gone on a business trip, wasn't he? Then again, he'd been planning to return about the same time as I'd finished the instance. In which case he must have already visited my room in the module center. If what Shantarsky had told me was indeed true, I'd been in suspended animation for quite a while. Also, I'd promised my wife to contact her as soon as I logged out, so she must have raised the alarm already.

In which case Dmitry would definitely try and contact Rrhorgus. Flint wouldn't keep his mouth shut either, I was sure of that. They must have already been looking for me.

Still, time was an issue. I had to do something—but what?

I reached for the chair, about to smash it against the window pane, when the door opened and closed again.

A hulk of a man towered in the doorway.

"Towered" being the operative word. He was a

good seven foot tall, built like a professional weight lifter... or a wrestler. No, a weight lifter. He didn't have the stoop typical of wrestlers and boxers and was much broader in the chest. Bulging with muscle, if you know what I mean.

I sort of deflated. Still, I kept clutching the chair, trying to shield myself with it.

"Excuse me, sir," the giant boomed, "please leave the chair alone and follow me."

"Follow you, where?" my voice broke. "My friends are looking for me," I added, trying to regain face.

"Don't worry," he interrupted me. "Keep your cool. I've come to take you out of here. Follow me."

He reopened the door and walked out first. No idea who he was or what his intentions were. I just knew I wasn't going to stay in this cage of a room for much longer. There was also a slim possibility of me giving him the slip on our way. I just hoped this troll of a man was indeed as muscle-bound as he looked.

I stepped to the door and peeked out. My rescuer's broad back hovered a few paces in front: he was striding away without even looking back. He didn't look as if he was escorting me to some torture chamber. He didn't even seem to care whether I followed him or not.

The sight of the goon by the door gave me hope. He was still sitting there, his arms crossed on his chest. His head hung listlessly to one side. His eyes were closed. Was he asleep?

I must have stopped in my tracks. The giant's calm voice brought me back to my senses,

"He'll live. But we need to hurry."

The elevator dinged. The giant was already inside, holding the door open for me. I looked around, shrugged and followed my surprise escort.

"Did my brother send you?" I asked, hoping against hope.

I watched the floor panel surreptitiously as he pressed the button for level -1. We must have been heading for the underground parking. The floor numbers on the shimmering blue display began to dwindle.

"No, he didn't," he said. "But that's where I'm taking you."

"But-"

"The person who sent me means you no harm. On the contrary. You'll see in a moment."

I drew in a deep breath, then exhaled slowly. The moment the elevator opened, I would dart for freedom. I was still weak but this guy was heavy. And if I ever got out of this mess, I'd make sure nothing like this would ever happen to me again.

The elevator's display panel finally blinked. The elevator jerked to a halt. I tensed myself and prepared to bolt for it.

Slowly the silvery door slid open. I didn't bolt. In fact, I froze. A light poke in the back brought me back to my senses.

"Please step out," the giant boomed.

I did so, but—was this a dream or something? I was facing a wheelchair. Not any old cheap one, either: I'd seen my fair share of wheelchairs over the last few years.

A girl sat in the chair. Or rather, a young woman. Slim and petite. Slender wrists. Pasty face. Pallid lips. She reminded me of a frail pot plant, brittle but struggling to survive.

She sat motionless in her wheelchair that next to her looked heavy and unyielding. Her chest barely rose with her each breath.

Then her eyes met mine.

The emerald eyes, heart-wrenchingly alive. I remembered them. I didn't need words to tune into her sadness. Into her concern. Her warmth. Her regret.

The car sped along the highway. It whizzed past road posts, trees and the oncoming traffic, ignoring the blurry faces of roadside vendors offering their humble wares: wild mushrooms, hand-picked forest fruit and penny souvenirs.

The distant fields were one boundless sea of green grass. A clumsy tractor raised dust, rattling along the dirt track that ran parallel to the highway.

The car's interior was neither hot nor cold. The driver, a young guy of about twenty years of age, kept his eyes on the road, checking the mirrors but ignoring me entirely.

I sat in the back seat, rereading a brief printout,

Dear Oleg,

I'm very sorry about what happened to you. It's the first time in my life I disobeyed my father. For the first time in my life I'm ashamed of what he's done.
Please forgive us if you can.
This is all my fault. I shouldn't have stopped and talked to you.
I'm very sorry.
I do hope your daughter gets better soon.
Sincerely,

Isa

I prized myself away from the letter and sucked in a deep breath. I couldn't think about anything just now. My head was a mess. My heart was heavy. I closed my eyes. I'd have loved to drink myself senseless.

I awoke when someone gently shook my arm.

"Here we are," the driver said. "This is the place, right?"

I sat up, rubbing my eyes. The driver was right. We'd arrived. I could see the familiar poster and the sign above the door. My brother's office.

"Thanks," I said, opening the car door.

"It's not me you should be thanking," the driver echoed.

For a moment, I watched the dark sedan pull away and disappear round the corner. Then I headed for the door.

The familiar guard posted by the entrance

stared at me as if he was looking at a fruitcake. Of course. I was still wearing my hospital duds. My unshaven face was a mess. My hair was standing on end.

Still, he flagged me through. As I walked up the stairs, I hear his voice below,

"He's here, sir... Yes. Already. He's coming up."

My brother met me by his office door. Surprise filled his eyes. He was trying to say something when I interrupted him, "You have some alcohol?"

Then I corrected myself. "Sorry. Not now. First I should call Sveta. Then I'll get drunk."

Chapter Twenty

"The administration of the strongest clans of Light," Dmitry smiled, repeating my words. "They have some imagination. Wish I could say the same about myself."

I only shrugged as I wrapped myself up in the familiar blanket, then downed the remaining brandy.

I'd stayed on the phone to Sveta for a good forty minutes. I did my best to reassure her, piling lie upon lie. What was the point in upsetting her?

As it turned out, I had been absent for about ten hours. Which was even less than Shantarsky had told me, even though technically his phrase, "less than twenty-four hours", was correct. I'd gotten away with a dressing-down and a lecture on the importance of being careful.

Then I'd told Dmitry the truth: every word of it. He was furious. He made a few phone calls, including one to the head of the module center security from where I'd been kidnapped. It seemed to have calmed him down a bit.

About twenty minutes ago we'd had dinner and were now working our way through a bottle of Hennessy.

"I found out you were gone about half an hour before you arrived," Dmitry said. "I was just looking through the logs of your misadventure."

"Right after you were back from your business trip?"

"Sure," he nodded. "I was back three hours before you logged out. I had an urgent virtual meeting. My telephone was switched off. Naturally, it took me some time to crawl out of the capsule and take a shower. When I finally switched my cell phone back on, it was flooded with missed calls from your wife and her messages saying you'd gone AWOL ten hours previous."

"And what about Rrhorgus?"

"He's been offline for the last forty-eight hours. He doesn't answer his phone, either."

"I hope he's all right," I said.

He dismissed my suggestion. "Please. Who would do that? Shantarsky? He may be wealthy and connected, but not connected enough to start creating problems."

"Are you sure? What about me, then?"

"You were a different story. He really put his foot in it this time. I seriously didn't expect him to do something this stupid. Jesus Christ! The 'administration of the strongest clans of Light', of all things! One might think you're some legendary hero! Trust me: you've no idea of the kind of money they deal in on a daily basis. For them, you're nothing. Don't look at me like that. I mean it. You're nothing. Sorry. Your Shrewd Operator is one hell of an ability. I'm not questioning that. So Shantarsky, the bastard, probably thought he had his future all sorted out. If you look at it in a different way, there was a certain logic in what he did. He'd never have been able to take you to No-Man's Lands, but renting you out to some stronger groups among the top clans—surely he could do that. So he'd have had himself an Expert Digger all leveled up—a perfect cash cow, no risks involved. A contract would have chained you better than any slave's collar. By the way, do you know that Expert level isn't the limit? The game keeps evolving. New resources are being introduced all the time. You have some space for growth, trust me."

"If I'm still around."

He smiled. "Relax. No one's gonna do that. You are an experienced player now, in all respects. Congrats on your new level, by the way! There's one thing I agree with Shantarsky on: you found a very elegant solution. Beautiful!"

I waved his compliment away. Still, it felt good. I wasn't as jittery anymore. Could have been the brandy; could have been my brother's tone. Or both.

"So what's gonna happen with Shantarsky now?" I asked.

"Good question. Even though he left someone

to guard your room, I don't think he expected you to escape. And he definitely couldn't have expected his own daughter to interfere, either. Heh! Who would have thought!"

"D'you know anything about her?"

"Virtually nothing. I heard something about the car crash. Her mother died, the girl lived. If you can call that a life."

"Do you think she'll have problems because of me?"

"Nah. From what I hear, he absolutely dotes on her."

"Is he dangerous?"

"Forget it. He's small fry in the large scale of things, but he's still a power to be reckoned with. For the time being, I suggest we leave it as it is. I might do a few things but we can't confront him openly, that's for sure. We're just not in the same league. What a shame. Had it not been for Somov, he'd still be shifting papers in his bank."

"I think I remember something. Shantarsky was deputy manager when I got my first loan with them."

"Exactly. It all started when Shantarsky Jr. met Somov's daughter online."

"Who's Somov?" I asked.

"President of Industrial Mega Bank and the leader of the Gold Guild clan. A very big shot. I mean, *very*."

"That's strange. A very big shot like that could have surely found a better match for his daughter."

Dmitry shrugged. "Apparently he couldn't. I

just can't work out all the machinations of their soap opera. From what I heard, Somov's little girl is as ugly as they come. Did you see Shantarsky Jr. online?"

I nodded.

"That's exactly what he looks like in real life. Tall, handsome, broad shoulders. Cover boy material."

"I see."

"And as for Shantarsky," he went on, "I don't think he'll start making waves. You can forget about him for the time being. Just keep your eyes peeled. He may be small fry but he has teeth too. A piranha is tiny compared to a shark but if it attacks you, you'll know all about it. So if he does do something, it'll be on the sly. Publicity is the last thing he needs."

"I could say the same," I added. "Actually, my work contract expires today. So I don't owe him anything, anyway."

Dmitry nodded. "The loan which you already have, you can still pay it off bit by bit. But I don't think you can get the big one now. Shantarsky will take care of that. By the same token, you're an Experienced Digger now. You won't have problems finding a new job. By then you might decide on a new bank too. Getting a long-term job contract is key."

He paused. "My wife and I, we've visited our bank recently. Because we have a mortgage on all our properties. Apart from our summer cottage, that is, that's been remortgaged to use as equity for our city apartment."

I tensed. "What are you driving at?"

"I'm just telling you we've been looking at some possible ways to help my niece."

"But Dmitry-"

"Oh, do shut up," he said with a good-natured smile. "My Natasha and your Sveta got on like a house on fire. So you and I, we have no say in the matter: our better halves have already sussed it all out. In any case, my mortgages prevent me from becoming your guarantor. So we have some thinking to do in this respect. If push comes to shove, I could raise up to twenty-five grand by selling a few assets. That's the best I can do."

"But Dmitry-"

"Dmitry what? What are you trying to say? We're family. We should stand for our own. Natasha and I, we haven't been blessed with children. In this respect, Christina is like a- never mind."

We fell silent. What else was there to say?

"I have another one in the cooler," Dmitry pointed at the empty bottle. "Shall we?"

I nodded.

He reached into the cabinet and filled our glasses with the amber liquor. The tangy woody aroma embraced my nose. We took a sip.

"I've been to the Moon yesterday," Dmitry announced.

I choked on my drink. "Excuse me?"

He grinned. "Been to the Moon, I'm telling you."

"I heard you the first time. I thought I was hearing things."

"Our company is facing some major changes," he began to explain. "Most importantly, we're about to sell the majority stake to the government. That's it. End of my freedom. My bosses just don't cut it. The whole thing proved too big for them."

"It was to be expected," I said.

Dmitry nodded. "This is the proverbial mountain coming to Mohammad."

"What about the Moon?" I reminded him.

"Not just the Moon. It's also Mars and Jupiter," he began to ramble. "They're working on several projects, both major and minor ones. Mirror World is only the beginning. Not everyone is into sword and sorcery, you see. A lot of people would prefer shooters and all sorts of star wars. Others don't want to fight at all. They want a game where you can create a character and just live there in peace with no need for swords, spells, starships and all that bull. A few new games are being tested even as we speak. One, as I've just said, is a space war simulator. Another one is a post-ap. There's also one based on the two world wars."

"Oh. What about the minor projects?"

His eyes lit up. "That's where it gets interesting. It's going to be some sort of funfair ride. Like an imitation of a trip to other planets, for one. Everything will be real: the launch site, the spaceships, the spacesuits—the lot!"

"If they're as real as Mirror World, they will go through the roof," I said.

"Oh trust me they are," Dmitry assured me. "Just think of all those dreams coming true! Space travel! Journeys to other planets! No need to pay a king's ransom for a premium account. It'll be single-use rides. They're going to create a special client database to log in their medical checks results and all that."

"Wow."

"You think someone would refuse to take their family on a Mars weekend? Or try one of our Animal World shows where you can soar in the sky with eagles or become a dolphin plowing through the seas? We have Stone Age, The Era of Dinos, Ancient China, Ancient Rome and Medieval Europe. And our Children's World, packed with ponies, Disney characters and Barbie dolls! The mind boggles. Would you like to go to a Beatles show?"

"You bet," I said.

"So you see? Only a game, you said?"

"More like a new industry," I agreed. "Something's brewing, I can feel it. Something very special."

We fell silent again.

"Listen," Dmitry finally perked up. "It's no good me doing all the talking. You still haven't told me what you plan to do now. Don't you feel sorry about your loan?"

"Not at this price," I said. "Not now that I can finally see this game's potential."

"I told you it wasn't a game anymore, didn't I?" he grinned. "Mister escape artist."

I chuckled. "Talk about bad luck. I thought I had it all sorted, and now I'll have to start all over again. And time is an issue."

"You don't need to 'start all over again', do you?" he said. "And even so, not many have a jump start like yours! You're an Experienced Digger, man, and that's no 'starting over' at all! So what's your plan?"

I rubbed my temples. I felt tired. "I've been considering several options," I began. "At first I contemplated the idea of joining the Dark side, but then I realized I might actually be giving Shantarsky a carte blanche. You're nodding—so you probably agree with me. Then I asked myself a question. Where can I work in peace without having to fear all these Slayers and other psychos? I came to the conclusion that I needed to find an influential land owner, preferably one who belongs to a top clan. Like Lady Melorie from the Steel Shirts."

"Oh," Dmitry rubbed his chin. "I was about to suggest Egan from the Untouchables. He is a very influential person in Mirror World, and his clan is one of the strongest. Melorie, the Lady of Storms! Hm. Actually, you might be right. She is Arrid's wife..."

I nodded. "Arrid is the clan's leader."

"You're a clever bastard, are you?"

"You bet," I grinned. "I'll join her workforce as an ordinary Grinder and just keep leveling, nice and quiet. She won't even notice me. She has hundreds of workers like myself—thousands even. I checked her out once at some forum. She's a major land owner too."

"And then what?" Dmitry asked, curious.

"Well, considering that a major loan implies a long-term work contract, I'll be working toward that end. I can always sell myself into slavery if it comes to that. But now I need my independence. I need a free hand."

"That's right," he nodded.

"You see," I began, "when Christina's body rejected the donor heart, we lost everything. We'd already sold everything we'd had. Thank God we'd had it! We'd hoped it would solve the problem. As a result, we lost everything—and the problems just kept piling up. God forbid you ever feel as helpless as I did then!"

We paused, each thinking his own thoughts. Dmitry was the first to break the silence,

"You still haven't told me whether you have other banks in mind."

I shook my head. "Zilch. I've been with Mega Bank for ages. My credit history, you know... The moment I find another job I'll start shopping for a new one."

He rubbed his chin. "Listen... If you don't mind me saying... You do have an account at Reflex Bank, don't you?"

"Reflex what?"

"It's Mirror World's in-game bank."

"I see... Yes, I used it to channel real-world money into the game. I must still have about a hundred left there. Why?"

"There's something you need to know. Reflex Bank isn't just a money-shifting machine."

I hurried to wipe my glasses. "Tell me."

"To put it short, they do loans too," Dmitry said. "Just don't hold your breath. At the moment, you can forget it. Both your account type and the narrow time frame are against you. But, say, in a year's time..."

I tensed like a greyhound. Dmitry must have

sensed what I was feeling.

"Look at him," he said mockingly. "Never mind. I'll explain it now. The bank where you keep your in-game currency is indeed only a cash dispenser with a few very basic functions. That's all it is. If you want something more sophisticated, you need to address yourself to their head office in Mellenville—Mirror World's capital city. I'm not sure if you know but low-level players aren't even allowed within its city limits. But you've already sorted that problem out for yourself. When I realized it, I immediately thought about Reflex Bank."

"Wait a sec," I said. "This doesn't add up, does it? An in-game bank capable of giving out wads of Monopoly money which you can then exchange for the real thing? Please."

"It would have been—had it not been for one peculiar detail. Reflex Bank is a baby of some five or six—can't remember the exact number now—of the world's biggest banks. When receiving an in-game loan, you choose one of them as your creditor."

"So the money *is* real."

"Of course. Basically, you're signing a loan agreement with a proper bank, only you do it in Mirror World. If later you quit the game for some reason, you're still under the same obligation to pay the money back in real life."

"Hm," I murmured. "The question is, where's the catch? Would I be correct in suggesting that in order to get a loan, I first need to earn a certain reputation? Is that right?"

He nodded. "Exactly. And not only that. There's

a number of conditions you're supposed to meet, otherwise they won't even talk to you."

"Which are?"

"An extended immersion without logging out for at least a month, for starters."

I whistled in astonishment.

"If you do log out, you'll have to start it all over again. Next thing. All these employer-paid communal modules won't cut it anymore. You'll have to shell out for a state-of-the-art capsule and medical support. It's not as expensive as you might think, but still. Plus your own health, of course. Having said that, an Experienced Digger's gear can keep the player in the game for even longer periods."

"That's not all, is it?"

"Oh, no. Far from it. They won't even talk to you in the bank unless you have a registered Mellenville address. Normally, a player can just come and live there, no red tape involved. But *you* must have one. You can't afford to buy a place, that little is clear. So you'll either have to rent a room or stay at a hotel. And to have your address registered, the property owner has to sign for you. If ever you decide to go that route, you won't get bored, that's for sure."

"Why all this song and dance?"

"The city's reputation. The higher your own reputation, the more opportunities you'll have all around the city. And that means at the bank too. You'll be obliged to do certain tasks and quests—some simple, others quite complex. You can go and check the forums to see what everyone has to say about Mellenville. Just don't expect to find any answers.

"Why so?"

"There're no guidebooks on Mellenville. All the quests are individual and random. And one more thing. You really need to be on your best behavior there. Mellenville is an NPC city."

"What city?"

"A city controlled by Non-Player Characters. Artificial Intellects. Robots, if the word can help you grasp the concept.

"I see," I suppressed a yawn.

"Just don't think you'll be greeted by some primitive pieces of scrap metal. Right," Dmitry slapped his shoulders and clambered to his feet, looking tired. "More on this tomorrow. Beddy-byes time. What a day! Try to get some rest now. The bedding's in the wardrobe. The couch is quite comfortable. I've slept here on a number of occasions. I still have a few phone calls to make."

"Thanks, Dmitry. No idea what I'd have done without you."

He waved my words away and added in a rough voice, "Off to bed now... escape artist."

Chapter Twenty-One

Surprisingly, I slept like a baby that night. This is probably what happens to everyone who's just made a life-changing decision like I had.

I was going to do the extended immersion thing. Sveta hadn't liked the idea at all. Still, when I'd laid all the pros in front of her, she'd finally given in—but only because she had no idea of my last-night's adventures. Dmitry, on the contrary, accepted my decision. I even got the impression he'd expected it from the start.

My move to the new module center was nothing to write home about. I'd been living out of a suitcase for the last few years anyway so I'd become quite immune to that sort of thing. A month's subscription had put me back thirteen hundred bucks. More expenses—but at least I hoped it was worth it. Thank God I had money on my account! Between the ten grand transferred by Rrhorgus, all my starting money and whatever I'd earned in the last week, I hadn't had to borrow from my brother.

By the way, Flint had managed to declare their last haul. As a result, I'd earned six hundred gold from that instance. Excellent. All because we'd had lots of bonus crystals that day.

I really didn't want to part with the guys. They were a good team. Dmitry had told me they'd found another employer, somewhere closer to the frontier with the Darkies. Apparently, Flint and Co. had filed an official complaint against Slayer. Shantarsky pretended he'd known nothing about the Wild West nature of the situation in his cluster and had publicly kicked Slayer out of the clan. That was the end of it.

Apparently, Flint hadn't had a chance to delete me from the group. Slayer had done his best to stop them too. By the time they'd got their act together, I was already engaged in combat while Flint stood by the entrance to the grotto trying to disband the group. Imagine his surprise when I dropped out of the instance, then quit the game!

I just hoped he understood enough to keep his mouth shut. At some later date, we might meet up and discuss it all. But not now.

Admittedly I couldn't even remember how I'd quit the game. It was irrelevant, anyway. I had other things to worry about. My main objective was to raise a hundred and eighty-five grand.

Time to start all over again. My "extended

immersion" was looming. Perusing the multitude of forums and blogs had only added to my confusion. The amount of contradictory and superfluous information on Reflex Bank was mind-boggling. It gave me the impression that seventy percent of it was a clever decoy. It made one thing clear though: it wasn't going to be easy. Especially for me with my humble Grinder's account.

But as far as NPCs were concerned, the information on them was pretty clear-cut. The so-called 'Glasshouse NPCs' were considerably different from their counterparts in other computer games. Mirror World's developers had created a special program called A Mirror Soul. This was a truly grandiose concept that allowed the Non-Player Characters to go far beyond their usual "emotion imitation" stuff. Instead of just generating joy, pleasure or fear, these NPCs could express their own attitude toward the situation and their role within it. Basically, a Mirror Soul was nothing other than a high tech clone of the human mind.

Jesus. A virtual world. A virtual mind. The more I learned about this place, the less comfortable I felt. I had a hunch that something had changed—that the world had moved on while I was lagging behind, choking on the dust raised by the avant-garde.

"Are you ready?" my brother asked me.

"Yeah," I nodded, suspended in the jelly-like substance.

Now more than ever he reminded me of Dad. I'd been eight at the time; Dad had taught me to ride a bike. The same emotionless face and the same vivid eyes filled with care and concern.

"Make sure you don't do anything stupid," he said.

I grinned. "Will do my best."

"Good luck, then!"

"Likewise."

Noiselessly the lid of my "coffin" slid shut. I found myself in the familiar pitch darkness. A piercing light assaulted my eyes. I was back in Mirror World.

A large 3D inscription hovered before my eyes,

Greetings, Olgerd! Welcome to Mirror World!
Please choose your entry point.

I stared at a list of some fifty major towns within Mirror World's realm of Light, supplied courtesy of the game's administration. I suppressed a sarcastic chuckle. How very nice. Freakin' do-gooders. It's the thought that counts, anyway.

I chose *The Outskirts of Verdaille City*. Leuton was more or less off limits for me now.

I heaved a sigh. That was it. I was in it for a month. No way back.

I was standing with my back to a forest, facing a neat corn field. The clock showed 7 a.m. The sun was just kissing the horizon.

I turned around. The forest was still dark and damp. The moist grass felt cold on my bare feet. Oh. I'd love to know who was wearing my boots now. They must have already flogged them for a nice bit of profit, as well as the gloves. What a shame.

Never mind. Once I got to the nearest city shop and compared their prices with the auction, I could kit myself out again.

Oh, before I forgot. I opened my Friends list. Nobody online yet.

Would you like to delete yourself from your Friends list?

Sure. This way they'd have no way of locating me. Sorry, Rrhorgus, Greg and Sandra. It was for your own good. Seeing me now wasn't a healthy idea: you were still in Shantarsky's employment. One day we might meet up and discuss it all over a nice long drink. At least I hoped we might.

Now, the clothes. Oh. That Steel Widow had done a nice job on me. My damaged gear wasn't worth anything now. But what could I do? It was a good thing I still had something to wear.

Wait a sec. What was that now? How could I have ever forgotten? Actually, no wonder. I'd been too busy thinking of other things.

The Apps tab was blinking orange. Let's have a look.

Would you like to install the Der Swyor app suite?

Oh, no. No need to rush. A new surprise from Pierrot was the last thing I needed right now. Later, all later.

I'd completely forgotten all about the clan's ring and the app that came with it. What a shame. I couldn't even pick Dmitry's brains on the subject now. Actually, I hadn't asked anyone's advice before downloading the file, had I? So it was only fair I had to use my own head. I was still kicking myself for having stayed behind in the cave that day instead of leaving with the rest of the group.

"Never mind," I mumbled. "Time to get going. I have lots to do still."

I walked along the road past golden corn fields, watching the farmers heading off to work. They all smiled. I could hear them joking. The air rang with women's laughter. Someone had already got down to work, singing. For a brief moment I had the illusion I was back in my childhood home, standing amid the boundless corn fields of Ukraine. I could almost hear the voice of Grandpa Stephan asking me to fetch him some water.

I shook my head free of the unwelcome memories and squinted at the workers for a better look, making out the pointy ears of Alven women and the Dwandes' impressive fangs.

The loss of my boots and gloves hadn't affected my mood that much. My speed hadn't dropped. Even incomplete, the Seasoned Digger's gear set allowed you to comfortably travel the vast expanses of this world. I remembered the trials and tribulations of my

---

first-day journey. That had been a feat!

After fifteen minutes of brisk walking, I checked my Energy levels. I'd only spent 20 pt. Excellent! That was a drop in the ocean. And if I set the bot to economy mode, I wouldn't even need to check it: it would restore Energy levels automatically.

I could see the city walls from far away. Verdaille, if the truth were known, was just another one-horse town. Same as Leuton really, only with a bigger population and three times as many mines.

The Outskirts of Verdaille City was a location controlled by the Steel Shirts clan. Or, to be more precise, it was Lady Melorie's domain—the clan leader's wife's. Even if you disregarded her high standing, The Lady of Storms was a very influential figure in Mirror World. A level 270-wizard, she obviously wasn't the kind of woman to indulge in needlework in the safety of her own castle.

Once again I congratulated myself on my choice of seigneur. It meant safety for me too. She wouldn't even know I was there. The less I stuck my neck out, the better. I had to level up my skill first, and then we'd see.

The city gates were pretty crowded. I'd never seen so many people in one place here before. The air hummed with voices. My eyes watered from all the loud colors and the glittering of armor. Domestic animals crowded the road: horses of every race and size, clumsy cows and bleating sheep. I noticed quite a few identical carts, heavy and unyielding—apparently standard-issue transportation. I focused on one of them.

Name: Wooden Cart
Durability: 3554/5000
Restriction: Requires the Slow Coach skill.

"Eh, she's not as she used to be," the driver said, noticing my interest in his vehicle. "I'm gonna get her some new wheels at the market and add a few points to the shaft, then you won't know her! She'll roll off the road like some freakin' Mercedes, by God! Only I need to sell my beasties first."

"Good morning," I hurried to greet him.

"Same to you," the man answered. He spoke almost in a singsong, with a soft and melodious Ukrainian accent. I glanced at his tag. *Zachary.*

I did a quick check on him. A Daily Grinder like myself. A Farmer. Race: Human. Level: Prosperous. From what I remembered, it was equal to Seasoned Digger. Did I have access to the driving skill, I wondered, or was it only available to farmers?

I took a look around me, focusing on every driver. Lots of Farmers among them, but also quite a few Herbalists and Fishermen. Which meant that the skill was available to everyone. I'd have to check it out later. What a shame the game didn't have Internet access. That would have simplified a whole bunch of things.

"Excuse my asking, dear sir, but what's actually going on here?" I said, walking next to his slowly advancing cart. "Why all these people?"

"There's a fair today, isn't there?" he answered eagerly. "It's like this every six months."

I could see he was in the talkative mood. Such long, slow queues usually make one disposed to shoot the breeze.

"I see," I commented. "How long does it last?"

"The whole week, what do you think?" he grinned back.

The man was positively beaming. He probably hoped to sell his "beasties" for a good profit.

"How are things overall, then?" I asked. "Is it quiet here? Any robbers or highwaymen?"

Zachary shrugged off my suggestion. "Forget it! What would they want with us? The idiot hasn't been born yet who'd mess around in Lady Mel's lands! She'd make quick work of any evil-doers."

I breathed a sigh of relief. This was exactly what I wanted to hear.

Noticing this, Zachary asked sympathetically, "You must have had it rough in other parts of the world."

With a sad smile I nodded at my feet, "You could say that. Even my boots are gone."

The farmer threw his hands up in dismay. "What kind of creature is man? You tell me! Always trying to profit from others' misfortune!"

I sighed. "Sort of."

"Why won't you stay here with us?" Zachary suggested. "I can see you're a Seasoned Digger. We have lots of work for the likes of you. Plenty of mines around."

I smiled back. "That's exactly what I've come here for. I'd like to make a new start."

"Good decision. You won't regret it."

"Actually," I asked, "where does one go here to look for work?"

"Well, if it's the dwarves you want, their office is in the Craftsmen's Quarter."

I shook my head. "Sorry, sir. I'd rather apply to Lady Mel. I liked how you spoke about her."

The farmer beamed like a newly-minted gold coin, puffing out his cheeks. My compliment had struck the right chord.

"I thought you were going to join your own," he said. "In this case you need to go to the high street. That's exactly where I'm heading. Get in, I'll give you a lift. No good marching barefoot on the cold stone."

Did he need to ask? A few saved Energy points were always welcome.

Apparently, Zachary must have taken me for a dwarf. Ennans did bear some resemblance to those fabled creatures. He must have glanced me over without bothering to check my tag. A short guy with a beard and a Digger to boot—he had to be a dwarf. I didn't mind. He'd also called me a Seasoned Digger— probably judging by my clothes. I had yet to get myself some new gear.

Wait a sec. And what if?.. Without even knowing it, the farmer had just given me an idea. Nothing major but it was worth trying. I'd have to look into it when I had the time.

As I entered the city, I received the standard system message and the offer to download the free map and the city's history. Plus lots of other offers for paid apps. Okay. I couldn't say no to freebies. The rest I didn't need.

It took us about twenty minutes to get to the city center. Remarkably, the town turned out to be much bigger than I'd assumed from forum discussions. Leuton wasn't a patch on it. Broad streets. Three and four-story buildings. Lots of shops, inns and taverns. It wasn't even eight in the morning and the sidewalks were heaving with people.

I actually might like it here. I absolutely had to check their fair stalls for any new clothes. The shop and the auction would have to wait. I just might find something cheap and cheerful.

"Here we are," Zachary stopped his cart. "You see that green building with wide windows over there? The one with the bird on it? That's where you need to go."

I nodded. "The bird" was an Aquila—the picture of an eagle spreading its wings. The Steel Shirts clan had simply copied the Roman legion's emblem.

"Thanks a lot, man. You've really helped me out."

He grinned back. "My pleasure. Come and see me at the market."

"Absolutely."

Eight o'clock: logically, the office must have already opened. Last night I'd checked their schedule on the site, just to make sure.

The doorway was completely blocked by players: dwarves, gnomes, Dwandes and humans. I also noticed a few Horruds and Rhogghs. About eighty percent of them zero-level, the rest Seasoned. I didn't see any Experienced ones. The beginning players in their start-up kits were an eyesore. They were standing apart from the rest, coveting the Seasoned players' gear. Others stared openly. The Seasoned ones, in their turn, stood there as if the whole world belonged to them. They didn't check out anyone; they just hung out talking calmly, casting an occasional ironic glance at the beginning players. I received the same kinds of stares: arguably even more scornful than if I were a bare-chested newb.

I checked my reflection in the window. I could understand them. I looked like a scaled-down dwarf, shaggy and disheveled. Although my stats were private, my clothes—whatever was left of them—betrayed me as a Seasoned Digger. My bag, boots, and gloves were missing. Even the new players looked better than I did.

I didn't give a damn. This wasn't Paris and I wasn't on an haute couture catwalk. I took another look at them, noticing that all of the Seasoned players had their stats available to all. It felt weird—really as if they were part of some beauty pageant.

There was nothing particularly special about their gear: just some standard-issue tools and runes. Only three of the Dwandes stood out. Their gear was top of the range and virtually unused. Not a single empty item. They stood apart from the rest, casting searching glances around as if looking for someone. They must have been a team. Their gazes scanned me en passant with a disdain reserved for a pigeon that had just shat in their soup.

Then the crowd perked up. Five dwarves were approaching the building from the direction of the square.

"The Ironbeards' headhunters," a zero-level Dwand commented.

"Yeah. They'll start hiring in a minute," a Cave Rhoggh agreed.

I cast a curious glance at the three Dwandes. They stood up straight, bright-eyed. Were they counting on this job? Then why hadn't they gone directly to the dwarves' office? Never mind. Why should I care? We'd soon find out.

The dwarves were only a few paces away from the front door when it swung open, letting out the powerful shape of a Cave Rhoggh. Everyone turned to the sound. The Rhoggh looked over the crowd as if it already belonged to him.

Having noticed the approaching dwarves, he scowled, "Breon, did anyone tell you that you look remarkably like a hyena?"

The smallest of the five dwarves hid a smirk within his fat beard. "Don't worry, Weigner, you'll have plenty left for yourself!"

He looked over the crowd, studying the workers. His mocking stare rested on me. Or rather, on my bare feet. He turned back to the Rhoggh and shouted, nodding at me, "I'll leave you the best ones, don't you worry!"

His friends guffawed. The crowd joined in. Even the newbs were laughing their bare backsides off. I didn't care. Let them laugh. You couldn't surprise me with a brownnose here anymore. Their kowtowing was only witness to their own worthlessness. What else could a useless person do? They might be thinking they were gaining something by it: something worth the humiliation. They might realize they weren't a pretty sight; they might even hate themselves for doing it. But as the famous French mathematician Blaise Pascal once said, *"the pureness of a goal justifies the perversity of the means"*. Which allowed me to take any and all such scorn philosophically. Now the fact that I'd been waiting here for a good ten minutes was much harder to take. I was losing time. I still had lots to do today.

Ignoring the useless dwarf, I looked up at the Rhoggh. Surprisingly, he was the only one who hadn't even smiled at the joke. That was good. The guy had character. Silently he opened the doors wide, turned around and walked back in. Apparently, it was supposed to mean that the office was now open.

To my surprise, no one seemed to have noticed it. All the mine diggers stayed outside, watching greedily the five dwarves who were walking through the crowd as if they were shopping for a couple of old cart horses.

I seemed to be the only one not interested in working for the dwarves. Excellent. It meant I wasn't going to languish in the long line at the PR office as I'd expected. How lucky was that?

I hurried to climb the steps in the Rhoggh's wake. Breon the dwarf was just talking to the three Dwandes. Our eyes met. He gave me another smirk and went right on talking.

In the meantime, Weigner the Rhoggh was already climbing the stairs to the first floor, muttering something under his nose. The sound of my voice made him turn round,

"Excuse me! Could you please tell me where I could sign a work contract?"

"Ah, it's you," he chuckled. "Decided to join us? Simply because those midgets won't hire you? Don't you worry, all those idiots will be back in a minute. But today, you're gonna be the first. Hurry up. I've lots to do."

Without saying a word, I tagged along.

His office proved too small for his bulk. A giant of his proportions needed more breathing space. Actually, it was the second time I'd seen an office worker of his dimensions. Was this the current trend? Or the company's policy? Or could it just be that the player was too puny in real life so here he lived life to the full, scaring any potential clients with his fangs and his booming voice?

"Shut the door," Weigner grumbled. "And take a seat. I'll make out the contract."

I closed the door softly. I hate doors being slammed. It's just some sort of a nervous tick I've had since early childhood.

Noiselessly I moved my chair closer to the desk and sat down. Been there, done it. I knew what was going to happen next.

The Rhoggh touched a dark wall panel with his clawed paw. A translucent screen materialized above the desk top. While the program was loading, Weigner was going through some paperwork, muttering deliberately loudly under his nose to make sure I could hear his every word,

"It's the same thing every month! One might think the dwarves' mines are paved with gold. Okay, so they pay a better wage, so what? Who would need their flippin' circus? They're not Ironbeards: they're Cheekyfaces."

It was probably time for me to butt in. "Why, what's going on in here?"

He squinted at me, disbelieving. "Quit playing the fool, you!"

I shrugged. "I'm not. I'm just curious what this hoo-ha is all about. That's the only reason I asked."

Weigner froze, his tiny yellow eyes boring a hole in me. His gaze sent shivers down my spine.

"Are you saying that you've no idea that the Ironbeards keep on coming to our front door every month offering jobs to players of other races?"

"I had no idea, honest," I replied, then added with a smirk, "Since when are they so generous?"

Weigner sat back, his stare still pinning me down. He paused, then spoke,

"There was this stupid discussion at some forum where the forum members accused the dwarven guild of being racist. People claimed they only hired dwarves and gnomes. I don't know about the Stonefoot, but the Ironbeards decided to teach everybody a lesson. Now every month their scouts arrive at the offices of those forum members who were particularly outspoken in that discussion, and pick workers from other races."

"But what about Lady Mel?" I asked.

"Well, she was the loudest. And the fact that they keep coming to her doorstep, she actually considers it her victory."

"So that's what it's all about."

"That's exactly it," he grumbled, then added, fuming, "And she doesn't seem to give a damn about them stealing our best workers!"

"The rich and their whims," I summarized. "Do the dwarves really pay higher wages?"

He shrugged. "Indeed they do. And they have better working conditions. They're a guild, what do you want? They're interested in making money first and foremost. And the Steel Shirts are a military clan. Admittedly one of the richest and most influential in Mirror World, but some of those clan members, while not exactly have-nots, have no idea of how to manage their riches. Or rather they don't want to."

I wasn't going to tell him about all the possible solutions to their money-making problems. If the truth were known, I didn't give a damn about all these "useless bosses vs. stupid rulers" conversations. What was the point? Why would I care about other people's problems? I had more than my fair share of them. It was time to fold up this discussion.

"Had I wanted to work for the dwarves, that's where I'd have gone to."

"And you think they'd have hired you?" his voice rang with sarcasm.

"They might," I said, unveiling some of my stats.

Chapter Twenty-Two

Watching the change come over his pallid fanged face was admittedly funny. He stood up in his seat, reading my characteristics. Naturally, I didn't allow him to see my Shrewd Operator. He seemed sufficiently impressed with my Experienced level, anyway. I don't think they had many diggers of my caliber here.

I flashed him a friendly smile. "So shall we sign me in? I'm a bit pressed for time."

I left his office at nine in the morning. Not bad. I'd thought it might have taken longer than that. The corridor was already packed with sour-faced players lining up. Apparently, not many had been "lucky" enough to get a job with the dwarves. I didn't see the three Dwandes anywhere. I was pretty sure the dwarves had hired them. I'd have done the same. A well-knit team is worth a lot. I knew this from experience.

I had signed their standard contract of my preferred piecework type. Two weeks. My level gave me no preferential treatment. Well, that was to be expected.

According to Weigner, Experienced Diggers didn't stay in town long. They inevitably found a strong group and moved cluster in order to start mopping up instances. That was fine with me too. The fewer people down the mine, the more space for me to swing my pick.

Still, I wasn't yet ready to join any mop-up groups. At my level, the minimum raid duration was six days. I wasn't quite prepared to be stuck in some cave or grotto for almost a week without the chance of getting out. Firstly, because at this work pace I risked leveling up prematurely. You never know with my Operator. So as I wasn't planning on blowing my cover, I'd have to work in a regular mine, slowly but surely. That also gave me the chance to check Zachary's idea out, even though he knew nothing about it.

Secondly and most importantly, if my char's Reputation with Mellenville wasn't up to scratch, the in-game bank wouldn't deal with me at all. And in order to level it up, I had to perform daily or long-term tasks within the city limits.

That decided it. I had to work in Lady Mel's emerald fields. That would fetch me about fifteen hundred gold a week. No doubt I could have earned way more doing instances but at the moment, reputation was key. Plus I was desperate for a long-term work contract. If I failed to get a loan with Reflex Bank, then I'd have to go cap in hand to real-life banks. So the longer my working experience, the better. The main thing was to make sure I didn't pop my clogs too soon. Nor do anything stupid. I had six weeks to raise a hundred eighty-five thousand dollars.

My next port of call was Mine Diggers Guild. I paid the weekly due of twenty-five bucks, this raising my Reputation with the guild 50 pt: 100 in total.

As I left the guild's building slapping my bare feet along the marble tiles, I could hear giggles and quips. Enough! I could stand a lot if absolutely necessary but there was a limit to everything.

Thus thinking, I headed off to the market. Time to do some shopping. Admittedly I did look like a tramp.

"Holy Jesus," I uttered, watching the central square transform before my very eyes.

I had surely expected to see some semblance of a market. The kind of market I knew in real life, that is. But this... Had I ventured in, I could have easily spent a week there.

My eyes watered with all the colors. The bright miscellany of tents and pavilions formed uneven aisles crowded with carts, kiosks and stands. I could hear the inevitable music playing.

They probably sold *everything* here. In an aisle off to my right, a big dwarf fronted a stand selling weapons and armor. To his left, a slim Alven lady boasted her embroidering skills; not two paces away from me, a fat Rhoggh was busy baking golden loaves of bread for everyone to marvel. The air was thick with music, vendors' voices praising their goods, the howling and bellowing of animals... What a crazy place. At nine in the morning, mind you. Where would I go? Where was I supposed to find what I needed?

"Aquamarine dust! Aquamarine dust for sale!"

"Hares' pelts! Wolves' tails! Boars' fangs! Bear claws!"

"I'll buy your gear!"

"I'll buy class-two herbal infusions! Price no object!"

"Hey, mister! Need some boots?"

At first I didn't even realize he was addressing me. "Pardon?" I managed.

A ginger-haired guy of about twenty-five patiently waited for me to focus my stare on him. "Just wondering if you might need a pair of boots. I can see you ain't got no gloves either."

"No, I don't," I hurried to reply, embarrassed by my momentary lapse of concentration. "What have you got to offer?"

"Over there," the guy waved somewhere to his right. "Stall nine. My uncle has some gear to sell. Froll's the name. Understood?"

I nodded. Not waiting for me to reply, the guy stole deeper into the crowd. As I began moving in the direction he'd indicated, I couldn't help hearing his voice,

"Hey, ma'am! Need a jacket?"

This was scary. A person with money wasn't going to leave this place empty-handed. By the time I made my way to stall nine, I'd been offered all sorts of things, from needles to legendary-class swords. Had I had to move a bit further on, I was pretty sure I would have stumbled along a tank vendor.

Froll's stall wasn't that hard to find. It was groaning under piles of clothes, footwear and various accessories. I'd never been a big market shopper so I was completely out of my depth here. Sveta, she'd always enjoyed this sort of thing. She would have loved it here.

As I studied the goods, I cast a quick glance at the vendor. His nephew hadn't taken after him, that's for sure. They might have been related in real life but here in Mirror World it would have been a bit over the top.

Froll was a Rock Dwand. His stats were hidden. Broad-shouldered, wearing town clothes. Not a Grinder.

I coughed to attract his attention.

He turned round and beamed, seeing me. "How can I help you, dear sir? I just happen to have an excellent Strength kit," he immediately switched to the offensive.

"No, thanks. I'm interested in Energy ones," I said.

"Excellent. Hardy Digger will fit you just fine. I have both new and second-hand ones."

I shook my head. "I'm afraid not. I need something more advanced."

For a brief moment, his expression betrayed surprise. Then his face dropped.

"Something wrong?" I asked.

"Not really," he breathed a sigh of disappointment. "Thing is, I don't trade in items for your caliber. I'll tell you more: I don't think this market has anything to offer someone like you."

"Why not?"

"In this backwater? What do you expect? Experienced workers all move closer to the capital. If you take me, it's not worth the trouble for me to stock items I can sell once or twice a year if at all. My cart and my storeroom can only hold a limited amount of items. Pointless lugging around something I can't even sell."

"I see," I said. "But why would you lug them around? Can't you just auction them?"

He smirked. "That's what you think. Auctions charge a fee on every submitted item regardless of whether it sells or not. And here I only pay my custom duty, then I can sell till the cows come home."

"I see."

So that's how it worked, then. I'd had no idea. You never know, it might be useful.

I bade my goodbye and was about to leave him when a jaunty female voice called behind my back,

"Excuse me, Sir Olgerd!"

I turned around. This was an Alven Archer girl. A pretty face; a pair of childishly blue eyes, slightly slanted. Black hair. Slim to the point of being fragile. A fancy bow and a quiver were slung behind her back. A knife and a dagger dangled from her belt. Her name was Saimie.

"I'm sorry to delay you," she hurried to add. "I just happened to overhear your conversation."

I smiled gallantly and shook my head. "It's all right. We're at the market, aren't we? You've something to sell, haven't you?"

She beamed. "Exactly. No clothes for your level, unfortunately, but I have some interesting jewelry. It's on my stall over there, if you don't mind."

She nodded, motioning me to follow her. I shrugged and followed, hoping I wasn't getting into something I might later regret.

Her tent was comparatively small but neat and tastefully decorated, mainly in the shades of green that matched the vendress' own clothes. A small round table stood at its center, surrounded by several small three-legged stools.

She pointed at one of them. "Make yourself comfortable."

Without saying a word, I perched myself on the stool. Saimie produced a small canvas bundle and unfolded it on the table. "Have a look if anything takes your fancy."

Right. What did we have there? I had a funny feeling I knew her line of business. After my memorable conversation with Shantarsky I'd checked a few forums and done a bit of research on No-Man's Lands. There was a lot of eye-opening information there, especially about the likes of her.

"Are you a scavenger?" I asked.

"Sure," she nodded. "Why, does that bother you?" her voice tinged with sarcasm.

"In a way, yeah. Are you White or Black?"

She smiled. "Sure I'm White. Do you think I'd be standing here selling had I been Black? Black scavengers sell everything via their own channels. My business is perfectly legal."

"Can't you do your own looting?" I asked.

"Hey, those are No-Man's Land mobs. I'm not exactly in the same league," she paused, then offered the iron-clad argument used in virtually every forum discussion, "Ninety percent of all Mirror World players are scavengers. That's just the way it is. You've any idea of all the stuff lying around there unclaimed?"

"Unclaimed? Really?"

"Of course. Imagine a group of level 100+ players. To cross the location, they're obliged to mop it up. They don't even look at all the loot from the low-level mobs. They save the space in their bags for much bigger game. Clan raids, that's different, there's virtually nothing left after them as they have their own newbs to feed. But there's plenty of stuff left after the loners too. Personally, I sign a contract with a group and do my job. Waste not, want not."

"I see," I said. "You sure you never robbed any corpses? I wouldn't want to buy some charm or bracelet off you only to be hunted down by its legitimate owner afterwards."

"They're clean!" Saimie said, indignant. "Here, look, they're not marked!"

"Marks are easy to remove."

"Do I look like I have tons of money to pay wizards for doing that? Are you going to have a look or not?"

It looked like I'd overdone it a bit. "Sure," I mumbled. "I'm terribly sorry. I'll take a look now, only it might take some time. I'll have to compare the prices with the auction's. Is that all right with you?"

"Of course. I'll be there at the counter if you need me."

She cooled off a little. I made a mental note to mind my tongue in the future. Apparently, not everything they said in blogs and on forums could be taken as gospel.

Let's have a look. What had she got there?

Name: The Bone Bracelet of Gadang
Effect: +15 to Defense
Race restriction: Only Cave Horrud
Level: 10

Defense had something to do with combat skills, didn't it? I opened the info portal. Aha. It reduced Physical Damage. That was good. Unfortunately, not for me. Some of the item's stats made it useless in my particular case. Next.

Name: Bear Tooth Necklace
Effect: +10 to Strength
Race restriction: Only Forest Dwand
Level: 15

Not for me. Next. What else did she have?

Name: Rock Charm of Torrk
Effect: +15 to Speed
Race restriction: Only Cave Rhoggh
Level: 15

Having checked about twenty items, I finally found a couple of runes: one of bone, the other of stone. Both with +15 to Capacity: one for my future bag and the other for a belt. That was all. The rest were all wrong classes and wrong levels. I checked the auction but didn't find any similar runes there. So I might take them just in case. You never know, I might need them some day. Now we had to discuss the price.

"Saimie? I'm done."

She materialized next to me as if on cue. "Found anything?"

Without saying a word, I pushed the two chosen runes toward her.

"Good choice," she said. "It'll be two hundred gold."

I couldn't believe my ears. What a cheek!

"You sure you're okay?" I asked. "Two hundred gold for two miserable runes?"

She seemed so surprised that she lost her professional manner. "Are you freakin' nuts? These are Capacity runes from No-Man's Lands! You try and level your reputation with geologists first and then you speak! These two runes are actually the most valuable items in my entire shop! *Miserable runes*, he says!"

She seemed to be sincerely upset. What a shame I couldn't check out the authenticity of her claims. I had no access to forums. The info portal didn't offer any intel. It was possible that the admins purposefully removed all information, editing the manuals and other players' comments. Never mind.

Not that I really needed them. I wasn't prepared to splurge on some totally unknown and untested items.

"Do you have anything else?" I asked, expecting a negative answer.

In a moment, she'd say "no". I'd bid my goodbye and be on my way. Neither of us would gain anything from this encounter. She seemed to understand it too. She didn't look too happy about it.

Silently I rose from the table and headed for the exit. I hated shopping. Sveta would have already haggled the shop owner into submission. What was I saying!—she would have never been attracted to such irrelevant items to begin with.

"Actually," her voice softened, "there is something I have... but I don't think it's worth your while."

I turned around. That was weird. She sounded upset. I felt out of sorts too. The conversation had left a bad aftertaste. I had this tendency of putting my foot in it before I even knew all the details. I didn't want to leave it like that.

"Take a look," she reached into her bag for some item or other and offered it to me.

I peered at it. Snuggled in her hand lay something resembling a bird's feather: either a charm or a pendant. Okay, why not? It was pretty. It looked like silver. Simple but tasteful. It wasn't inlaid with precious stones—but the craftsmanship was amazing. You could see the feather's every barb and quill. The craftsman was a genius. Then again, what was I saying? This was Mirror World. How about its stats, then?

Name: [unavailable]
Effect: [unavailable]
Race restriction: [unavailable]
Level : [unavailable]

I looked up at the girl, uncomprehending.

"Haven't you ever seen a hidden-stats item before?" she sounded surprised.

"No, not really," I mumbled, taking the silver feather from her.

She chuckled. "I see. To open them, you need to go to Mellenville and find an artifactor. It's gonna cost you. But if the item turns out worth your while, you can make good money out of it. Of course it can also be junk. It's the luck of the draw, if you know what I mean."

"Why can't you unlock it yourself?"

"It's in Mellenville. I've still some leveling to do to get admission. Also, artifactors' services cost an arm and a leg."

"And where do such thingies come from?" I kept grilling her.

"They don't. Not anymore. I was on a raid with this group of guys doing some hunting in the Misty Mountains just next to No-Man's Lands. So we found this nest made of rocks, huge like you can't imagine. Absolutely packed with bones inside. Well, I decided to check it. Found a few bits of steel and this feather. It was still attached to one of the skeletons. When I found it I thought, that's it, that's my lucky ticket."

"And?"

She shrugged. "As if! Had it been a sword or a piece of armor, that's different. You can take them to artifactors no problem. You'll always get your money's worth. But a dicey charm like this, who would need it? The auctions have already returned it to me a few times. I paid their lodging fees for nothing. So I'm obliged to lug it around like an idiot. It just takes up space."

"It might go if the price is right," I suggested.

She raised her head. "What price would be right for you?"

I winced. I hated tricks like that. It felt too much like manipulation.

I shrugged. "This is a strange situation, don't you think? You're offering me a pig in a poke and expect me to name my price?"

She looked up at me sullenly. "Not even twenty gold?"

I winced again. Enough. I was fed up with her childish attitude. Time to go. I had more pressing things to do.

"Fifteen!" she offered pleadingly, watching me turn away.

I heaved a sigh. "All right. Give it here."

She'd talked me into it, hadn't she?

Chapter Twenty-Three

Barefoot, I left the marketplace as I'd entered it, feeling I'd wasted both my time and my money. Sveta would have laughed long and hard: I'd been shopping for some shoes and ended up with a useless trinket.

It was almost ten in the morning and I still had clothes to buy. The experience had left a strange taste in my mouth. Weird girl. I'd have to look into these runes and especially into these private-stats items.

I opened the map. The city store was one block away from the square.

It didn't take me long to get there. Remarkably, the shop's interior design was identical to that of Rrhorgus Digger's Store. Only the player manning the counter was a stocky dwarf who went by the name of

Doryl. Black beard, small closely set eyes. A bulbous nose. A large wart on one cheek. A typical dweller Under the Mountain any way you looked at him.

He sized me up and down, then chuckled. I could swear he was about to say something about the state of my footwear.

"Aren't your feet cold?" he guffawed, his toothless mouth grinning.

What did I say?

Ignoring his quips, I dictated him a list,

"I need a full Reflection kit, a Sturdy Bag, a Sturdy Sword Sling, four sapphire runes of Strength and three of Stamina. I'd also like you to show me whatever tools for Experienced Diggers you have. Some Capacity runes and maybe also some jewelry. Just show me whatever you have."

With my every word the dwarf's jaw seemed to drop lower. Finally it must have reached some limit. I heard his teeth clatter, followed by a voice shaking with excitement,

"I'm afraid, sir, we don't carry any tools, Capacity runes or jewelry to suit your level..."

I dismissed his excuses, all the while studying my virtual toes. "It's all right. I might get something in Mellenville. How about the rest of my list? I'd hate to spend three days hitchhiking to Mellenville for nothing."

My last words must have become the final straw for him. He darted into the back of his shop. No wonder: he was looking at some nice profit today. A sapphire rune alone cost about eighty gold. On average, a seven-piece kit for an Experienced Digger was two hundred and fifty. It all added up, but it was worth it. Absolutely.

The night before, my heart had been bleeding as I'd transferred two grand to my in-game account. I had to. In order for my plan to work, I had to invest in it first.

The dwarf kept disappearing into his storeroom, dragging out more and more items from my list. The heap of clothes on the counter kept growing.

I started with the Reflection kit. It brought up Strength and Stamina 45 and 35 points respectively. The seven-item kit bonus also made me 30 pt. speedier.

I glanced at a small open box and the neat row of deep blue tablets inside. Gingerly I took one out.

Name: a Sapphire Rune of Stamina
Effect: +15 to Stamina
Restriction: Only Experienced Digger

So it worked out that just one such rune increased my Energy 300 points. That opened up some excellent prospects. I fought with my desire to buy four of them instead of three. But I promptly remembered Rrhorgus' instructions issued when I'd bought those malachite runes off him and decided to stick to my plan. So I bought three Stamina runes and four of Strength 17 pt. each. Balance was key.

Next he brought out a nicely-made leather knapsack with carved fastenings.

Name: A Sturdy Knapsack
Capacity: 150
Durability: 90

Lastly, a sword sling. Made of a dark brown fabric with leather inserts, it had 90 pt. Durability and twenty-five slots.

The dwarf zoned out temporarily, then hurried to inform me, "All in all, that'll be nine hundred gold forty-five silver with the discount."

I heaved a sigh. More expenditure. Still, it had turned out much cheaper than I'd expected it to be before logging in.

I paid, then asked him, "Will it be all right if I change here?"

The dwarf was beaming like the desert sun at noon. "Absolutely! We have a fitting room here. And a mirror too."

I walked into the large fitting room and stopped, facing a large mirror. "Jesus," I mumbled. "What a state to get into. No wonder everyone was poking fun at me."

I smiled sadly, remembering Walter White the way he looked in the last episode of the fifth season of *Breaking Bad*. Quite a semblance, really. The shaggy beard, the tired eyes... I needed a makeover really badly.

It took me only a few minutes to change my clothes. That was it. All done.

The familiar Ennan stared back at me from the mirror, looking quite the same. Only, how can I put it... he was sort of *pimped up*. His leather clothes were of good quality, his boots with thick strong soles hugged his calves nicely. The hat resembled one of those funny Alpine hats with a tapering crown jauntily pinched on top, its medium-width rim turned up at the back and pulled down in front. It made me look like the epitome of a Bavarian climber. All I needed was a long feather tucked into the headband.

Right. What I looked like wasn't really the point. My stats were. And I had to admit that the said stats were quite pleasing to the eye,

Strength, 116
Stamina, 83
Speed, 34
Kit's Durability, 150
Energy, 1700/1700

It even made it easier for me to breathe, as if I'd dropped twenty years or so. What a feeling! Now all that was left for me to do was choose some tools, a few Capacity runes and some jewelry.

I stuffed my old clothes into the knapsack. After a moment's hesitation, I hung the silver feather around my neck. It might be a dark horse but it would make a nice pendant for the time being.

I gave myself another once-over. No. That just didn't look right. I needed to sort myself out properly before heading for the big city. Really. At the moment I looked like a tramp who'd robbed a well-to-do townsman.

I scrambled out of the fitting room. The dwarf was still smiling. Still, as I approached the counter, his smile faded. His jaw locked. He glared at me from under his bushy eyebrows. What was going on? Just a moment ago he was all cute and cuddly and now he looked like a thunder cloud?

I tensed. "Everything all right, sir?"

He drew his eyes away from my chest and glared at me, sniffing. When he finally spoke, his cold, level voice rang with a threat,

"Black scavengers have no place in my shop."

His announcement dumbfounded me. What the heck? "I'm afraid there must be some misunderstanding," I did my best to sound calm and confident. "What makes you think I'm a scavenger and a Black one at that?"

He sniffed his indignation. "Grave robbers have no shame! You're walking in flashing a relic artifact that can only be taken off a dead body, and you're asking me what's wrong!"

So that's what it was, then. I looked down at the silver feather. So the girl *was* a thief, after all. Still, something didn't add up.

The dwarf kept glaring at me, his eyes livid with rage. I locked his stare in mine and answered calmly,

"Firstly, you've just insulted me. I can actually file an official complaint with the admins now. And once they check the logs, they'll see that your accusations have been both hasty and unfounded. Secondly, I bought this so-called 'relic artifact', as you say, at the market today. It cost me all of fifteen gold. This can also be checked. Thirdly and fourthly... but that's enough for you, I think, at least until I hear your apology complete with your side of the story."

He sort of deflated under my stare. His face betrayed confusion. "I, er, all I wanted... you know..." he kept mumbling.

I shrugged. Crossing my arms on my chest, I stared at him. Deep inside, I was shaking with agitation. If the truth were known, it was my brother who'd told me about "the logs". He'd said this was one of the magic words in Mirror World. Apparently, you could solve any argument by applying to the admins for a copy of your "logs". It did cost you but this seemed to be the most effective tool in the game's judicial system. The game's server registered everything that was said or done, so my determination to contact the admins in order to provide them must have shaken the shop owner's conviction. He sort of shrank.

The vendor sighed. I could read confusion in his face. "Please accept my apology. I can see now that I was wrong. You don't look like a scavenger even though you're in quite a state."

I grinned and tried to keep my voice level, eager to take the edge off the situation. "I understand. I'll tell you more: had I been who you thought I was, your stance would have deserved every respect."

His gaze warmed up to me as I went on, "But could you please be ever so kind as to explain what exactly prompted you to think so ill of me?"

He groaned. "It's that thing on your chest, sir. I literally turned to stone when I saw it. Private-stats items are extremely rare in Mirror World. That's what players call relics. Now where would a common

Digger, even of your level, lay his hands on something like this?"

I froze. "I see. Oh."

"Actually, now I understand," he went on. "Had you indeed been a scavenger, I'd have never seen you wear it. Besides, those rats only keep these things because they want to sell them. And you wore it in broad daylight."

"The more I speak to you, the more questions I have," I replied with a sad grin.

He chuckled. "That's another thing confirming that you're not what I thought you were. You've put the charm on. Now you won't be able to give it away— neither for money nor as a gift. It's non-transferable. It has no Durability. In other words, it's eternal and it's yours alone. Relics are non-transferable first and foremost. Or rather, you can try and give it to someone else—until its new owner tries to put it on."

I forced a smile. "You can call me a noob."

He smiled back. "Or a very rich Experienced Digger."

So he hadn't believed the price I'd paid for it. Still, it gave me an idea. The whole situation rang a few bells... it was almost a déjà vu. I had to go back to the market place.

"Mind if I give you some advice?" the dwarf asked. "You'd better hide it away from prying eyes. Till better days, if you know what I mean. I don't want to offend you but this type of item only looks good on a level 200+ player."

I hurried to follow his advice, burying the feather in my new knapsack. "Okay," I kept sponging more free intel off him, "so what am I supposed to do with it now?"

"There's only one answer to that," he said. "Make an appointment with Aldor of Mellenville, the wizard. He'll open it for free."

"For free? Really?" I asked, remembering what Saimie—or whoever she was—had told me.

He grinned. "He'll open it for free, no catch there. He charges for the appointment itself, not for the service."

"Oh. So much for my lofty illusions."

"Heh! You know nothing about prices yet! Are you ready?"

"The way you say it already makes me sick."

"So!" he continued. "Jewelry: prices start at ten grand. Weapons and armor: twenty. And so on and so forth."

"Oh. So what's so valuable about them?"

He shrugged. "That I can't tell you. Simply because I've no idea. I remember reading in some forum or other that apparently some of the relics are quest-bound. But this is pure speculation. There are no guides available on them. As I've just told you, only top players are in possession of these kinds of items. And as you can well imagine, they're not in a hurry to divulge any information about them. I'd think they must be extremely pricey even though I haven't yet seen one at auction in the entire year I've been in the game."

Dammit! What had possessed me to put it on? Once a noob, always a noob. I wanted to smash something against the wall—preferably, my own head.

The dwarf must have read my state of mind as he added soothingly, "Don't get so worked up about it. I don't think you'll lose anything by having it opened. This thingie must cost a fortune."

I sighed. "I wish. It's about time I learned how to handle unknown items."

We didn't even notice as we switched to friendlier tones. We chatted for another quarter of an hour, discussing the game and the world beyond it. He was all right. I needed to strike a few new friendships. I still had at least another month in front of me, digging in this hole. Finally, we agreed to meet the following night over a few beers in one of the city's numerous taverns. Then we parted—if not as good friends, then at least as buddies.

Chapter Twenty-Four

"This girl, she put up her tent right here, see. Then she brought you in. And once you were gone, she packed up and left, and that was the last we saw of her."

That was all I'd managed to find out about the scavenger girl. The place where her tent used to stand had already been taken by a ginger-haired farmer selling agricultural tools. His neighbor, a square-shouldered Dwand, kept telling and retelling me the story of the girl "packing up her stuff and disappearing".

He squinted knowingly. "Has she ripped you off?"

"Not really, no," I muttered. "I can't really tell you what it was."

He raised his eyebrows. "Women!"

For the second time I left the market with mixed feelings. I had zero intel. Her motives were clear as mud. I had my suspicions but I tried not to even think about them. Time would tell. Basically, I had to keep my eyes peeled. Preferably grow another pair in the back of my head.

As I walked past a large shop window, I couldn't help seeing my reflection. It made me cringe.

I opened the map. Immediately I saw something I could use. *Lyton's Tonsorium.* I looked the word up. Apparently, it stood for a barber's shop. Excellent. Time to sort myself out.

At first I thought that the satnav had brought me to the local branch of the Red Cross. The benches in front of it were packed with shaggy individuals. The only things missing were soup canteens in their filthy knobbly hands and streaks of gravy dripping from their thick beards.

I was about to turn round and leave when a neatly dressed dwarf appeared in the doorway, his own beard trimmed and plaited. His hair was nicely styled. Dandy being the operative word.

Immediately one of the shaggy characters ducked into the doorway past him. So that's what it was! I seemed to have come to the right place. If this dwarf used to look as scraggly as the others did, this was the place for me.

When I took another look at them, I noticed that judging by their clothes, most of the queuing customers were Seasoned Grinders—although their professions differed, of course.

I took my place in line, perching myself on one of the benches. The virtual sun warmed my body. I threw my hands behind my head and closed my eyes. Even so I could sense several pairs of eyes staring at me. The Reflection kit was a statement in itself. My hair might be a mess—no more than theirs, actually—but at least I was dressed to the nines.

I decided to put the unexpected pause to good use. I opened the action tab and auctioned off the remaining items from my Hardy Digger kit. Reserve: fifty gold. Bid deadline: twenty-four hours. I didn't think I'd have any problem flogging them. Every item had a malachite rune installed. Their Durability wasn't as good as that of new ones but still quite decent. In any case, any of the runes cost fifty gold in its own right.

A hand touched my shoulder, followed by an impatient voice, "Are you getting your hair cut or what?"

"Yeah, sure," I hurried to reply as I ducked into the shop's doorway.

I expected to see a standard barber's layout but this was nothing of the kind. A small room harbored a small table and two chairs: one for the owner, the other for his clients.

The barber was an Alven guy. It didn't surprise me in the slightest. This particular race stood out from other Mirror World denizens through its finesse and style. I focused on his name tag: Lyton.

Without saying a word, he pointed to one of the chairs. His slanted green eyes stared at me, impassive. "What would you like?"

"What can you offer?" I countered his question, making myself comfortable.

"Eh?" he sounded surprised. "Won't you ask me to "just give it a trim" or to "tidy up the sides"?

"Oh, no," I said. "You're the king here. It's up to you to decide."

His eyes lit up. The guy seemed to be fed up with mediocrity. I just hoped I wouldn't regret my decision.

The already familiar transparent screen rose between us.

"I'd like you to remove your hat and sit up straight," the barber said. "Please don't move. It's only a second. I'm taking a screenshot... that's it! All done. You can breathe now."

I saw myself on the screen—or rather, a picture of myself.

"The engine will now generate several images and you'll be asked to choose one," Lyton explained, beaming. "All I'll have to do is process it."

In less than a minute, I heard a soft ping. The screen filled with... er, with myself. Sort of. Lots of me, depicted in all kinds of colors and styles.

"You can browse through it now," the barber suggested, adding a background to the images. "You have a few minutes."

"Thanks," I mumbled.

Firstly, I discarded everything too loud. The pink, acid green and other psychedelic versions of me went straight into the Recycle Bin. They were followed by all the hipster types, even though admittedly I liked the one with the Mohawk. He looked formidable but... I still had to go to the bank. *Delete.*

I spent the next five minutes leafing through the catalogue until I realized that I needed to follow my plan and blend in with the crowd. Right. I opened the picture of an Ennan wearing classic Dwarven hair. This was what I needed.

"All done," I said.

The barber hurried to switch off the background. The impression of insulted incomprehension froze on his face.

"So that's what you want," he mumbled. "Standard issue. You shouldn't have wasted all that time."

"You need to understand," I began, "you might have already noticed that I belong to one of the dead races. I'm trying to avoid the limelight. How would you feel if you were walking down the street and every five minutes someone stopped you and asked you about your stats, abilities and other trivia? Every day. I can see it in your face that you know how it feels. So what would you do? Exactly. You'd go to an expert stylist."

I know, I know. I'd turned the whole thing on its head and flattered the boy shamelessly in the process. But you wouldn't expect me to tell him the whole truth, would you?

My arguments seemed to have worked. Once again the barber's eyes lit up with enthusiasm as he began to fine-tune the chosen image. He spent the next five minutes perfecting the screenshot.

"D'you like it?" he finally asked.

"Excellent."

I seriously liked what he'd done. A dwarf stared

back at me from the screenshot—a dwarf with an Ennan's eyes. I thought I even detected a hint of reproach in his stare.

Come on man, cool it, I said to him mentally. *This is only a temporary measure. Once we did a bit more leveling, we'd be strong enough to wear what the heck we want. Traditional Mayan dress, if you want to.*

My beard had been trimmed and plaited into several braids, each ending in a tiny steel cylinder covered in fine ornamental script. My hair was brushed back, some of it tied into the semblance of a ponytail.

"No one will tell you from an Experienced dwarven Digger," the barber commented. "Are you choosing this one?"

I nodded eagerly.

"That'll be five gold with the matrix and virtual makeover. Payment upfront," he said.

I nodded again.

"I would ask you to sit up straight and be still," he said.

Gently he pushed the screen in my direction. A 3-D copy of my head left the screen and floated toward me.

A message materialized,

Would you like to install a new image?
Price: five gold
Accept: Yes/No
I accepted.

Your avatar has been updated with a new image.

Effect: +5 to Trust
Duration: 7 days

"All done," Lyton summed up, then added bitterly, "What a shame no one will see this coiffe in a mine."

Gingerly I felt my face. "They will. I'm going to Mellenville first."

Lyton sat up. "That changes everything! How long are you going to stay there?"

"I'll have to live there, I'm afraid," I said, "but I'll be working here."

He threw his hands up in excitement, "Aren't you the lucky one! Would you like me to enter your matrix into our database?"

I tensed. "What for?"

"What do you mean, what for? Once your seven days have expired, you'll have to come back to me. This way we'll have your image already created and set up. Updating it will only take a moment."

"Aha. I see."

"You might want to focus on leveling up your reputation with Mellenville, am I right?"

"You are. Why?"

He smiled. "I just happen to know that certain characteristics although utterly useless for mining somehow work wonders in the capital. I mean Winsomeness, Tranquility, Endearment, Inspiration and the like."

I rubbed my forehead. "That's weird. The

forums don't mention anything of the kind."

He snorted. "You bet! There're no guidebooks on Mellenville. I'm pretty sure the developers have something to do with it. One thing I do know, though: if a characteristic exists, it means it can affect something."

"How am I supposed to level them up, then?"

He shrugged. "Lots of ways. Jazzing up your clothes might work. Alternatively, having your hair cut like you've just done can do the trick too. Basically, giving your char a makeover in whichever way you can think of."

Pensively I rose from the chair. "Thanks for the tip."

"My pleasure. So are we saving your matrix?"

"Why not," I replied. "It's not gonna hurt, is it?"

He chuckled bitterly. "I don't think so. Good luck!"

I walked out onto the street and temporarily zoned out, thinking. So that's how it was, then? By having my hair cut, I'd accidentally found out that looks were an important detail in Mirror World. I had indeed read about all the places where they could glam you up, but I'd believed it to be a useless whim.

"Jazzing up one's clothes," I repeated. "How's one supposed to do that?"

I decided against going back to the barber's. I wasn't going to waste my time standing in line again simply to pose one last question to the owner. I might try another way.

I opened the map and activated the search. Got it! Oh wow. So many of them! *Alice the Seamstress,*

Alanis' Tailored Suits, Liseanne's Fashion House and so on, and so forth—at least fifteen search results. No, enough for today. I was too tired. First the market, then the shops and now fashion houses? I don't think so!

I headed for the portal.

Chapter Twenty-Five

When I could finally make out the outline of the so-called Portal Station far ahead, I thought it at first to be some sort of a local railway station. The building seemed to be fashioned out of a single chunk of white marble with a massive gate, thick walls, wide windows and a huge square tower at its center.

The waiting room met me with an impeccably polished floor and walls. Row after row of comfortable seats. Lots and lots of ticket counters—at least thirty or forty.

I happily accepted their offer to download the station's floor plan. Freebies are always welcome. I opened it and gasped. Some station! It boasted twenty restaurants alone.

I looked around me. The place was crowded

with players. Most of them Grinders, all well-dressed. Some belonged to higher paying plans. For the first time since I'd joined, I saw a level-210 wizard. Some of his stats were made public. I could understand him. He saved himself some time by making everyone kowtow to him. That's status for you. You just couldn't avoid these things.

I also noticed one particular herbalist, definitely the same level as myself. His stats were private but he sported some very pretty decorative inserts on both his jacket and pants. Aha. They didn't come with the clothes, did they?

I slumped into a seat and hurried to open the auction tab. My idea was simple. According to the rules, an auctioned item's stats had to be made public. That made it a perfect place to do some market research.

I started by setting the search filter to Experienced Herbalist. I then narrowed it further down to Outer Garments. Yes! Just as I thought it would be. Most of the jackets weren't decorated at all. Then I finally found something similar.

Name: Funny Ribbon
Effect: +10 to Endearment
Restriction: Only Experienced Herbalist

"I see now," I whispered.

There was one last thing left to verify. I changed the Search settings to Experienced Digger. The search immediately produced a few hundred Reflection jackets. At least thirty were decorated with fancy bits of embroidery.

I closed the auction window, leaned back comfortably in my seat and gave it some thought. It looked like I'd jumped the gun. If all these people saw fit to adorn their clothes, they must have had a good reason to do so.

I slapped my knees and rose. Better safe than sorry. Lyton was right. The game developers didn't add new characteristics for nothing. I had to go back to town.

It didn't take me long to find the shop of Alice the Seamstress. Why there? Firstly, because it was the closest to the station and secondly, because I had a funny feeling that she and her colleagues must have shared the same profession level, the names of their shops being the only difference between them. I just hoped I could afford it.

Alice's establishment looked like a regular haberdashery outfit so popular with the fairer sex. Whenever I entered these kinds of places, I felt terribly out of my depth. Now too, the moment I walked in, I froze like a pillar of salt. This was assortment gone crazy.

My head turned. Trying not to look at all those spools of colorful cotton, reels of thread, scissors, needle kits, samplers and whatnot, I walked over to the counter and coughed to attract the owner's attention. "Alice?"

The storeroom's door swung open, letting out a slim woman in a colorful frock.

"Hi, Olgerd," she said with a cute smile. "How can I help you today?"

I faltered. "I... you know... I need... how can I say..."

"Keep going," she encouraged me, still smiling.

"I need something to decorate my clothes with," I winced as I said it. It sounded as if I wanted to decorate a Christmas tree.

"What characteristics do you have in mind?" she asked, all businesslike.

Her question caught me by surprise. Either I was a total noob or this was common practice here.

"*Trust*, maybe?" I didn't sound too sure.

No idea what all those characteristics could do. So I decided to level up the one I already had.

"How many items would you like to decorate?"

So *decorate* was the right word, then. "How about everything I have on? Can you do it?"

"Of course," she said. "The belt and the knapsack too?"

I tried to test the waters. "Is it worth it?"

Alice shrugged. "You must be heading for the capital, otherwise you wouldn't have needed to improve the whole kit. That's what some people do. In my opinion, the more items you have decorated, the better. You shouldn't think I'm only saying this to attract new custom. This is what I believe to be the answer to your question."

I mockingly raised my hands. "I didn't even mean to upset you. I've never done this before, see."

She nodded. "I've never been to the capital. And I don't think I will in the foreseeable future. My level's not up to it. We don't have much information at all, only whatever rumors reach us occasionally. For instance, they say that you shouldn't expect new characteristics to work miracles."

"How interesting," I mumbled.

"Some people try to stuff their kit with as many various characteristics as they can. Some stick to only one as you've done."

"Which characteristics can you increase?"

"The standard ones. The same as all the city's craftsmen of my level. Trust, Courage, Beauty, Endearment, Inspiration. Speaking in terms of your profession, I craft Seasoned-level items," she smiled again, then added, "I don't think you'll find a higher-level craftsman here. I'm the top."

I chuckled. "Excellent. That means I don't need to shop around. As for the characteristics themselves, I might have given it some consideration had I known what exactly there was to consider. It's all too vague. I'd love to ask someone who'd already been to the city. That would have made my decision so much easier."

"Don't even think of doing that," she warned me. "No one will say anything. They might even hurt you—verbally or otherwise."

"Oh really?"

"Sure," she nodded. "This is a taboo subject."

"Thanks for telling me," I said pensively. I already had a theory. Now I had to go there and see for myself. "I think I'll stick to *Trust*. It sort of sounds more specific than the rest."

She nodded. "All of your items?"

"Yes."

"That'll be nine ornamental ribbons. Have a look."

A small ribbon appeared on the counter, covered in a simple floral pattern.

Name: Flower Band
Effect: +10 to Trust

That would be +95 in total. Another pig in a poke. Still, it was probably worth it.

"Ribbons are a bit like runes," Alice explained. "One ribbon per item."

I nodded. "I see. How much do I owe you?"

"Sixty gold each," she said with a humble smile.

I burst out coughing. This way I'd be penniless by the time I got to Mellenville!

"That's including the discount," she drove the last nail into the coffin. "You can check it if you want. Those in the auction cost a lot more."

I pulled myself together and forced a smile. I'd have to buy them.

My virtual wallet had grown 540 gold lighter. With Alice's permission, I immediately installed all the ribbons onto my clothes and checked my reflection in the mirror.

There was one good thing about it. My shaggy Ennan now looked like a respectable dwarf. Hopefully, also trustworthy.

On my way back to the station, I met three dwarves. One of them was none other than Breon, the Ironbeards' headhunter. All three nodded to me politely. Breon's eyes betrayed nothing but respect. Which was weird. He probably hadn't recognized me.

Or had forgotten my nickname. Then again, it was perfectly understandable. Who would dream of putting a ragamuffin's name to the face of an honorable dwarf? The former a Seasoned Digger, the latter an Experienced one, apparently on his way to the capital to do some urgent business.

This little incident had admittedly boosted my morale. I nodded back to them and continued on my way, fighting off the desire to turn around and double-check on them.

The ticket counters turned out to be terminals similar to those I'd used back at the mines. I stopped next to one of them. In the next moment, the terminal sprang to life.

Greetings, Olgerd!
This is Portal Terminal # 5778
Would you like to buy a ticket?

Sure I would.

Please choose your destination.

I scrolled through hundreds of place names for Mellenville West. According to Dmitry, this was the area with the cheapest rent.

Price: 10 gold
Warning! The effect of teleportation will cause
your Energy level to drop 500 pt.
Confirm the purchase: Yes/No

Yes, sure.

Pillage and plunder! My daily commute was going to cost me an arm and a leg plus a serious drop in Energy. According to some forum, every trip would increase my reputation with Portals. The number of reputation points depended on the distance of the trip. Once I leveled it up, I could start using the portal shop which offered quite a few interesting goodies, like discounted season tickets and special portal charms that contained enough Energy for the jump, among other useful stuff. Provided you could afford them, of course.

Thank you! Your name has been added to the Portal listings. You can teleport when ready. Have a good trip!

I sighed and headed for the portal module. Guided by the floor plan, I entered the station's North wing. That's where the portal itself was installed: a giant mirror, its frame of white marble bejeweled with precious stones of every size and color.

The mirror pane was divided into two sections. They must have been both entrance and exit. The portal's smooth, dull silvery surface reflected nothing. Occasionally it rippled whenever a player crossed over. I wouldn't have said that the place was packed with potential travelers. Then again, this was one of the backwater clusters: the outskirts of Mirror World. I may have been wrong but I hadn't yet seen one player exiting the portal.

I could see those walking in front of me

disappear inside the mirror. It didn't feel good. I knew this was a game and all that, but still.

Finally, I was the first in line. I closed my eyes—don't ask why—and stepped in.

It felt as if I'd plunged under water. All the sounds were drawn out. I moved as if in slow motion. It lasted maybe a couple of seconds. Then a cacophony of voices assaulted my eardrums. I opened my eyes. My jaw dropped.

I had thought that today's market square had been busy. Well, that was nothing compared to what I was now witnessing. The waiting area of Mellenville's portal station must have held at least several thousand players. I'd been told many times that the number of the game's registered users was massive but only now had I realized how seriously large it was.

I received the standard system message complete with the offer to download a few apps. Strangely enough, I found it reassuring.

Using the freshly-installed scheme, I navigated the crowd toward the exit. I was quite happy to discover that the 500 Energy they'd charged hadn't at all affected my wellbeing. The 100+ Strength points took care of my regeneration just fine. According to Dmitry, by the end of the month I might find it harder but at the moment I shouldn't sweat it.

Mellenville met me with a bright sunny day and the brilliant splendor of shop windows. I was deafened by the tolling of bells, the clopping of hundreds of horse hooves and the midday chiming of the clock on the donjon.

If someone asked me to describe it all in one

word, the word would be *city*.

Carts and carriages of every shape and form scurried about. Flocks of colorful birds fluttered amid groomed trees and shrubs. Children ran around the many fountains and flower beds...

Yes! That's what it was! All the time I'd been in the game it felt as if something was missing. But only now I knew what it was. Until now, I'd not seen one child in the whole of Mirror World. But here, wherever I turned I could hear children's happy screaming, laughter and angry whining.

Young mothers promenaded up and down the boulevard, pushing prams and strollers. Newspaper-reading fathers occupied the park benches keeping a watchful eye on toddlers crawling in the grass playing with their colorful toys. Two young students walked past me, engrossed in a passionate discussion. All these babies, children and teenagers made the world of Mellenville so much more real.

I opened the map. According to Dmitry, I should be looking for either a hotel or a player-owned boarding house. The ideal scenario would be to find one owned by an NPC but at the moment I couldn't hope for that. The interface box of my reputation with the city was displaying a glowing zero. From what I'd read in forums, you had to level up your relationship with NPCs slowly, little by little. It was a bit like building a card house which might tumble at any moment. And one's reputation with Mellenville was, in the eyes of NPCs, a very important factor indeed. The higher it was, the higher your chances of receiving a nice quest with a hefty reward. Having said that, my reputation with the Portals had already grown 10 points. Not bad for a start.

I entered "property to rent" into the Search box. Oh. The search came back with posh villas, imposing mansions and any number of luxurious hotel suites. The prices were outrageous. One night at the Pearly Castle Hotel cost twenty thousand gold. Its screenshots hurt your eye with its rooms' regal splendor. But twenty grand!

I sorted the search results by *Price: lowest first* but failed to study the outcome. Someone kept tugging at my sleeve, gently but insistently. Excuse me? I looked down. What did we have here?

Two huge blue eyes. A tousled head of ginger curls. A smattering of freckles on the child's nose. He was about six years old, dressed in a funny pair of shorts and a dark green singlet. When he saw that his tugging had finally forced me to look down, he began explicating politely, pointing his plump little finger,

"'xcuse me mister, but my ball it's dropped in the fowntin over there and Mom don't let me get my feet wet..."

I smiled and ruffled his hair. "Your Mom is right. You should listen to her. Where is she?"

""She's gone to fetch some ice lollies," he said.

"Well, ice lollies are important business indeed. Where's your ball, then? Show me."

The kid darted off to the nearby fountain, skipping and hopping, all the while pointing his finger at it.

The "fowntin" wasn't deep at all. The water didn't even reach my knees, so fishing the orange ball out of it presented no problem. As I climbed out, I noticed that the area was truly busy with players. What had prompted the kid to approach me of all people? I'd been standing at least ten paces away for the fountain. Had he asked everyone around but hadn't got anyone help him? Hardly. Never mind. No skin off my nose. The kid was happy, that was all that counted.

"Thank you, Uncle Olgerd!" the kid shouted and bolted off, skipping and hopping down the boulevard.

A 3D message unfolded before my eyes,

Congratulations! You've just completed a hidden quest: The Unsinkable Ball.
Reward: +5 to your Reputation with Mellenville
Congratulations! Your reputation with the city of Mellenville has grown 5 pt.!

Warning! The forces of Dark never sleep! Their spies are everywhere! You must swear a solemn oath that you will never tell anyone about the origin of your reputation! In the name of the forces of Light, vouch to never disclose anything you know about Mellenville!

Do you swear: Yes/No (Obligatory)

Oh wow. The further it goes, the messier it gets. Mechanically I pressed *Yes*. There was no other way, really.

Immediately the system treated me to another

message,

Warning! If you break your oath, you'll lose all your Reputation points with Mellenville already gained. An oath-breaker will find it very hard to regain respect in this city.

While this new fact was sinking in, I overheard a happy child's voice not far away,

"Mommy! Mommy, look! Uncle Olgerd has rescued my ball for me!"

Chapter Twenty-Six

"Good morning, sir!"

A young woman in a pale blue dress stood a few paces away from me. My young friend was clinging to her hand while devouring his "ice lolly" with abandon. The family resemblance was obvious. A shock of unruly ginger hair escaped from her cute lacy bonnet. Her large bright blue eyes shone with gratitude.

"Good morning," I said. "Sorry I don't know you na-"

"It's Mila," she offered, smiling. "I'm so happy to meet you, Olgerd. Tommy has already told me about your valorous deed. I'd like to thank you for your patience and apologize for my little rascal."

Congratulations! You've just completed a hidden quest: Good Deeds.
Reward: +5 to your Reputation with Mellenville

I watched as the woman and child's names appeared on the tags over their heads. So that's how it was here, then. Apparently, wherever you turned, you might walk into some hidden quest or other. Couldn't have been better. Ten points Reputation in five minutes, how cool was that?

"It's all right, Mila," I smiled. "Nothing to apologize for. I have a daughter too. I really enjoyed helping your little boy."

"Still, I apologize. I hope you weren't too busy with more important things."

"Nah," I shrugged. "I was checking the property market, that's all."

"Are you considering settling down here?" she asked, immediately interested.

"Sort of. Just looking for something temporary."

"Oh!" she exclaimed. "If you haven't decided yet, I suggest you go to my cousin Ronald. His inn is only two blocks away. It's very clean and quite affordable."

"Perfect," I said with a smile.

She was rather naïve, this one. I still had some leveling to do before I could attempt approaching NPCs' establishments. It would be great though. According to Dmitry, signing into an NPC hotel gave one +30 Reputation every 24 hours. Automatically, mind you, just for the pleasure of living there.

"That's sorted, then," she perked up, "It's called the Footworn Traveler Inn. It's quite easy to find. Tell Ronald that I sent you. He might give you a discount."

New quest alert: Searching for an Inn
Reward: Unknown
Accept: Yes/No.

What did I say? New quests everywhere you turned.

I pressed *Yes*. You never know. Something might work out.

I bid my new friends a warm goodbye and hurried to the inn. These were the first NPCs I'd actually interacted with here. Mirror Souls, as they were called. Artificial Intellects. But as far as I was concerned, they were perfectly human. The constantly popping system messages had considerably ruined the pleasure of meeting them. The announcements seemed to remind me I was dealing with pieces of software.

Actually, everything seemed too simple. I'd completed two quests without even breaking into a sweat. I'd done a bit of reputation leveling. Now I was on my way to complete a third quest. It might just work, you never know.

I imagined the expression on Dmitry's face when I told him about my Mellenville feats. He had actually warned me to be prepared for a long and boring climb through the ranks. According to him, initially I'd have to run errands for the so-called "admin NPCs": all those gate guards, pompous clerks and the like. But somehow his advice disagreed with what I observed around me. What a shame he had no access to any information on Mellenville. This wasn't his prerogative, apparently. Oh, well. The proverbial company policy.

The Footworn Traveler Inn proved easy to find. The building was rather nice: a four-story with a pale yellow stone façade. You couldn't miss the burgundy of its window frames and roof tiles. Okay, let's see it from the inside. Provided they let me in, of course.

The front door was guarded by two players: Brand and Tyx. Warriors, judging by their gear. Levels 88 and 90. Guarding the door must have been their job.

I was only a few paces away from the front steps when I heard the level-88 one, Brand, speak calmly,

"Hey, man. I don't think you need this place. It takes a thousand Reputation to stay here. You can try of course but-"

The other one, Tyx, poked his fellow guard in the ribs by way of stopping him. "Let the gentleman try," he said with an affable smile. "You can see he needs to get in."

I hated his smile. It wasn't nice. I could see he was lying. It was the kind of smile that promised nothing good.

Brand shook his head, apparently disapproving of his comrade's behavior just as much as I was. "I shouldn't if I were you," he warned. Then, seeing me take the stairs nevertheless, he added, "You can do what you want, I don't care."

I nodded my gratitude. As I walked up the steps, I caught a glimpse of Tyx's nasty smile. What was he so happy about? What was going on in here? It felt as if I was about to enter a dragon's lair, not a freakin' inn! And another thing. How did they know I didn't have much reputation yet? Could it have been my clothes? Doubtful. My account? Somehow I didn't think so. Lots of questions, and not an answer in sight... yet.

Followed by two pairs of watchful eyes, I walked in. Immediately a system message popped up, offering me a free download of the inn's floor plan, the restaurant menu and a list of the services available. I pressed *Accept.*

I turned around and saw two dropped jaws. Another question to add to my list.

Actually, I received an answer to this one almost straight away. "What the hell's going on?" Tyx demanded. "Is it a bug or something? Brand, what d'ya think? How could a yellow tag cross the barrier?"

"A yellow tag," I repeated. "Meaning?"

"You see?" Tyx vented his indignation, completely ignoring me. "He's a flippin' noob!"

I couldn't agree more with him.

Finally Tyx glared in my direction, furious. "Mind my word he's a cheater! I've had these freebie lovers up to the eyeballs! You spend months busting your hump to add a few crummy points to your Reputation and then a yellow noob comes and walks in as if he owns the place!"

Brand had already overcome his initial surprise and was grinning at the scene. Apparently, he found the sight of his furious partner much more entertaining than the appreciation of my failure to enter the inn. He laid an assuaging hand on Tyx's shoulder,

"He's not a cheater, no way. Had he been one, d'you really think he'd have been so overt in front of us? Aha! I can see you get my point."

"In that case..." Tyx mumbled, sounding confused.

"In that case he probably has a quest," Brand finished his phrase for him. He turned to me. "No offense, man. He's about to log out soon, that's why he's all screwed up like that."

I shrugged, turned around and headed for the reception desk.

True, the two guards' name tags were dark green. I studied mine. I wouldn't say it was *yellow*, more like a lighter shade of green. It probably did look yellow from a distance. I needed to check it out once I was back in a public place. Apparently, for some reason of their own, the game developers wanted the city dwellers to differentiate between old-timers and newcomers.

A *barrier*, was it? That could explain Tyx's nasty smile. Most likely, the "noob vs. Reputation barrier" encounter held a promise of free laughs for the onlookers.

The reception was staffed by a blonde girl in a stern navy suit. "Hello," she said. "How can I help you?"

"Hi," I said. "I'd like to have a word with the owner of this excellent establishment."

"Oh!" a male voice boomed behind my back. "I'm flattered by your high opinion of my modest guesthouse!"

I swung round. A large ginger-haired man stood not two paces away from me: at least six foot four, with cheerful blue eyes and a generous smattering of freckles all over his face. Little Tommy was bound to grow into his carbon copy—provided that NPCs were capable of growing up, of course.

"Not at all," I answered. "I'm telling the truth. Your place is exactly what Mila told me it would be... Sir Ronald."

Okay, so I'd dressed the truth up a bit, so what? It was for a good cause.

"Do you know my cousin?" he asked.

"Yes," I nodded. "It was her who sent me here to see you, Sir Ronald, when I happened to mention I was looking for a room."

Congratulations! You've just completed a hidden quest: Searching for an Inn.
Reward: +15 to your Reputation with Mellenville.

Twenty-five points already, excellent! I'd only been here for less than an hour, but my Reputation points were mushrooming like crazy. It might actually be easier than my brother had imagined.

The innkeeper's name appeared in a tag over his head. Grinning, he offered me his hand. "Welcome, Olgerd! I hope you'll like my Footworn

Traveler."

Congratulations! You've just completed a hidden quest: Invitation to Check In.
Reward: +150 to your Reputation with Mellenville
Reward: 5% discount to all services provided by the Footworn Traveler Inn

Trying to look impassive, I replied with a courteous smile, "I'd be delighted."

A hundred and fifty rep points and a discount! I couldn't believe it! I just prayed I could afford it. If only I could afford it...

Ronald gave me a friendly slap on the shoulder. "Excellent! I assure you, Olgerd, you won't be disappointed. Now, unfortunately, I'm forced to bid you my farewell. You can discuss all the details with my assistant."

He gave me a wink and walked out, leaving me in the care of the blonde receptionist.

"So what kind of room do you have in mind?" she asked, smiling.

"The cheapest," I blurted out, then hurried to add, "I live and work away from family, see. In my case, simplicity and affordability are key."

She nodded her understanding and began leafing through a thick tome. Soon she raised her head. "A one-bed, second floor. Very minimalistic. Breakfast and daily cleaning. Do you need a residence registration?"

"Yes, please," I said trying not to betray my

excitement.

"That'll be twenty gold a night."

I suppressed a sigh of relief. I could have done much worse. "Excellent. I'll take it."

"Duration of stay?" she asked, all businesslike, as she began entering something into her book.

"A month," I said. "I'll pay upfront."

That was something else Dmitry had taught me. A month's stay was the minimum requirement in order to apply for a hotel residence registration. And it had to be paid in advance.

"Minus the 5% discount that'll be 570 gold for the whole of this month."

Once I confirmed the transaction, I received a new system message,

Congratulations! You've just rented a hotel room and received a month's residence registration in Mellenville!

Reward: +200 to your Reputation with Mellenville.

From this moment on, you'll be receiving a daily bonus of +30 to your Reputation with Mellenville.

There you go! You help a kid to get a ball out of a fountain and in less than an hour they shower you with 400+ rep points. By the same token, I'd managed to spend more than two thousand dollars over the course of the same morning. I had two hundred ten gold and thirty silver left on my virtual account.

"Enjoy your stay," the girl smiled, offering me

the key.

A name tag materialized over her head: *Miranda.*

* * *

Dear Olgerd,

We're sorry to inform you that you cannot view the Loans page of the Reflex Bank site. Viewing it requires 1000 pt. Reputation with Mellenville.

Enjoy the game!

I reread the terminal's message, swung round and headed for the exit. The Reflex Bank HQ reminded me of one of those Las Vegas slot machine halls, only instead of one-armed bandits it was lined with row after row of the already-familiar "parking meters". These terminals decided who would get the loan. They also determined its size. All they were interested in was the user's personal information and gaming history. I didn't even have enough Reputation to check out the Loans page. That was the way they did business here, sending me a clear message: if I wanted to get what I needed, I'd have to immerse myself into the game long-term. Another thing I'd realized was that I'd have to get a grip and try to remain sane.

According to Dmitry's and my plan, I still had one last port of call before returning to the market town of Verdaille: Mellenville's city hall. That was where players could get repeatable reputation quests.

The good news was, both the bank and the town hall were located on the same street. Admittedly both buildings looked rather modest next to some of the others. Their interior design wasn't much to write home about, either.

In the town hall too I was obliged to deal with a terminal.

Greetings, Olgerd!
This is Mellenville administration Terminal #312
Would you like to check the Reputation Quests available?

I groaned with fatigue. *Yes*, please.

From tomorrow on, you will have the following Reputation Quests available:
Daily Reputation Quests: 3
Weekly Reputation Quests: 2
Monthly Reputation Quests: 1
Enjoy the game!

I walked out and took in a lungful of fresh virtual air. I seemed to be hungry. Dmitry had told me not to suppress my brain's signals. My capsule-bound body and my game-located mind had to function in unison. Okay, suppress I wouldn't. I might have dinner in Verdaille before heading into the mines to do some work. I still had two portal jumps in front of me before the day was over. That's thirty gold. Emeralds, here I come! I need you to replenish my bank account ASAP.

Chapter Twenty-Seven

My room in the Footworn Traveler's was small with a tiny bathroom: a shower and a toilet. Perfect. It was indeed Spartan: a bed, a wardrobe, a comfortable soft chair and a side table, that was it. Not that I needed much.

The window offered a view of the night city. Mellenville was getting ready for bed.

I'd spent the rest of the afternoon in the mine trying to make up for the time lost. I'd met my quota—largely thanks to my Reflection kit which had facilitated the job no end. I hadn't even needed to use the elixirs although by the end of the day my fatigue had begun to show.

Part of my brain tried to make me remove my clothes and jump in the shower. Without my stuff, I'd have to suffer an energy drop but it was only for a quarter of an hour.

Strangely, as I offered my body up to the cool jets, I didn't notice any energy pressure. All sensations were perfectly lifelike. I closed my eyes, enjoying the moment, then glanced at the energy bar.

Energy: 100/100

Oh. This was actually my start-up number! Wasn't I supposed to feel exhausted the moment I removed my clothes? I rubbed myself dry with a fluffy towel and walked back into the room. I felt just fine.

Right. And what if... I opened the room door and took a peek. The corridor was empty, excellent. Let's experiment.

I stepped out into the corridor. Oh! An invisible force pressed down on me. My Energy dropped 20 pt.

I ducked back in. Better safe than sorry. Immediately the vertigo and the unbearable pressure were gone. So that's how it was, then? The room created some sort of microclimate for the lodger? Excellent. Very good. I'd had trouble imagining myself having to sleep fully dressed every night. Back in the Spider Grotto it would have been perfectly acceptable: a raid dictated its own lifestyle. But spending a month sleeping in my hat and boots wouldn't have been nice, that's for sure. Kudos to the game developers for finding a way around it. It's the small mercies that count.

I opened the wardrobe. A neat stack of bathrobes sat on the middle shelf to my right. I unfolded one. So!

Name: a terrycloth bathrobe
Type: Non-transferrable
Style: unisex
Effect I: +1000 to Energy
Effect II: +1000 to Comfort
Life span: 24 hours since first worn

Warning! This item is a Fragile Artifact. We strongly advise against taking it out of the room.

Should I try it on, maybe?

Oh wow. It was so soft, warm and comfortable. How on earth did they manage to control my brain to this degree?

Then again, what did I care? I yawned. "Doesn't matter, does it?" I mumbled to myself. "It feels so good, that's all that counts."

I studied the rest of the wardrobe. Much to my delight, I discovered also some pajamas and a pair of house slippers on the lower shelf. Their stats weren't as impressive but were equally soft, warm and comfortable. Thank God for life's little pleasures. It would have been so much more miserable without them.

I walked over to the window and took in the view of the night city. It looked beautiful. Tomorrow morning, back to the daily grind for me. The whole month's worth of it: completing quests in the morning and going down the mine in the evening. Jesus. I'd have given anything to have my family here with me.

Never mind. We didn't have much to wait. Very soon I'd see my dear girls again.

Then something totally unexpected happened. A 3D message materialized in front of me,

In order for the system to work correctly, the compulsory installation of the Der Swyor Clan app suite will be initiated.

Would you like to install it now or wait till the end of the countdown?
00:59
00:58
00:57...

Feeling my face turn pale, I whispered, "That can't be right!"

Whether it was Pierrot the cunning programmer or the system itself, either left me no choice. I had to remind myself that I'd approached the carving in the cave on my own accord. It had been me who'd brought the ring to the statue; me who'd downloaded the app suite. I had no one to blame. That was it. That was the end of the line.

I sighed and closed my eyes. For several minutes nothing else happened. Then I began receiving messages,

Success! You've unzipped and installed The Der Swyor Clan app suite.
Success! You've installed the Ancient Map of the Der Swyor Clan's Trade Routes.
Success! You've installed the List of the

Legendary Elders of the Der Swyor Clan.

Success! You've installed the Floor Plan of the Twilight Citadel property of the Der Swyor Clan!

Success! The app has been activated and synchronized with the game engine.

Enjoy the game!

Mirror World Administration

The message was followed by a small postscript,

That's it, noob! You sort it out!

At this point I think I'd stopped breathing. I was trying to take in some air and couldn't. It felt as if I'd received an almighty whack to my solar plexus. Everything had started so well! My plan had seemed to be working. My Mellenville start had proven easier than I'd expected. My chance encounter with the little boy had been followed by a chain of very decent reputation tasks.

Apparently, by pulling the ball out of the fountain, I'd triggered some complex quest which had already resulted in some very pleasant bonuses I wouldn't have even dreamed of otherwise—at least not for the next few weeks.

I was already ahead of the schedule I'd set up for myself. That was good news. But what had caused it? Could it be the omnipresent Andrew "Pierrot" Petrov again, the wayward programmer? Was he indeed so powerful that he could have arranged my meeting with the six-year-old NPC right in the middle of the game's capital city? Honestly, I had my doubts. The market girl who'd sold me the feather—yes, definitely. But as for little Tommy... he didn't seem to fit into this jigsaw puzzle. Let's think again.

But what if Tommy had been attracted to me by my 95 Trust points? Then again, why not? It wasn't too unlikely. My level of Trust must have drawn the boy to me. After all, all these Mirror Souls were little else but bits of binary codes. Granted, they were complicated to the point of being perfect, but codes nonetheless. The "boy" must have analyzed dozens of bystanders until his choice fell on the most suitable candidate: myself and my Trust levels. Which could only mean one thing.

It meant that the "souls" of the game's NPCs mirrored the players' stats. We could affect their behavior. Or rather, their algorithms chose the right behavioral patterns by analyzing our stats. Had the said algorithm located another player by the fountain whose levels of Trust had been just one point higher, I could have kissed all this Reputation good-bye.

But why Trust? Why not Courage or whatever? In any case, I had a theory. Now I had to check it by daily practice.

Okay. That had reassured me a bit. Now I had to sit down and give it all a good think through. It didn't look as if I was going to get any sleep. I had to look into it. What new surprises did this nutty programmer have in store for me? What was he trying to achieve, anyway? What was the point of his messages?

So: where do we start? The List of Legendary Elders? Good idea. I could study the maps later. So what do you want from me, Mr. Pierrot?

Predictably, the Legendary Elders app didn't contain any of those lengthy stories of ancient races, bygone days and other useless trivia. It was concise and to the point. The writing style admittedly tried to imitate the game's general tone, but the whole app consisted of just one page of several laconic paragraphs.

Having finished reading, I sat motionless for a long time, lost in thought. The thing that Pierrot was driving me to didn't sound nutty at all. On the contrary: I was beginning to understand that my brother must have omitted some very valuable detail. Not even omitted really: it must have been something he'd forgotten or simply ignored.

Never mind. I'd think about it later. I needed to study the text again.

From the dawn of time, the Ennans' society had been governed by councils of Elders. The great Der Swyor Clan wasn't an exception. In order to acquire harmony and balance, Ennans could only be ruled by those whose achievements in their respective occupations knew no rivals. Only acclaimed experts were eligible for seats on the Council.

In doing so, the entire Ennan society looked up to the Legendary Elders of Der Swyor—the most powerful clan Under the Mountain.

Master Satis was the wisest of the wise. He went down in the annals of history as the Greatest

Lord of Force.

Master Axe the Terrible. Which Ennan child hasn't heard the legends of this Slayer of a Thousand Monsters? Master Axe is the epitome of courage and valor!

Honorable Master Grilby, the crafting pioneer. It was him who uncovered the Power of Stone and sampled the greatness of Isilird, the heavenly steel. And it was he who managed to combine these two unruly elements!

Good Master Adkhur whom posterity hailed as the patron of the Younger Race.

These are the names of Ennans who will live forever in the hearts of all folk Under the Mountain!

That made four of them. Now what had Mr. Pierrot wanted to say by that? Why would I need to know? What was the significance of this information? Never mind. Let's open the trade routes map and see what it has to offer.

It didn't take me long to work out why I needed the information about some long-departed Legendary Elders. It turned out simple. Their former dwellings were flagged on the map. Curiouser and curiouser...

With a sigh I sat back. If I wasn't mistaken, my programmer patron was nudging me in the right direction. I double-checked the map. Two of the Elders, Grilby and Adkhur, were located in the so-called Lands of Light. The others were in No-Man's Lands. And so was the Twilight Citadel, the seat of the Der Swyor Clan—and I was the lucky owner of its floor plan. To be precise, it was situated in the very heart of the neutral zone. As I opened the plan, I already knew what I was about to see.

Of course. The Throne Room, the Armory, the Treasury... the works.

An experienced player would have already been dancing a jig, celebrating these new opportunities. But not I. It didn't feel good.

Your load might prove too much for me to bear, Mr. Andrew "Pierrot" Petrov.

I had this gut feeling I might have bitten more than I could chew. Or rather, that someone might chew on me instead. What was that King Solomon had said about much wisdom breeding much grief? I knew of course this wasn't what he'd meant but somehow it seemed pertinent to my situation too.

I dreaded to even think about someone like Shantarsky getting hold of this kind of information. The intel Pierrot had shared with me must have been truly unique—and valuable.

A faint flicker of doubt stirred in my heart. Should I have followed Dmitry's advice and chosen another char? No. Too late. My time was running short. Or rather, Christina's time was. It was all my own fault. Why, oh why had I had to download this wretched app? Then again, I should have already known that whenever Pierrot wanted to slip me something on the sly, he always succeeded.

Wait, I said to myself. This wasn't the way to go about it. Firstly, I needed to calm down. Secondly, nothing had happened yet. I was still safely in my room, snug as a bug in a rug.

I had to get a grip and think it over. The

situation called for a good ponder. My paranoia seemed to be getting out of hand. It wasn't good. It prevented me from thinking clearly. And that might result in me making mistakes.

So what had actually happened? Currently I was in possession of important intel about some bountiful area. I also shouldn't forget about the decidedly rare artifact tucked away in my bag. True, its stats were unknown. Lastly, I also had my Operator. What could this all mean? It might mean, firstly, that Pierrot wasn't as nutty as everyone believed him to be. And secondly, that we just might have mutual interests in all this. Both of us seemed to be interested in my char's development. Don't ask me why though I already had a couple of ideas. And as for my next move... I might need to see a few people in the morning.

Chapter Twenty-Eight

Greetings, Olgerd!

This is Mellenville administration terminal #572.

Would you like to check the available Reputation Quests?

Yes, please.

It was 7 a.m. and I was already busy pestering the administration terminal for quests. First thing that morning, a system message had happily informed me of my 30 pt. Reputation. Things were looking up.

You have the following Reputation Quests available:

Daily Reputation Quests: 3

Weekly Reputation Quests: 2

Monthly Reputation Quests: 1
Display all: Yes/No

No. You couldn't hurry these things. I decided to open them one by one, starting with the dailies.

The terminal paused, thinking, then generated three new quests,

Seek out Mattais the Guards' Captain and do what he asks of you.
Reward: +5 to your Reputation with Mellenville
Seek out Valdemar the Notary and do what he asks of you.
Reward: +5 to your Reputation with Mellenville
Seek out Litius the Scribe and do what he asks of you.
Reward: +5 to your Reputation with Mellenville

All three were as alike as... as three peas in a pod. Each offered the reward of 5 pt. Reputation: fifteen in total, provided I completed them. Most likely, the quests were of the "go fetch" kind, involving lots of running around. Predictably so.

Right. Let's open the weeklies. Strangely, it took the terminal less thinking to produce them,

Seek out Vertetio the Alchemist and bring him 50 Swamp Mushrooms.
Reward: +25 to your Reputation with Mellenville
Seek out Theodore the Pharmacist and bring him 50 blades of Blue Grass.
Reward: +25 to your Reputation with Mellenville

Two farming quests, good. These weren't as time-consuming but might prove quite costly. They would fetch me 50 pt. Reputation in total.

Let's have a look at the monthly quests, then. The terminal zoned out, thinking, then offered,

Seek out Nikanor the Lawyer. Objective: to sign a short-term work contract with him and complete any tasks he might have for you for a month.

Reward: +750 to your Reputation with Mellenville.

Oh. I had a funny feeling I knew now what those two, Brand and Tyx, had been doing guarding the inn. They must have been busy completing their monthly quests.

Almost eight hundred Reputation for a month's work for some yet unknown NPC. It looked like the game developers were bent on keeping the players busy.

In my case, my motivation was perfectly clear: I was here to get a loan from the bank. But what was forcing other players to diligently complete Reputation quests? Why did they do it? Were they desperate to get a loan too, all of them? Unlikely. Then what would it be?

Very well. Just another question without answer... yet.

I had one last quest left: the repeatable one. I opened it.

The terminal zoned out for a good five minutes.

Come on, buddy, find me something nice. You're a good machine, I know it. Make it worth my while, please.

My pleas must have worked as the machine happily offered,

Go to the Maragar Citadel. Objective: seek out Captain Gard and offer him your services defending the Maragar Pass from the powers of the Dark. Become a Citadel guard!

Duration: 90 days.

Reward: +2500 to a guard's Reputation with Mellenville every 30 days.

Warning! In order to complete the quest, you will have to temporarily lodge in the Maragar Citadel barracks. Those players already registered in Mellenville retain their right to receive their daily 30-pt. bonus to Reputation.

Warning! The quest must be completed in full. The failure to do so will result in losing all points already earned.

Warning! In order to receive a new quest, a player must complete the previous one.

Very nice, thank you very much! What's that for a quest? Becoming a Citadel guard? Just something I had in mind... *not.*

The fact was, the terminal didn't care what account type I had. I'd wanted a quest, so it had issued me one. I'd love to know how it expected me to defend the Citadel from the powers of the Dark. Was I supposed to brandish my pick? Could I defend anything at all with my account type?

The forums abounded with all sorts of information about the place. It was the so-called "front line of the Powers of Light". The Citadel's gate opened onto the wild lands of the neutral zone. No-Man's Lands.

From what I'd heard, the Citadel's walls were stormed daily by monsters. Only very well-trained warriors chose to go there. Every now and again it was attacked by players of the Dark—top levels normally. They came there craving blood, seeking to level up Valor and Fury. Citadel was one nasty place, I tell you. But it looked as if it might need some regular Grinders too.

Actually... did they have mines there? I opened the map. Oh. Lady Mel, my very own employer, seemed to own some land in the vicinity of the Citadel. Very well, let's have a look. What did we have here... mines, mines... where are they... Got it! Emerald fields! Two of them!

I closed the map and shook my head. Not a good idea. This Citadel was hell. Definitely not the right place for the likes of me. Forget it, Olgerd. Just forget it.

I did some more math. If I stayed in Mellenville proper and completed all the required quests, I'd still have about 1400 pt. Reputation a month. And I shouldn't forget that I might come across more of these surprise quests every month. How many little boys were there in this city who liked to play by its fountains? What if one of them needed to save a kitten from a tree?

The difference between the two schemes was 1100 points. In the course of the previous morning alone I'd already earned 400. What was the point in risking my butt on the front line? No. If the truth were known, something didn't feel right. It just didn't. What if my yesterday's success was a glitch, pure and simple? A bug, as Tyx had suggested? That raised another question: why would level-100 players choose to guard some useless little inn instead of joining the battle on the Citadel's walls?

This was difficult to fathom. Too many things to consider. One thing for sure: I shouldn't jump the gun. What was it the Roman Emperor Octavianus Augustus a.k.a. Julius Caesar had said? "Make haste slowly". That was exactly what I had to do: make haste slowly. To continue Mr. Octavianus' quotation analogy, my idea was not to repeat the mistake of that fisherman who tried to fish with a hook of gold.

For a start, I had to accept all quests apart from the last one. Then we'd see. Let's check the resources first.

I opened the auction and entered Swamp Mushrooms into the Search box. What did we have here? Hundreds of offers, all of them in bundles of 50. Oh-kay. It looked as if the quest kept coming up time and time again. Not good news for Dmitry who used to tell me that every quest was unique in Mellenville.

The prices were more or less the same. I didn't notice any drastic disparity.

The blades of blue grass and the swamp mushrooms cost me fifty-five gold in total. The weekly quests would come to about two hundred. And that was the best-case scenario.

By 5 p.m., I'd finished all the errands, having earned 65 points. I'd also signed a contract with Nikanor and even completed two of his tasks. The lawyer had turned out to be a grumbling old bastard constantly unhappy about something. Actually, what did it matter? I'd met worse humans. And he wasn't human even—just some miserable NPC.

I hadn't come across any more surprise quests though. Most likely, what had happened on my first day in town must have indeed been a glitch. All the NPCs I'd come across today were extremely friendly with me—but that was the extent of it.

The portal station met me with a bustling noise. My emerald fields awaited me. Once I was back in Verdaille, I'd have to buy some sandwiches for a quick snack on my way to work. I still had my quota to meet. Last night, my skill level had reached 109. The game developers had reacted by upping the ante to 270: the level necessary to become a Master Digger. With a little help from my Operator, I might do it within a week. No idea what I would've done without it.

While I queued for the ticket, I opened the Map of the Der Swyor Clan's Trade Routes. The Elders Grilby and Adkhur lived in the lands controlled by the forces of Light. The former, "the crafting pioneer", had his residence in the Gray Cliffs. The other one—the patron of some "younger race" or whoever he was— lived in the Woods of Lirtia. Judging by the map, both locations were quite close to the capital. Even

Verdaille was further than that. I'd have to check the ticket prices.

By then, I was first in the queue. I "greeted" the terminal, then entered:

Gray Cliffs

So! Not bad. The jump to the settlement nearest to the location would cost me ten gold. Same as Verdaille, basically. I checked the Woods of Lirtia. Same story, the distance slightly greater.

So, Sir Olgerd, what do you think? Should you pay a visit to the crafting pioneer? Now was just as good a time as any. Should I make haste slowly? I still had enough time to do my quota in the mine. The jumps were going to cost me, but I just hoped it was worth it. I was almost sure that Master Grilby was an NPC created by my hyperactive patron programmer.

That decided it, then. I had to go and visit him.

Malburg turned out to be a neat quiet town. I had once been on a business trip to a one-horse Spanish settlement clinging to the foot of a mountain. That's exactly what Malburg looked like. The effect was identical: the Cliffs were still at least a half-hour brisk walk away but they seemed to be rising up just behind the town wall.

I set my satnav to Gray Cliffs and walked out of Malburg toward their darkening range. The guards by the town gate greeted me respectfully, their curious stares following me. Apparently, the mine diggers of my caliber were a rare sight here. Then again, what did they care where this experienced Dwarf prospector was heading?

The higher I climbed, the narrower the road grew. Once I reached the cliffs it had turned into a barely visible trail. It must have once followed the bed of a mountain river that had at some point in the past changed its flow due to some geologic shift higher up.

I was almost there. Finally, my satnav reported the end of the route. I could see it myself. I stood facing the dark mouth of a cave. Not a single terminal in sight, which meant there were no resources to mine here. I hadn't received any system messages announcing my arrival at an instance. Was it just a regular cave, maybe?

I reopened the map. The location was correct. This was where I was supposed to find Master Grilby who'd "uncovered the Power of Stone and sampled the greatness of Isilird, the heavenly steel".

I took a deep breath and stepped into the cave's gloomy depths. Still no system messages. Very well then. Let's continue. This looked like a regular cave indeed. I could stand upright even though I had to squeeze my way through the narrow passage. The good news was, Ennans' eyes adapted to darkness easily.

The rocky corridor was heading downward—I knew I couldn't feel it but still I did.

I kept descending like that for several minutes. This Elder liked his dwellings deep, didn't he? How on earth did he live here? If this was the only entrance to his halls, I didn't envy him. Imagine having to squeeze yourself through piles of rock day in, day out. Personally, I'd have found myself something more convenient.

Ah! I glimpsed the dull flicker of a light. The tunnel was growing wider and lighter.

Was it my imagination or could I really hear someone groaning weakly? I hastened my step. That's right: someone was groaning here. I darted forward.

Soon I found myself in a small cozy cave. An enormous fireplace faced the entrance. No, not a fireplace—a forging furnace. I could see an anvil with its hammer, some pliers and other tools. This was a smithy. And judging by a small bed in the corner, a low table and some shelves holding tiny pots and plates, the blacksmith lived here too. But where was he?

A weak groan came from the direction of the bed, indicating the location of the cave's owner. I'd failed to notice his frail little body amid the rags.

I hurried over.

An Ennan. An *old* one. He was emaciated beyond belief. His eyes were closed. His parched lips kept mouthing something. The old boy seemed to have fever.

The weak fire in the furnace was expiring. I shivered. The place seemed to be getting colder. The old man wore some filthy rags. He was shuddering.

He needed to get warm. I pulled off my jacket and wrapped him in it. That's better. My Energy levels had dropped but that was irrelevant. I dragged the bed closer to the fire. The cave echoed with the screeching sound of its legs scoring against the rock floor. Now, now. The old boy seemed to be getting warmer—but the fire was dying...

I looked around me. If I didn't find any firewood, I'd have to burn what meager furniture was there. Wait. What was that?

I saw a small pile of something dark in the corner next to the furnace. Could it be coal, maybe? I walked over and focused on it.

Name: Fire Stones

What, was that it? No stats, no effects? Apparently, I'd have to act by trial and error. I picked up a stone and flinched as a system message unfolded before my eyes.

You've received a resource: Fire Stone
You've received +1 to your Skill.

Excuse me? I picked up another one.

You've received a resource: Fire Stone
You've received +1 to your Skill.

What was going on? I picked up another one.

You've received a resource: Fire Stone
You've received +1 to your Skill.

I dropped to my knees and began scooping up the stones into my knapsack. Only when it was packed to the brim did I force myself to stop. Actually, no. I still had one more slot left.

My hands shook as I produced the feather and

hung it around my neck. Now I had space for one more stone.

You've received a resource: Fire Stone
You've received +1 to your Skill.

That was it. My knapsack was well and truly stuffed. My head spinning with excitement, I checked my stats.

Current skill: 259 pt.
The maximum skill limit for your current profession level: 270.

There were still about twenty stones left on the floor. I was panting as if I'd just run a hundred meters. I still couldn't believe my luck.

A weak groan reminded me why I was here and what I'd been going to do.

I scrambled to my feet and walked over to the furnace. It was nearly out. Fire Stones, you say? Could they be what the old boy used for fuel? I had to try.

I picked up a stone and threw it into the furnace. The orange flames reluctantly licked its dark little body. At first I got the impression that it had only doused the fire further. But immediately the flames sprang back to life, coloring the black "coal" bright red.

That's what it was, then! Excellent.

I opened my knapsack and poured its entire contents into the furnace that roared, happy with the unexpected offering. The cave grew noticeably warmer. After a minute, you could barely breathe with the heat.

I glanced at the old man. He stopped groaning. He didn't seem delusional anymore, either. The heat must have helped him, poor wretch. Good.

Actually, what if I gave him a drop of my elixir? It couldn't hurt him, that's for sure.

Holding the old man's head, I slowly poured the entire contents of the vial into his mouth. If this stuff helped me, it would surely do him some good.

Poor man. He was all skin and bones. Of course he was an NPC but still he was a sorry sight. Once he regained consciousness, I'd give him another elixir.

I perched myself on the edge of the bed and adjusted his miserable excuse for a pillow, all the while trying not to look at the stones. What if the old man got angry with me for having thrown so many of them into the fire?

What was I like? Pierrot and his tricks! Who would have thought? And I'd been a right piece of work, pigging out on the stones like a junkie on a fix.

"Brolgerd? Is that you, my boy?" a crackling old voice made me jump.

I turned round. Two eyes pale with age stared at me.

"No, sir," I said soothingly. "I'm not Brolgerd."

"Who are you?" the old man whispered.

"Just a traveler," I said. "I've come to see the legendary elder of my people..."

"And what you saw was a bag of old bones," he

ended my phrase for me, smiling weakly. "What is your name, traveler?"

"You can call me Olgerd, Sir."

"Sounds almost like Brolgerd..." he heaved a sigh. "Give me your hand."

I obeyed. The master's hand turned out unexpectedly strong as if forged from steel.

"I can feel the callouses of a mine digger," he said.

"That's right."

He chuckled. "I can also feel you wear something made by my apprentice. I'd sense this metal anywhere. Brolgerd was the only one who succeeded in combining silver and heavenly Isilird."

I ripped the charm from my neck and offered it to the man. My heart missed a beat. He didn't take it though. His fingers touched it lightly.

"That's right," he said. "This is it. The Feather of Hager the Night Hunter.

I glanced at the charm, hopeful.

Name: the Feather of Hager
Effect: [unavailable]
Restriction: only Ennan race
Level: 0

The effect? What was its effect?

My virtual heart was about to jump out of my chest. "You don't happen to know more about this item, do you?" I mouthed, my lips dry.

Master Grilby shrugged. "Brolgerd made it for Tobold I, the king of Ennans. That's all I know..."

I sighed, disappointed. Having said that, I shouldn't complain really.

The old man went on, "When I was young I used to toil in the mine too. It was a long time ago. We all start by getting to know the stone. Brolgerd, my best apprentice, used to go down the mines with a group of prospectors, studying the underground veins," he shivered. "I seem to be a bit chilly. Could you add some fire stones to the furnace? Let it burn nice and hot. I want to get warm before I leave."

Mechanically I headed for the remaining stones and started collecting them. What did he mean, 'before I leave'? Where did he want to go in his state?

I placed the last stone into my bag. A new system message barely registered in my mind,

You've received a resource: Fire Stone
You've received +1 to your Skill.
Congratulations! Your professional level has grown! You're a Master Digger now!

That was it. I was a Master Digger now. I must have broken every profession-leveling record in history. Had the admins been following my progress? What was going to happen to me now? Would they delete my account? Somehow I didn't think that Pierrot hadn't made a provision for that. If he'd allowed me to level up just like that, it probably wasn't as bad as it looked.

This was crazy. I made Master! In ten minutes flat!

Pensively I scooped the remaining nine fire

stones which had brought me one point skill each.

"Olgerd?" the old man called weakly. "Where are you?"

"I'm here, Master. I'm coming."

I glanced at my stats,

Current skill: 279 pt.

The maximum skill limit for your current profession level: 690.

For some reason, Pierrot had only provided me with 170 of these cheat stones. You'd think he could have left a nice big pile here, enough for me to make Expert level too? So apparently he didn't want me to stick my neck out too much. Then again, how was I supposed not to, if my levels kept mushrooming out of all proportion? He probably knew more about me than I could ever guess. For all I knew, he might be keeping his tabs on me 24/7: both in the game and in real life.

I poured the remaining stones into the fire and produced another vial, "Master, I have something here to make you feel better."

He shook his head. "Don't waste your precious elixirs on me. Nothing can help me now. I'll warm myself a bit by the fire, then I'll be on my way. Sit here next to me, please. I have something to tell you."

What was he talking about? He couldn't go anywhere in his state! Still, I obediently plonked myself down next to him.

"Every Ennan can evolve from an ordinary journeyman into a Lord of Elements. Not everyone can do it but those who do, go down in the history of our people. My eyes may be blind, but I can still see that you're hardworking, strong and kind-hearted. I'm not going to ask you this question again. Are you ready to start on the hard road to true craftsmanship?

My throat rasped. "I... I am, Master."

He laid his hand, heavy with fatigue, onto my shoulder. "Very well, my boy. It's a shame I can't be with you on your path. You'll have to learn the ancient lore all on your own. But don't you worry. You can work hard, and that's the main thing. Promise me to remain strong and kind-hearted. Here, take this."

He reached under his tattered cloak and, as if by magic, produced five scrolls. "These are the blueprints of my five greatest inventions. You'll only be able to grasp one of them. The remaining four are yet beyond your comprehension. But don't you despair! As long as you study the first one and practice building it, the other four will cease to be a mystery. I'm sorry... my time is up... I must return to the Lord of the Underworld. Remember, my boy: you must work hard. Then you can achieve your goal. Fare thee well!"

He lay back on the pillow and closed his tired eyes.

I didn't expect what happened next. The body of Master Grilby, the Legendary Elder, vanished into thin air. I was left alone in the cave.

It took me some time to notice a new 3D message,

Congratulations! You've completed a hidden quest: Secret Knowledge!

You've received a second profession: Engineering Designer!

You've received an item: Blueprints of a Replicator

You've received an item: [unavailable]

You've received an item: [unavailable]

You've received an item: [unavailable]

You've received an item: [unavailable]

Chapter Twenty-Nine

It was the third day of my Mellenville stay and I was completely done in. First thing in the morning, I'd completed a quick quest run, seeing as Nikanor the Lawyer didn't overwork me at all. We seemed to be developing a nice working relationship—if you can call it so, of course, considering my employer was an NPC.

He was a grumbling old sort, you had to give him that. But at least he seemed to approve of my fervor. Every morning at 8 a.m. on the dot I was in his office awaiting his orders.

Last night I'd even managed to complete my mining quota. Emeralds were definitely the way to go. I still had the two-week contract with Lady Mel to work off. And then we'd see...

One thing I definitely wasn't going to do was

change my gear for that of an Expert Digger. Exposure was the last thing I needed at the moment. Besides, my old kit was good enough. Emeralds provided an excellent source of income. I needed stability, so I wasn't going to change anything any time soon. Surprisingly, my skill levels kept growing. Not as fast as they would have, had I switched to Expert resources, but still.

So now it was the evening of my third day; I'd completed my mining quota and come back to the inn earlier than expected. What I needed was a meal, a shower and some well-deserved rest. I'd have to visit Elder Adkhur some other time. Tomorrow or the day after, maybe. I already had my hands full with what I'd already received.

So I was the proud owner of a second profession. I was an Engineering Designer. It sounded cool but rather incomprehensible. What was I supposed to design? A spaceship? A tank? Or the latest-generation state-of-the-art toilet bowl?

When I'd finally "studied" the first scroll last night, I'd been rubbing my hands with glee, but today I wasn't as optimistic. Firstly, because I was supposed to use it to build some weird machine called a Replicator. Secondly, because—apart from the fact that I had no idea what the hell it was supposed to do—putting the thing together might take a few days.

The whole assembling procedure consisted of five stages, each of which was dedicated to creating one particular element of the design. In other words, the blueprint consisted of five smaller ones which in turn contained lists of ten ingredients each. The procedure was simple: by collecting all ten ingredients, you could activate one element of the design. Easy peasy.

So that's what I was doing now: rummaging through the auctions for the resources I needed. You had to give Pierrot justice: he'd chosen the cheapest and most accessible of ingredients. Who could have told me that you could create a Sensory Spiral by mixing Sticky Yellow Potion, Rose Tea, Bone Dust of a Grroggr and other such junk?

In total, all of the ingredients had cost me eighty gold. All I had to do now was activate one of the secondary designs, and I'd have the first part of the machine. The biggest problem was that activation was going to cost me thousands of points of Energy. For that reason, the building of the machine was going to take several days.

I opened the blueprint and chose design #1. A system message helpfully informed me of the ingredients necessary. It was followed by an alert,

Warning! Building a Sensory Spiral will deprive you of a 1000 pt. Energy!
Accept: Yes/No.

With a sigh, I clutched a Stamina elixir and prepared for the worst. No idea what could happen next: I might collapse in a heap for all I knew. In any case, an Energy drain like that was going to affect me, that's for sure. I pressed *Yes*.

Congratulations! You've created an item: Sensory Spiral.

You've received +25 to your skill.
Current skill: 25
Maximal skill pt. for your current profession level: 200

My vision faded. My head went round. It felt like being squashed by a gigantic press. I gulped the elixir and sat back. Some profession! You could pop your clogs just by leveling.

A new message appeared,

Cooldown alert! You can create the next part of the design in 07:59:59... 07:59:58...

I struggled to scramble out of the soft chair. Jesus. This didn't feel good. Groaning like an old man, I hurried to change out of my kit into the pajamas. The bed welcomed me.

I remembered how back in the Spider Grotto the other guys kept dreaming about acquiring a second profession. According to them, that was a totally different ball game. It turned you into someone of a much higher standing.

Maybe. But personally, I didn't feel any different. Last night I'd entered *Replicator* into the auction search and found nothing. Mirror World's market knew of no such product. So this freshly-minted Engineering Designer had better learn to be patient.

As I was falling asleep, I thought that I might have been better off choosing some other profession. How about a Master Mitten Knitter? I'd have spent my evenings churning out pair after pair of wooly gloves without a care in the world...

* * *

"I knew it!" Weigner slammed his ham of a fist on the table. "That's typical! I told you that workers who show promise don't stay here long."

This was the sixth day of my extended immersion. We were all sitting in The Stickleback Inn: Weigner, Doryl the dwarf, and myself. The place was decent, the food was good. Most importantly, it was affordable.

"What makes you think I'm leaving?" I asked him.

"Doryl, did you hear that?" the Rhoggh bellowed, furious. "First he asks us all sorts of funny questions and then he's upset when I put two and two together!"

"I only asked you whether my contract with Lady Mel was valid in all her territories. That's all I asked."

"Doryl, say something!" Weigner persisted. "Can't you see he's going? Mark my words! I won't be surprised if he's already packed his bags!"

I could understand his predicament. He'd just reported that he'd successfully recruited a new worker with potential—and before you knew it, the said worker was already looking for greener pastures.

He was right, to a point. My contract was

expiring in a week. My trial period was almost over. The duration of my future contract partially depended on Weigner's recommendation. My idea was simple: sign a contract with Lady Mel here in Verdaille but work somewhere else. I had plenty of reasons to do so. Firstly, it was about time I moved on to class 3 resources. None of which were available here, unfortunately. Secondly, I shouldn't flash my new status around.

Dammit. It looked like my Operator had doomed me to never put down roots.

"Give it a break, man," Doryl tried to pour oil over his indignation. "Sooner or later it would have happened anyway."

Weigner waved his words away. Doryl turned to me. "You have a plan already?"

Did I have a plan? You could say so, I suppose.

"You see," I began tentatively, "I was just curious. Let's presume I like my employer but for some very serious reason I have to, er, leave my current position. Let's presume I have to move town..."

"And let's presume your current employer owns some mines in the town you've moving to," a smiling Doryl completed my phrase for me.

I nodded. "I can see you know what I mean. What I want to ask is whether my contract is only valid in one particular location?"

"It's not," Weigner grumbled.

"By signing a contract with Lady Mel you can indeed work in any one of her mines," Doryl agreed. "Doesn't matter where."

"She has lots of emerald fields," Weigner said softly. "She even has a few diamond ones."

I tensed. I'd spent days poring over the map trying to locate a single diamond field—to no avail. You could buy diamonds at auction but you couldn't find any diamond mines. How was this possible? And I couldn't even do a quick forum search. What a shame. Just when I needed the information the most. So basically, it was one big mess as usual.

Doryl grinned. "She's a prudent old girl, is our Lady Mel. She must have laid her manicured hands on the juiciest locations already during the clans' turf wars."

"You bet," Weigner chuckled. "Now all she has to do is reap the dividends."

"And so she should," Doryl said. "I dread to think how much those wars cost them."

"Quite a bit," Weigner agreed.

"Not even counting the Blackout spell," Doryl added. "You have any idea how much she paid the wizards for casting that?"

"Don't want to know," Weigner replied. "I've got to save every penny to pay for my son's studies while they... never mind. They're too spoiled, that's all. You see *them* living on a wage?"

Doryl guffawed. "Depends what you mean by a wage. According to statistics, most people need fifty thousand dollars a year to be happy. Happy not as in, celebrate their luck. I mean *happy* happy: a long-term satisfaction with their quality of life."

"That's about four grand a month," Weigner commented. "The question is, can money make you happy?"

"It might," I said pensively. "It's sort of two-way relationship."

"Sure," Doryl said. "A well-fed European is happier than a starving African."

"That's not what I'm talking about," I said. "What I mean is this momentous shift in a family's life when tables turn. When people who used to be dirt poor finally reach financial stability. When they can at last get their hands on a decent car, when they can take the kids to the movies every Sunday, get nice new clothes for everyone and stop freaking out about putting food on the table. I'm talking about basic human needs here."

"Middle-class needs," Doryl added.

"Exactly. But then they enter the next stage. They get used to this particular level of income. It doesn't make them happy anymore."

"What did I say? Spoiled!" Weigner said. "So it's not the fact of having the money, it's how much money you have."

I chuckled. "So I don't think happiness has anything to do with the size of your paycheck. It's more to do with the work itself and the meaning it adds to your life. What I want to say is, as long as you keep working and making progress, as long as you try new things and fight obstacles—that's what makes you happy. Provided you move forward, there's hope for a better life for your loved ones. My happiness is in my family's health."

We paused, pensive. Finally I said, "There's one thing I don't understand. If class 3 resources are not

---

disclosed, how is a humble Master Digger supposed to choose an employer? Why make them secret in the first place?"

The other two burst out laughing. "A humble Master Digger! Did you hear that? He's something! That just made my day!"

Weigner slapped his clawed hand on the table, guffawing. The cups and plates clattered their protest.

Doryl offered a reserved smile. "Just imagine I called him a black scavenger the day we met."

"A humble Master Digger!" Weigner repeated, still laughing. "You're something, you!"

"Sorry, Olgerd, no offense," Doryl said. "You need to understand us. The thing is, there're quite a few Master Diggers in Mirror World. But there's no such thing in Mirror World as a *humble* Master Digger. They're anything but."

Wegner had already calmed down. "All Masters are the property of their clans. Strong clans. All such players live in closed settlements that belong to various rich influential players."

"Give it some time, seven to eight months normally," Doryl added, "and if you keep working at this pace, you're bound to receive an offer-"

"... which you will find hard to refuse," I finished his phrase.

"Yeah, sort of," Weigner nodded. "This isn't a game, Olgerd. I'm very happy you realize it now."

Doryl chuckled. "One might think you're talking of selling him into slavery. Yes, sure, all clans view their top-level workers as some sort of strategic resource. You can't deny it. Just don't forget that usually all such top-level workers are very comfortable with their agreement."

"As comfortable as their powerful employers want them to be," Weigner's voice rang with sarcasm. "What's lost is the illusion of freedom. You stop feeling as if you can take on the whole world."

"That's exactly what it is: an illusion!" Doryl exclaimed. "There is no freedom. That's fiction. A free man doesn't last long. He's either eliminated or shoved back into the pen. So his quality of living depends on the price tag he puts on his so-called freedom. We've been told all sorts of noble lies about lofty goals, but that's just wishful thinking. An illusion, if you wish. So my advice to you, Olgerd, would be this. When the day comes, try and squeeze your future employer for every bit of money he or she can offer you. Otherwise you might live to regret it."

"He will," Weigner added with a sarcastic grin. "They'll work him into the ground for every promise of a comfortable life he might get."

As I walked back to the inn, I kept pondering over the best course of action. I could try to contact the leader of the strongest clan in the entire Mirror World and offer him my services. Or I could try and sell myself to the highest bidder. This seemed like the most logical solution. But was it the best one? Dmitry and I had discussed it already. They would turn me into a pack horse, locking me up in some mine or other where I'd be free to bash at the rock and fill the great clan's vaults.

Would such a clan profit from my offer? You bet. How about me? Unlikely, regardless of whatever terms I managed to negotiate for myself. That's provided I'd be allowed to negotiate at all. Who was I in their eyes, after all? I was exactly nothing: someone without a face nor clout or protection.

Now: Andrew "Pierrot" Petrov. He wasn't as simple as everyone believed him to be, was he? Definitely not the nutty type, that's for sure. Why, oh why had he started all this? He must have known how I'd feel once I opened the apps. I just refused to believe he'd done all this simply to piss off the game developers. And even so, how could I possibly hurt them? They don't even seem to notice me. They had their hands full with other things.

What did Pierrot gain from my selling myself into slavery? This scenario would have brought all his efforts back to zero. And Pierrot sought profit first and foremost, didn't he? There. I'd figured him out. Only how was he going to pull it off?

Difficult concept. The four NPCs he'd so helpfully planted in my way—this had to be the clue. Why not just say so? Was he wary of the logs? What was his plan? Judging by the maps he'd provided me with, I had only one place to go. No-Man's Lands.

Chapter Thirty

The morning of my seventh day met me with the already habitually sunny weather, the chirping of birds and the buzz of an awakening city. My day off. However desperate I was to work daily, Dmitry had banned me from it. Otherwise, he'd said, there was no chance of me lasting the whole month. I'd have to log out before completing my contract.

Only a moment ago, the system had showered me with thirty more Reputation points. That made 680 pt. in total. A few more days, and I'd get access to the Loans page. And then we'd see what the bank had to offer me.

I had a few things on my agenda for the day. Last night I had finally completed the fifth and last part of this Replicator thing. So this evening I could finally put the beast together. I'd spend the morning doing my usual quest runs, after which I hoped to check out the Woods of Lirtia.

I made myself presentable and walked downstairs into the lounge. Oh. It was packed solid. I carefully threaded my way through the crowd into the inn's lounge. It was even worse. The variety of players was astounding: knights in shining armor, wizards in their navy attire, archers, swordsmen and quite a few high-level Grinders. Commotion and happy guffawing filled the room. Serving girls in canary dresses fluttered amid the tables that groaned with food and liquor. Was that what they called breakfast here? I had a funny feeling I must have missed something.

Ronald was beaming by the counter. No wonder, considering he was going to make a month's profit in one morning.

Noticing me, he flashed me a smile. "Sir Olgerd! What would you like? Your usual?"

I smiled back. "Yes, please. And if you don't mind telling me... What's going on here?"

He seemed sincerely surprised. "You don't know?"

I shrugged. "Too much work."

Ronald nodded his understanding as he handed two frothy beer mugs to a couple of bearded dwarves. "Today the portal to the Barren Plateau finally opens."

I looked around me. "Do you want to say that all these people are heading there?"

Ronald laughed heartily. "In your dreams! *These people* had better keep out of there. The Barren

Plateau is a location for real warriors."

A dwarf sitting next to me sniggered. "You don't mean you've never heard of mass PvPs?"

I shook my head.

"I see," the dwarf said. "You're one of those who're too busy to peek out of their mines and see what's going on in the world."

"Exactly," I chuckled. "I can see you're nearly finished with your beer. Mind if I call it my round?"

"No, I don't!" he happily slammed his hand on the table. A beer mug overflowing with golden liquid materialized in front of him.

I focused on his name tag. The dwarf went by name of Smith.

"The portal to the Barren Plateau opens once every six months," he began explaining. "This is the ancient battlefield of Light and Dark clans. The two strongest armies in Mirror World. This is some PvP, man, I tell you. Only top level fighters. Players below level 200 don't need to bother. The stakes are too high."

"So it's sort of a show," I mumbled.

"Exactly," Smith agreed. "We may not have football or the Olympics but we do have our share of good shows. The Barren Plateau PvP is one of them. You see now why it's so busy? The live stream will start in two hours. You can watch it here in Mellenville. The recording will be available in a few hours."

"Where can you watch it?" I asked.

"You can either watch it on the big screen in the city center. Or you can download the Glasshouses app and watch it anywhere. Personally, I'm staying here. Ronald will switch on the screens in a minute. This time there's only three of our clans participating, as opposed to four Dark ones. Last time it was the other way round."

'Why?"

"It's randomized. Ten clans had submitted applications but the system only chose three of them. Still, the total number of players is the same on both sides. So technically, it's fair."

"How many participants?"

"Five hundred from each side. If you haven't yet seen a mass PvP—man, you ain't seen nothing yet! Hollywood, eat your heart out. But our guys won't have it easy this time. The Steel Shirts are out. The Gold Guild and the Untouchables are both strong and experienced, but the Dead Clan has never been engaged in anything of this caliber before. And all the four Dark clans are top ones, just to please. There's no way our guys can win."

"Don't speak too soon!" a ginger-bearded dwarf next to him butted in. According to his tag, his name was Pete. "I'm sure they'll put up a good fight. The Dead Clan has grown a lot. They've got lots of excellent warriors now."

Smith grunted. "I wish! Had the Steel Shirts been with them, they might have prolonged the agony. But they're not there..."

The room hummed its approval. I looked around. The whole inn was listening in on our conversation. I wasn't surprised. Smith the dwarf had this soap-box kind of voice.

"You wanna bet?" the ginger-bearded Pete squeaked.

Smith guffawed. "Right! You offered it, not me! What's your bet?"

The room exploded in an uproar,

"Me too!"

"And me!"

"I'm betting!"

"Put me down too!"

The noise was such you'd think you were in a Chinese market. Ronald didn't miss a trick, either. "Gentlemen, please! As the landlord, let me remind you that my duty is to guarantee everything that carries on is within the law! For the paltry one percent of the winnings!"

"Okay! Take our bets!" the crowd shouted.

I suppressed a smile. Trust the admins to get their pound of flesh.

Ronald stood up tall, arms akimbo. "So what are we betting on?"

A burly Horrud answered for everyone, "Victory!"

"I bet a hundred gold that our guys will make a quick job of the Darkies!" the ginger-bearded Pete offered.

The room hummed its disagreement. Someone called him a crazy; another voice sneered, suggesting he gave the money to the poor instead.

"I bet a hundred that this time the Darkies will give us a good drubbing," Smith said firmly.

The room cheered its agreement. Bets started pouring in.

They offered me to join in, so I bet twenty gold on the Lighties. I'd always done my best to avoid such situations so this was the first bet in my entire life. I might have said no but then I wasn't really losing anything. I bet on the Lighties simply because they were "our guys". The support-the-good-guys mentality must have kicked in too. Besides, the Dead Clan was in it as well—and my Ennan was almost one of them.

Strangely enough, many of those present bet on the Lighties too, so there wasn't much disparity.

They brought me my breakfast which I took to a far corner of the room. The two hours that followed were worth it. You should never underestimate the informational value of large gatherings. Mainly such information was just a pile of junk but it was still worth digging through for an occasional glitter of gold.

As an example, a snippet of conversation between two Alves at a nearby table explained to me the mystery behind the players' eagerness to do Reputation quests. They didn't say it expressly, of course, apparently for fear of disclosing the secret, but I got the general idea. Mellenville's treasury. That was every player's wet dream. The more Reputation points you had, the more items you could buy there. I didn't have access to it yet but once I raised my Reputation to 2000, I fully intended to check it out.

I'd also found out that apparently Dmitry had been mistaken about in-game blogs and forums. There were quite a few around but you had to look for them. They also probably charged for access. Once I logged out, I might look into that too.

The two hours had gone quickly. I was

finishing my second cup of coffee when Ronald activated a wide screen hanging over the bar. For a split second, it felt as if I was back in the real world, sitting in some British pub about to watch a local game.

The audience cheered. The setting up of the screen was accompanied by their cheeky banter about the fate of ginger Pete's savings.

The portal would open in ten minutes. I was toying with the idea of going back upstairs to watch the battle in the quiet of my room but reconsidered. I didn't want to strip myself of the pleasure of feeling the intense nature of the crowd's emotions.

"It's starting!"

"Shut up, everybody! It's starting!"

"The portal's opening!"

The room calmed down somewhat. A picture of the Barren Plateau filled the screen. I immediately thought of Dasht-e-Kavir, the great salt desert in central Iran. It felt as if the game designers had borrowed some of its grandiose landscapes.

Almost simultaneously, the Dark and Light players poured out of the portals. The room dissolved in cheers.

"They're all mixed up!" someone shouted.

"Why did they do that?" others voiced their disappointment.

No one could understand anything. As far as I could make out, the forces of Light had decided to march out as one army. The uniform ranks of heavy footmen paraded first, closely followed by swordsmen. The wizards and archers kept slightly behind.

The Dark clans, however, had chosen to march out separately each under their own colors. They looked the same, actually: humans, Rhogghs, gnomes and Alves. The only difference was that they supported the so-called Powers of the Dark.

"The Lighties are finished!" Smith guffawed. "They shouldn't have done it! The Darks will make quick work of them!"

I glanced at Pete. He bit his lip in disappointment. His eyes betrayed his dismay. Personally, I couldn't understand what Smith was so happy about. Never mind. Let's see how it was all going to end.

The battle began without warning. The Dark ones charged. Almost immediately it became clear that the Light ones were going to deploy defensively. The first arrows and spells zapped through the air. Wow. I wouldn't want to be the one stuck in that mess. Even though admittedly the show was top rate.

The Darks split up. The Lords of Chaos and the Dark Legionnaires left their positions and moved out to the flanks. The Independent Clan and the Caste kept advancing toward the center of the Light ranks. The Darks' strategy was rather clear: first to knock their wizards and archers out of action and then close in on the heavy footmen.

A sigh of surprise ran across the inn. Instead of trying to stop the enemy's flanking them, the Light ones formed a square and ensconced all their wizards and archers in the middle. Had the terrain of the Plateau been more restrictive—had it had some natural obstacles like hills, groves, or little rivers—the generals of Light might have chosen a different tactic. But seeing as it was lifeless and flat as a pancake, such a step was in my eyes probably the best one.

No one seemed to share my view. The audience raged, calling the Light generals all sorts of unflattering names. If you listened to the room, one had to be an idiot to allow the enemy to surround you so stupidly.

Couldn't they see that this breakthrough had cost both the Lords of Chaos and the Dark Legionnaires an incredible amount of energy? They'd performed their stunt while being showered with arrows and spells while the main forces of Light just stood there behind the safety of their magic shields.

Finally, the Darks closed in. This signaled the start of the melee. The heavy footmen joined in the battle. The ranks of Light quivered under the pressure from the Caste and the Independent Clan. It looked as if they were going to break any minute now.

Some of the more faint-hearted supporters were already leaving the room, spitting in disgust and waving disappointed hands at the screen. As in, *there's nothing left to do here, we might just as well kiss our money goodbye.* Those who'd bet on the Darks were rubbing their hands.

I shrugged. Strange people. Couldn't they see that this breakthrough was the beginning of the Dark ones' agony? Even I, a humble interpreter-turned-mine digger, could see that the Darks had had it.

A few minutes later, the inevitable happened. The Lights counterattacked.

The swordsmen who'd been hovering behind

the heavy footmen's backs now infiltrated the formations of the Caste and the Independent Clan. Dying, they made sure they took a few archers and especially wizards along. The giant red-skinned Narkh assassins brandished their curved sabers in their four arms, eyes furious, froth dripping from their fangs. This kamikaze strike on the part of the Light swordsmen had stripped the enemy's heavy footmen of their magic backup. That was basically it. The colors of the Independent Clan turned gray, followed by those of the Caste.

I heaved a sigh of relief and eased back in my chair. Now the defeat of the Lords of Chaos and the Dark Legionnaires was only a question of time. My heart was pounding as if I too were in the thick of the fight.

The top-level Dark players lasted the longest. They huddled together, clumsily trying to deflect the blows. But after some time they fell too.

Smith was a sorry sight. He stared at the screen in disbelief, watching the winners celebrate their triumph.

The inn was in turmoil. Red-bearded Pete was dancing a jig on the table to the accompanying rattle of pots, mugs and whatnot. Those who'd bet on the Light side were beyond themselves with joy. Admittedly, as was I. My wallet was now five and a half hundred gold heavier. Many of the losers gave Smith the evil eye as they walked out.

What were they like? What had Smith got to do with it? Yes, he was the loudest but he hadn't forced anyone to bet on the Darks. Human nature! Everyone wants to blame someone else for their own mistakes.

Some of the losers sincerely cheered the Light ones' victory. And a fine victory it was, too. Later I found out that almost every member of the Dead Clan had fallen in that battle, allowing the others to finish off the Dark survivors.

I didn't feel like leaving the inn at all. Seeing my state, Ronald gave me an encouraging wink. He handed me a small wine flask, a nice fat slice of piping-hot bread and a chunk of yellow cheese.

In the meantime, the inn was just beginning to celebrate. Patrons dragged the tables together while the serving girls clad them with large serving plates groaning with starters. Even out in the street I could still hear their happy voices, the clattering of the plates and the cheerful music.

I heaved a sigh and headed for the administration center.

Chapter Thirty-One

The freshly-installed Woods of Lirtia free app kindly informed me that I was about to visit one of the game's largest locations that took up about 25% of Mirror World's total area. Had I not had a detailed route to Adhur's dwelling all mapped out, it might have taken me a few months to have found my way out of the woods.

Talking about which, Master Grilby's cave in the Gray Cliffs had disappeared from the trade routes map. Which meant I only had three NPCs left to visit. Two of them were located in No-Man's Lands. I'd have loved to know what Pierrot had been thinking when he'd come up with this layout.

I couldn't help thinking about old Grilby. Sure, he was an NPC, a bit of binary code, but still it was weighing heavy on my heart. It had been too real.

Trying to distract myself from unwanted thoughts, I began tinkering with my satnav settings. It didn't take me long to synch it. Next thing I knew, the machine offered me an optimal route plan.

The woods turned out to be quite a busy place. I caught glimpses of other players among the trees. Herbalists toiled away in the numerous open spots, mainly Alven women whose racial characteristics must have had bonuses for herbal medicine.

I also saw plenty of hunters, mushroomers and woodcutters. I even walked past a group of fellow mine diggers busy heading into the woods. In other words, the place was buzzing with life.

My satnav guided me along the main trail, bypassing dangerous areas and the lairs of various monsters. Confronting them wasn't on my agenda today. True, my heart would miss a beat every time I noticed the giant beasts that looked like mutated wild boars. When an enormous black wolf crossed the trail not twenty paces away from me, I very nearly swung round and ran for dear life. Luckily, I noticed some herbalist girls farming herbs nearby. If they didn't show any fear, things couldn't have been that bad.

I sighed and kept going. I was almost there, anyway.

In another ten minutes, the trail brought me to a grove. It looked admittedly gloomy. I sort of didn't feel like entering it. The gaps between the tree trunks seeped darkness. So scary. But my satnav, as if on purpose, insistently invited me to enter it.

I sighed and took a few tentative steps. The

wall of trees devoured me like a starved monster, closing behind my back. I walked in the shade, casting wary glances around. Everything was quiet. The air was surprisingly fresh. It smelled of tree sap, of rotting leaves and forest blossoms.

Gradually the path narrowed to a deer trail. Every now and again I noticed enormous clawed footprints on the ground. I just hoped Pierrot wasn't luring me in to feed me to some forest giant.

After some time I noticed a light behind the towering trees. Finally!

I hurried on, leaving the last trees behind.

The trail had taken me to a large opening overgrown with lush green grass. After the darkness of the grove, my eyes couldn't get used to the light. A large tree towered at its center. It would have taken several people to encircle its trunk. It gave the impression that the grove had stepped back in fear, awed by the giant.

I took a better look. That was strange. Why hadn't I noticed it earlier? A small hut clung to the base of the tree. If you asked me what the dwelling of a forest spirit looked like, I'd tell you to come to this place and see for yourself. It had log walls overgrown with yellow moss and a tiny window—a dugout rather than a hut.

Then I saw its owner. Correction: I heard him first.

"Get down! Get down, I tell you, little trouble-maker!"

A forest spirit indeed. He looked like a big fat mushroom with a long gray beard, clad in a green robe. A wide-brimmed straw hat was perched on his head. The image was completed by lots of twigs, pine needles and bits of dried leaves littering his clothes and beard.

He stood by the wall of his hut trying to reach the roof with a long stick. Or rather, trying to reach *something* that was there. A little black animal was thrashing along the roof's edge, hissing and baring its fangs. It looked like a marten.

A cat the size of a panther, red with darker spots, watched the scene with lazy indifference. It had lynx-like tufts of fur on the tips of its ears. The cat's tail kept swishing across the grass. I thought I knew whose footprints I'd just seen on the trail.

I took a few more steps and stopped. I had to attract his attention somehow. All I could think of was give a little cough. "Greetings, Master Adkhur!"

All of them, the marten included, turned toward me. Without moving, the enormous lynx focused its predatory yellow stare upon me. The old man hushed it down.

His gloomy eyes sized me up. "Nice day to you too. Where do you think you're coming from? And how come you know my name, dammit?"

Faking surprise, I replied, "Who the hell doesn't know one of the four Legendary Elders of our people?"

He frowned. "What do you mean, *your people*? Are you sure, traveler, that you haven't hit your empty head on a tree on your way here? I suggest you go back from whence you came, sir, before I tell my animal to see you off! He likes having travelers' balls for breakfast!"

Honestly, I was in shock. Pierrot must have overdone it this time. Never mind. I didn't care. I had no business starting flame wars with nutty NPCs!

I was about to turn round and leave when I remembered. But of course! My appearance! Hadn't I updated my looks in Lyton's shop? Didn't I look like a dwarf now? No wonder Master Grilby sounded so pissed off. He'd seen nothing yet.

I made my stats public. What would he say now?

His jaw dropped. "No! Dammit..."

"I'm sorry I didn't do it at once," I said. "Enemies are everywhere. I have to keep a low profile."

"Oh yes, yes, absolutely," he hurried. "Please forgive the old man. I've grown completely out a touch here. Can't tell a decent Ennan from a hole in a wall. This is crazy, dammit..."

The little black marten squeaked his indignation, leaping around the roof like a hyperactive wind-up toy.

The old man glared at him. "You make sure the roof stays in one piece! Crazy critter..."

"You need help?" I offered.

He sighed. "I really don't know if you can do it. It's a Black Grison, you see. All the way from the Steely Mountains."

"Oh really?" I played along.

He answered very seriously, "He might be the last of its kind."

"Why?"

He chuckled. "You're funny, you. You seem to know me—and yet you haven't heard of Black

Grisons!"

"I'm sorry, Master Adkhur," I began to ad lib. "I grew up far from this part of the world, you see. I'm a Der Swyor in spirit but I know regrettably little about my own people."

He startled when he heard the clan's name. "So your parents managed to rescue you? Did they raise you abroad? Is that how you escaped the terrible fate of all the others?"

I nodded. I had to tread carefully here or I might say something I might later regret.

"I see," he whispered, thoughtful. "What's your name?"

"I'm Olgerd."

He chuckled. "How weird. Sounds almost like Brolgerd."

"That's what Master Grilby said."

The old man startled. "Do you know Master Grilby?" he whispered.

I nodded. "I do. He's my mentor."

The old man grabbed my shoulders and shook me. "Where is he? How is he? When did you see him last? Come on, say something!"

I waited until his torrent of questions subsided. Once the old man calmed down a bit, I said, "The Lord of the Underworld summoned him."

Master Adkhur slumped. He aged instantaneously, gaining a few more years before my very eyes. Tears glistened on his furrowed cheeks.

"No," he whispered. "What's going to happen to us now? Brolgerd is missing. Grilby's gone. Satis and Axe the Terrible must be dead too. What will happen

---

to our secret lore? But... wait... didn't you say that..."

He looked up at me. "You said Grilby was your mentor, didn't you?"

I nodded. "He passed on to me the designs of his most important inventions."

He grabbed my shoulders again. Then he gave me a bear hug. I didn't expect that at all. When he stepped back, the expression in his eyes had changed. I thought I caught a glimpse of hope in his gaze.

"Well," he said with a smile, "let's see if you can tame this little prankster."

New quest alert: Black Devil
Reward: unknown
Accept: Yes/No

Definitely *Yes!*

Master Adkhur stepped back with a strange smile on his face, leaving me to it.

Okay, let's see. I walked over to the hut and focused on the little trouble-maker. He was busy digging. Bits of straw and turf were flying everywhere.

I glimpsed the interested stare of the large spotted cat focusing on me. The marten or whatever it was, noticed my advance and paused. He tilted his sly little head to one side. His beady black eyes stared at me with curiosity.

I immediately remembered something my next-door neighbor Aunt Luba used to say: *A cat and a fridge are never too far apart.* The creature on the roof admittedly looked nothing like a cat. But I wouldn't lose anything by trying, would I?

Closely watched by three pairs of eyes, I slowly lowered my knapsack to the ground. I was pretty sure I had some cheese in it somewhere. I broke off a tiny piece and showed it to the beastie. He was already at the roof's edge, craning his neck, his tiny moist nose busy detecting the new smell.

I smiled. "Come on, kiddo, get down. Cheese... yumm..."

Without a moment's hesitation, the grison covered the distance between us in a few long bounds. Wasn't he fast! His long lithe body was beautiful. His black fur shimmered in the sun.

Very slowly so as not to alarm him I lowered myself to one knee and offered him the bit of cheese in my outstretched hand. Come on, take it. No need to be afraid.

The grison straightened his neck. His right leg hovered in the air. His ears stood up.

In an almost imperceptible swoop, he snatched the cheese from my hand and leapt back to a safe distance. Then he sat there savoring the treat.

That was it! I had him! Just look at him, squinting with delight! Apparently, he loved cheese now. And it wasn't for nothing I'd only given him a tiny bit. Now he'd be back asking for more.

I was right. The grison made quick work of my offering and looked back at me. By then, I had a second bit of cheese ready. Only this time I placed it on my shoulder and stood up. What would he do now?

The grison tilted his cute head, thinking, then dashed toward me. Two powerful leaps later, he was sitting on my shoulder holding the bit of cheese in his front paws. I could hear him purr next to my ear just like a cat.

To capitalize on my success, I offered him a third piece, a bigger one this time. Then I turned and gave Master Adkhur a victorious look.

He grinned. "What are you like! Just don't tell me that cheese is all you've got!"

* * *

"These days, they tell lots of weird stuff about those times. Some people believe it. Others don't. Believing is safer, I think."

Master Adkhur was already slightly the worse for wear. He'd had his fill of Ronald's wine. We'd been sitting in his hut for a couple of hours already, drinking wine and chasing it down with cheese, bread and cured ham.

The Black Grison had proved to be a glutton from hell. He'd already necked a quarter of the cheese and was now sleeping on the table, resting his cheeky little head on my arm.

"Most people now say," Master Adkhur kept reminiscing, "that Der Swyor masters created a terrible weapon and didn't want to share their secret with other clans."

I nodded. "That's exactly what I heard."

He squinted at me. "You see! They portray our honest Ennan clan as a bunch of bloodthirsty animals, dammit! They claim we were greedy and merciless. They say we couldn't wait to conquer the rest of the world!"

I shrugged. What could I say?

"Not many people know," he went on, "that when the King of Ennans died childless, our clan leader Stromwold the Steel Axe was the next in line."

I nodded my understanding. "Power games."

"Exactly. They know no mercy. Also, the rumors of the mysterious weapon weren't exactly groundless. So the Clan Council Under the Mountain sentenced us all to death. Each and every one of us: women, children and old folk."

He cast a sad glance at the sleeping grison. "They even culled all of these."

I didn't understand. "Why?"

"Unfortunately for these cute little animals, the Der Swyor Clan's coat of arms features a Black Grison. The Council decreed that nothing should ever remind that we ever existed. Even if it took the annihilation of an entire animal race."

He smiled. "But as you can see, they failed. You and I, we're still around. And so is this little fellow," he paused, pensive, then looked up at me. "You know what? Take him with you! He won't leave me in peace anyway, dammit. Just look at him! He really likes you, doesn't he?"

I snickered. "He likes my cheese, that's what it is!"

He shook his head. "Don't say that. You don't understand. Once a Black Grison has chosen a master, it's... it's *for good*."

As if in confirmation, the little brute stretched in his sleep and hugged my finger with his tiny paws. I looked at him closer. Christina would have liked him. Decisions, decisions...

"But what do you want me to do with him?" I asked. 'Where do I keep him? If he's always so hyperactive, I won't last very long."

"Hyperactive?"

Master Adkhur reached into his pocket and pulled something out. I thought I noticed a faint bluish glow enveloping his clenched fingers. The Grison disappeared. Into thin air. Just like that.

I stared in disbelief at my arm where this little bandit had been fast asleep only a moment ago.

"That's it!" Master Adkhur offered me a small shiny round object. "Take it, dammit! It's yours now!"

Congratulations! You've just completed a quest: Black Devil.

Reward: a Black Grison Summoning Charm

Chapter Thirty-Two

We spent some quality time talking about the clan and its history, about life underground and the joys of mining. Master Adkhur literally buried me under a cartload of historical facts. True, it might be of little use for me personally. Ditto for the little charm I kept fumbling with. What was I going to do with my new pet, tell me, Mr. Pierrot? Was it a new addition to my collection of useless junk like this Replicator I was supposed to put together the same evening? Where exactly did the nutty programmer's offerings simplify my life? The Shrewd Operator and the Master level, now that was different. I was eternally grateful to Pierrot for those. Problem was, I shouldn't stick my neck out. The second profession—the stuff of Flint's group's dreams—had proven to be a

---

major waste of time and energy. And the feather... wait! The feather! How could I've forgotten!

My hands shaking, I reached into my knapsack and offered the silver feather to the already drowsy man. "Sir Adkhur, do you know what this is?"

He peered shortsightedly at it. "Oh, yes," he hiccupped. "This is the feather of the Night Hunter. A gift to King Tobold I. If I'm not mistaken, it was Brolgerd who made it."

My virtual heart thumped twice as quickly. "You don't happen to remember its properties, do you?"

He shrugged. "I'm sorry, my boy..."

I suppressed a sigh of disappointment.

Master Adkhur must have understood how I felt. "Mind if I ask you a question? Where did you get this from?"

So I told him the whole story.

When I'd finished, Adkhur paused, thinking, then began mumbling, half-asleep, "The Misty Mountains, you said... Why not? You never know..."

He must have come to a decision as he yawned again, "I think that's where you might find the answer."

New quest alert: Journey to the Misty Mountains!

You must find the Nest of Rocks and inspect the remains of the last wearer of the Royal Charm. Then come back to Master Adkhur and tell him everything you've seen.

Reward: Unknown

Accept: Yes/No

I double-checked the task and pressed *Yes*. My satnav pinged, suggesting a new route. I opened the map. The red line of my future journey led toward No-Man's Lands. That's where these Misty Mountains were located. Oh. Talk about all roads leading to Rome.

The sound of healthy snoring filled the room, distracting me from the map. Master Adkhur had already snuggled up in his chair, oblivious to the world. The clock showed 6 p.m. I'd way outstayed my welcome. Time to move it.

Slowly so as not to disturb the old man, I rose from the table. I really should have found something to cover him up with as it was possible that he might not move from his chair all night.

I looked around and noticed a comforter on his bed. Just what the doctor ordered. Gently I covered the old man with it. The comforter was soft and smelled of herbs. Good. But... Of course he was only an NPC and still he'd done so much for me already. What could I give him in return? Then again, what *did* I have?

Having said that... I might leave him two Stamina elixirs. One of them seemed to have worked for Grilby.

Two vials left my belt and floated onto the table. Good. That's it. Time to get going.

I made sure the door didn't slam as I closed it and walked out. The beautiful spotted cat still lounged by the entrance. Funny but now it didn't look as dangerously predatory. Two friendly yellow eyes followed my every move.

"See you around, kitty," I whispered happily and headed toward the grove.

I was so deep in thought that later I couldn't remember how long it had taken me to get back. When I came round, I was already standing inside the Portal Center. So! This Pierrot sure knew how to get a man thinking.

The portal jump was predictably easy—routinely so. Lots of things in this virtual world had already become part of my daily life. I wasn't yet sure whether this was a good or a bad thing.

Nighttime Mellenville buzzed, partying, as the capital celebrated the Barren Plateau victory. Many passersby clutched colorful little flags with the winning clans' logos. Wherever you turned, you could hear upbeat music and cheering for the generals of Light. The sky exploded with fireworks. The game designers were having a ball! I lingered, taking in the magnificent scene.

The inn was the same as I'd left it, as if I'd only popped out for a couple of minutes. It was packed solid. I got the impression that there were more serving girls, too. The screens kept replaying the morning's victory from every possible angle: apparently, some players had already uploaded their videos to the local net. Wow. I absolutely had to watch the whole thing again. But now I had work to do.

My room was strangely quiet. The walls blanketed out any noise. Why couldn't they do that in real life? I'd been to Barcelona once on a business trip. I'd arrived late at night and had a meeting with a client early the next morning. I'd have given anything for a good night's sleep. Just my luck: that same night, the local team defeated Real Madrid. Long story short, everyone arrived at the meeting red-eyed from lack of sleep. The city went on celebrating for another week.

Peace and quiet was exactly what I needed now. A Stamina elixir in hand, I made myself comfortable in the chair. Right. Last stage. Let's assemble this mysterious Replicator thing.

I opened the blueprints.

Warning! In order to assemble Replicator, you will need:
A Sensory Spiral
A Steel Stand
A Support
A Condenser
A Crystalline panel

Warning! In order to assemble Replicator, you need 1500 pt. of pure Energy!

Would you like to assemble Replicator: Yes/No

Oh. It wasn't going to be easy. Never mind.
I pressed *Yes.*

Congratulations! You've assembled a Replicator!
You've received +75 to your skill.
Current skill: 200

Congratulations! Your professional level has grown! You're a Class 1 Engineering Designer now!

The maximum skill limit for your current profession level: 400.

When I finally came back to my senses, I realized I was holding a smallish object that vaguely resembled a microscope. Oh. That Energy drop had really crushed me. But if you think about it, it wasn't that bad after all.

I fidgeted with the gizmo for a bit, then shoved it in my knapsack. What about the blueprints?

Indeed there was a new design available! Great. Let's get going!

Congratulations! You've studied a design: Unworked Charm of Arakh

To build an Unworked Charm of Arakh, you will need:

A fragment of Blue Ice.

My satnav kicked back to life,

Would you like to locate the source of Blue Ice?

I had a funny feeling I already knew where that might be. Still, I clicked *Search*.

So, Sir Olgerd! Let's take stock of what we'd done. On one hand, I hadn't deviated from the original plan. I'd say more: I was currently ahead of schedule. I'd had myself registered in Mellenville—and in an

NPC inn, no less. My Reputation with Mellenville kept growing. Soon I'd be able to apply to the bank for loan instructions—but that only after I signed a new longer-term work contract. This was my sole trump card. I had neither property nor guarantors left.

On the other hand, nutty Pierrot kept sending all sorts of weird items and quests my way. Even this Replicator...

I reached into my knapsack and produced the freshly-assembled machine. What on earth could it be? It did indeed look a bit like a school microscope. But that was only from the outside. In reality, it was nothing like. It had no buttons or little wheels, no lenses—nothing of the kind.

Replicator. A Replicator. Could its name be the clue? It could be anything, really. It could copy things. Duplicate them. It could clone stuff. Another funny thing was, I hadn't yet received the activation message. Putting it plainly, I'd just assembled God knows what.

Now, the second design. Blue Ice, it said? I opened the auction. A quick search produced exactly nothing. According to this search, there was no such resource in Mirror World, period.

Okay. Let's see what my satnav had found.

Of course. Just what I thought it would be. There was only one place where you could farm Blue Ice: the so-called North Mine. Had it not been for the Map of Der Swyor Clan's Trade Routes (courtesy of Pierrot), my bot would never have found it on its own. I made a mental note to check all the forums for any No-Man's Lands maps as soon as I logged out. I should have done it earlier. No wonder: before, I'd only been interested in mining locations. But things seemed to be taking a very interesting turn...

Now the location itself. That was the most interesting thing about it. The North Mine was located in the neutral zone. It was the farthest-flung, God-forsaken hole at the furthermost periphery of Mirror World, to be precise. No idea how I was supposed to get there. Most likely, even the crème de la crème of Mirror World players weren't interested in going there. So it looked like I hit a brick wall in this particular direction.

Oh. Bummer. What could I say? I'd have to keep on mining, wouldn't I? All that time wasted on assembling a stupid machine!

Never mind. What was it Master Grilby had said? *Do not despair...* Okay, so I won't. Now the feather. What had the other Master said? The Misty Mountains.

I checked the map. That looked more doable... sort of. The location was just next door to No-Man's Lands. Wait, wait. This was a stone's throw from the Maragar Citadel, the one that Terminal #572 had so insistently invited me to. Yes, that's right... look... here's the Raldian Ridge... the Black Stream... and to their right, the Misty Mountains.

I sat back, deep in thought. What was the probability of me, a humble Mine Digger, finding the said Nest of Rocks without getting into trouble? If the truth were known, trouble was my middle name. On the other hand, I only had one characteristic of the Feather left to open. Three I knew already—without spending a penny, mind you. If, by some miracle, I discovered its effect, it just might bring me closer to my objective. You never know. All I could do now was hope for the best.

And talking about the Ennans' Elders, I had two more of them to visit: Satis and Axe the Terrible. According to Pierrot's prompt, all these NPCs were experts in their professions. Grilby was more or less clear. He was an Engineering Designer who'd given me his passion for his lifework. Now if I only knew what his lifework had been about...

Master Adkhur was a forest spirit. What did the description say? He was the Patron of the Younger Race. He too was more or less clear. He lived in the forest and seemed to be happy with his lot. It looked like he was the lord of the animal realm. Or something along those lines. Pierrot, my tireless well-wisher, had placed these two in the lands of Light. Apparently, he'd wanted me to start my search here. Unlike Grilby's, Adkhur's name hadn't disappeared from the map which meant we had to meet again.

Next. Master Axe the Terrible. The valorous monster slayer who wore his underpants on the outside. He might try to beknight me. If he did, he'd be disap-nted. I was a Mine Digger, and no mistake. Here in Mirror World, a Grinder was supposed to stick to his trade.

Axe the Terrible resided in a location known as Sleepy Valley, not far from the Twilight Citadel which I'd have loved to visit. Still, at the moment it was out of my league.

The fourth Elder: Master Satis. He seemed to

control some kind of force or element. Also, apparently he was a very smart guy. A warlock, if I'd understood correctly. His Ice Tower was located to the north of No-Man's Lands. That entire region was colored white on the map. Incidentally, that's where my Blue Ice was located too.

That seemed to be it. I heaved a sigh and produced the round silvery charm Adkhur had given me. A curled-up marten had been minted on it. The charm's reverse side featured what I believed to be the coat of arms of the Der Swyor clan: a triangular shield being at its center, supported by two Black Grisons. Unlike my little bandit, they looked strong and threatening. Dangerous.

I couldn't work out the motto. The language looked like nothing I'd ever encountered. I had a funny feeling there was no dictionary in the world that could translate this.

Now. What else?

Name: The Black Grison summoning charm
Effect: Allows you to summon your pet
Restriction: Only Ennan Race

And how was I supposed to summon you? Hadn't Master Adkhur clutched the charm in his hand?

I copied his actions exactly as I remembered them. Yes!

Would you like to summon your pet: Yes/No

Aha. *Yes!*

Before I could blink, the lithe black body materialized out of thin air and dumped itself onto the bed. Was it my imagination or did I glimpse a slightly bewildered expression on its face? Still, the first shock hadn't lasted. Three minutes later, the grison had already inspected the whole of my room. I had the impression he'd sniffed every corner at least twice.

"That's right, buddy," I chuckled. "I'm afraid we'll be stuck here for a while."

While he'd been prancing around the room, his stats chart had appeared in my mental view. So! This little fellow was actually a char in his own right!

Main Characteristics:
Name: [...]
Race: Black Grison
Type: Relic
Level: 0
Satiety: 50/50
Experience: 0/50

Now that was interesting. Relic, you say? I wondered if common Grinders like myself were even allowed to have a pet. I couldn't quite wrap my head around all these latest developments! Let's check his settings.

Abilities: None (Available from Level 1)
Experience received: 10% of the owner's combat experience without detracting from it.
Nourishment: The owner can feed his pet at any

given time by sharing some of his Energy with it.
   **Warning! A pet's level may not exceed that
of its owner!**

I scratched the back of my head. This looked like a Catch 22 situation. You, my little critter, are doomed to remain an ordinary animal. Seeing as my type of account wasn't entitled to receive combat XP, my pet's level wasn't going to grow any time soon. So basically he was a nuisance and a liability. Even though if the truth were known, I was happy to have the company—even the company of such a restless and ill-mannered little brute.

So should we give you a name, then? Judging by what Adkhur had said, this little monster was a male. Oh. Actually, I did have an idea. We used to have a tomcat, just as black and just as big a lover of cheese, too. When still a kitten, he used to raise a hell of a lot of mischief. Over time, he'd sort of grown out of it. He'd lived in our country house. All the neighborhood dogs knew better than to mess with him. To be fair, he'd never provoked anyone. He was a very laidback animal. But still his early-life escapades had earned him the name of Prankster. Later, no one could understand what had ever possessed us to give such a name to this calm and civilized cat. That's irony for you.

Oh... it felt like another life. Had it really been me then? The university... The slim engagement ring I'd presented Sveta with... Her emotional *Yes!* Our modest wedding, followed by years of traveling the world. Her sweet round little belly, followed by the birth of Christina.

I sighed and closed my eyes. As if sensing the state I was in, the grison jumped onto my lap, his moist nose nudging the palm of my hand.

"So, buddy?" I whispered. "Mind being Prankster for a while? Why not? At least it suits you... for the moment."

The grison lifted his head and pricked up his ears. Two beady black eyes watched me intently.

That's sorted, then. I entered the name: *Prankster*. The system zoned out, then presented me with the acceptance message.

I smiled. "Christina would have been on top of the world now. I'm sure you'd have liked her too. Actually, you must be hungry."

I opened his interface. There! The *Satiation* characteristic. When I'd summoned him, it had been at 50 points. I checked the clock. It had been almost fifty minutes ago, and Prankster was already 10 pt. down. That sounded like a lot for a tiny critter like himself. But considering the fact that he'd never stopped bouncing around since, it was probably normal. What was 10 pt. for me, with my Strength and Stamina readings? Peanuts.

Right, let's try and feed you, then. I searched for the Nutrition tab. Got it.

Would you like to feed your pet?
Energy required: 10 pt.
Accept: Yes/No

I chose *Yes*. His Energy bar began growing

until it filled to its limits. Had I read gratitude in his beady black eyes? Couldn't be. Must have been my imagination.

The system addressed me again,

Congratulations! Your pet is well fed!
Warning! Make sure you feed your pet regularly!
You might simplify the feeding process by synchronizing it.
Would you like to synchronize the feeding process: Yes/No.

What was that now? Synchronization? What about it? Actually, *simplify the feeding process* sounded rather reassuring. Very well, then. I pressed *Yes.*

Once again the system zoned out, then reported,

Synchronization successful!
Congratulations! From now on, the feeding process will proceed in automatic mode. Check your interface for changes.

I followed its advice and opened my profile. Found it. There was a smaller Energy bar just under mine, with Prankster's tiny cheeky face next to it. I see. So every time he got hungry, the system would feed him out of my resources. Admittedly, for me it was a drop in the ocean. It also saved me quite a bit of time. Which was becoming more of an issue with every passing day.

Chapter Thirty-Three

The morning promised no surprises. A cold shower. A breakfast downstairs in the inn. Doing my daily quest runs. The epitome of Groundhog Day. Just like actor Bill Murray, I was stuck in a time loop.

Still, I shouldn't grumble. I kept advancing toward my goal—slowly but surely, as with every passing day my knowledge of Mellenville kept growing. Of course, it had been the bot that controlled my char most of the time but I had disabled it on occasions, too. And this morning, I'd forgotten to activate it at all.

Admittedly, I was beginning to understand why they needed all these Reputation quests. They introduced a player to Mirror World, allowing him of her to take the plunge into this weird and wondrous world that followed its own rules.

Over the last eight days, I'd already built up a certain circle of NPC acquaintances. For the most part they used me as an errand boy, and even that only within one particular block. The program might soon move me to a different area of the city. No idea whether this was good or bad. I seemed to be getting used to it. Besides, I also seemed to have a good relationship with local NPCs. No more surprise quests, though. Which was a shame.

By 11 a.m., I was already freed up. You could say I was lucky: the lawyer had called in sick. I just hoped I'd still get the credit, so I'd reported to his office just in case. A failed quest was the last thing I needed. Now, in principle, I could head for the mines. But before doing so, I felt like treating myself to a coffee. There was a nice cozy tavern on the corner of Theater Street I sort of frequented whenever I could. It wasn't that their coffee was the best, but it was definitely the cheapest.

I entered the already-familiar tavern as usual and headed for the bar. There you could always find a pile of newspapers and magazines reporting on the NPCs' life and news. You might think that this was just a bunch of virtual scrap paper, but for long-term players who found themselves stuck in Mellenville it was a veritable treasure trove of information. Most Reputation quests relied on players' reading them. A couple of days ago, my lawyer had issued me a task I'd have had no chance of completing had I not checked one particular article in the local rag. He'd sent me to deliver some paperwork to some old baron or whoever. When I'd arrived at the address, they wouldn't even let me in. So I went back to my lawyer and explained the situation. He didn't want to know: according to him, I had to deliver the papers and that was that. And if they didn't want to talk to me, they'd better give a good reason.

So I went back and was shown the door again. By then, it had been two hours of me running to and fro; I was quite tired so I decided to have a quick coffee in this very tavern. And what did I see but this newspaper on the bar. Apparently, the old baron had kicked the bucket and his brats were busy sharing out his money. That's why they hadn't let anyone in. Armed with this intel, I hurried back to my lawyer who was more than pleased with the news and dismissed me for the rest of the day.

So you see. These days I tried to pop in and check the papers whenever I could. Just in case, you know.

I was about to place my order when I heard someone in the room call my name. A woman's voice. I'd heard it before.

I turned round. Of course. This was Mila— Tommy's mom. Remember Tommy, my innkeeper's nephew? She stood by the staircase smiling wearily, all pale and red-eyed—either with tears or from lack of sleep.

"Hi, Olgerd," her voice was tired, lifeless even.

"Morning, Mila," I said. "Great to see you. I've just popped in for a coffee. Would you like to join me?"

She shook her head. "Thank you, Olgerd.

That's very nice of you. But I'm in a bit of a hurry. Tommy's sick. He's at home now. Ronald's wife is looking after him. And I still have to rush to the other end of town to see the pharmacist. There's an herbal doctor who lives above the inn but he doesn't seem to have the medication I need."

"Is it serious?" I asked.

Her eyes filled with tears. "My boy gets worse by the hour. The medication is very, very rare."

"Can I help you? Tell me what it's called. I'll go look for it and you go back to Tommy."

Hope glistened in her stare. "You might be right. I can use all help I can get, that's for sure. The medication I need is Millefeuille Tea.

New Quest alert: Searching for a Rare Medication
You must locate a serving of Millefeuille Tea and bring it to Mila.
Reward: Unknown
Accept: Yes/No

I clicked *Yes* and assured Mila I'd do everything possible. Having double-checked her own address, I hurried in search of the nearest pharmacy.

If my satnav was to be believed, I was already within a ten-minute walk from it when I froze in my tracks and slapped my forehead.

"What am I doing?" I mumbled. "What's the pharmacy got to do with it?"

I opened the auction tab. Hah! There it was! Millefeuille Tea wasn't at all rare—nor expensive. Two gold. I clicked *Buy*. My inbox flashed with the confirmation message.

That was it. Off I went to save the kid. Rare medication, yeah right!

It took me about fifteen minutes to get to Mila's. She looked genuinely surprised when she answered the door. I'd done it in no time as I'd promised.

Once I handed her the medication, the system showered me with 100 Reputation. Excellent. Wish it happened more often.

Mila didn't want to let me go just like that. She asked me to wait for her in the lounge. While she was busy giving the medication to Tommy, I studied their family pictures on the wall. So strange. These *Glasshouse NPCs* really had lives of their own. Just like in the real world. The funny thing was, I was already getting used to it.

One of the pictures showed Mila and Tommy, accompanied by a military officer in a crisp uniform. Broad shoulders. Tall but not burly. He looked more like a gymnast: all sinew and muscle. Serious face. A stern but strangely happy smile. Sharp cheekbones. A firm chin. A scar ran across his right eyebrow and cheekbone. His eyes weren't damaged: an enemy sword must have missed them by a hair's breadth.

I took a closer look. Tommy bore a definite resemblance to the man.

"That's Tommy's dad," Mila's voice said behind me.

I turned around and smiled to her. "Like father, like son. Where is he now?"

She sighed. "He's serving on the border."

"I see. How's my young friend?"

"The fever's almost gone," she nodded gratefully. "He's fast asleep now."

"Excellent," I said. "Let him sleep. He needs to recuperate. I've got to be off, actually. I need to get to work."

"Thank you so much, Olgerd. I've no idea what I'd have done without you."

"That's nothing. I'm happy if I can be of help."

I bade a warm goodbye to two other women—Ronald's cousin and his wife—who too came out to thank me for my help, then walked out onto the street. For today, my Groundhog Day was over. Something new had just happened. Why hadn't I thought of befriending the inn keeper's family? Was it real-life inhibitions kicking in? Had I been wary of intruding or being in the way? And now the game had blatantly pointed me in the right direction. I had to meet Mila's husband too. You never know, all this might result in surprise quests happening more often.

I'd barely taken a few paces when a new system message popped up before my eyes. Judging by the way everybody flinched, I wasn't the only one who'd received it.

Denizens of our glorious capital!

Yesterday's victory over the forces of evil fills our hearts with joy.

To honor this undoubtedly outstanding event, the administration of Mellenville have decided to offer every city dweller a free gift to remember this day!

Congratulations! You've received +300 to your Reputation with Mellenville!

Congratulations! You have seven days to acquire any item from the city treasury depending on your Reputation ranking! Hurry to claim your 15% discount!

Attention all those who opted for repeatable Reputation quests! Mellenville administration considers this category of players worthy of a special offer. For the next 24 hours, the reward for accepting such quests doubles! All players who're still considering this type of quest—now is the time to accept it!

I reread the 3D message, then looked around me. Other players all seemed to be scurrying off somewhere, grinning happily. Wow. I opened my stats. I had 1160 Reputation points! Yes! I could go to the bank!

I flew off to the Reflex Bank building. Hope gave me wings. I looked for a free terminal and opened the Loans page.

Greetings, Olgerd!
Would you like to apply for a loan: Yes/No

I pressed *Yes.*

Available services by Reflexbank:
Express Loan:
Maximum 3000 gold for up to 10 months.

Medium Term Loan:
Maximum 20,000 gold for up to 6 years
Long Term Loan:
Amount: negotiable
Term: Negotiable

I held my breath and selected *Long Term Loan*.
The system replied straight away,

We're sorry to inform you that you can't view the
Long Term Loans page of the Reflex Bank site. Viewing
it requires 5000 Mellenville Reputation points.

All my attempts to view the other types of loans
failed, too.

I left the bank with a heavy heart. Where was I
supposed to get 5000 Reputation in one month? This
was a terrible blow. And that was simply to view the
page! What would they ask me to do next? And my
tribulations might only start there. Had everything
been in vain—this stupid registration, these
ridiculous quests? All that errand-running I'd done...

Calm down, I told myself. Keep your hair on. I
still had the contract which, once extended, offered
me the chance of getting a loan in a real-life bank.
Now of all times I was quite ready to face the Steel
Shirts leader in order to be shoved back into the pen,
as Doryl had so eloquently said.

This wretched, disgusting frustrated feeling.
How I hated it! Could I ever do something on my own?
I closed my eyes. Think, man, think. There was some
very important detail in there somewhere that kept

eluding me. Some tiny little fact, very butterfly-like: the harder you tried to catch it, the easier it fluttered away from you. But the moment you stopped thinking about it, it would alight onto your shoulder, soft and gentle.

Wait! I found it!

I swung around and dashed for the administrative building. Today it was especially packed. No wonder: everyone was in a hurry to cash in on repeatable quests. Lots of sour faces around: apparently, their missions proved too much for them.

I finally grasped the thought that had kept eluding me. I remembered my system message and the city administration's promise to increase rewards for completing repeatable quests.

Go to the Maragar Citadel. Objective: seek out Captain Gard and offer him your services defending the Maragar Pass from the powers of the Dark. Become a Citadel guard!

Duration: 90 days.

Reward: +2500 to a guard's Reputation with Mellenville every 30 days and an additional +2500 bonus in commemoration of our victory over the forces of the Dark.

Warning! In order to complete the quest, you will have to temporarily lodge in the Maragar Citadel barracks. Those players already registered in Mellenville retain their right to receive their daily 30-pt. bonus to Reputation.

Warning! The quest must be completed in

full. The failure to do so will result in losing all points already earned.

    Warning! In order to receive a new quest, a player must complete the previous one.

I accepted the quest. Didn't they say that all roads led to Rome? In my case, all roads seemed to be leading to No-Man's Lands.

End of Book One

About the Author

Alexey Osadchuk was born in 1979 in the Ukraine. In the late 1990s his family moved to the south of Spain where they still live today.

Alexey was an avid reader from an early age, devouring adventure novels by Edgar Rice Burroughs, Jack London and Arthur Conan Doyle.

In 2010 he wrote his first fantasy novel which was immediately accepted by one of Russia's leading publishing houses Alpha Book.

He also used to be a passionate online gamer which prompted him to write the story of a man who joins an MMORPG game hoping to raise money for his daughter's heart surgery. In 2013, the first book of *Mirror World* was published by EKSMO, Russia's largest publishing house. The original Russian series now counts three novels. The second book of *Mirror World, The Citadel,* is now being translated into English.

Want to be the first to know about our latest LitRPG, sci fi and fantasy titles from your favorite authors?

Subscribe to our NEW RELEASES newsletter:
http://eepurl.com/b7niIL

Thank you for reading *Project Daily Grind!*
If you like what you've read, check out other LitRPG
novels published by Magic Dome Books.

Dark Paladin LitRPG series by Vasily Mahanenko:
The Beginning
The Quest

**The Dark Herbalist LitRPG series
by Michael Atamanov:**
Video Game Plotline Tester
Stay on the Wing

The Neuro LitRPG series by Andrei Livadny:
The Crystal Sphere
The Curse of Rion Castle

**The Way of the Shaman LitRPG series
by Vasily Mahanenko:**
Survival Quest
The Kartoss Gambit
The Secret of the Dark Forest
The Phantom Castle
The Karmadont Chess Set
The Hour of Pain (a bonus short story)

Galactogon LitRPG series by Vasily Mahanenko:
Start the Game!

Phantom Server LitRPG series by Andrei Livadny:
Edge of Reality
The Outlaw
Black Sun

**Perimeter Defense LitRPG series by Michael
Atamanov:**
Sector Eight
Beyond Death
New Contract

In order to have new books of the series translated faster, we need your help and support! Please consider leaving a review or spread the word by recommending *Project Daily Grind* to your friends and posting the link on social media. The more people buy the book, the sooner we'll be able to make new translations available.

Thank you!

Till next time!

63832578R00241

Made in the USA
Middletown, DE
06 February 2018